DUAL REALMS
BOOK TWO

THE BLOOD
CURS

PAIGE AD

IS
1.
2.
Print
First Ed

The Blood Curse (Dual Realms Book Two)

Editing services provided by The Pro Book Editor
Design services provided by Streetlight Graphics

ˈigeaddams.wordpress.com

N: 978-1-7331081-2-6
ain category—Fiction
ˈer category—Paranormal Romance
ˈn the United States of America

ɔn

For my amazing husband, the love of my life, David,
who actually finds my brand of crazy endearing.
Hathun eri, navoj. Iyo kawey eri.

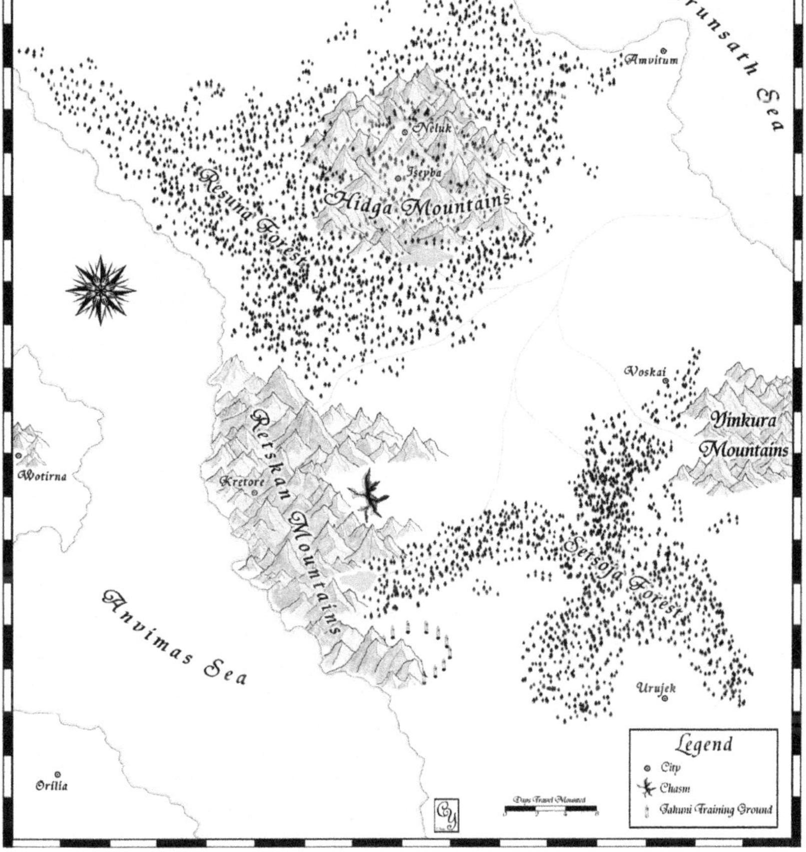
The Lands of
Ejoma
Majit
Senira Desert
Krunsath Sea
Amvitum
Neluk
Iseyba
Resuna Forest
Hidga Mountains
Voskai
Yinkura Mountains
Retskan Mountains
Kretore
Wotirna
Setsoja Forest
Anvimas Sea
Urujek
Orilla
Legend
City
Chasm
Jahuni Training Ground
Days Travel Mounted

Excerpts from Shima Historical Tomes

In the Beginning...

God stood at the center of creation after completing His masterpieces, men and women in His image. Seeing that there was both light and dark in them and knowing the pain in store for them, He separated His beloved creations. These children, each an aspect of God, were scattered. Divided into two realms, human and shima were separated by a wall of energy that became known as the arute.

The human realm, Thavos, became a world of science and machines. Always striving to invent new things and understand the world around them, humans became strong. They learned to distinguish themselves from one another and divided into smaller groups. They separated themselves by hair, skin, and eye color; where they were born and what language they spoke; and the different names and ways they learned to call and worship God.

But they forgot their shima brothers and sisters.

Lost to human history, shimana became nothing but folktales and fantasy passed down through the years.

Ejoma, the shima realm, became a world of magic and energy devoid of machines. Shimana strove to keep balance within themselves and the world around them, knowing their powers could be dangerous when unleashed. Immortal, they filled their countless years with learning. Shimana saw their differences in the kind of power each wielded, but this did not divide their society. The ten shima aspects learned to keep the balance, each holding both light and dark within to varying degrees. They spoke one language and called God by one name, worshipping Him in the same ways.

They never forgot their human brothers and sisters, and curiosity drew them to their human counterparts on occasion throughout the centuries, giving birth to human legends about magical creatures.

For more on the people, traditions, and history of Ejoma, please visit paigeaddams.wordpress.com.

PROLOGUE

Shima realm
The city of Orilia

ASHRIEL TELESHANI STRUGGLED AGAINST HIS captors. His body was battered and exhausted, but he wasn't going to make this easy for them. Even if he could break free, there were too many warriors—besides the two dragging him down the castle corridor—to take on by himself. But he'd be damned if he wasn't going to fight until he physically couldn't anymore.

"Get your fucking hands off me!" he shouted, trying to wrench himself free.

Restrained with magic-dampening shackles, hands behind his back, he threw his body weight into one of them, but they barely seemed to register his resistance. They stumbled and just kept going, regardless of his efforts. Nothing he'd said or done so far had raised any sort of reaction from either of them. He'd fought them with everything he had, magic and hand-to-hand combat both, but they'd just kept coming, no matter their injuries.

The warriors' expressions were eerily blank as they

trudged forward, hauling him into the throne room. He took note of the handful of warriors positioned between the three pillars on either side of the carpeted path to the throne. Stopping before the dais where two Jiruna would normally sit, they shoved him to his knees in front of the throne.

He lifted his head to glare up at the usurper in front of him, Enalel Otharo, sitting in one of the two matching ornate, high-backed chairs beside her twin brother, the true ruler. Although the Jiru had given up his immortality after his mate died, and had begun to age as a human would, they shared the same dark-blond hair, Enalel's falling in curls to her waist and the Jiru's cut short, and had identical light-gray eyes. But where Enalel wore a smugly satisfied expression, Jiru Otharo was as silent and seemingly lifeless as the warriors Ashriel had been captured by. He resembled some kind of disturbing puppet, slumped in the matching chair beside Enalel, eyes unfocused. The only sign of life was a telltale tremor that briefly moved through the Jiru's body.

This was dark magic. It permeated everything around Ashriel and clung to Enalel so strongly he felt like he would gag. Bile rose in his throat as he recognized the signs of what she had done.

The creepy doll-like stillness when not following a command. Silent, unquestioning obedience. Blank stares and tremors. He'd seen mind control before, but never like this. Not on this scale.

Mindful of the ribs he was sure were broken, Ashriel carefully sat back on his heels. His armor, severely damaged with burns and dents from magic and weapons, creaked as he shifted his weight. Shaking wavy black hair out of his face, sticky with blood from a cut near his temple, Ashriel assessed his surroundings with narrowed dark-violet eyes, praying he was wrong.

Wincing, he spat a mouthful of blood onto the pristine, white-stone floor and scowled up at Enalel. "What have you done?" he said, repulsed by the empty stares of the dozen or so warriors stationed around the large throne room. "You're the Jiru's sister. These are your people too."

"Are they?" she said, her dark laugh unsettling in the unnaturally silent room. In her gown of pure, shimmering white, she should have been glorious to look at, but all he could see was her cruelty. "First, they were the Junak's pawns. Aimless. Purposeless. So scared of their true powers, they happily suppressed them to keep in line with the Junak's laws, which serve no one but the Junak. Little better than humans," she sneered. "Now they belong to me. I see no significant difference."

"You've taken their will!" Ashriel growled, disgusted by her abuse of power. "The Junak—"

"The Junak knows nothing," she said lightly, completely unconcerned. Leaning against the arm of her chair, she propped her chin on her fist and studied him as if she were bored by the whole ordeal. "I have nothing to fear from them."

Her absolute confidence gave him pause. As a warrior, he dealt with the Junak often, assisting them in the human realm on behalf of the city he served, and had heard nothing. For months, a rogue shima faction had been growing, attacking seemingly random cities, kidnapping people, and unleashing strange void creatures that had never been seen before. With these recent attacks, the entire realm was focused on tracking them down. He wished he could believe it was impossible, but if she had moved carefully enough, her crimes against Orilia could have gone unnoticed in the realm's chaos.

Dark magic, in its most insidious forms, could be hidden if it were done carefully enough. The mind control was on a level he'd never seen before, however. How had she managed it in such numbers, and with so much success?

Every shima could tap into small amounts of dark magic, but it was a dangerous gamble that not many dabbled in. It was too easy for a shima to become addicted to the power. In small amounts, dark magic was tolerated, but based on what he'd seen so far, what had happened in Orilia was far beyond what would ever be allowed.

"Why are you here?" she continued, assessing him with shrewd eyes. He got the impression she was asking more out of curiosity than any real fear of being discovered by the Junak. "Who sent you?" When he didn't answer, she sighed and leaned back in her chair. "They found you in the dungeons," she said in a bored tone, examining her nails. "What were you looking for?"

Ashriel kept his mouth shut, staring up at her silently as she met his gaze again. Whether he talked or not, he was sure she was going to try and force herself into his mind to get the answers she wanted. Hopeless as his situation seemed, he couldn't let that happen.

Twisting his wrists against the cuffs slowly, he tried to see if he could disrupt their magic-stripping effects somehow. All he needed was an opening. Any small give in the cuffs would do.

Enalel narrowed her eyes, leaning forward slightly in her seat. "Or perhaps I should ask *who* you're looking for? The dungeons would be more of a place to locate a 'who' than a 'what,' after all."

Ashriel clenched his teeth, keeping his silence. She was getting too close to the mark for comfort. He couldn't risk giving her leverage to get information out of him.

Could he truly refuse her if it meant sparing his friend, Darenai? Bound as he was, and completely out of alternatives, he wasn't very confident he could.

"Our laws are in place for a reason," he said, trying to sound far calmer than he felt. "You can't just—"

"Please," she nearly purred, smirking at him coldly. "Continue telling me what I can and can't do while you're bound and bleeding in the middle of my throne room floor." She stood then, laughing softly to herself as she gave a languid stretch. "No. On second thought, this is getting boring. Let's get on with this."

Enalel approached him without any fear, and he got the impression from her blasé attitude that she mistakenly believed he was going to let this happen quietly. A low growl rumbled in his chest, wrists flexing against his restraints as he tested them again.

"Yes, I know," she said breezily, rolling her eyes as she stopped within arm's reach of him. "You are a terrifying creature, even on your knees. Consider me intimidated."

He was determined to find a way to wipe that smug look off her face, if it was the last thing he did. The way things were going, it probably would be. He kept his eyes on her, sensing where the other warriors in the room were in relation to him.

Close, but not enough to stop him from one last act of defiance while his mind and body were still his own. He carefully gathered what was left of his magical energy, pushing uncomfortably against the limits his shackles set on him. The strain made him tremble, his head going fuzzy and his chest aching, but he ignored it all.

It wasn't much, but it was something. He waited for what he knew was coming.

She raised a graceful arm, pale hand hovering inches above Ashriel's head. He sensed her energy reaching out for him and prepared himself.

"Stop!" A figure materialized out of the shadows, angrily moving into the room from behind the cover of a pillar.

The warriors nearest the man didn't react, awaiting Enalel's command, but Enalel stiffened, head whipping in the newcomer's direction as she took a battle stance and stretched out her hand toward him, ready to throw a spell if need be. When she saw who it was, Ashriel noticed how tense she remained. Nobody had seen the man slip into the room, even Enalel, and it must have made her nervous.

Ashriel watched as the man looked around the room quickly, only to stop dead as his gaze settled on the Jiru. When he looked back at Enalel, he was outwardly composed, but Ashriel could feel the violent energy pouring off him.

The resemblance to the Jiru was obvious in his facial features and shoulder-length, light-blond hair as he swept the edges of his dark-brown cloak open. He wore no armor, only a simple linen shirt and brown hide pants and boots, but it was clear by his stance and the way he clenched the handle of the dagger at his belt that he was ready to fight.

Enalel sighed, dropping her hand as she turned to face the man. “Banen—”

“No,” he interrupted, pale-green eyes narrowed in disgust. “You don’t get to address me so informally, like I should still consider you family after what you’ve done here.”

“Fine then,” she said with a smirk and a mock bow to the future ruler of Orilia. “Sijo Otharo. I wasn’t expecting you.”

The Sijo unsheathed his dagger, and Ashriel saw a new opportunity as Enalel foolishly turned her back to him, fully shifting her attention to the other man. Carefully, he changed his position to kneel with one knee up. If they hadn’t been robbed of their ability to think for themselves, the warriors still standing on either side of him may have reacted, or at least noticed his movement, but as they were, they remained silent and still. Staring off into space until called upon. As long as he didn’t make any big movements, they probably wouldn’t do anything.

“Because you’re my aunt, and you were close to us once, I will give you one chance to escape,” the Sijo said with a quiet, deadly edge to his voice. “Release these people and leave now, or I will do whatever it takes to free them from you. Even if that means killing you.”

“Aw, what a sweet sentiment, Sijo,” Enalel said, and although her back was to Ashriel, he could practically hear the derisive smirk in her tone. “I don’t suffer from the same weakness. You are here alone," she said calmly, and as the Sijo tensed, Ashriel waited for his opening. "You are not enough to stop me."

The Sijo leapt at her, dagger flashing in the light as he made a downward slash at her. She took a hasty step back and lifted a hand to put up an invisible energy barrier between them. The Sijo's dagger stopped just short of her chest, sparkling embers of magic skittering over the barrier from the contact as the weapon stuck, and she laughed, signaling her warriors closer with her free hand. "Always so direct, Sijo. You never could hide your intentions from me."

Light and sparks moved over the surface of her barrier as the Sijo's dagger stayed embedded in it, his muscles trembling as he pushed against the unseen force with all his strength, and for the briefest of seconds, the Sijo's cold gaze shifted to Ashriel over her shoulder.

It was all the signal Ashriel needed. They had a common enemy, and that was good enough for him.

The Sijo teleported behind Ashriel, channeling his energy into Ashriel's shackles to release them, and chaos erupted all around them.

"Seize them!" Enalel shrieked, going straight for the Sijo with her bare hands, dark magic empowering her strikes.

The Sijo met Enalel head on, casting offensive spells and slicing at her with his dagger, but she seemed to absorb every spell he threw at her. They were a flurry of movement as they teleported around each other, fighting to get the upper hand.

Ignoring the searing pain in his body from the injuries he'd sustained fighting to free himself, Ashriel rose to his feet to take on the warriors coming to Enalel's aid. Saving his energy, he disarmed the first one and used that warrior's sword to take down anyone who came near.

The Sijo's shout caught Ashriel's attention, and he turned in time to see a hulking creature, made of black smoke, with bloodred irises and black where the eyes should have been white, slice into the Sijo's back as he tried to strike Enalel.

The Sijo was hurled away, and she advanced on the Sijo with the creature at her side. Weakened by the poisonous, cloying void energy pouring off of them and seeping into the bloody, ragged claw marks in his back, he Sijo struggled to rise to his feet, reaching futilely for his dagger.

There was a sickening sensation in Ashriel's gut, and he realized this was one of the creatures he'd heard rumors of. The void clung to it, tainting anything that got too close. That meant this wasn't just some power grab. She was working for the same rogue shimana who had been attacking the cities, for Tairi knew what reasons.

He raced toward the Sijo, praying he wasn't already too late to save him. A hard blow to the chest was all it took to get past the only warrior who was immediately in the way. He heard others rushing behind him, trying to get to him before he got to Enalel.

She finally turned at the commotion behind her, and was caught by a blast of energy he hurled into her chest. Taken by surprise, she was flung to the ground, far away from the Sijo. Ashriel dodged the creature as it swiped at him, using his pulse spell to knock it back and slow it down. He was on Enalel in seconds, kneeling over her, one hand clenching her throat, the other palm raised to her face, inches away from her nose.

He could feel the creature's void energy leeching away at his powers as it quickly closed in on him from behind, and he knew he had only seconds, if that. His eyes met Enalel's between his outstretched fingers. "Now," he growled. "Let me see you absorb this."

Even as he focused all of his power into his hands, he felt her draw on her own energy, and a split second later, there was an explosion as they both released their spells at the same time. His body was hurled through the air like a rag doll, the air forced out of his lungs. Blinding light flashed in front of his eyes, the presence of the void creature at his back eased as it was flung away from him, and he could hear the screams of the remaining warriors all around him.

By the time his vision cleared, the Sijo had disappeared, hopefully having managed to escape the throne room, and Enalel was limping toward him. Her face was swollen, her eyes streaming tears and reduced to slits. Deep gashes marred her previously perfect face, blood dripping steadily from them. She moved very carefully, as if her body ached, raising her right hand to clutch her other shoulder, which was hanging at an unnatural angle.

He felt the beginnings of hope in having been able to injure her at least. If she could be hurt this badly, then she hadn't consumed nearly as much power as he had originally thought.

"You will pay dearly for your interference," she said menacingly, her narrowed eyes smoldering with rage. He could feel the nauseating energy of the creature as it prowled in the shadows, eyes trained on him as it awaited Enalel's command.

Coughing, his lungs labored for air. "You'll never catch the Sijo in time," he said with a choked laugh. He had no strength to stand, so he just stayed where he was, flat on his back on the hard, stone floor at the end of the room in front of the throne, knowing his time was up. "He'll bring the entire Junak down on you."

She gave him a twisted smile. "No, he won't," she said with far too much confidence for comfort. "You'll make sure of that."

"Like hell, I will," Ashriel said weakly. The room was starting to spin, little black dots floating at the corners of his vision.

She lifted a hand to hover over his head, and he gritted his teeth, trying to fight the blackness pulling him under. He had to resist her. He couldn't let her into his mind.

"When I'm done with you, you won't have any other choice," she said, the dark energy around her intensifying until it was enough to choke him.

There was a flash of light, and the last thing he felt before he lost consciousness was a searing pain as if his head were slowly being ripped open from the inside.

CHAPTER ONE

A small town in Thavos, the human realm
One month later

IF HE COULDN'T ANNIHILATE HIS enemies with his bare hands, at the very least he could go out of his way to disrupt every one of their plans.

Bits of glass crunched beneath Ashriel's boots as he crossed the room, and he took great joy in grinding them into the hardwood floor. It could only help his cause. What he was searching for could appear to be anything, anywhere in that house.

Futile, considering his hopeless circumstances? Absolutely.

Childish, even to his admittedly questionable standards? Definitely.

Did he give a shit? Not at all.

Held captive, his powers reduced to almost nothing, he was trapped in this hellhole of a needlessly massive, enchanted house where all the damned rooms moved and so little light was let in that it felt claustrophobic and smelled musty. He figured he wouldn't be living long, so he had to take his pleasures where he could get them. And, as pointless as it was, it wasn't in him to just give up and wait to die.

He knew his enemies would refill the house with random items every day, no matter how many he broke or tore through, both to make it more impossible to find what he was searching for and to distract him from the humans they brought in. But they seemed to have underestimated just how stubborn he could be. Or maybe they were so confident he could accomplish nothing that they simply didn't care.

Pausing to kick an end table over with a satisfying *bang*, he scanned the offending furniture with his limited senses. He wasn't surprised when he didn't find what he was looking for. He moved on, but not without a second kick to the end table for good measure, sending splintered pieces of wood flying in different directions.

Finding things to destroy was such good stress relief. And to think, it even served another purpose beyond the obvious. What was that human saying? Something about two birds and a stone? Whatever. Darenai had always been better at remembering those sorts of things. He supposed that was beside the point. As long as there was blood and spattered body parts at the end, it was a fitting enough analogy.

"I don't have to put up with this," a sharp voice snapped from the doorway behind him. "I didn't sign up for this, and if you don't stop, I *will* quit!"

Ah, perfect timing. And now for the kill...

Ashriel smiled diabolically, turning to meet his opponent's gaze. Her black hair was pulled back in a ponytail, and she wore jeans, old running shoes, and a T-shirt. Her blue eyes narrowed, and she glared at him.

He'd done his best not to bother remembering her name, or the names of any other humans who wandered into the hellhole he was currently stuck in. It was better that way. He'd made the mistake of giving a shit a couple times, and it had bitten him in the ass. So the number of humans he was on a first-name basis with was down to one. And since that one was on her way out soon, he could focus on the task at hand.

The human trying to stare him down at the moment, his captors' live-in housekeeper for the past two weeks, was at her breaking point. Right where he wanted her. They seemed to need to drain the humans slowly to accomplish their goals, luring humans in to live in the mansion on the outskirts of town under the pretext of work, and it had taken him far too long to begin undoing the spell this housekeeper was under, splitting his limited magic between the different humans they'd targeted besides her. His enemies were becoming stronger, while he spread himself too thin and weakened a little more every day.

But perhaps it would be enough. Maybe he could still save this one if he just pushed a little further. That enough of her free will had returned to allow her to be angry with him was a promising sign. At least she wasn't drooling on herself and walking into walls like the last one.

"And leave me without the pleasure of your uplifting company?" he asked in as pleasant a tone as he could muster, using her frustration to distract her while he reached out to her vulnerable human mind with what was left of his tattered magical abilities. "I so look forward to our time together. I even put serious thought into ways to keep you busy." He gestured around the room, honestly proud of the level of destruction. It was early yet, and he already had such a good start. "I wouldn't want you to get bored, after all."

She planted her hands on her hips, and he fondly imagined she was beginning her daily routine of silently talking herself down from saying what he assumed were some very unladylike things.

He didn't have anything against her personally. She was nice enough, for a human.

He briefly, but only *very* briefly, considered toning it down a bit. After all, he didn't want her head to explode. And her complexion was almost...

Purple wasn't a normal human color, was it?

The human took a deep breath before she spoke again, rubbing at her temples as though she had a headache building, and even with his diminished senses, he could tell his intrusion into her mind was taking a toll. "Look, since I'm going to be living here, we have to find a way to get along."

He immediately crushed all those passing thoughts of taking it easier on her. She would see no mercy from there on out. He pushed as far into her mind as he dared, latching onto the insidious dark magic that had left its mark on her.

"Ah, I guess you have a point," he said pleasantly, smiling in a way he knew made her nervous.

A wave of lightheadedness hit him as he worked to untangle the spell she was under, then a slow, slicing kind of pain spreading through his skull, and he barely managed to breathe through it without letting it show on his face. Odath and Petrin's spellwork was as careless as ever, without concern for the damage they could cause. Like the sticky threads of a spider's web, their compulsion was wrapped so tightly around her mind that he was afraid he would hurt her unraveling it. Although he didn't particularly care for humans, he didn't want to be the one whose clumsy trampling through their brains turned them into vegetables.

He kept talking, as much to distract himself from the pain as to keep her in the room long enough for him to do what he needed to. "In fact, I think we should celebrate our new friendship with a feast. Your people do that, right? Cook food over open flames?" He tilted his head, watching her with narrowed eyes.

The confusion in her expression wasn't enough. He would have to do better if he was going to free her. It was for her own good, after all. If he found humor in her reaction to his provocation, that was merely a bonus.

"Just as a show of my determination to make your life easier, and to prove my commitment to our new truce—" he brought a hand to his heart, attempting a look of sincerity "—because I am so fair and rational."

Obviously sensing danger, her eyes had become so wide that he began to wonder if they were going to pop out of her head.

"I feel I should warn you that as soon as I leave this room, I'm going to raid your cleaning supplies and set them on fire." He smiled broadly, dropping his hand. Just a little more. He had to keep her there just a few moments longer. He could sense the fractured places in her mind fusing back together as his magic worked on her. "But don't worry too much, since you know in advance you have plenty of time to buy some food to roast over the flames." He frowned as if a thought had just occurred to him. "Maybe we should send out invitations and make a cozy little *housewarming* party, so everyone in town can be my new best friend and share flame-blackened food over the inferno of this giant bonfire."

"You're lying," she said incredulously, rubbing at her temple with a slight frown. His lack of power made him clumsy, but he couldn't afford to be gentler with her. She narrowed her eyes at him, despite what was probably an annoying headache building in her head. "You wouldn't."

He held her gaze firmly as he felt the last of the spell controlling her dissipate. She seemed to freeze in place, wide eyes locked on him and body trembling like a small, frightened animal. Clenching his teeth against the pain, he placed a small compulsion of his own in her subconscious.

"Leave," he whispered into her mind, commanding her to do as he said with every ounce of his waning power. *"Now."*

"Have I ever," he asked out loud, continuing their conversation as if nothing unusual had happened, "in the short time you have known me..." He very deliberately picked up a discarded book and began to slowly tear out pages. Balling them in his fist like he would kindling, he tossed them aside, more than ready to give her all the incentive she could ever need to run away from him and never look back. "*Not* followed through on something I told you I would do?"

Her reaction was everything he could have asked for in that moment.

Jillian Mitchell looked up at the imposing structure before her. Standing outside this huge house in the middle of the woods, she felt as if she were at the opening of some horror film and any second a crazed murderer would come screaming out of the trees. Just looking at the place made the hairs on the back of her neck stand on end.

The mansion itself was beautiful, with its perfectly kept lawn and pristine, white paint. It should have felt as welcoming as the nearby town did, but it felt cold to her somehow.

Sometimes she would get a feel for a place, or for a person, and she just *knew* if the situation would work out or if it wouldn't. She chalked it up to good instincts, and was grateful for it.

But she had never had such a strong feeling of foreboding before.

It wasn't as though she had a lot of choice in the matter, however. She wanted to stay close to her family, only a couple hours away, and her previous employers had moved out of state. She wanted to be able to drop in and see her parents from time to time, especially since her two younger siblings were off at college and her dad, a construction foreman, was off work with a broken leg after an onsite accident.

She wasn't in a bad financial situation, but she soon would be if she didn't get a new job. There was a position available here. End of story. The creepiness factor of the place would have to take a back seat to her need for things like food and money, and not worrying her parents when they had other things on their plate.

Squaring her shoulders, she continued up the walkway to the door.

It opened before she got there, and a black-haired woman with angry blue eyes stormed past her, suitcases in hand. “Good luck, lady,” she muttered with a narrow-eyed glance behind her.

From the beginning, it had seemed too good to be true. Not only would she be splitting the work with other housekeepers, which was an unusual but welcome change of pace, but also her new employers were offering a lot of money for the position of live-in housekeeper.

Almost a ridiculous amount, she reflected as the woman threw her bags in the back seat of her car. She was clearly shaken, climbing into the car with a clumsy kind of desperation, before speeding off down the driveway.

What have I gotten myself into? Jillian wondered with a quiet sigh as the car disappeared from sight. She’d assumed they were offering a crazy amount of money and had hired her as additional help because the place was so huge, but it wasn’t that much larger than the last house she’d worked at. She was starting to worry there was something else going on that she didn’t want to get involved in.

She jumped at the sound of someone clearing his throat behind her, and quickly turned to see a man standing in the doorway. He couldn’t have been too much older than she, maybe early thirties.

He was a good deal taller than her own five-eight frame and had a wiry build. His skin was pale, except for faint circles coloring the skin beneath his light-brown eyes, as if he’d had one too many late nights in a row. Shaggy dark-red hair curled around his ears and brushed the collar of his blue hoodie. Leaning against the doorframe with his arms crossed, casual in fashionably distressed jeans, he could have been considered attractive if not for the coldness in his eyes that belied his smile.

He held her with his stare, the corners of his mouth turned up in a grin, and she wasn't sure she could look away. There was an oily quality to his friendly expression that made her a little uncomfortable. She was getting the same feeling from him that she had from the house. There was no warmth in him.

A chill of apprehension raced down her spine, but she tried to suppress it. She felt a little dizzy suddenly, holding his gaze, but couldn't look away. It felt like she imagined it would if she locked eyes with a predator in the wild.

"How can I help you?" he asked, his tone holding a hint of amusement, as if he knew he unnerved her.

Raising her chin, she met his gaze. "I'm here to see Petrin Sadil," she said coolly. She wasn't about to let him intimidate her. "I'm the new live-in housekeeper, Jillian Mitchell." She extended her hand, determined to give this place a fair shot. As she forced herself to focus and not dwell on her uneasiness, the strange dizziness faded as suddenly as it had come.

He narrowed his eyes then, studying her with a calculating smile that did nothing to reassure her. Slowly, he straightened and reached for her hand.

"Odath," a woman's voice said warningly from somewhere behind him.

Odath paused just before he was about to clasp her hand, then lowered it to his side once again. Unexpectedly relieved to have an excuse to back out of taking his hand, Jillian shoved her hands in her pockets.

"You must be Jillian?" the woman said, stepping forward out of the shadows of the darkened hallway beyond the door. She didn't get closer to offer her hand, and neither did Jillian. "I'm Petrin," she said, smiling in a way that made Jillian want to follow that first woman's cue.

What was it about this place and these people that put her so on edge? She felt as though she were being stared at by two vipers.

Petrin was just as beautiful as Odath, and her exotic, dark-gold eyes were also just as cold. Pale, blond curls flowed in waves down to her waist, a stark contrast to her black sweater and jeans. The gaudy dagger pendant she wore on a thick, gold chain around her neck, with a little dragon wrapped around the hilt, made her look like some sort of modern pagan goddess.

"Please," Petrin said, stopping just before the patch of sunlight that hit the marble floor of the foyer. "Come in. Let me show you around, and then you can unpack."

Odath barely shifted to the side to let Jillian pass, that cold smirk still in place as he watched her, and her creep meter nearly went off the charts. Grabbing the handles of her two rolling suitcases, she skirted around him to follow Petrin, giving him as wide a berth as she possibly could.

Not a good start, she thought grimly to herself, resisting the urge to look back at him and make sure he wasn't following. She was already doing the math in her head of how long her savings would stretch before she could get another post through her agency.

Petrin instructed her to leave her bags by the stairs before starting a quick tour. Walking quickly ahead of Jillian, Petrin paused every now and then to gesture down a hallway and describe what rooms were in that general direction. The house was uncomfortably dim, with most curtains closed. Structurally, the mazelike layout made no sense. There was no straight path to anywhere, and it somehow felt much bigger inside than how it seemed from the outside. How had they managed to cram so many rooms into one space? She was beginning to see why they needed more than one housekeeper.

Whether it was intentional on Petrin's part or not, Jillian barely had time to glance into rooms as the tour continued. Only about half of them actually seemed to have a purpose. There was a library, study, kitchen, dining room, bedrooms on the second and third floors, and a bathroom on each floor. The others sounded like they were just there to fill up square footage. Some rooms were completely empty, and looked as if no one had even been in them in years.

The effect only reinforced the whole horror movie atmosphere.

"We have a guest staying on the third floor, but that part of the house is off limits," Petrin said. "It's under construction, so it isn't safe."

"Got it," Jillian said, already planning in her head how best to tackle the first two floors and get everything done. She didn't outwardly question why someone would stay in a part of the house that wasn't safe, trying to be optimistic in her assumption that their guest was in some kind of profession where they could determine the safest place for themselves if they *had to* stay up there for whatever reason. But some nagging instinct in the back of her mind wouldn't let her lie to herself. It didn't make sense. So she filed those questions away for later.

"And this is Raelyn, the cook and occasional housekeeper," Petrin said, stopping to gesture again as a woman in an apron came walking around a corner.

"Hi!" Raelyn greeted them. She was in the process of tying her long, dark-honey-blond hair back. Nodding cheerfully, her smile warmed her dark-brown eyes in an openly friendly manner. "Call me Rae," she said, reaching out to shake Jillian's hand.

"Nice to meet you," Jillian said, trying to hide her relief as she shook Rae's hand. Finally, someone who *didn't* make her uncomfortable.

Still getting things ready for dinner, Rae didn't have much time to talk, but she invited Jillian out to check out the town with her and her friend, Mindy, on their next day off.

"You'll meet Mindy at some point too," Petrin said as Rae disappeared down another hallway. "She'll be helping you with your housecleaning duties, although she won't be living here. The other housekeeper who was supposed to live here didn't work out. I believe you might have seen her on her way out," she said, and something about her tone made Jillian a little uneasy again. She almost sounded amused. "So we'll have to find a replacement."

Jillian nodded noncommittally, remembering the woman who had stormed past her earlier. "Okay," she said, but she was seriously doubting whether she would even make it a whole day working there herself. Normally, she would never turn her nose up at a job, and she certainly wouldn't quit day one, but this was beginning to feel like too much.

Maybe she was being paranoid, but she was getting a strong impression that this wasn't a safe working environment.

"This way," Petrin said with a beckoning motion as she turned to head down another hall, and Jillian shoved those thoughts out of her mind. "You have one more person to meet."

This time when Petrin spoke, it was clear she was enjoying herself. Jillian decided right then and there that if this last person was as awful as Petrin and Odath, she was done.

She led Jillian down a long corridor that branched off from the main hallway. "His name is Ashriel. You should probably do your best to avoid him." She laughed softly, and Jillian felt like her skin was crawling. "Or think of him like furniture, and just ignore him."

"Why is that?" Jillian asked, her voice deliberately bored, wanting to make it clear that she didn't scare so easily. At least, she *usually* didn't.

Petrin shot a smirk at her as she stopped at the last door. "Because he's insane," she said calmly, almost pleasantly. "He suffers from severe delusions and is prone to tantrums where he likes to break things."

Jillian met her mocking gaze with a benign smile, forcefully reminding herself how much she was going to be getting paid to deal with these people if she stayed. "I think I'll be okay," she said more optimistically than she felt.

Petrin's smile broadened, more like a bearing of teeth than anything else. "Yes, I'm sure you'll be just fine." Grasping the handle, she pushed the door open and, scowling, moved quickly to the side, away from the open doorway. Instead of preceding Jillian into the room, Petrin gestured for her to go in by herself.

Jillian stepped through the doorway and immediately froze. The sun was at just the perfect angle to shine through the open window across from her, blinding in contrast to the otherwise dark room. No lights were on to help counter this effect, but she could see that the room within that bright patch of light was completely destroyed. A coffee table had been overturned, cushions pulled off of couches and chairs, torn books and shattered trinkets littered the floor.

She took in the destruction and asked herself if the money was really worth it after all. Somewhere in the background the doorbell rang, but she barely noticed it.

"I think I'll just let you get started," Petrin said, and was already gone by the time Jillian glanced behind her.

Now what? Go unpack? Or clean this up first?

One day, she thought with a sigh. *I'll give it one day, and see how I feel about it tomorrow.*

Unable to find a light switch by the door, Jillian squinted as she turned to face the room again. Raising a hand to shield her eyes, she stepped out of the glaringly bright patch of sunlight to try and get a better view of the room.

"Geez!" she gasped, nearly jumping out of her skin again as her eyes adjusted and she caught sight of a figure several feet away from her. A man leaned casually against the wall across from her, so still he had blended in with the shadows where the light couldn't reach. Even though he didn't introduce himself, she knew this had to be Ashriel.

All she could make out at first was the dark silhouette of his body, but she could see a little more as he moved out of the shadows to stand in front of the window. He was tall, with a lean, muscular build. He was dressed casually, in a dark-green T-shirt and blue jeans. Black hair fell in waves well past his shoulders, framing a face that she still couldn't quite make out. There was an eerie stillness in his posture, some mysterious quality to him that made him seem almost otherworldly.

She knew she should say something. Hello. Nice to meet you. Anything. But she couldn't seem to find her voice.

His features slowly came into focus and, considering his expression, she was relieved she wasn't the subject of his attention at the moment. He watched the doorway behind her silently, arms folded, obviously having seen Petrin duck back into the hallway after opening the door. He seemed to smolder with a barely suppressed rage, cold calculation in his eyes, and the promise of vengeance for some unspoken act of evil on Petrin's part.

She couldn't tell what color his eyes were, but she could feel their intensity as they finally came to rest on her.

His gaze was like a physical touch against her skin, and the unfamiliar sensations moving through her had nothing to do with feeling uneasy in that moment. The malice she had seen in him was fading as he studied her, being replaced by something else. Something more powerful. It felt like the world was tilting, like she was being coaxed toward him by some invisible force.

Attraction felt like too mild of a word for it. It was only strength of will that kept her from moving closer to him, wanting to touch him despite knowing better. Her fingertips tingled to discover those finer details of his face that she couldn't clearly make out. She wanted to clench her hands against the temptation, but she somehow knew those watchful eyes would catch that telltale movement.

Not used to that kind of reaction in herself, she tried to shake the feeling off.

For a long moment, they just stared at one another. Then his mouth curved up at the corners in an enigmatic smile that had her heart racing in her chest. Unfolding his arms, he began to move toward her, his eyes never leaving her, analyzing her as if sizing her up for battle. She noticed a faint scar on his neck, as though something had been wrapped around his throat, cutting into his skin. She didn't have much time to wonder about it, though.

All of his considerable attention seemed to be centered on her. As though they were the only people in the universe in that moment. His expression still held a challenge, but there was something else there too. Something that could've been similar to the inexplicable attraction she felt.

"So," he said softly, "you're my new babysitter?" He chuckled mockingly, walking a slow circle around her, and his tone helped to cool her head a little.

An involuntary shiver ran through her at his nearness, despite her resolve. His low voice seemed to reach across the space between them, enchanting her, a faint accent she couldn't place coloring his words.

Raising her chin, she met his eyes squarely as he came to stand in front of her again. "I don't know what that's supposed to mean," she said firmly, determined not to be swayed by how hot he was. "I'm the new live-in housekeeper."

Purple. His eyes had almost looked blue at first, but she realized they were actually *purple*. Mysterious, they spoke of something hidden. Something just beneath the surface that she couldn't understand.

She had never seen eyes like his before. They had to be contacts, right? They seemed to draw her in somehow, taking away her will to look anywhere but at him.

"I'm not impressed," he said, as if he hadn't heard her.

She frowned, annoyed by her own distraction, and mentally bit her tongue to keep from telling him exactly how high on her list of priorities impressing him was. What was wrong with her? This guy lived with her employers, and he was supposed to be a complete maniac. Judging by the state of the room, she had to assume that was true.

Luckily, she wasn't getting any serial killer vibes from him. Her instincts were telling her his brand of destructive only applied to inanimate objects, and she prayed this would be another case of them being right. He made her uneasy, sure, but she felt bizarrely unafraid of him, given the circumstances.

She was determined to try and make this work, regardless of her misgivings. There weren't that many job openings in the area, and she didn't want to move too far from her family, especially with her mom trying to balance her own work and taking care of Jillian's dad at the same time. Trying to be professional and willing to give him the benefit of the doubt, despite the strange tornado of emotions he inspired in her, she went against her better judgment and extended a hand to him. "Nice to meet you. I'm—"

"I don't care," he interrupted, the initial coldness she'd seen in him creeping back into his voice. "Trust me when I say this isn't the job for you." He made a shooing motion, blatantly ignoring her outstretched hand. "Go back to wherever you came from."

His attitude was like a bucket of ice water to the face, finally drowning out the unexplainable attraction she had felt moments before, and she dropped her hand to clench it at her side. Who did this guy think he was? The fact that he was probably the sexiest man she had ever seen was quickly paling in comparison to the fact that he was also the rudest.

"Sorry you feel that way," she managed, holding back what she *really* wanted to say in that moment.

Maintain calm, she thought. *Deep, healing breaths... in with the good air, out with the bad...*

Smiling evilly, as if he had heard her thoughts, he reached over and plucked a figurine off the remaining end table that hadn't been tipped over.

"I assume you'll be starting with this room as soon as you're unpacked?" he asked, his voice lowering menacingly.

She nodded, not trusting herself to speak. *Thou shalt not beat thy employer's guests with blunt objects.* Her temper had always been her downfall, but she'd never had a problem keeping it in check at work before. Not until that very moment.

He extended his arm, holding the delicate trinket between his thumb and forefinger. "I'll be moving to the library next," he said darkly. Then he dropped the trinket.

To her, this amounted to throwing down the gauntlet at the same time.

She stared down at the splintered pieces of glass and deliberately counted back from ten in her head. Then started over again at ten thousand when that wasn't enough. He was trying to get to her for some reason. He was actually *trying* to make her angry. He seemed to be going out of his way to do it.

He's trying to scare me off, she finally realized, her anger cooling to a more manageable level now that she had him figured out. Crazy or not, she wouldn't be pushed around by anyone. She still wasn't sure if she was going to stay, but if she did, she wasn't about to set the standard that he could get away with this.

She lifted her gaze from the shattered remains and gave him her most dazzling smile. She bowed deeply at the waist, as if bowing to royalty.

"Third door on the left from the main hallway, isn't it?" she asked cheerfully, barely suppressing saying, "Your Highness," at the end. "Shouldn't take me too long to get there since you've saved me the trouble of dusting all those tiny little things."

"Fantastic," he said, brows snapping together in a scowl, and she could tell he was wondering where she as going with this. "Can't wait to get started."

She turned on her heel and walked casually toward the door. Grasping the doorknob, she glanced back to look at him again. "By the way, do you do the rooms in any particular order?"

He gave her a blank look, and she found a great deal of pleasure in knowing she wasn't reacting the way he had obviously hoped.

"Just thought I'd check, so I could see about maybe childproofing a few things before you get there." She was about to leave, but hesitated, debating on how straightforward she should be with him. But if her new employers couldn't handle her setting boundaries with him, then this definitely wasn't the place for her.

"Since you didn't hire me, you don't get to decide if this job is right for me or not," she added, enjoying the dumbfounded look on his face. "It doesn't seem like Odath and Petrin care if you tear everything apart, so I won't either. If they want me to follow you around like a nanny chasing a misbehaving toddler on a rampage, then I'll do it. Be as obnoxious and destructive as you want, if that's how you get your kicks. I don't have to take you seriously, or care about your opinion, to get my work done."

Bowing low again, she shot him a challenging look as she walked out and closed the door on him.

Ashriel stood staring at the closed door for a long moment with no idea how she had turned the tables on him. For the first time in centuries, he was surprised. By a *human*, of all people.

Just when he'd been congratulating himself on getting rid of one human sacrifice, another had strolled right in. Completely different from any he'd met before, and twice as stubborn as the last, apparently. Lucky him.

Were human senses truly so dull that they couldn't feel any of the evil in this place?

He tipped his head back on a sigh, closing his eyes briefly to pray to God for patience. Divine intervention. A miracle. Anything.

Not now, he prayed. *Tairi, please, not now.*

Resigned, he opened his eyes and looked around himself, no longer quite as satisfied with his progress. As fun as breaking things was, the situation had just gotten more complicated, and he was nowhere near finding the means to free himself.

He righted a chair so he could sit and gather himself. Slouching down in the seat, he scrubbed a hand tiredly over his face. The new housekeeper was going to be a problem. A really big one.

Even as dulled as his senses were, the moment she had set foot in this hellhole his entire being had focused on her in a way that made him extremely uncomfortable. Even though he couldn't quite make out her words, the soft cadence of her voice as she'd moved around the house had arrested his attention immediately, and for a moment he'd forgotten what he'd been doing. His world had narrowed down to only her.

He'd wanted to know the curves of her face, and the expression she wore that went with the swirling emotions he could feel within her. Emotions that he was annoyed not to be able to perceive with his limited senses.

Some instinctive, primal desire he'd never known he had, buried somewhere deep inside himself, had responded to her presence, and it scared the hell out of him. As much as he wanted to dismiss it, even she had felt the undeniable pull. He'd seen it clearly in the way she had returned his gaze, as hyperaware of him as he had been of her.

For a human, she was uncommonly pretty and, unfortunately, he had noticed every damned detail. Pale-blue eyes, full of a fire that called out to him in a way that nothing ever had. Dark, rich-brown hair that curled loosely at her shoulders and made him want to sift his fingers through the strands. She was taller than most women, but still only came up to his chin. Delicately curvy, with full hips and breasts that he had no business noticing, but still had.

Whether he wanted to acknowledge the attraction or not, he had a feeling he was seriously fucked. He had no idea what *it* was supposed to feel like. That glorious, life-altering *it* that every shima searched for. He sure as hell hoped this wasn't what he was feeling, but he'd never felt *it* before, so how could he tell?

Cursing in several languages, he clenched his left hand, desperately trying to ignore the tingle in his wrist. Could he just lie to himself, and force himself to believe he had an aversion to housekeepers, or some freak allergic reaction to humans? He refused to consider the sensation in his wrist had anything whatsoever to do with the first symptoms of the legendary *it* that he had no damned time for or interest in at the moment.

"Oh, this is just fan-fucking-tastic," he muttered to himself. Maybe he was insane after all, and all the frustration and anger had finally made him delusional enough that he was imagining this logic-defying fascination with a human. One could hope. That option would actually be preferable, under the circumstances. "Of course, it might be happening now. Now is perfect."

Human or not, and regardless of whether this was it, he couldn't deny he wanted her. Badly. All he wanted to do was pull her into his arms and hold her against him, so close he could taste the vulnerable skin at the base of her neck and hear her sigh. He wanted to kiss her until they were both senseless, and nothing else mattered.

All the more reason to keep a distance between them, and get her the hell out of this place as quickly as possible. The sooner the better. Before she ended up like the last human who had stayed too long.

And he sure as hell was going to stick to his self-imposed rule about not learning her name especially. It was bad enough that her face would haunt him if he failed her. God help him if he let himself get too close.

Unfortunately for him, her natural mental barriers were stronger than a normal human's. Probably traces of shima ancestry in her blood, who knew how many generations back. After getting rid of the other housekeeper, he couldn't even begin to give Jillian a compulsion to leave. Since she was infuriatingly stubborn, and didn't appear to scare easily either, he was going to have to work a lot harder to get her out.

For the first time since the whole ordeal started, he wasn't looking forward to plotting ways to get rid of this latest human.

Chapter Two

Jillian was still groggy when she woke up the next morning. The day before had been a complete blur after she'd met Ashriel, and she dreaded the idea of starting all over again.

He'd been true to his word, sweeping through the entire downstairs like a madman. For reasons unknown, he seemed to get some strange kick out of demolishing everything in his path. Considering how huge the place was, that was saying something.

It made her wonder how many times her employers had replaced their belongings, and why they even bothered if they insisted on letting Ashriel live there. Maybe that was why some of the rooms were empty. Honestly, she was kind of relieved because if there wasn't anything left for him to rip apart or smash it would make her life a lot easier.

Sighing, she got out of bed and stretched. Her still-packed bags were sitting by the door and she eyed them dubiously. Honestly, after the day she'd had, she was hesitating over whether or not to even bother unpacking. She had wanted to give the new position a fair shot, and see how she felt after a day of getting used to things, but between the creepy, dimly lit house and the crazy, rude people, her nerves were constantly on edge. She'd felt like she was being watched all day as she followed Ashriel's trail of destruction from room to room, and it was only by the grace of God that she'd even managed to find her own room.

She wondered whether or not it was really a good idea to stay, but...

I'm fine, she thought automatically. She could stick it out for another few days to decide if she should stay or go.

Momentarily surprised by how firmly that answer came into her mind, she shook her head at herself. Feeling kind of off in a way she couldn't put her finger on, she pulled some fresh clothes out of her bags and got ready quickly, throwing on jeans, an old band T-shirt, and some beat-up sneakers. Her new employers hadn't asked her to wear any kind of uniform, and told her to wear what she liked, so she figured she'd just dress comfortably.

Grabbing her cell phone from the dresser and unplugging it from the charging cord, she made a quick call to her parents. She'd told them she would once she settled in at the new house, and she'd totally forgotten.

When her mom picked up on the third ring, she smiled to herself. Her mom was a worrier, watched more true crime TV than was probably healthy, and was forever warning Jillian she'd eventually end up working for serial killers. So this was going to be a fun conversation.

As expected, her mom was already imagining her employers were hiding a body somewhere by the time she was done describing her first day. "I'm fine, Mom, don't worry," Jillian rushed to reassure her. "They're a little weird—"

"A little?" her mom said doubtfully.

"But everything's fine," Jillian insisted. She heard a beeping noise over the line. "Hold on, Mom," she said, and quickly peeked at the screen. Frowning, she put her ear back to the phone. "Sorry, my battery's dying. I could've sworn I charged it last night."

"I'll let you go," her mom said, and then there was a pause where Jilliann could hear the muffled sound of her dad's voice in the background. "Your dad says to come over on your next day off if you can. And be careful!" her mom quickly added. "The news has been talking about unusual animal attacks in your area."

"Really?" Jillian frowned, bending down next to the dresser to check that her charger was plugged into the outlet all the way. "Well, don't worry, I still hate hiking," she said, trying to lighten the mood. Everything seemed fine with the outlet, so why was her phone not charged? "I won't be going into the woods for any reason."

They said their goodbyes, and Jillian promised to call again soon. After she hung up, she put her phone back on the charger and waited until she saw the little charging icon in the corner before she put her phone back on the dresser.

Sighing heavily, she studied herself in the mirror as she pulled her dark-brown hair back into a messy ponytail, a few loose curls framing her face, too short to be tied back. For the hundredth time, she asked herself why she couldn't just leave. She was worried about her parents, and her brother and sister were too far away and too busy in college to help out, but she knew she could probably manage to find another position not too far from them.

"I'm fine," she said to her reflection. It was a litany in her head. *I'm fine. I just have to be patient, and everything will work out fine.*

Turning away from the mirror and her confusing thoughts, she tried to focus on something more productive as she went to unlock her door. She felt like crap, but she had a job to do. She hadn't slept well at all, tossing and turning all night, and the prospect of dealing with Ashriel again made her head begin to hurt.

I'm fine, she thought again, confusingly. Shaking off the unusual fogginess in her head, she left the room and made her way to the kitchen to get some breakfast.

Ejoma, the shima realm
Resuna Forest, to the west of the Hidga Mountains

"Focus," Odath said, giving Ashriel a hard shove from behind.

Stumbling a little, Ashriel sighed as he walked through the dense forest. At least he was outside and could breathe the fresh air again. "Enalel said the Sijo was here?" he asked, although he really didn't care either way. He planned on being as unhelpful as possible.

"He was," Petrin said, looking through the trees to the west. It went without saying that none of them would be heading east, toward the Hidga Mountains.

Dim sunlight filtered down through the canopy high above, a mix of blue and purple leaves, shining off Odath and Petrin's dull silver armor as they searched.

They wore no insignia of rank or city, for obvious reasons.

They were traitorous pieces of dark magic addicted shit.

Unconcerned with whether he lived or died, they'd left him weaponless, in his human blue jeans, boots, and dark-red T-shirt. They probably also knew giving him a weapon would only ensure he used it on them at some point, regardless of his limited magical abilities. Their decision led him to grudgingly admit they weren't completely inept.

Ashriel stopped and turned to look at them, tilting his head slightly as he raised an eyebrow. "And how long ago was this? The trail is cold. I don't know why we're here."

"He's most likely to go to the Junak for help," Petrin said, touching the leaves of a vine wrapped around the trunk of one of the trees. He felt her magic shift as she scanned. "Not that it would do him much good even if he got past us."

"So again, why are we here?" Ashriel said. Bored, he leaned back against a tree and folded his arms across his chest as he looked between the two of them. "Let your people on the inside kill him."

If the rogue shimana had truly infiltrated the Junak, the Sijo was as good as dead. It would take at least a day to gather the members of the Junak, and in that time whoever was involved would silence him long before he could do any real damage to their cause, whatever it might be, assuming the Sijo even knew anything of value aside from Enalel's involvement.

"That's not what Enalel wants," Odath said.

"And you obediently follow," Ashriel said mockingly.

Odath narrowed his eyes at Ashriel, but Petrin merely sighed.

"I believe you were told to focus," she said, including Odath in the sharp look she gave Ashriel before continuing her own search.

Straightening away from the tree, Ashriel walked on ahead a few feet, pretending he intended to put some effort in. They probably knew he was dragging his feet, and he assumed they thought it was too much work to search while forcing him to do as they asked, so they let him be as long as he didn't make trouble for them. He'd be there, ready to kill on their command whether he liked it or not, when the time came anyway.

Glancing around, he vainly hoped they were near a road or pathway, but there was nothing as far as he could see except for trees. He wasn't sure it would do him much good if he could get a random passersby's attention, however, and he didn't like the idea of getting anyone else killed.

Not far enough away for his liking, Ashriel could feel the disgusting, leaching dark energy that clung to the void creature Enalel had sent to aid in the hunt for the Sijo. Glancing over uneasily, he could see the large cloud of black smoke that made up the creature's mass, almost perfectly still, and the fact that it was vaguely shima-sized creeped him the hell out. He'd seen this particular creature in action when he'd been captured. He knew it was watching him while it also searched for the Sijo.

"Hey, I have an idea," he said, glancing back at Odath. "Why don't we search in the mountains?"

"That won't be necessary," Petrin said. "We have his teleport stone."

They all knew the real reason. There were powerful creatures in those mountains to the east, and they'd be attracted to the darkness in Odath and Petrin. The orblike wendjana, so pretty on the surface with their bioluminescence, protected Neluk and Iseyba, concentrating on Iseyba especially. Known for luring unwary travelers off the path to satisfy their hunger, the creatures wouldn't let his captors get far, and Ashriel, with his relatively normal, low levels of darkness, might be able to escape while Odath and Petrin fought to the death in a vain attempt to get away.

What did it say about his life that he'd gotten to the point where his dearest fantasy was to watch two people get maimed? Not that they didn't deserve a serious maiming, but still.

"How'd you get your hands on that?" Ashriel said, putting his palm against a tree and lazily scanning his surroundings with his senses. His powers had been let off the leash just slightly more than usual so he could search effectively, but that didn't mean he planned on going along with what Odath and Petrin said. Unless he was strictly forced to by the magic binding him, he had his own agenda there.

Waste as much time as possible, be useless, and piss everybody off.

The more time they were in the shima realm, the more time they were away from the humans under the influence of the spells in the house he was being kept in. Without the hassle of trying to protect a bunch of oblivious humans from death and worse, he could focus just on freeing himself for a while. Careful not to be obvious about it, he watched Odath and Petrin as they searched, but hadn't seen them carrying any sort of object they could have tied his curse to yet.

He laughed when they both ignored him. "Don't tell me," he said, trying to get under their skin as he turned to face them. He already knew which of the two of them would cave first, but it was still fun. "You had him, and then you fucked up and lost him again. Bet Enalel wasn't too pleased with you guys."

Odath clenched his hand on the hilt of his sword, but a swift glance at Petrin quickly had him back in line.

Ashriel smirked at him when he met the other man's gaze, and deferred to Petrin just to piss Odath off. "Where do you want me to search next, Petrin?" She was in charge, under Enalel's orders, and Odath didn't like that one bit.

"North," she said absently, not paying attention to the tension building between Odath and Ashriel.

"Which do you think would win?" Ashriel asked, picking up a random branch and looking at it closely, as though the Sijo's whereabouts could be discerned by studying it. He wandered in a generally northward direction, keeping Odath in the periphery of his vision. "The void creature or the creatures in the mountains?"

"The void creature," Odath said, kneeling to place his hand to the dirt to scan.

"Feel like testing that theory?" Ashriel said, grinning as he absently picked a bright-purple leaf off the branch he was holding.

"We're not going into the mountains," Petrin said stiffly, clearly starting to get annoyed.

Ashriel shrugged. "I suppose you're right. Odath probably wouldn't make it through."

Odath glared at him, rising to his feet. "There's not enough of a trail left here to follow. The Sijo was here too long ago, and he hid his energy too well," he said to Petrin.

"I believe I already stated that," Ashriel pointed out. "Stop making me have to compete to out-useless you."

Odath was in front of him in an instant, the edge of his sword at Ashriel's throat, but Ashriel didn't even flinch. He'd known Odath would be the first to break, so he just raised an eyebrow, pressed the jagged, broken end of the branch he still held against Odath's stomach a little harder, and waited calmly. He felt Odath tense when he realized his mistake, finally noticing Ashriel held a weapon of sorts.

"Odath," Petrin said warningly, and her authoritative tone only seemed to irritate Odath further. "He can't fulfill his role if you kill him now."

Odath's eyes flicked to her, the hint of a challenge in his gaze as he backed away from Ashriel. Petrin didn't unsheathe her weapon, but she was clearly ready, hand resting lightly on the hilt of the sword at her waist. A silent moment of tension passed where Odath and Petrin stared each other down, before Odath turned his back on her and Ashriel and trudged off into the trees to the south, angrily shoving his sword back into its sheath.

Ashriel smirked. If nothing else, he could rely on stirring up the power struggle between these two to amuse himself.

"Keep scanning," Petrin said as if nothing had happened, releasing her grip on her own weapon. She glanced briefly at his makeshift weapon before walking a short distance away, toward the west, apparently dismissing him as any kind of real threat to her.

Ashriel stole another look at the creature before returning his attention to the task at hand—the fine art of just barely keeping up the pretense of doing something while very obviously being content to waste everybody's time. Honestly, he was only there on the off chance that they found the Sijo's trail anyway. It specifically had to be him that murdered the Sijo for some reason. He had his suspicions as to why, but the why really only mattered if he managed to get away and do something about it.

Using the end of his branch, he rifled through some leaves at his feet before moving on. Petrin and Odath didn't have to worry about him running off. The magic that bound him kept him from leaving whatever area they chose, so unless they were eaten by a wendja, or he freed himself, or some other horrible fate befell his enemies, he was stuck.

Resigned to several more hours in the company of his captors and the void creature, Ashriel decided to try and enjoy his time outside of the stifling house. There wasn't anything else to do anyway. So he kept walking until he started to feel the spell he was under react to his distance from the others. A tightness over his skin and a pressure in his chest. Any farther and there would be pain.

Sighing, he put a hand against the nearest tree, ready to sit at its base and do nothing until Odath and Petrin had searched the area. A very faint but familiar energy hummed in the bark of the tree beneath his palm and he paused, mid-crouch. Straightening, he slipped behind the cover of the tree and used his magic to scan the area, making sure the others were still a good distance away.

He sensed that they were still hunting elsewhere, the void creature not too far from Petrin, off to the west. The energy he felt was stronger to the east, and he quickly followed the weak trail, unafraid of wandering too close to the mountains.

The farther he got from the others, the more uncomfortable the pressure in his chest became, but he ignored it. Who knew how long he had before they noticed he wasn't where he was supposed to be?

As the leaves of the trees and undergrowth began to darken from different shades of blue and purple, to the much darker blue of the crystal trees found in the mountains, and the tree trunks began to be veined with crystal, he could feel the spell he was under pulling at him. Leaching away at his magic. It was a warning, but he couldn't afford to let that stop him.

Moving silently through the forest, Ashriel took note of any anomaly in his surroundings. Disturbed earth and destroyed plants to his left, where magic had missed its target. He'd only fought beside the Sijo briefly, but he recognized this magic as his. Gashes in a tree to his right, where some large creature had taken a swipe at something, saturated in void energy.

The Sijo had done an excellent job of hiding any signs that he'd been there, but Ashriel could tell he'd been in a hurry. After a little searching, he could see why.

The tainted stench of void energy hit him like a slap in the face just before he reached a little-used path that led into the Hidga Mountains. The Sijo must have been ambushed by a void creature. Maybe two, based on the amount of energy he sensed.

Pain sliced through his chest, sharp and hot like he'd been slashed with a fiery blade, and it stole his breath for a moment. Dizziness swept through him, and he stumbled to a stop, trying to reorient himself, but the magic binding him was too strong. This was as far as he could safely go from the others.

Kneeling, he brushed the leaves on the ground aside so he could rest his palm against the soil. It wasn't much, but he could at least cover the Sijo's trail and make it a little harder for Odath and Petrin to track him.

Just as he was channeling his energy, ready to erase any sign of the Sijo, he heard a low growl uncomfortably close to his ear. Void energy surrounded him, almost choking in its intensity, and all the hairs stood up on the back of Ashriel's neck.

Staying perfectly still, he clenched the branch he still held in his right hand, but he knew it would barely even slow the creature down if it were ordered to attack. The formless mass of black smoke circled around him to position itself between him and the mountains, brushing his shoulder as it passed, and his stomach dropped with a sickening lurch as a sensation so cold it was painful seared through him from the contact. Without a solid form, the creature's touch had been nothing more than a moment of heaviness against his shoulder, but it had sucked a large amount of magic right out of him, leaving him momentarily dizzy again.

"Clever beast," Ashriel said, warily rising to his feet and taking several steps back. The pain from the spell he was under eased, but that was the least of his worries. He didn't dare take his eyes off the hulking creature, even when he heard the telltale calls of a wendja not too far off in the mountains, like a beautiful song. The wendja must have sensed the darkness in the creature in front of him and had come closer in the hopes of a meal, but the void creature didn't react at all.

It didn't sit well with him that the creature had figured out what he was up to. It wasn't like the mind-controlled warriors he'd seen in Orilia. Its intelligence was in tact. It watched. Learned. Strategized. Just as he'd been studying Odath's reactions throughout their conversation earlier, the creature must have been silently analyzing Ashriel's.

It wasn't long before Petrin found them, but it felt like forever while Ashriel waited for the creature to do something. The wendja's song grew closer, and he could tell Petrin was tense because of it from the way she kept a white-knuckled grip on the hilt of her sheathed sword, and her gaze searched through the trees before landing on him.

"You finally found something," she said.

"Thrilled to have been of service," Ashriel said sarcastically.

"Go regenerate," she said, but not out of any true concern. These were part of Enalel's orders. To keep him alive until he'd fulfilled his purpose. As long as he didn't step foot outside the house in the human realm, he wouldn't be affected by the magic that forced him to stay close to Odath and Petrin, so he knew he could count on at least a couple hours of time to himself while they reported what they'd found to Enalel.

Petrin reached out and placed a hand on his shoulder, and for once he didn't think of slapping her hand away. He couldn't stand to be anywhere near the nauseating void energy pouring off the creature, or the darkness he could feel in Odath and Petrin. He needed a break from it, however short it might be, even if that meant being cooped up in that miserable house again.

She said a quick spell under her breath, then there was a flash of light and a sensation like pins and needles sweeping over his entire body, and then he was suddenly in the human realm, standing in the shadowy corner beside the stairs, facing a blank wall across from the front door, on the first floor of the house he was being kept in with the humans.

Petrin seemed not to care at all if a human happened to see him appear in a flash of light. This was the point he always returned to when she teleported him. He felt so drained from his proximity to the creature though, that he couldn't summon the energy to be annoyed about it.

Holding his arms away from his body and wishing he didn't have to breathe so he wouldn't smell the fumes coming off himself, he felt like he'd just been bathing in something unspeakably foul for the past several hours. All he wanted to do was shower, purify himself of the dark magic clinging to him, and go into his regenerative sleep. Not that Enalel would let him completely heal, but at least it would be something.

"Disgusting," he muttered to himself.

"Hey," he heard a voice say behind him, and he spun around, ready to take someone's head off. When he saw it was just the new live-in housekeeper, he was almost relieved.

Almost.

"Why are you still here?" he demanded, too exhausted to deal with her right then. She made him feel all sorts of things he didn't want to be feeling, and at the moment she was looking at him with such a look of concern in her wide, light-blue eyes that he wanted to be nice for once and reassure her.

What the hell was wrong with him? He should pick her up and chuck her out the door, except that he knew javelin throwing a human probably wouldn't end well.

"Just making sure you're all right," she said, giving him a funny look as she crossed her arms over her chest.

"I'm great," he snapped. "Amazing even."

She looked unconvinced. "Sure," she said dryly. "Whatever you say."

So maybe from her point of view he *had* just been standing in the shadows, facing a blank wall, but he wasn't going to be swayed. He couldn't afford to be nice, even if she was trying to be.

They couldn't be friends. He didn't even want to be acquaintances. And he sure as hell wasn't going to acknowledge that standing within five feet of her like this was making his wrist tingle again.

Fucking hell!

Could this day get any worse?

He was about to brush past her, something rude on the tip of his tongue, when he sensed there had been a subtle change in her energy. He was already so overly aware of her presence and her effect on him that he couldn't help but notice.

Stopping beside her, much closer than he should ever allow himself to be to her, he gave her a hard look, scanning her with what was left of his magic. Just one touch from the creature had drained his already weakened body.

And for some damned reason, she raised her chin and stared him down with a raised eyebrow. She didn't back away from him, or get scared or intimidated. She looked at him fearlessly, brows furrowing in a frown. "Look, I realize we're not going to be buddies or anything, but you don't look too good."

"Don't worry about me," he said, detecting some magical tampering in her brain already, even with his own magic failing him. "It's *you* that you need to be focusing on." Sighing, he tried something he'd tried dozens of times with other victims in that house. Something he would never ordinarily do, if things weren't so dire, because there were strict laws against telling humans these things unless it was a special circumstance. The truth.

"Odath and Petrin aren't human, okay? And I don't mean in a they're-so-cold-blooded-it's-inhuman sort of way. They literally are not humans," he said, and she stared at him with wide eyes, not saying a word. This was going about as well as expected. "They want to drain you dry of all your energy, sacrifice you, and possibly drink your blood just for the rush. The influence their spells have on you will only get worse with each passing day. Now is the time to leave, before they get back. Don't grab your bags. Just get the fuck out while you can."

"Wow," she said, looking at him like he was a complete psycho. She did take a small step away from him then, however, like she was waiting for him to start breaking things. "That's...creative."

"I know you feel the danger here. You're stronger than most humans," he said, trying to maintain his composure in the hopes that he could get through to her. Drawing on the last pathetic drops of his magic, he levitated a small vase from the narrow entryway table and brought it to hover between them, practically right in front of her face so she couldn't possibly miss it or try to rationalize it. "There are monsters here who want to kill you. Get out!"

She froze, breath stalling and eyes going glassy. "I'm fine," she said, but her voice sounded hollow and unnatural.

It was just like what he'd witnessed in Rae and all the other humans Odath and Petrin had lured to them. Normal one minute and a puppet the next, until one day they were just staring off into space, their minds completely broken and under their captors' control. Then they disappeared soon after.

"I fucking hate that word," he said to no one in particular, because she certainly couldn't hear him wherever the hell her consciousness had flown off to when the spell she was under activated. Even though he could tell she had shima ancestry somewhere in her family line, and was stronger than a normal human, she was still far from being any kind of match for Odath and Petrin's magic. "Wake up," he said, snapping his fingers next to her ear. "Human! Snap out of it!"

When she didn't respond, he almost reached out to shake her, but stopped himself at the last second. He dropped his arms back to his sides, clenching his hands into fists. Touching her was the last thing he should *ever* do. Sighing, he released the magic holding the vase in midair and it landed right at her feet with an impressively loud shattering noise.

There was roughly a two second delay, and then she yelped in surprise, jumping back. “What the heck! What are you doing?” she demanded, scowling up at him, and he wondered how much she remembered.

“Dunno,” he said, watching her for any signs of slipping back under the spell. “What *was* I doing?”

Rolling her eyes, she turned her back on him and walked away, giving a wave over her shoulder. “Good-night, Ashriel.”

CHAPTER THREE

A WEEK HAD PASSED, AND RATHER than being the live-in housekeeper, Jillian had resigned herself to being Ashriel's live-in babysitter. When he wasn't causing some form of chaos, he was silently brooding somewhere. Normally in a room he had just gotten done destroying. Usually just watching her as she cleaned up after him. Not saying anything. Making her feel uneasy. Probably on purpose.

Despite her determination to figure out what was going on with him, she had learned not to look at him. Because every time she did, their gazes would meet and a whole new insanity would befall her.

She was actually attracted to him. Brooding, scowling, rudeness and all.

She was fighting it tooth and nail, but she'd caught him in a couple rare unguarded moments, when he wasn't breaking things or being a jerk, and her resolve had weakened. She could've sworn his expression softened just the tiniest bit a few times when he looked at her, and she wondered if he might be battling the same bizarre fascination with her.

She instinctively knew getting involved with him

would be trouble, not to mention more than a little unprofessional, but she was curious about him. After unwillingly spending a whole week in his company, she'd come to realize that all of his destruction and anger wasn't actually about her. He also wasn't the criminally insane ax murderer Petrin kept hinting he was. He was having some sort of war with Odath and Petrin that she didn't understand.

More than once she had gotten the impression that he was actually searching for something. Whenever she asked, though, he just blew it off or said something snide.

Heaving another sigh, she mentally prepared herself for the inevitable chaos of the day ahead. Strangely exhausted, simply getting ready felt like a chore. Her movements were sluggish as she went downstairs, finding her way to the kitchen for a quick breakfast after getting lost a couple times. Chatting with Rae for a few minutes while they ate woke her up a bit, and she felt a little more cheerful after she finished.

"Hey, what's up with the electricity in this place?" Jillian said as she brought her plate to the sink, bringing up something that had been bothering her for a while. "The outlets in my room aren't working right. Have you noticed anything?"

"Petrin said the wiring in this place is a mess," Rae said, shrugging. "She didn't seem concerned, but none of the electricity in the house works correctly."

"I can't keep my phone charged," Jillian said, digging it out of her pocket to check the battery's charge percent. As expected, it was low.

"I don't know if that's the bad wiring so much as this house being outside of town. Nobody's phone works that well here. Maybe it's the terrible reception too?" Rae said, taking Jillian's empty plate off the table to clean it.

"Thanks," Jillian said, putting her phone away in her pocket.

"Ashriel told me to try keeping my phone off while I'm here, and it actually helps," Rae said.

"Weird," Jillian said, wondering what that was all about.

"Yeah," Rae said. "Petrin said they called an electrician, but I doubt she's really going to do anything about it."

"Probably not," Jillian agreed. Her employers seemed content to be in the dark constantly anyway. "I'd better get to work. Ashriel waits for no one."

Rae laughed at that. "Yeah, he's in a mood this morning. Good luck."

"When isn't he?" Jillian said with a long-suffering sigh. "Thanks for breakfast," she said, getting up from her seat at the island in the middle of the kitchen. "See you at lunch."

"See ya!" Rae called cheerfully as Jillian walked out into the hallway.

Feeling better with some food in her stomach, she went to collect her cleaning supplies and headed for the library. The morning was starting out crappy, and it only got worse when, after a few wrong turns, she managed to locate the library and realized Ashriel was already there.

Stopping in the doorway, she glanced around the room in front of her in horror. She should be used to this buy now, but it was still a shock every single time. How? And why? But mostly, *how exactly* had Odath and Petrin managed to fill the room with more vases and lamps and candles again so quickly after Ashriel's daily rampage? Every day since she'd arrived the same thing had happened, and it made no sense. Did they have a storehouse somewhere she was unaware of? If the rest of the house had been refilled, she might finally quit.

I'm fine, she thought incongruously, even though she simultaneously wished she could be anywhere else besides that house. *Everything's fine.*

She was about to sneak away and head to a different room to postpone the inevitable, but Ashriel had already spotted her. He smirked briefly, as if he'd guessed what she'd been thinking, and she knew it would be pointless to try a different room. He'd made it clear each day that he would follow her just to annoy her.

Squaring her shoulders, she took a deep breath before entering the room. "Good morning," she said in a cool voice, giving him a bright, careless smile as if she didn't want to pounce on him every time she saw him.

Lounging indolently in a large chair in front of the cold fireplace, he silently watched her through hooded eyes, apparently brooding about something already. Dear lord, he was gorgeous. His long black hair was down, slightly messy in a sexy way. He wore faded jeans and a black button-up shirt, untucked, with the sleeves rolled up. His clothes were rumpled like he had just rolled out of bed.

She felt like she'd enjoy rolling him right back in.

Feeling herself flush, she prayed he didn't see her reaction. She noticed the way his gaze warmed for just a moment, there and gone so quickly she might have imagined it, and her knees went weak. And then he was back to his usual.

"Good morning," he nearly growled, obviously annoyed about something.

Trying to ignore him, she walked to a shelf and started removing objects so she could dust, but she could feel him staring.

"You seem tired. I think you should leave and find work elsewhere. Anywhere that suits you better," he said, launching into his favorite topic.

"I'm fine," she said, and for some strange reason her response seemed to irritate him.

"You're not fine," he grumbled, but she ignored him. "And why are you starting so early?"

It made no sense for that question to sound mildly accusatory, but it did.

"Meaning, before you had a chance to destroy anything in here?" she said crankily, glancing at him.

His lips twitched in the beginning of a smile. "It's very disappointing, you know. My whole schedule for the day is out of line now."

"Inconsiderate of me, isn't it?" she asked mockingly, deciding it was best not to look at him directly. She refocused on her work.

"Very," he said, sounding distracted.

As much as she tried to concentrate only on what she was doing, she was so conscious of his gaze on her, she could barely pay attention to anything else as she replaced the trinkets and moved on to the next shelf. Desperately wishing she'd managed to escape earlier, she glanced over her shoulder, unable to help herself, and caught him watching her with his usual scowl.

"Can I help you?" she asked, feeling a little nervous with his eyes fixed on her. She couldn't tell what he was thinking, but she could practically feel the tension in him, and it was putting her even more on edge than she was before.

"That would be beyond your limited abilities, human," he said cryptically.

"Do you hear how weird that sounds when you call me human like it's my name?" Even after all this time, he refused to call her anything except *human* or *pain in the ass human* or *idiot human* for some variation.

"Am I wrong?" he asked, raising an eyebrow. "Noticed any recent manifestation of supernatural powers? Telepathy? Control of the elements? Shapeshifting?"

She stared at him blankly, fully aware he was being sarcastic. Of course. Thank God she'd decided he wasn't really a psycho, and couldn't possibly believe any of those things he'd mentioned were real. This sure would be awkward if she still thought that he was crazy in a small place in the back of her mind. "Not recently, no. You?"

That permanent scowl of his softened fractionally, unexpected warmth creeping into his expression, and he seemed oddly amused by her question. "Not today, but you'll be the third to know if I do."

While his comment made absolutely zero sense, the genuine, fleeting half smile he gave her did devastating things to her blood pressure. She cleared her throat and quickly looked away, moving her dust rag over the surface of the shelf in front of her. Lying to herself about the butterflies in her stomach, she tried to force herself to think about this rationally.

Keeping her job. Good.

Jumping her employer's guest, in her employer's library, on her employer's chair. Bad.

Steering clear of complicated men with unpredictable natures. Good.

Lusting after broody bad boys that made her knees weak...bad?

"Petrin told me that the third floor is under construction, and isn't safe," she said, just making conversation to fill the silence. She wished her voice didn't sound so breathless.

"I suppose, if she says so," he said noncommittally.

She risked glancing at him again, arching a brow. "You suppose? Then why do you sleep up there?"

The small smile he gave her then was humorless. "There is no safe place in this house," he answered quietly, rising to his feet.

"Isn't that a little melodramatic?" she said, raising her eyebrows as he moved toward her.

"Maybe a little," he admitted, stopping in front of her. "But it's true. You shouldn't stay here."

"Why not?" she asked, her breath catching a little as he raised a hand to brush a stray curl behind her ear. She stood perfectly still as the warmth of his fingers brushed across her temple with the action, and found herself tempted to turn her face into the caress.

"You aren't safe here," he said unevenly, dropping his hand. He frowned as if he were as surprised by his actions as she was.

"What is it you think I need to worry about?" she said, trying not to notice the way her skin seemed to tingle where he had touched her. Something in his tone made her think he was referring to whatever his deal was with Odath and Petrin, in his own roundabout way.

He was quiet a moment, studying her with an unreadable expression, and she wondered if she was finally getting somewhere with him. Maybe she could find a way to understand him, if he'd only open up to her and tell her what was going on.

"So when are you leaving?" he asked brightly, abruptly changing the subject. He turned his back to her, pacing a few steps away to put some much needed space between them.

"Are we really going to talk about me staying again?" she asked flatly, heaving a sigh. She knew she shouldn't feel so disappointed. If he wanted this distance between them, he was doing them both a favor.

Never mind that she was still on the fence about staying, she wasn't crazy about the heavy-handed way he was trying to get her to leave.

Besides, she was fine. Everything was *fine.*

"I'll even help you pack," he continued as if he hadn't heard her. "It will be fun."

He said the last part with a perverse kind of pleasure that made her narrow her eyes at him.

"Would this be the same kind of packing—" she used little air quotes when she said this, emphasizing the word *packing* as she arched a brow at him, "—that you help Odath and Petrin with everyday?"

He chuckled, casting her a sideways glance as he walked around the room. Trailing his hand over an end table, he carelessly swept a lamp to the floor before moving on.

Like that was completely normal, logical behavior. No big deal. Just breaking things again. Whatever.

"I don't have to break things. I can be very gentle," he softly promised as he faced her again.

She narrowed her eyes at him, feeling her cheeks flush and hating the telltale sign. Oh, she knew very well that he could be gentle, darn him, but he seemed to prefer being a jerk. Several times over the past week he'd seemed to be looking out for her. Grabbing her elbow to steady her when she tripped over something he'd hurled to the ground and then pulling his hand back like she'd burned him. Automatic, polite gestures that didn't feel as out of character for him as they should, like opening a door for her when her arms were full or picking up something she dropped. Or the way he'd noticed she'd been under the weather all week, and couldn't seem to help asking how she was feeling, even though he always asked with a big scowl on his face and followed up with some sarcastic comment about this being further evidence she should quit.

But the second she started seeing him as anything other than crazy in his brief flashes of normalcy, it was like a switch flipped, and he went to extreme measures to show off just how insane he could be.

She eyed him doubtfully, unable to shake the idea that there was more to him and his weird back and forth behavior than there seemed. "You keep saying you want me to leave, but sometimes I get the feeling that's not entirely true. Then you push me away again," she said, the words slipping out before she could stop them. "I don't think you really know what you want."

"Unfortunately, I do," he said enigmatically. While she was wondering how to take that, he made a show of lacing his fingers in front of him and cracking his knuckles loudly. “Shall we get started on this room?” he asked way too cheerfully for her comfort.

She crossed her arms, scowling at him. “Besides me leaving, was there something you needed?” she demanded, praying he would act like a normal human being, take the hint, and leave so she could work. She raised an eyebrow at him and waited.

He tilted his head, lips curving up in one of his knee-melting smiles. “What makes you think I need anything besides the pleasure of your company?” he asked smoothly.

“Yeah, because I’m just so interesting to you,” she challenged.

“You say interesting things when you’re angry.”

She sighed. “Ashriel,” she said, her voice edged with annoyance. “It’s too early for your games, and I’m not going to play along.” She glared at him, eyes narrowed, and turned away to begin wiping down the desk, shifting things as she worked, trying to distract herself.

“Who said I’m playing?” he said quietly, and she tensed, knowing she wasn’t going to like whatever else he had to say. She didn’t turn around, but she could feel him watching her again. “I will do whatever I have to do to get you to leave this place. If that includes making your life hell, then I’ll have to make myself do it.”

“You’re telling me this isn’t how you usually get your kicks?” she demanded, not particularly caring if he heard the disbelief in her tone. “I’m just special?”

“No,” he admitted with a chuckle. “I do enjoy messing with people.”

“This isn’t going to work with me,” she said breezily, trying for indifference as she gave up and faced him again.

He gave her a menacing smile then. "I'll wear you down eventually. You have no idea how much time I have on my hands," he said with feeling, some hidden meaning in his words. He nodded toward the desk again. "Now, don't you have work to do?"

She clenched the dust rag in her hands, wishing she could strangle him. Noticing the way his gaze zeroed in on the reaction, she forced her fingers to uncurl from their death grip.

"You aren't going to break anything else?" she demanded, proud of how calm she sounded.

"Oh, no," he said pleasantly. "I'm still going to tear this place apart." He managed to say this with the same matter-of-fact tone someone else would use to discuss the weather. "I'm just going to wait until you're done dusting. Doing such detailed cleaning of those fragile things." The smile that curved his lips could have been friendly, if one managed to forget he was *trying* to make her lose it. "Putting all those little trinkets back exactly where they belong..."

Breathe. Just breathe, she chanted to herself.

"Well?" He gestured around them. "Let's go. I would say that I don't have all day..." Obviously knowing he had her right where he wanted her, he tilted his head, his grin widening. "But I do. I do have all day to spend with you. Following you. Giving you a helping hand with the chores. All day." He arched a brow, and openly continued to enjoy her reaction. "Every day until you leave."

And that was it.

That was the moment she finally lost it.

It was a losing battle anyway, and she knew it. This had to be the most ridiculous situation she had ever been in, and there was nothing else to do about it, so she just laughed. She laughed so hard and so long that her stomach hurt, and he actually started to look a little concerned.

Wiping her eyes, she shrugged, moved behind the desk to face him, and swept her arm over the surface, knocking everything to the ground. "I keep forgetting no one seems to care anyway," she said, sounding strangely calm even to her own ears. "Go for it. It's not my house. And if they don't care, I have no reason to worry about it."

She shrugged again, and another bubble of laughter escaped. "From now on, I'll just save myself the time if it's all the same. Go ahead and destroy everything. Sweeping is easier than rearranging things while I dust. So from now on, *I'll* just follow *you* around the house. It will be much easier, and much faster, that way. Now—" she gave him a cold smile, bracing her hands on the desk as she stared him down "—for the last time, I'm not leaving," she nearly growled, unable to keep the calm in her voice no matter how hard she tried.

"Tease," he muttered.

"What?" She blinked at him, completely lost.

"Just when I think I've pushed you far enough, and I'm taunted with the idea that you might actually cave, you disappoint me." He sighed heavily.

"What is your problem?" she demanded, planting her hands on her hips. "Is this personal or something? Because it's really starting to feel like it is."

"Why do you want to stay so badly?" he returned,

all signs of humor fading. His brows snapped together in a frown.

She looked away from him, unable to meet his gaze. "The money is good," she lied stiffly.

"Kaitsa dahuj hano!" he growled through clenched teeth, slipping into his native tongue as he completely lost his patience.

He moved so quickly then that she couldn't contain a small cry of surprise, dropping her dust rag and automatically stumbling away from him, hands coming up between them defensively. One second he had been several feet away, and the next, he was looming over her, grabbing her by the shoulders to steady her, looking very much like he wanted to shake her while he was at it.

She flattened her palms against his chest, some instinctual part of her a little frightened of him. She hadn't seen him move. He was just suddenly there.

"Finally!" he growled, his gaze burning into her. "You should be scared! You have no idea how dangerous this is!"

"So explain it to me!" she yelled, hands curling into the front of his shirt. She didn't like the feeling of being in the dark.

"Don't you understand that I can't?"

"Won't," she stated flatly, glaring at him. She dropped her hands, intending to put some distance between them, but he didn't seem to notice when she tried to pull away. His grip didn't hurt, but he still easily kept her close.

"Can't," he insisted, firmly correcting her.

He gave her a long, searching look. His hands softened on her shoulders. "And I think you know that this *is* personal," he said darkly, his mood doing another dizzying one-eighty.

Again, with the ambiguous, crazy-man answers. But she could feel the change in him. He wasn't messing with her. All pretenses were gone, and he was finally being honest.

She swallowed hard, taking a deep breath before she nodded. "Okay."

Her instincts had been right. Something was wrong there, and the more Ashriel said, and didn't say, she was beginning to think she actually was in a dangerous situation. But every time she considered leaving, she just...couldn't. Something stopped her every time. Her worry for her parents. Her weird attachment to Ashriel. Both could be addressed even if she worked somewhere else, but she was never able to follow through with what her instincts had told her that first day. She should leave.

I should stay. The thought popped into her head automatically. A brief wave of dizziness came over her, and then—

What had she just been thinking about? She couldn't remember for some reason. All she knew was that she had to convince Ashriel she really wanted to stay.

Ashriel was frowning at her for some reason, and she tried to recall what she might have said to annoy him this time. When his hands moved, one shackling her left wrist, the other sliding around her waist, she didn't think of struggling. Her free hand drifted up to rest on his shoulder again, but she couldn't decide whether it was to maintain a small distance between them or to keep him close. All she knew was that she was inexplicably comforted by his nearness.

"I'm fine," she said, trying to convince herself as much as she was him. "I appreciate your concern, but I'm staying."

Ashriel gritted his teeth against the urge to find the nearest inanimate object to vent his frustration on. He'd never felt so beyond words, out of control, enraged in the entirety of his existence, but he managed to reel himself in for the human's sake. He'd already seen the evidence that Odath and Petrin were messing with her head, he was next to useless when it came to doing anything about it, and she didn't even know why he was angry.

"Stop saying you're fine!" he snapped, wishing he could just throw this maddening human over his shoulder and carry her out the door himself. "Saying you're fine is just proof that you aren't!"

"What does that even mean?" she said, annoyed because she didn't understand, and he couldn't explain. "I'm fi—"

"Don't," he said angrily. "God help me, if you say you're fine one more time, I'm going to set the entire house on fire."

"You weren't already planning on that?" she shot back. "And why is breaking things always your answer?"

"Because I can't kill the people I want to instead."

Probably trying to decipher if he was serious or not, she narrowed her eyes at him. "So reassuring."

Realizing he was still holding on to her, he forced

himself to let go and took a quick step back. *Fucking bond,* he thought to himself. It made him so damned hyperaware of her, keeping his distance was becoming increasingly difficult.

Who was he kidding? Human or not, he would've been attracted to her even without the bond.

"Wasn't trying to be," he said, wondering what he would have to do to convince her to leave. Odath and Petrin had already started targeting her, and unlike himself, their magic was at full power. They could easily force themselves into her mind. *I'm fine* could mean she was actually doing fine, or it could be just like when he'd levitated that vase in front of her. "I'm not going to make things easier going forward, you know?"

"Doesn't matter," she said, retrieving her dust rag from the floor and tossing it on the desk. "And it's fine by me. I'm not participating in whatever weirdo game you're playing with Odath and Petrin. I'll just wait until you get bored and move on to the next room." With that, she grabbed the arm of the office chair behind the desk, pulled it to her, and flopped down in the seat. Leaning back comfortably, she propped her feet on the corner of the desk, crossing her ankles. "You have fun now," she said, making a shooing gesture at him before patiently folding her hands in her lap. "I'll be here when you're finished."

Ashriel groaned in frustration, scrubbing his hands over his face as he lapsed into his native tongue. "Iyo gan ith jerutoj."

"Right back at you, buddy," she said, picking up on the feeling he put into that phrase, despite not knowing what the words meant.

He tried to collect himself. Took a deep breath. Looked at her, and saw the stubborn, challenging look in her eyes.

Could he just burn the house down? He'd failed before, but would it be possible this time? Would the curse binding him stop him again? This particular human obviously didn't have the sense to leave unless there was no house to live in, so this was his only logical option. Clearly.

He turned on his heel and stalked toward the door, intent on his mission.

"Where are you going?" she asked, but he didn't even pause.

"To burn the fucking house to the ground," he nearly growled. "Hopefully, if you smell smoke, you'll be smart enough to get the hell out." He slammed the library door closed behind him before she could say anything else that would drive him insane.

Fuming at how helpless he felt, he went straight for the cleaning supplies in the hall closet near the kitchen. He knew it was futile, but he had to try. Saving up enough magic to attempt putting a compulsion on a human to do it was out of the question. He'd tried that once, and he'd regret it for the rest of his life. Human or not, he wouldn't put anyone else in the line of fire again. He could only hope his connection with the frustrating new housekeeper had strengthened him just enough to resist the spells controlling him.

When he got to the closet, he wrenched the door open, nearly ripping the heavy oak door right off its hinges in his haste. The knob hit the wall hard, leaving a large crescent-shaped gash in the drywall. He reached for the first flammable thing he saw, feeling hopeful. But then he felt the moment the spells activated, tightening their hold on him like invisible shackles. His hand stopped midway, his body frozen. He tried to fight it, pushing against the magic with his own pathetically depleted powers, but he couldn't even make a dent in it. Sighing, he stood there and silently waited for the ax to fall.

He didn't have to wait long.

"Again?" Petrin said from behind him, sounding distinctly bored.

"Until I'm successful, obviously," he said, gritting his teeth when he sensed her move closer, until she as standing inches behind him. The natural revulsion he felt at the dark energy clinging to her was only part of the reason he felt like vomiting. The other part was just her personality. "Don't suppose you could fuck off? I'm obviously extremely busy right now."

"Oooo, so cranky," she said, her breath warm on his neck. She was a threat on several levels, her sathra nature being the most immediate at the moment. Unlike Odath, she actually needed blood to survive, but that didn't mean she was above taking when she didn't need to. "I keep asking myself why Enalel won't let us just kill you and get it over with. Your outbursts force me to divide my attention too much."

"Wow, I feel so bad about that," he said without inflection. He was beginning to feel uneasy with her behind him, but he wasn't about to show her that. If nothing else though, at least Petrin's attention was away from the humans for the time being. Sensing that the new housekeeper had gone farther away, deeper into the house, he was thankful she wouldn't walk in on this by chance. The less she knew, the safer she'd be. "What can I do to make your life easier? Because I sincerely care about what you want."

"So glad you asked," she said, and he realized he'd screwed up. She wasn't in the mood.

She kicked the back of his knee hard, forcing him to kneel in front of her. His knees hit the wood floor so hard it made him wince, but he refused to give her the pleasure of hearing him react. Her small hands gripped his shoulders, nails digging into his flesh, and a fiery pain ripped through him as she bit down on the side of his neck.

Repulsed, he fought against the magic still holding him, but it was no use. He weakened as she grew stronger, her greed taking over. It wasn't just sustenance she wanted. It was the power in his blood. Shima blood was so much richer in magical energy than a human's. It would give her the strongest high and temporary boost to her own powers.

After she'd had her fill, he stumbled his way to the third floor, desperate to regenerate and cleanse her darkness from his skin.

Chapter Four

Jillian couldn't help looking over her shoulder again as she made her way down the second-floor hallway, trying to locate her room again in the ridiculous labyrinth of a house. It was early still, just before sunset, and she was finally considering getting around to finishing unpacking before dinner. After a couple weeks of being there, nothing had really improved, but she just couldn't seem to make a clean break and leave. If anything, things just got stranger and stranger.

She was considering drawing herself a map of the house, because she could never find her way anywhere on the first try, forever getting turned around. As if the place wasn't hard enough to navigate, the house was dark and stale-smelling because she wasn't allowed to open the curtains or windows. Ever. It made it rather hard to clean, but no one seemed to care.

Her cell phone had officially stopped working altogether. When she plugged it in, she didn't even get a charging icon anymore. Rae had been right. The house was like the Bermuda Triangle of electricity. Nothing worked, not even electronics brought into the house. She'd picked up a new charging cord and cell phone, and tried to remember to keep it off unless she needed to make a call.

Petrin and Odath were secretive and always watching her. She almost felt like they were toying with her sometimes.

Almost as if to confirm that, every day, without fail, rooms Ashriel had previously destroyed would be full of items again. She had no idea how or why, and had pretty much given up on trying to figure that out. Somewhere in the house there had to be a storage room the size of a museum to replace everything.

And Ashriel was still maintaining the same darkly sarcastic, brooding attitude at all times. He rarely smiled, and when he did it was full of mockery and disdain. As the days passed, he seemed to be trying even harder to make her want to leave. And she hadn't seen that more mellow side of him since their argument in the library either.

He had caused more damage to everything than she had thought would be humanly possible. And yet, every day, without fail, there were still more things lined up on the shelves he had emptied the day before. More little figures for him to hurl to the floor. More messes for her to clean up. If there really was a room full of replacement items, she wanted to take a page from Ashriel's book and destroy everything herself.

The only bright spots in her days so far had been chatting with Rae, the only sane person she'd met so far. Mindy had been off work since she'd arrived, which was strange, but what wasn't in that house, so the jury was still out on her. From what Rae had said, she sounded nice.

"Finally," she muttered, seeing the staircase to the

third floor up ahead. From there, she knew her room wasn't far. Probably.

She was beginning to wonder if she was losing it herself. A couple times that day, she'd turned down a hall she swore she recognized, only to feel like it had changed somehow and the rooms had moved around.

Sighing, she tried to get her imagination under control. *It's just the stress,* she thought. Either that, or Ashriel's insanity had rubbed off on her.

Just as she was about to continue toward her room, she found herself pausing. For some inexplicable reason, her gaze was drawn to the darkened stairs that continued their way up to the third floor. The only place off limits to her.

That was where Ashriel stayed. Just the thought of him had her breath picking up, in spite of everything. When she wasn't busy fantasizing about strangling him, she'd been fighting her curiosity over him.

She didn't understand him at all. He actually seemed fairly normal when he wasn't breaking things, aside from how massively rude he was. But what kind of person would go through someone else's house, destroying everything? And why did nobody seem to care that he was acting like a lunatic? Why was he still allowed to stay after all of this?

Why did she feel like this was all some extremely weird kind of game to Odath and Petrin?

Nibbling on her bottom lip, she considered whether the danger of getting caught was worth satisfying her curiosity about what was on the third floor. Did she even want to know? Hiding in her room felt more tempting by the second.

"I believe you were told the third floor was off limits?" Odath's voice whispered in her ear from behind.

Unable to stifle a yelp of surprise, she spun to face him, stumbling back several steps to put some distance between them as quickly as possible. A cold chill ran down her spine when she met his gaze, but she tried to play it off like she didn't have the same reaction to him that she did to particularly large, disgusting spiders.

"You scared me," she said, taking a calming breath as she warily straightened. Knowing he liked to make her uncomfortable, she met his gaze squarely, determined not to give him the satisfaction.

"Did you lose your way?" he persisted, moving in closer to crowd her space again.

She tilted her chin up, purposely giving him an unaffected look. "No, I know where my room is," she said evenly. Casually backing away from him, she tried not to be too obvious about putting several feet between them. "I was just curious."

He raised an elegant eyebrow. "Curious?" he repeated softly. He glanced toward the stairs, then back at her again. "All that's up there is Ashriel's room." His lips twisted in a parody of a smile. "The rest of the rooms are all empty, except for several inches of dust and cobwebs."

She cocked her head to the side, raising an eyebrow of her own. "And you want your housekeeper to stay away from them?"

There was something calculating in the way he watched her as he moved toward her. "It's for your own safety," he said smoothly, his voice lowering even more, taking on an almost mesmerizing note. "The floor up there isn't what I would assume it used to be. We wouldn't want you to be injured."

Unable to help herself, she backed away from him again. "I wonder why Ashriel stays up there then?" she asked, incapable of keeping her mouth shut.

She was leery of working for people who had too many secrets. For all she knew, they could be serial killers. She wouldn't doubt it with this household of psychos.

He shrugged. "You could say it's because he's crazy. Or that he wouldn't sue us if he were injured." He chuckled, his handsome face splitting into a disturbing grin that made her want to punch him and run for it. "Or we could just say that going up there puts your job on the line."

"Yeah, and about the whole Ashriel being criminally insane thing," she said, completely dismissing the threat of losing a job she still wasn't even sure she wanted. "Are you guys really cool with him breaking everything? Did you seriously just hire me to follow him around?"

Odath ignored her questions, extending his hand to her in a way that would've been polite, if it had been anyone else. "I'll show you the upstairs if you want."

The thought of taking his hand made her skin crawl. As uneasy as his oily, too friendly smile and twisted personality made her, she felt like there was something far worse beneath the surface that he hadn't shown her yet. There was nothing openly threatening about him, but she felt scared, nevertheless.

"Has something changed in the last few minutes to make it less dangerous?" she asked, blatantly ignoring his outstretched hand as she crossed her arms in front of her chest.

He shrugged, unimpressed by her thinly veiled sarcasm. "I'm just trying to put your mind at ease," he said, holding her gaze steadily. His tone dropped to a strangely hypnotic level. "If you'll just come with me..."

His light-brown eyes bored into her, his words echoing in her head. *"Come with me. Take my hand,"* his voice whispered into her mind, but she knew he hadn't spoken out loud. A shiver moved through her, and a dull headache began to throb at her temples.

Before she realized what she was doing, her arms relaxed to her sides, and her body leaned in toward him, her knee bending to take a step. Shaking her head to clear it, she blinked a few times before scowling at him, and a look of genuine surprise crossed his arrogant face.

Geez, I must be more tired than I realized, she thought.

"No, thanks," she said warily, trying to figure out a way to inch past him and get to her room. Seeming to guess her intentions, he stepped directly in front of her.

Screw this, she thought, envisioning spending her days cleaning up after Ashriel and dodging Odath and putting up with Petrin's cryptic comments. *Nope. No amount of money is worth it.*

She started moving backward, not caring anymore if he knew she was running, and he continued to casually pursue her until her back came up against a wall. Leaning down, he brought his face far too close to hers for comfort.

"Hey—"

As soon as she planted her hands against his chest to shove him back, a jolt of pure, freezing cold shot through her hands and up her arms like some weird kind of electric shock. When she tried to jerk away, he caught her wrists to keep her in place. She was just about to shove a knee somewhere that would wipe that smug look off his face *really* quick, when his gaze captured and held hers.

Pain sliced through her skull, but her body relaxed instantly. It didn't matter that in her head she was trying to fight him with everything she had. She couldn't move her arms and legs at all.

What is this? she thought desperately, panic growing in her chest. *Why can't I move?*

"I love the fear in you," he said with a twisted smile, releasing one of her wrists to trail his cool knuckles across her cheek. "It flavors your energy in the best way."

Repulsed by his touch, she flinched, unable to do more. *No, no, no.* Body trembling, heart pounding in her ears, she struggled to make herself move, but it didn't matter. *This can't be real!*

The pain in her head was growing to the point where she thought she'd pass out. *Please. Stop.* Resisting him was like wading her way through quicksand, and the harder she pushed the more her head pounded. *God, please, help me...*

Odath laughed, obviously enjoying himself.

"Stop!" her mind screamed, and suddenly, she was in control again. The pain in her head faded, and she jammed her knee up between his legs as hard as she could, clawing at his eyes with her free hand.

Yelling curses in some other language, he doubled over, releasing her.

"Get away from me!" she shouted, turning to run. The name she tried to call for help came so naturally she didn't pause to question it. "Ash—!"

Before she got more than a couple steps away, her body was lifted off the ground and slammed back against the wall, cutting off her scream. Her breath left her in a rush, little points of light dancing across her vision, and she gasped for air. Some invisible weight held her pinned, and she was forcefully immobilized.

"Impressive," Odath said, but some of his amusement had clearly faded as he came to stand in front of her again. Breathing heavily from her place on the wall, she was pleased to see he was limping and had deep, bloody scratches around his bloodshot right eye. "You must have a tiny bit of shima blood somewhere in your ancestry."

She jerked her head to the side when he roughly grabbed her chin, trying to bite him, but he was too strong. Remembering how he'd controlled her with his eyes before, she clenched hers shut to stop him from latching onto her again.

"Smart girl," he said, laughing darkly. Just as she opened her mouth to scream for Ashriel again, Odath's tone changed, an unbelievable pain stabbing into her brain as he spoke, his voice seeming to echo in her mind. "Look at me."

Whatever insidious power he had wrapped itself around her, and her body wasn't her own anymore. Her eyes opened, and he snared her with his gaze again. Her head buzzed with dizziness and pain, and she was sure she'd pass out any second. Her surroundings started getting fuzzy at the periphery of her vision. She struggled to stay conscious so she could try to fight, chest heaving as she labored for air, but she could feel herself growing weaker. Dimly, in the back of her mind, she realized this was part of his power too, draining her energy.

"That's enough for now, Odath. We don't want to kill her," she heard Petrin say from somewhere off to the side, but she couldn't turn her head to look. Her gaze was glued to Odath's, and there was nothing she could do about it. "A source as strong as her could be useful."

"If you insist," he said, hand moving from Jillian's jaw to her temple. "Sleep."

The moment he said that, darkness rushed up to claim her.

Jillian woke up feeling like she had a hangover the next morning. She hadn't slept well, plagued by some weird nightmare she couldn't quite remember. Her head was a little foggy, and she was exhausted, but she figured she'd feel better after some breakfast.

Pushing the thick gray-and-blue comforter off herself, she caught a stale scent, and added cleaning her own room to her list of the day's tasks. She yawned her way through her morning routine, showering and sluggishly pulling on faded jeans and a black tank top.

Catching sight of her still partially packed bags sitting next to the door on her way out, she got this nagging impression somewhere in the back of her mind that she was forgetting something. Hand on the doorknob, she stopped and just stared at them for a long moment. A dull throb started to build in her temples again, and she sighed, rubbing at them.

Oh well, she thought, shaking her head at herself. She was sure she'd remember later. She glanced at her fancy new cell phone paperweight on the dresser but didn't bother turning it on to check it.

Making a mental note to see if it could retain a charge any better than her old one, she headed for the kitchen, and the smell of breakfast wafting around the house had her stomach growling. She was starving, like it had been too long since the last time she'd eaten. Come to think of it, she couldn't really remember what she'd had for dinner.

Geez, I must be more tired than I realized...

The moment she thought that, she stopped in her tracks at the bottom of the first-floor stairs. The dull ache throbbing in her head was building. What was wrong with her this morning?

She was just about to continue on her way, when she noticed the mural on the back wall, opposite the front door. It had caught her attention when she'd arrived, but she hadn't really had a chance to study it. It looked like some sort of wood carving of a map she didn't recognize, with a language etched into it that she couldn't read.

She'd noticed other types of artwork throughout the house too, more so in the bedrooms than anywhere else. Some sort of spirally symbols, totally different than the mural. Frowning slightly, she wrapped her arms around herself. For some reason, whatever they were supposed to mean, they gave her the creeps.

The mural wasn't bad, though. She wondered what part of the world it represented, and leaned a little closer to scrutinize the small lettering she assumed made up the names of towns.

"Perfect," she heard a voice say behind her, and nearly jumped out of her skin. Spinning around, she came face to face with Ashriel. One look at his beautiful, scowling face had her disagreement with him in the library rushing back to her. How had she forgotten *him*, of all people? "This human's already broken."

"What?" she said, confused by him referring to her as *human* again. What else would she be, and why did it sound like an insult when he said it? And hadn't it been long enough for him to start using her name? Why he insisted on not knowing it was beyond her.

"If you didn't realize you've been staring blankly at the wall for the past five minutes, you've got bigger problems than I thought," he said, raising an eyebrow at her.

"Seriously?" she said, glaring at him. "Can't we have a truce until *after* breakfast? More specifically, after the *large* cup of coffee that's going to improve my mood?"

He tilted his head, pretending to consider. "Nope."

"Do we really have to be at each other's throats?" she asked, already foreseeing a *very* long day ahead of her. The dull pain in her head was turning into a splitting headache. "Can we start over?"

He looked at her silently a long moment, and then he slowly closed the distance between them. That sarcastic expression of his changed, a slight frown furrowing his brow as though he were concerned. It was probably her imagination, but it was enough to keep her still. Waiting to see what he would do.

"You look tired," he said, ignoring her question. He

spoke quietly, but she could practically feel the frustration in him. She had no idea what she'd done to bring that reaction on, but logic didn't seem to apply to him anyway.

"I'm fine," she replied, mystified that it didn't even occur to her to move away from him, and he frowned at her words, muttering something in his own language. Just like the other day in the library, he was standing so close, it should have made her uncomfortable. If Odath had tried this, she probably would've pushed him away and ran for it.

A sudden pain lanced through her head, and she winced, clenching her eyes shut. Unexplainable pressure gripped her skull like a vice. She automatically brought her hands up to clutch at her head, but Ashriel's were already there, his fingertips pressing lightly against her temples.

Holding onto his forearms for support as a wave of dizziness swept through her, weakness leeched away at her. She knew she was digging her nails into him, but the pain in her head was so intense she couldn't make herself loosen her grip, or even find her voice to apologize.

She sucked in a breath between her teeth when the pressure in her head abruptly increased, but then it changed. The pressure became a strange heat that flooded through her body, from her head down, easing until there was nothing but a comforting warmth.

"Breathe," she heard Ashriel say, and found herself following the even rhythm of his breathing as he took a deep breath with her. As she opened her eyes, his hands fell away from her, and he took a step back.

"Thank you," she said, actually glad he'd been

there, despite their differences. Whatever had come over her was gone. "I don't know what happened."

"Interesting," he said without inflection. "Your frail human constitution seems to be failing you. This is the perfect opportunity for you to leave and go to the hospital. While you're at it, maybe they could hire you, and then you could leave permanently."

"I'm fine." The words left her mouth automatically, and she had the strangest feeling that she'd been saying that a lot lately. She'd never been prone to headaches or migraines, so technically she *should* get checked out, but the moment the idea came into her mind it was immediately rejected without a second's thought.

He sighed, his frown deepening. "I knew you were going to be a pain in the ass," he said roughly, as though she had somehow brought the whole situation upon herself. "Why are you still here?"

Rolling her eyes, she turned on her heel and headed for the kitchen. "Moment of gratitude ruined," she muttered, praying he wasn't intending on following her.

But he did. Of course, he did. Because that's just what she needed. She was exhausted, grumpy, and her head was...actually, that was feeling better. But still, dealing with Ashriel when she felt like crap was the last thing she wanted to do.

He followed her down the winding hallways in annoyed silence for a few wrong turns, before taking the lead with another sigh. He grumbled something in that language she didn't recognize, but matched his pace to hers. She wondered if this was one of those rare moments where he was being nice, and if he'd slowed down so she wouldn't have to speed walk to keep up with his longer strides.

Honestly, she kind of appreciated the quiet between them, as awkward as it was. He was much more appealing when he wasn't busy being a jerk, and she could covertly ogle him all she liked since he wasn't looking at her.

The walk to the kitchen was too long and too short.

Her stomach growled again when they reached the kitchen, the sight and smell of food making her mouth water. Rae was still cooking, and already had milk, orange juice, and some glasses sitting at the breakfast bar attached to the island in the middle of the spacious kitchen.

Oddly enough, there were no windows in this kitchen, so all the lights were on to keep it bright and welcoming. Otherwise it was a nice kitchen, with white granite counter tops and fancy cabinets. It was clear no one except Rae really touched anything in there.

"Morning, Rae!" she said, feeling a lot better in the presence of breakfast and someone who wasn't insane.

"Morning, Ji—"

"Finish that sentence, and I swear I will break everything in this room!" Ashriel loudly interrupted, scowling at Rae as he brushed past Jillian. He plopped down onto one of the chairs at the island, muttering what had to be some colorful curses in whatever weird language he'd spoken before.

"Excuse you," Jillian said, stomping her way over to the island. He looked bored as she frowned at him, crossing his arms over his chest and raising an eyebrow at her. "I don't know what your problem is, but—"

"It's fine," Rae quickly interrupted, seeming to

sense the impending bloodshed. She glanced over her shoulder at them as she cooked at the stove. "He's got some freaky thing about names. You should have seen the way he spazzed out when I introduced myself to him."

"I never asked to know anything about you," Ashriel grumbled, returning Jillian's stare in a way that made it clear that comment applied to her too.

Jillian's stomach did a funny flip as he held her gaze. It was only for a second, but the direct way he was looking at her wasn't giving her the impression he wanted her to stay away as much as he claimed. An unwelcome blush stained her cheeks when his eyes narrowed on her, and the sarcastic comment she'd had on the tip of her tongue seemed to stick there.

"It's one of those polite, general human interaction things, Ashriel," Rae said, breaking whatever spell had briefly held them together. They quickly looked away from each other while Rae chatted and cooked, apparently unfazed by his insanity. "Don't worry. I'll be careful about your name phobia."

"Thank you," Ashriel said in a far politer tone than Jillian had thought he was capable of.

"So your brand of 'friendly' doesn't usually apply to Rae?" Jillian asked, slightly weirded out by the lack of sarcasm and disgust in his voice. She tried not to be too obvious about scooting her chair a little farther away from his as she sat down beside him at the island.

Ashriel shrugged. "She feeds me."

"We have an understanding," Rae said, turning enough to narrow her eyes at Ashriel as though remembering something unpleasant. She plated up some pancakes, sausage, and fruit for them, and brought them over to the breakfast bar. She set Ashriel's down with a meaningful clunk and a raised eyebrow, and then gave Jillian hers with a friendly smile. "He breaks things in here, he gets nothing but stale cereal I left out overnight. Right off the table, if all the bowls are broken."

"That, and she promised she's leaving," he added, returning Rae's glare before digging in to the pancakes. "Although I wish she'd go right now."

Rae rolled her eyes as she went back to the counter to make a plate for herself. "Yeah, yeah," she said breezily. "I'm on my way out the door at the end of the month."

"You're quitting?" Jillian said, disappointed she'd be left with only psychos for company.

"Wait, what? The end of the month?" Ashriel demanded, sounding like he was ready to start breaking things immediately, stale cereal or not. "You told me you were leaving at the end of this *week*."

Jillian took a bite of her blueberry pancakes and nearly died. They were so good she was totally content to let Rae murder Ashriel while she finished her breakfast. A girl could dream.

Rae shrugged, apparently so used to Ashriel's outbursts she barely batted an eye. "Things got delayed at the café," she said, setting her own plate on the island.

"You work at a café too?" Jillian asked, ignoring Ashriel's bizarre reaction.

"She's *opening* a café in town," Petrin said from the doorway, sliding smoothly into their conversation. Ashriel stiffened, leveling a murderous glare at her, and rose to his feet, food forgotten. Seemingly entertained by his reaction for reasons unknown, Petrin continued, "Her cooking's so good I know it'll be a great success."

"I'll have to stop by," Jillian said.

"Thank you, guys!" Rae said, eyes glittering with excitement. She started talking about her plans for different recipes and lunch combos, but the whole time Ashriel had his eyes locked on Petrin.

Jillian noticed the deliberate way he got up from the breakfast bar, leaving his food half eaten. He was subtle about it, going to the fridge to get a bottle of water he didn't need, but when he returned, he didn't sit. He stopped in the middle of the room to face Petrin, and for some reason it almost looked as if he was purposely situating himself between the two of them and Petrin.

And the weirdness continues, Jillian thought, wondering what that was all about. She kept her questions to herself as she finished off her breakfast, watching how things played out. Maybe she was reading too much into it, but it was starting to feel like there was a mutual dislike between Ashriel and her employers. *Why is he even living here?*

"I really wish I could convince you to stay," Petrin said, sparing Ashriel an amused glance before smiling brightly at Rae. Something about that expression gave Jillian the chills, and she found herself frowning.

"She's leaving," Ashriel said coldly. Hostile didn't even begin to cover the way he was looking at Petrin.

"Is she?" Petrin said cryptically. She tilted her head, giving him a chilling, devious kind of grin.

Jillian glanced between them, knowing she was missing something. Her head started to hurt again, and she rubbed at her temple distractedly.

Rae broke the tense silence that followed with her usual cheerfulness, like that whole exchange never happened. “I was going to run into town for some ingredients after breakfast,” she said, obviously trying to steer the conversation another direction. “Need anything while I’m out?”

“I was actually just about to ask *Jillian* to go out,” Petrin said, shooting another amused glance at Ashriel when she emphasized Jillian’s name. “It appears we need more cleaning supplies.”

Rae laughed as Ashriel’s expression darkened to homicidal levels of rage. Petrin seemed to know all about Ashriel’s name phobia too.

Jillian dropped her hand from her temple, more than happy for an excuse to get out of the house as she got up and brought her empty plate to the sink. “I’ll go with her. It’ll be easier with us both to carry everything together.”

Ashriel opened his mouth to say something, but Petrin cut him off. “Sounds good,” she said, pinning Ashriel with her stare as she swiftly raised a hand to grasp the unusual dragon dagger pendant she wore. Ashriel clenched his hands at his sides, but didn’t otherwise move as Petrin sauntered right past him and extended a hand toward Jillian.

She had an overwhelming urge to dodge Petrin, but didn’t want to be rude. Still, the moment her hand landed on Jillian’s shoulder, she felt cold sweep through her. Pain lanced through her skull as Petrin’s gaze locked with hers, but she couldn’t move a muscle.

“Come back quickly.”

CHAPTER FIVE

"Ji—"

Jillian heard a sound from far away. She was so tired, though, surrounded by nothing but chilling darkness, that she wasn't sure she could find where it came from. Immobilized, she felt like she was wrapped up tight by invisible ropes as she sank deeper into an abyss.

"Hey—"

I have to wake up, she thought distantly.

"Jillian!"

She felt warm hands clasp her shoulders, and a gentle shake. Pain tore through her brain as light flooded her vision and sound filled her ears.

The next thing she knew, she was staring up at a cloudy sky and Rae's worried expression from a hard sidewalk outside somewhere. She glanced carefully around, feeling weak, and realized they were in the middle of town, in front of a row of storefronts.

Rae was kneeling on one side of her, an older woman she didn't recognize on the other. The woman's white-streaked, light-blond hair fell around her shoulders as she examined Jillian, her hazel eyes sharp. Her hand was on Jillian's shoulder and, in her confused state, head still spinning, she could have sworn the woman was softly glowing.

"Are you all right?" the woman said, brows furrowed in concern.

A small crowd of people had gathered, and she heard someone on their cell phone calling for an ambulance. For some reason, her brain immediately rejected the idea of going to the hospital.

"I'm fine," she mumbled, even though she felt the exact opposite.

"Are you sure?" Rae asked, sounding relieved. "You scared me to death! I thought you were having a seizure or something. One minute I was talking to Noren and Hasenda, and the next you were on the ground. You've been acting so weird ever since we left the house—"

"Wait." Jillian shook her head as Rae and the older woman, who she assumed to be Hasenda, carefully helped her sit up. A knot of fear was forming in her stomach. "I don't even remember leaving."

"That's it. We're going to the hospital," Rae said firmly. "You kept telling me you were fine all the way here, and I knew you weren't telling me the truth."

"No hospitals," Jillian said automatically, then winced at the cold tone of her own voice. She hadn't meant to say it like that. "I'm so sorry. I don't know what's wrong with me. I didn't mean to bite your head off," Jillian said, shaking her head again. Her runaway brain quickly formulated a lie, and it was out of her mouth before she could stop any of it. "I get these migraines sometimes that make me fuzzy before and after. I'm fine, really. I promise. Let's just head back to the house and I'll take my migraine meds, and get some rest."

"Don't rush yourself," the older woman beside her said, and Jillian found herself staring at her. She was officially losing her mind. She had to be.

For some reason she couldn't shake the insane idea that this woman was inside her head, and *knew* she was lying.

"This is Hasenda. Do you remember? We were just talking a minute ago. She's a nurse," Rae said quickly, misinterpreting Jillian's silence. She gestured to the man standing beside Hasenda, with shaggy salt-and-pepper hair, and brown eyes that seemed to be watching Jillian very closely. "And her husband, Noren. They're family friends of mine."

"Thank you for helping me," Jillian said, trying to collect herself.

"Are you sure I can't convince you to get checked out?" Hasenda said.

"No, I'm sorry," Jillian said, still feeling really strange. "I think I just need to get back and rest, and I'll be fine." There was that word again. It kept repeating in her brain even though she knew better.

Rae exchanged a quick look with Hasenda, who hesitated, and then finally nodded. "Okay, if you say so."

"You both should come over when you're feeling better," Hasenda said kindly.

"Yes, we're having a barbecue next weekend," Noren said, the pressure of his gaze finally easing a little when he smiled. "Any friend of Rae's is always welcome. And invite Mindy, too," he said to Rae.

Rae and Jillian said their goodbyes, agreeing to see

them at their party, and hurried home. Jillian was glad Rae seemed to want to let her rest on the ride back to the house. She wasn't sure she could've kept up with any kind of conversation.

The second they got back, Petrin spotted them as they came through the front door.

"What happened?" she asked, and Jillian could only imagine she looked twice as crappy as she felt. Still, as foggy as her mind was, she could tell Petrin was only asking because that's what people were supposed to do. She didn't actually care at all as Rae explained the situation.

She did encourage Jillian to go to her room and rest for the day, however. So with Rae hovering at her side, she made her way sluggishly to the second floor.

"I promise, I'll be fine after I get some sleep," she said for the tenth time. There was that word, yet again. She couldn't get it out of her head.

I'm fine. I should just stay right here, and everything will be fine.

"Seriously," Rae said, a little exasperated. "You'd better call me if you need anything. And I *will* be checking on you, like every hour. And if you aren't better in a few hours, I will physically drag you to the hospital if I have to."

Jillian chuckled. "Understood," she said, forcing the word out even though the urge to say, "I'm fine," again was nearly overwhelming. She felt bad enough for worrying her new friend, and wasn't about to keep pushing her away when she was only trying to help. "Thanks, Rae."

"No problem," she said, still looking a little worried.

"You need anything right now? I can grab you something before I start prepping for lunch."

"I'm fine," Jillian said, then inwardly cringed. It felt more wrong every time she said it.

After Rae left, Jillian closed and locked her door. Digging her phone out of her pocket, she tried to turn her phone on, only to find that it was dead again. After putting it back on the charger, she made her way to the bed and flopped down on her back, fully dressed.

She had no idea what had just happened, or why she was so exhausted, or what her sudden aversion to hospitals was all about. Thinking about it only seemed to make her head spin, so she tried to close her eyes.

She couldn't shake a growing restlessness, though. The longer she laid there, the stronger it became. Frustrated with the contradictory symptoms she was having, she sighed loudly and opened her eyes.

She hadn't thought much of it before, but one of those weird, spirally symbols was etched directly above her bed. It was a lot bigger than any of the ones she'd seen so far, about the same size as the queen-sized bed she was on. The intertwining curves and lines made her think of a huge basket of serpents, and a chill worked its way up her spine.

Now that she'd noticed it, she couldn't focus on anything else. It wasn't an ugly symbol, but she still hated it for some reason she couldn't put her finger on. The longer she stared at it, the more she felt like she was sinking in quicksand. Her limbs grew heavier, and her head ached dully.

"This isn't helping," she muttered to herself, wondering if it was too late to switch rooms. Maybe not all of them were decorated with these symbols? She was sure she wouldn't be that lucky.

The room spun around her as she made herself sit up on the edge of the bed. She waited for everything to stop being all wobbly in her vision, before carefully getting to her feet. She couldn't stand to be in her bedroom even a second more. Whatever those symbols were, there were too many of them in there, and she couldn't shake the crazy idea that they were making her worse.

Ashriel stopped in his tracks when he saw Jillian dragging her feet as she wandered down the second-floor corridor. Conflicted, he kept far enough back in the shadows of the hall that he knew her human eyes wouldn't be able to spot him.

Jillian...

The last human name he ever wanted to hear. Of course, he couldn't forget it, no matter how hard he tried. It was burned into his memory as strongly as her face was.

The name that would haunt him the most.

He clenched his hands at his sides, forcing himself to stand still and just keep an eye on her. He wanted so badly to go to her, but he knew he shouldn't.

Sure, he wanted to burn the compulsion manipulating her out of her mind. He would use up every ounce of his diminished power if he could, but he knew it wouldn't be enough yet. However, he wasn't so much of a fool that he didn't understand wanting to free her of Odath and Petrin wasn't the only reason he wanted to go to her.

The inside of his left wrist tingled, and he viciously pushed down the emotions that came with that little sign.

Son of a bitch.

He was already moving toward her as she plopped down to sit at the bottom of the third-floor staircase. She slumped sideways, leaning her body against the bannister and closing her eyes, unaware of his presence even when he was right beside her.

For the first time in centuries, he hesitated. There was a reason his kind was careful about touching others, human and shima alike. There was always a certain amount of energy transfer, and shimana could read a lot about others through physical contact, intentionally or not. Unless it was a lover or family member, out of courtesy they generally shielded their minds to limit the transfer if they did touch.

He knew Jillian was different, however. As if his initial reaction to her hadn't been proof enough, he'd felt it every time he'd unthinkingly touched her. It would be a colossal mistake to let it happen again, possibly strengthening the tenuous bond already growing between them, but he didn't have a choice in the matter. She was stronger than most humans he'd come across, and Odath and Petrin had noticed that as well. They were using much stronger spells on her than they had the others, and she was getting too weak too quickly. If he didn't act, the compulsion might grow too strong for him to do anything at all.

Fucking hell...

Against his better judgment, he shielded his mind the best he could and knelt down in front of her. Gently grasping her shoulders, he helped her sit up straight.

A very small amount of her energy poured into him, warm and inviting. So different than anything he'd felt from a human before. Her pale-blue eyes fluttered open, taking a second to focus on him, and seeing her so weak made him want to murder everyone responsible. An unfamiliar possessiveness came over him, and again he fought the urge to drag her into his arms and carry her out of the house right that second.

If only that were an option.

"Why you?" he wondered out loud, knowing she wouldn't be able to answer that, even if she were fully in control of herself.

"Why *you*?" she mumbled with a furrowed brow, obviously half out of it, but still with it enough to try and argue with him. Her eyes slid closed again, her head starting to tip to the side. "I'm fine."

He gritted his teeth at those words, instantly pissed off. He'd heard that too many times from other humans in that house, and they were *never* fine.

"Look at me," he said quietly, willing her to obey without having to touch her further. Cursing under his breath when she didn't respond, he lifted a hand from her shoulder to cup her cheek. She turned her face into his palm with a sigh like it comforted her. "Tairi, gesja hano. Jillian, you have to look at me."

The longer she just sat there, unresponsive, the more a strange kind of desperation started to grip him. He felt protective. Fearful that he would lose her. And so frustrated with his inability to help her that he wanted to tear something apart with his bare hands.

He wouldn't let Odath and Petrin have her.

She was—

No. He wouldn't finish that train of thought. He couldn't afford to even think it.

Gritting his teeth, he took a deep breath, and did the only thing he could think of. Probably the stupidest thing he could possibly do. He dropped his mental shields.

Energy moved between them unchecked, the very beginnings of a bond linking them together, and he could feel that it strengthened them both. Jillian stirred a little as their mingled energy flooded her system, but still didn't open her eyes. He could feel how fractured her mind was, like big, jagged pieces of broken glass. Odath and Petrin had not been gentle with her.

No longer splitting his energy in half, he lowered his voice when he spoke, putting a small amount of compulsion behind his words. "Jillian," he said, working through her mind as carefully as he could while still trying to be quick. Odath or Petrin could show up at any time, and who knew how they'd react to him helping Jillian? "Please, look at me."

She finally turned her head, opening her eyes to meet his gaze. "Ashriel?" She seemed confused, unfocused, but he could already feel Odath and Petrin's hold on her weakening. He didn't have the power to free her completely, in one try, but this would have to do for the time being. "Where am I?"

"In an enchanted hallway, in a cursed house, in the human realm, under the control of a couple of borderline cannibalistic freakshows who like to play with their food," he said, believing she wouldn't remember a word of it. He dropped his hand from her cheek, clenching it at his side and regretting the life decisions that had led him there. Because, of course, he very much wanted to keep his hands on her.

Damn, damn, damn. He wracked his brain for the most heinous cuss words he could come up with, but was sure nothing could cover his current situation.

"Not funny," she muttered, surprising him. Still working on healing her as best he could, he could feel some of the broken pieces in her mind stitching back together. He instinctively knew it was that damned bond helping, but he was grateful.

Fighting the urge to curse in every language he knew, he took her hands and carefully coaxed her to her feet. "Wasn't trying to be. You asked. I answered."

"Well, somebody's cranky," she mumbled, frowning up at him. "Why are you always in such a bad mood?"

Mystified that she could find the strength to give him a hard time, he tried to lead her away from the stairs. "Breakable little humans shouldn't ask questions with answers that would make their heads explode. Time to go to bed."

"No," she said, but she made no move to pull her hands away from his. "I hate those—" she paused, searching for a word in her confused state "—things."

"Beds?" he said, staring at her. "Just when I thought you were waking up—"

"Not beds," she said, rolling her eyes. "The swirly things above the beds."

A knot of dread settled in his gut like a stone. "Show me," he said, pulling at her hands again. When she resisted, he cursed and just scooped her up in his arms. Who knew when Odath or Petrin would show up again? He didn't want to risk being caught helping Jillian.

“Put me down!” she said, trying to wriggle free.

“Nope,” he said, relieved that her strength was returning enough that she was a little harder to hold on to. Not that a human had any chance of getting away from him, but at least she was putting up a good struggle.

“Jerk,” she muttered, tiring quickly. She stopped fighting him, but he could feel the tension in her body as he held her.

“Yeah, yeah,” he said, trying to stifle his irritation when the hallway in front of him changed and he had to take a different path to her room. “Fucking house.”

“Agreed,” she said, reluctantly starting to relax against him. “Fricking house. It feels like a labyrinth.”

Mildly impressed by her intuition, he considered different excuses he could give her. “It is,” he said, momentarily dismissing the idea of lying. What was the point? She obviously wasn’t stupid and was more sensitive to these things than other humans he’d met. “When something feels like it’s different, stop and focus your mind completely on the room you want to find. Your instincts will lead you.”

“I’ll remember that,” she said, and when he glanced down at her, he could tell she was almost fully alert again, and would probably remember the entire damned conversation.

So much for the whole it-was-all-a-dream line he had been planning on giving her later.

When they reached her room, he gently lowered her to her feet. She grasped his shoulders, steadying herself, and looked up at him a long moment. He could tell she was trying to piece things together, even though none of it would make sense to her human mind.

"What happened?" she asked, expecting truth from him when he couldn't really give it to her. "I remember leaving my room this morning. Then I was in town somehow. My head was killing me," she said, her expression growing distant as she tried to remember. "I went to rest, but I couldn't. And when I left my room...I don't know. I just woke up with you in front of me."

"You passed out."

"I did?" She frowned, then shook her head. Narrowing her eyes, she pinned him with the same kind of analyzing look she'd given him before. "Sitting up?"

"And you're back," he said, laughing darkly. "Show me the things."

"Things?"

He raised an eyebrow, impatient. Who knew how long it would take Odath and Petrin do discover he was helping Jillian? "The swirly things you hate."

"Oh." She paused, confused for a second. He could see the moment it clicked. And then she seemed to realize she was still holding on to him. "Oh, yeah."

She released his arms and he ruthlessly ignored the urge to take her hand and connect them again. She turned away from him and opened her bedroom door. Leading the way in, she swept her arm out in a wide arc, like the "swirly things" were everywhere, but he couldn't see anything out of the ordinary.

The strong scent of dust. A window with old blue curtains. A dresser. Bedside table. A big bed with a gray-and-blue comforter. Jillian's suitcases. Everything looked normal.

"Point to one," he said, wondering if this was another effect of Odath and Petrin messing with her head, or if there was really something there he was missing. Either way, he wouldn't be surprised.

She raised an eyebrow like he was an idiot for not seeing something right in front of his face. She walked across the room and tapped a place on the wall with her index finger. "Right here."

"Stand back," he said, going to where she indicated. She moved back a step and he sighed. "Get behind me."

"You think it's going to explode?" she asked sarcastically, but did what he asked.

"Probably," he grumbled, blocking what he was doing from her sight with his body.

Careful to keep his right hand in front of him, he drew on the power of his aspect. Magic coursed through him, slightly stronger from his connection to Jillian, and his nails lengthened and morphed into deadly black claws. He hadn't attempted any kind of transformation since his magic had been diminished to nearly nothing, but he'd gotten slightly stronger because of Jillian, and had saved up enough energy to try for a short period of time. If Odath and Petrin found out he could do this, they'd put a stop to it immediately. He assumed the last thing they'd want would be for him to get strong enough to fully transform on his own.

He tore into the wall where she had tapped it, and a jolt like electricity shot up his arm. A pattern began to form right in front of his eyes. A powerful spell that combined binding and draining. "Fucking hell," he growled, angrily slashing into the wall again.

"What are you doing?"

"Stay back!" he said, shooting her a glare over his shoulder when she would have moved closer again. He was careful to keep his hand out of her line of sight. The last thing he needed was for her to see his claws out. "Where's the next one?"

She scowled back at him, hesitated a moment, then finally walked over to another place beside the window and touched the wall again. They went around doing this for a while, until Ashriel had clawed up over a dozen patterns on her walls, and one huge one over her bed.

He'd suspected they'd somehow made their spells invisible to him, but now that he knew for sure he felt even more hopeless than before. He was never getting out of there if he couldn't see the spells binding him.

Jillian was running her fingertips over one of the slashed-up spell engravings, her back to him. "What are these?" she asked quietly. He could tell she was still desperately trying to make sense of what was happening to her, but he had no answer he could give her that her human mind would accept.

She turned to face him slowly, determined to get some answers. He could sense the fear in her, and the uncertainty, and found himself admiring her ability to stay calm under these strange circumstances. "Why do I feel better now that you've destroyed them?"

Energy shifted between them, subtly transforming, and he knew it would only get stronger if he didn't distance himself. Even across the room, without touching her, he could already feel the tiny bond that linked them. Which was the last damned thing he wanted.

Not when he was trapped in that house. Not while he was under the thumb of a group of power-hungry murderers. And certainly not with this beautiful, fragile human in front of him.

Darenai, his closest friend, would be laughing his head off at the irony if he were there.

"You should get some rest," he said, not caring how obvious he was being about dodging her questions. "As soon as you're feeling strong enough, get out."

He turned and left quickly, not giving her a chance to ask anything else.

CHAPTER SIX

ASHRIEL COULD FEEL IT THE moment he closed Jillian's door behind him. He'd been caught, and there wasn't a damned thing he could do to stop what was about to happen. He glanced both ways down the darkened hallway, conserving what little was left of his magical energy, which was next to nothing. It'd taken nearly everything he'd had to snap Jillian out of her trance.

"There's something about her, isn't there?" Petrin said, materializing out of the shadows like the creepy stalker she was. "Some tempting shima blood somewhere in there that makes her stronger."

Ashriel stayed protectively in front of Jillian's door, subtly shifting his weight to take on a defensive posture. "Whatever you say. I don't see it."

Petrin smirked at him. "Liar. If you were being honest, you know you could just drain her yourself and restore some of your lost power," she said, apparently getting a sick thrill out of repulsing him.

"I'm not like you," he said, sickened by her suggestion. Even though the natural magic and energy in blood was powerful, he'd never been interested in it himself. Only sathrana were allowed to drink blood. They needed it to survive. For anyone else to do it, it was only to get the drug-like high.

"Only because you insist on acting like you're better than us," she said dismissively. "What's the big deal? It's not like you like humans anyway." She narrowed her eyes at him thoughtfully. "I've noticed you're sticking closer to Jillian than you have the others, though. Why is that, Ashriel, if it isn't the shima blood she carries?"

Ashriel shrugged, keeping his eyes on Petrin as he considered his options. Weakened as he was, they both knew he was no match for her, but he wasn't about to just let her into Jillian's room. "I do nothing but fill my days plotting how to make your lives difficult until you kill me. If you guys pay extra attention to a human, so do I."

He felt the magical shifting of the house again, rooms and hallways moving on the first floor, and heard a sound from below that made his blood run cold. Faintly, he heard a woman screaming. He sensed that she was lost. Being chased.

His body tensed, on the verge of following the sound, but he couldn't make himself move from in front of Jillian's door. Instincts fighting each other, he struggled with who to try to protect in that moment. Who would suffer more? The one he chose, or the one he left behind?

"What will it be, Ashriel?" Petrin said, amused by his indecision. Overly confident, she sauntered closer to him, not even bothering to shield herself against his potential attack. It was obvious she didn't see him as a threat anymore. Not without his powers. Someday he'd make sure that arrogance bit her in the ass. "I still need Jillian, so I won't kill her. But the same can't be said of the human Odath has right now."

Knowing what he had to do didn't make it any easier. He was dying inside as he shoved his way past Petrin, but if he allowed his connection to Jillian to supersede his logic, choosing to stay in front of her door when another human was in mortal danger, he knew Jillian would suffer much worse from Odath and Petrin because of his favoritism than any of the other humans before had.

So he forced himself to keep moving, ruthlessly pushing down his desire to stay close to Jillian. Petrin's cold laugh followed him as he raced through the house, clearly enjoying her perverse little game. Pushing the limits of his waning magical energy, he flared his senses out, searching for Odath and the woman as he ran.

Reaching the bottom of the stairs, he sensed them down one of the darkened hallways ahead. Knowing the house could shift randomly at any moment, he pushed himself faster, and found them outside the study just as his faltering power was exhausted. Cursing, he threw himself at Odath's back.

Odath barely turned toward him, holding up a palm and using a fraction of his power to place a barrier between them. Ashriel's body rebounded off the invisible shield, and he was thrown back several feet.

Scrambling to his feet again, he pressed his palms against the barrier, trying to draw on what energy he had, but it was no use. He was too weak, especially after helping Jillian. He couldn't even make a dent in the shield that stood in his way. Hopeless as the situation was though, he couldn't just walk away while someone was in trouble.

Ashriel ignored the sting against his skin as thin tendrils of electricity danced across the surface of the barrier where his hands touched it, but he couldn't get even a step closer to Odath and the human woman cowering at his feet. There was a sickening lurch in his stomach when he recognized her. Like all the others, he hadn't wanted to remember her name either, but he knew her face. It was Rae's friend, who he'd met only briefly. He'd been focusing his attention on Rae, since she'd arrived at the house first, and he realized too late Odath and Petrin must have noticed and shifted their attention to Rae's friend instead. He'd been careless, convinced by Rae's assurance that her friend was out of town, but he should have known better. Under the influence of the spells, Rae might not have even known her friend was actually missing rather than just out of town.

Ashriel could tell the woman was free of her mind control at the moment, probably for Odath's amusement. Her shoulder-length brown hair was messy from struggling against Odath, her green eyes were bloodshot, and her face was bruised and streaked with tears. "Let her go."

Odath tilted his head, giving Ashriel a quizzical look. "I wasn't expecting you this time. Not with Jillian taking up so much of your attention."

"Sick bastard," Ashriel said through gritted teeth. "You've drained her enough!"

"Which do you mean?" Odath said with a twisted grin. He grabbed a handful of the woman's hair, and she yelped in pain as he dragged her to her feet, forcing her to stand in front of him like a shield. Still holding her hair to keep her head tipped to the side, he snaked his other arm around her waist to keep her close. "The whimpering meat bag here, or the one waiting for me upstairs? That hint of magic spicing Jillian's blood makes me want her more."

A low growl rumbled in Ashriel's throat, the more feral side of his jahuni nature rising to the surface. He pounded a fist against the barrier, sending bolts of electricity skittering over the surface. "You don't need any of them," he said, wishing he had the means to wipe that disgusting smirk off Odath's face. "Instead of wasting time picking off humans, why don't you do what Enalel ordered you to do? Use me to settle things with Sijo Otharo once and for all, and leave the humans out of it."

"How sweet," Odath said dismissively, bringing his face close to the human's and taking a deep breath as if to inhale the scent of her fear. He laughed when she cringed away from him, but kept her locked against him. "You've changed. What a champion for the weak you've become. Darenai would be proud."

"Fuck off," Ashriel ground out, fighting the urge to throw himself at the barrier again. After tearing through Ashriel's mind, his enemies knew just enough about Darenai to use his friend as leverage.

"Walk away, Ashriel," Odath said with a sneer, keeping his eyes on Ashriel while he rubbed his cheek against the woman's hair. "As usual, there's nothing you can do."

The woman Odath held tried to jerk away from him again, but he kept her trapped effortlessly, enjoying her response. Ashriel knew he was running out of time. He had to divert Odath's attention away from her.

"You talk about their weakness, but it's yours I see now," Ashriel said, but Odath barely acknowledged him, drawn by the scent of his victim. He dipped his head down, ready to bite into her shoulder. "Your lack of control is pathetic. You're not a sathra. You don't need her blood, but the power in it is just too tempting for you. No wonder Enalel didn't trust you to take care of the Sijo yourself."

That finally got a reaction. Odath raised his head to glare at Ashriel, hands tightening on the woman. She gasped, frightened eyes silently pleading with Ashriel. "Coming from one of Enalel's playthings, that's laughable. You're powerless now, and you talk about my lack of control?" he said, but Ashriel could hear the undertone of anger in his voice. "You're alive only at Enalel's insistence that you'll be useful in killing the Sijo, but don't think I can't find a way around that. You might want to keep that in mind."

Ashriel knew he could get under Odath's skin easily, and focused on shifting his enemy's attention to himself. Although Odath was good at hiding the mild beginning effects of hajithra, the sickness that eventually overcame any shima who wandered too far into the darker side of magic, the level of his bloodlust gave him away. He was volatile. Constantly hungry for more energy, and for the purest source of that energy. The power of life itself that moved through the bloodstream.

Ashriel tilted his head, raising a mocking eyebrow. "I might actually take that uninspiring threat seriously if you weren't using a magical shield *and* a human shield to keep me away from you." He laughed darkly, measuring the impact of his words on Odath. “But I wasn’t talking about the cowardly way you take advantage of my powers being stolen. I was talking about the hajithra eating away at you. It’s sad the way you allow it to control you. If even I can see it in my current state, Enalel certainly can. Which brings me back to the point—Enalel doesn’t trust you to get the job done, so she left Petrin in charge.”

“The hajithra makes me stronger,” Odath said, a distinct growl in his voice. As a warrior, it was the same argument Ashriel had heard many times from other criminals who had chosen to give in to the temptation of dark magic, and it had some truth to it. But the cost of straying too far into the darkness eventually caught up with anyone who embraced the hajithra. “I’m not suppressing the potential of my powers, no matter what the laws of the Junak say, trying to take some ridiculous moral high ground—”

“You’re stronger for the moment, sure. But constantly giving in to that craving, letting it rule you, you’re almost as useless as I am. It’ll burn through you soon,” Ashriel said, intentionally goading Odath as he paced along the edge of the barrier between them. He would be ready if Odath was distracted for even a second. “They see your weakness, as I do, and use it against you so easily it’s actually kind of depressing to watch. You’ve been collared almost as effectively as I have by Enalel, and handed off to Petrin like another of her playthings.”

“Don’t put me on the same level as you,” Odath said, taking a threatening step forward, the girl nearly forgotten in his grip. “I could rip you apart, and easily take care of the Sijo myself.”

"Ooo, now I'm frightened," Ashriel pushed, sensing Odath's control of the barrier slipping. "Why don't you free my powers before you talk shit?" He tilted his head, and it was his turn to smirk. "That's right, you can't. Petrin wouldn't approve, would she?"

His provocation worked, and Odath shoved the woman away from him. More than ready for a fight, Ashriel rushed the dissipating barrier between them as the human ran in the opposite direction.

Focused on Odath, he felt Petrin's presence a second too late. Just before he could get his hands on Odath, he was jerked off his feet and thrown backward down the hall. Slamming hard into a wall, the wind was knocked out of him as he crumpled to the floor. The weight of her power kept him on his hands and knees. Struggling with all his might against the magic holding him, he gritted his teeth.

"Careful, Odath," Petrin said, stepping gracefully around Ashriel. "You're letting him manipulate you again."

Odath hesitated, bloodlust clear in his gaze as he stared at Ashriel. There was a satisfying tic in his jaw, and Ashriel could tell he was struggling to hold himself back.

Ashriel smiled mockingly from his place on the floor. "Looks like you're not just Enalel's bitch."

Odath growled, moving to attack.

"Odath," Petrin said warningly when he tried to pass her, freezing him in his tracks with her cold tone. "We really do need him for our mission."

Probably sensing he was pushing his luck, Odath got himself under control again, and Ashriel chuckled to himself. They all knew Petrin was slightly stronger than him. Just enough to give him pause. And she had Enalel's favor for the moment. Cursing under his breath, he tore his attention away from Ashriel, and in the blink of an eye he was gone, disappearing down the hall as he raced after the human.

"Stop this, Petrin," Ashriel said, muscles tensing against the power holding him immobilized. "You don't have to kill this human to get what you want."

"I don't *have* to," she agreed easily, tilting her head. "But I *want* to." She laughed in the face of his disgust. "We both know the hajithra, when controlled properly, is a powerful kind of magic. While Odath may be consumed by it, I flourish in it." Erecting a barrier between them, she spared him once last glance over her shoulder before she walked away to follow Odath. "I'll bleed this entire town dry to feed it."

The moment he could move again, he leapt to his feet and focused all of his remaining energy on getting through Petrin's shield. He could sense the human's heart pounding somewhere ahead of him in the house. Just out of reach. Then he heard a scream, quickly choked off.

He pounded a fist against the barrier, sending streaks of electricity across the surface. "Petrin!" Roaring in fury, knowing he was powerless, he hit the barrier again and again out of frustration, ignoring the burning pain, only stopping when the unmistakable smell of fresh blood reached him.

Fists clenched, he fought the urge to vomit. The darkest kinds of magic left a nauseating stain on everything they touched. No shima who didn't suffer from hajithra could stomach it.

He swore to himself that he'd find a way to spare

Rae and Jillian from this fate. Whatever mixture of spells Odath and Petrin were using to drain the humans, they seemed to require time, but the length differed depending on the strength of the human. He could only guess how much time he had left to work on freeing Rae and Jillian.

That Rae didn't live at the house gave him an advantage with her at least. Odath and Petrin concentrated more of their time on the humans living in the house, and used the others more slowly.

When there was no human heartbeat ahead of him anymore, he said a silent prayer for Rae's friend, as Darenai would have done, before leaving to check on Jillian. Knowing Petrin had just come from her room, a knot of fear settled in his gut, and he couldn't rest until he knew Jillian was all right.

Jillian watched Ashriel leave the room with a million questions spinning in her head. None of what she could remember of their conversation made any sense. Something about cannibals and enchantments.

Her gaze was automatically drawn to one of those symbols he'd slashed. Before, looking at them had been enough to give her the creeps. Now that he'd destroyed all of them, however, they didn't really bother her anymore. Frowning, she touched the jagged edges of plaster and wood that he'd somehow torn through.

"How did you do this?" she wondered out loud. It wasn't like he'd been carrying a knife or anything. Matching her fingers to the longer, deeper gashes, she couldn't shake the impression that they looked like claw marks from some kind of large animal.

Goosebumps rose on her skin, and she took an instinctual step back, hugging her arms to herself. Whatever was happening, with her weird fainting spells, the symbols, and her strange employers, she knew Ashriel was right. She needed to leave as soon as possible.

No sooner did she have the thought than a searing pain sliced through her head. Sucking a breath in between her teeth, she clenched her eyes closed, holding her head in her hands.

I'm fine. I should stay right here.

Panic squeezed at her chest as the pain faded and she opened her eyes. She remembered how adverse she'd felt to going to the hospital earlier with Rae, and started to feel like she really was losing it. The thoughts coming together in her head with what she could remember...none of it made any sense.

"This isn't real," she whispered to herself. "It can't be. It's not possible."

Heart pounding in her chest, she tested her theory, feeling like a crazy person. Almost *hoping* she was losing her mind, and none of this was real.

She took a deep breath and tried to brace herself. "I'm leaving." Pain instantly ripped through her brain again, and she doubled over.

Words whispered through her mind in a voice that sounded eerily like her own.

I'm fine. I'm staying.

It was chilling how calm that voice was. It felt like her own thoughts. Like she could change her mind if she wanted to.

Her eyes fell on her suitcases, and she walked purposefully toward them, only to be brought up short before she could grasp the handles. Arms shaking from the strain, she suddenly just stopped moving. Dropping her hands, she tried again.

"I have to leave." Immediate pain brought her to her knees, and a wave of dizziness hit her so strongly she nearly blacked out right there.

I have to stay. I'm fine.

"This isn't right," she whispered, horrified. Struggling to catch her breath, she got to her feet and stumbled over to sit on the edge of the bed. "What's wrong with me?"

She sat there for a long while, trying to calm herself down and get her thoughts together. The fear was still there, sitting like a stone in her stomach, but she couldn't just hide in her room and wait for something else to happen. Forcing herself to think things through, she tried to remember as much as she could about what she'd seen since she'd started living there.

Entire patches of her memory were missing. She didn't remember dinner the night before, or going to bed. With a jolt, she realized that wasn't the only night she didn't remember. She'd gotten lost many times, and as soon as she reached her room...nothing. She couldn't remember a thing.

She also didn't remember leaving the house with Rae that morning. Or what had happened on the stairs with Ashriel.

"Ashriel..."

She got unsteadily to her feet and made her way to the door. She needed to understand what was going on, and he wasn't going to get away with a few vague, disturbing comments and telling her to get out as if it were that easy. As if whatever was going on in her head would actually *let* her leave.

She wrenched the door open and stopped dead in her tracks. Dread filled her as she found herself staring right at Petrin. The thought flitted through Jillian's head that Petrin knew Ashriel had been talking to her, and she must have been waiting to see what Jillian would do.

Instinctively, she took a careful step backward. Body shaking, she was ready to fight if she had to, but Petrin was completely composed. She smiled at Jillian before glancing into the bedroom behind her.

"Someone's been busy," she said lightly, and the laugh she gave made Jillian's skin crawl all over again. She knew Petrin was looking at the slashed-up symbols, but didn't dare take her eyes off her. She sensed that would be a huge mistake.

"Excuse me," Jillian said, hoping Petrin would let her by. She didn't like the idea of getting too close to the other woman. "I need to—ugh!" Pain sliced mercilessly through her skull, legs buckling beneath her, and she was on her knees again. Just thinking about leaving was enough to cause it.

Petrin casually approached her, seemingly used to this kind of situation. "Interesting," she said, looking down at Jillian with a smirk. "You're even stronger than I gave you credit for, if Ashriel's meddling can bring you back to your senses so quickly." She shrugged. "Not that it'll matter in the end. It's rare that he manages to get anyone out in time, but it's so fun to watch him struggle."

Jillian's blood went cold at the calculation in Petrin's eyes. "Just let me g—" She nearly choked on the words, clenching her eyes closed as she clutched at her head. Pain cut into her so hard, little dots danced behind her eyelids.

"Haven't you learned yet? I know this is all new and scary, but you can't be that dense." She heard Petrin laugh from somewhere above her, and lifted her head defiantly to meet the other woman's mocking gaze.

Breathing heavily, Jillian struggled to her feet. She was so focused on not thinking about anything that would bring the pain back, all she could do was glare at Petrin. It was like holding eye contact with a smiling predator.

Seeming to sense Jillian's determination to fight, Petrin sighed. "Humans are such poor, magic-deficient creatures. It's almost endearing, the way you scurry around, tinkering with your machines and patting yourselves on the back for your 'advances' in technology." Jillian tried to move when Petrin reached for her, but her body wouldn't obey.

The other woman's hand landed on her shoulder, and a sensation like cold and electricity mixed together moved through Jillian. "But in the end, you're all as helpless as babies. Even the strongest among you." Her cold smile was terrifying in its calmness, and Jillian's head began to swim with dizziness. "Resist me all you want. It won't change anything."

Jillian tried to fight it, but then her body went numb, and all at once her mind was blank. Peaceful. Why had she been afraid? Everything was fine.

CHAPTER SEVEN

JILLIAN WOKE UP FEELING AWFUL. She still wasn't sleeping well, there was a dull ache in her head, and she felt weak. She'd fainted the day before, running errands with Rae, and the fever from whatever flu bug she'd caught must have been so bad she'd slept through the rest of the day. Everything after breakfast was just a blur.

She considered getting checked out at the hospital, but quickly dismissed the idea.

I'm fine, she thought, getting sluggishly out of bed. She'd probably feel better after a shower and some breakfast. Her stomach growled like she hadn't eaten in ages, her mouth watering in anticipation of food.

Yawning, she started to stretch when something on the wall across the room caught her eye. Long, claw-like gashes. Glancing around the room, she realized with a start that every one of those spirally designs on her walls had been slashed up, including the big one above her bed.

"What—?" A sudden stabbing pain in her skull had her sucking a breath in between her teeth and cradling her head in her hands.

It took a minute for the headache to start to fade back to a manageable throb. Lifting her head, she looked at the marks again, a chill of apprehension moving through her.

I'm fine. The reassurance flitted through her mind immediately. *Odath and Petrin told me about them remodeling, I just forgot. Everything's fine.*

Pushing the unease out of her mind, she managed to get ready, but she felt so crappy she was seriously wondering if she could get her work done. She threw on her comfiest beat-up jeans, and a random band T-shirt from her suitcase, and wondered for what felt like the millionth time why she hadn't gotten around to unpacking yet.

"Ugh." One look in the mirror confirmed she looked as rough as she felt. There were dark circles under her blue eyes, and she seemed paler than usual. Yawning as she tied her hair back, she resigned herself to another day of following Ashriel's trail of destruction with a dustbin and broom.

Trudging down to the first floor, her limbs felt stiff and heavy, but she just ignored it.

I'm fine.

These words just kept echoing in her head, even though she felt anything but fine. Pausing on her way to the kitchen, she tried to get her bearings, feeling strangely disoriented. She took a deep breath, briefly closing her eyes. The air shifted around her, growing heavy, and the creaking of the old house seemed louder than usual. Her head swam dizzyingly for a moment, but she breathed her way through it, leaning heavily against the wall.

When she was ready to move again, she opened her

eyes, only to realize she had no idea where she was. She could have sworn she was near the kitchen. The hallway stretching out in front of her seemed unfamiliar, completely different than it had before she'd closed her eyes moments ago. She could see the open door of the study ahead of her, which was nowhere near the kitchen.

Probably.

Sighing, she was about to turn and go the other way, when she was stopped by the sound of hushed voices coming from the direction of the study. She hesitated, recognizing them as Rae and Petrin.

She couldn't make out what was being said, and she had no desire to talk to Petrin, but the tremble in Rae's voice worried her. Unsure if she was intruding, she made some noise as she approached the study, not wanting to seem as though she were eavesdropping. Peering into the large room, she knocked softly on the doorframe. Standing at the far end of the room, in front of a large wooden desk, both women looked over at her.

It was clear Rae had been crying. Her brown eyes were puffy, and her cheeks were red and tearstained. Petrin was standing close by, her hand resting on Rae's shoulder in what should have been a friendly gesture. Jillian had no idea why, but she had the insane urge to slap Petrin's hand away from Rae immediately. Pushing down the strange impulse, she stepped forward and took Rae's hand instead.

"Rae, what's wrong?" she asked, worried for her friend. She tried to ignore how uneasy she felt with Petrin so close, glancing uncertainly at the other woman, but Petrin seemed perfectly composed, her delicate features softened into a convincing look of concern. Choosing to ignore the weird vibes she was getting from Petrin for the moment, she focused on Rae. "What happened?"

Rae sniffed, swiping at her tears with the wad of tissues clutched in her hand. "It's Mindy," she said shakily. "She was killed."

"What? Oh my gosh, Rae, I'm so sorry," Jillian said, her stomach sinking. She forgot all about Petrin, reaching out to hug Rae tightly. She felt the other woman tremble. The dam seemed to burst as Rae clung to her, and it wasn't long before she felt the dampness of tears on her shoulder. She held onto Rae, rubbing her back soothingly until she had calmed down a little.

Looking over at Petrin, who was silently watching their exchange, Jillian tried to find a polite way to get rid of her. "I'll sit with her a while," she said, hoping Petrin would take the hint and leave.

"Of course," Petrin said smoothly, giving another one of her chilling smiles. "I'll come back later."

Jillian had to bite her tongue to keep her true opinions from slipping out. *Please, don't,* she thought, but managed a polite smile and a nod for Petrin before she left.

"I'm sorry," Rae said, pulling away from Jillian. She sounded calmer, but it was clear she was trying to put on a brave face.

"There's nothing for you to apologize about. Here, let's sit down," Jillian said gently, leading Rae over to the leather sofa in the middle of the room.

"Thank you," Rae said, dabbing at her eyes again as she sat at one end. "Mindy was a good friend. I wish you had gotten the chance to meet her."

"I wish I had too," Jillian agreed. She turned on the lamp on the end table next to the sofa, trying to make the study less gloomy, and sat down next to Rae.

"I hadn't heard from Mindy in a while, but I knew she was taking a couple weeks off, so it didn't seem weird," Rae said, sniffling. Jillian just let her talk, not wanting to press her. "They said it was some kind of animal attack, but that doesn't make any sense. Mindy didn't like to go hiking or do outdoorsy type things." She shook her head, brows furrowing in a frown. "I could rarely even get her to go running with me in the park. Why would she have been out in the woods?"

An involuntary shiver worked its way through Jillian. For the briefest of moments, she remembered one of the nightmares she'd been having. Predatory eyes staring into hers. Being paralyzed by some unknown force. The gashes on her walls from remodeling that looked too much like claw marks for comfort. Shaking the unwelcome memory away, she focused on Rae.

Rae shuddered, squeezing her eyes shut for a moment. "There have been so many of these strange animal attacks lately." She frowned at Jillian, confusion in her expression. "I mean, the woods are full of wild animals, so everybody knows to be careful. But it's never been like this," she insisted. "They've never singled humans out as food."

"Yeah, they usually tend to avoid humans," Jillian agreed.

Rae sighed, sounding a little calmer. "Usually. Rarely, a hiker might get attacked if they go really far into the woods, or if someone's out messing around where they shouldn't be." She crumpled the tissues in her hands. "But now it seems like they're actually hunting humans." She shook her head. "What other explanation could there be for so many attacks recently?"

"I don't know," Jillian admitted.

"And the way they've left these victims..." She shuddered again, going a little pale.

"Why don't you take a little time off?" Jillian quickly suggested, trying to steer the conversation away from the gory details of Mindy's death. "She was your friend. You should take some time for yourself."

Rae nodded, looking down at her fisted hands. "Maybe it's time I finally quit," she said. "The café's almost ready anyway. Besides, this place gives me the creeps sometimes. And..." she trailed off, shaking her head with a self-deprecating sigh.

"And what?" Jillian urged.

"I know it's all in my head," Rae said, trying to shrug off whatever was bothering her. "I don't know." She rolled her eyes at herself. "It's silly. I feel like I'm being watched or something all the time. Or like I'm being followed when I'm working."

Jillian had to fight off another shiver. She didn't want to alarm Rae with her own experiences, but she had been feeling the same way. She considered how best to respond to that.

"I told you it was silly," Rae said with a forced flippancy and a strained laugh.

"No, not at all," Jillian said, hoping she wasn't scaring Rae further. "I've felt the same way sometimes." All the time. "It's probably just this house, you know?" And the extremely creepy people in said house. "It's like the perfect setting for every haunting movie you've ever seen."

Rae chuckled, giving her a teary-eyed smile. "No kidding," she agreed, glancing around the room as she spoke. "All it needs are some unidentifiable stains that won't wash away."

"Oh, I'm sure Ashriel will create some," Jillian said darkly.

"Give me time," a deep voice interrupted, startling them both.

Jillian's heart leapt in her chest. She didn't have to look at the doorway behind them to see who it was. It could only have been one person. The only person she had ever known whose dark voice captured her attention every time she heard it. She saw Rae's eyes widen and knew she was right.

"But where are the whispering voices following us down darkened hallways?" Ashriel continued before either of them could get too embarrassed about being caught talking about him.

Jillian took a deep breath, finally turning her head to look over at him. The words died in her throat as their eyes locked, and she instantly knew something was wrong. This wasn't the same Ashriel she'd been verbally sparring with for days. He was quieter than usual, without the bite she was used to in his tone, and his eyes lacked their usual intensity, like there was something on his mind. Her instincts were giving her the strong impression that he was shaken, but trying to hide it.

Was this strange somberness because of Mindy? She'd assumed it was only Rae he was on good terms with, but maybe she'd been wrong.

He was the first to look away, turning his attention to Rae. "And I think you're right, by the way," he said, using a gentler voice than Jillian had thought him capable of. "You should go to your café. Get out of this place, and go where you can be happy. I think you know staying here isn't good for you."

Rae exchanged a quick look with Jillian, apparently not used to this more mellow side of him either. She nodded as if coming to some sort of decision, sighing deeply. "Yeah, I'm not particularly attached to this place, and I don't really want to work for Odath and Petrin anymore." She dabbed at her eyes one last time, and a little bit of anger began to creep into her expression. "They didn't even seem to care what happened to Mindy."

"That's horrible," Jillian said, but she wasn't surprised. She'd gotten the impression that Odath and Petrin didn't really concern themselves with others.

Rae grew quiet for a moment, lost in her own musings. "It's so weird. I've considered quitting before, but for some reason I just couldn't bring myself to do it."

For some reason, Rae's comment made her strangely uncomfortable.

I'm fine. Everything's fine.

"Thank you for listening," Rae said. Glancing over at Ashriel, she smiled hesitantly. "And thank you for your advice."

He nodded and made small talk, speaking gently with Rae to cheer her up, but Jillian was so caught off guard by how pleasant he was being that she lost track of the conversation. The corners of his perfect mouth curved up in a smile, and it was her turn to sigh. Him acting all normal and kind like that only made her notice all over again how gorgeous he was.

For one insane moment, she wondered what those lips would feel like against her own.

And then for several completely call-the-people-with-the-white-coats moments, she wondered how many kisses it would take to keep him smiling—and imagined it in great detail.

As if he sensed her staring, he looked over, and she tried to pretend like she hadn't just been having inappropriate thoughts. "Could you get a glass of water for Rae?" he said.

"I'm okay," Rae said, shaking her head.

"Let me be nice," Ashriel said gently. "This rare mood probably won't strike again for a while. Take advantage while you can."

Rae laughed a little, finally nodding, and Jillian caught Ashriel's subtle glance. It seemed like he wanted to speak privately with Rae. Feeling an inexplicable sting in her chest, Jillian quickly left.

What am I thinking? she wondered as she looked for the kitchen. It almost felt as if she envied Ashriel's kindness to Rae. *Ridiculous. What's wrong with me?*

Rae was in pain, and Ashriel was being nice for once. She refused to acknowledge the small part of herself that wished he'd be nice to her too.

After a few wrong turns, she finally found the kitchen again. She grabbed the water and rushed back the way she'd came. She heard Ashriel's quiet voice as she approached the study, and she hesitated. There was that gentle sound again. A tone he never used with her.

Her steps slowed, and she wondered if she should wait a little longer. So far, Ashriel had only really been kind to Rae. For the first time, she wondered if there was actually something between the two of them.

She was about to turn away, that unwelcome ache throbbing in her chest again, when some of Ashriel's words brought her up short.

"You will leave now," he said, a clear command in his voice, even though he spoke softly. "And you will never come back."

"You will stay," a voice echoed in Jillian's head. A memory from one of her strange nightmares. The voice was so much colder than Ashriel's, and a shiver moved through her. She was frozen to the spot as the image of Odath's cruel gaze popped into her mind out of nowhere. *"You're fine."*

A dull pain seared Jillian's head, and she rubbed at her temple. Unable to help herself, she crept toward the doorway of the study. Some instinctive part of herself knew something was wrong. Heart pounding, she wanted to run for some reason, but she couldn't make herself do it.

The sight that greeted her when she looked into the study made her blood run cold. Ashriel was leaning close to Rae where they stood in front of the sofa, staring deeply into her eyes, his hands on her shoulders. Any other time, Jillian would have thought he was moving in to embrace her, but the blank look on Rae's face told Jillian it was nothing like that.

"If you see Odath or Petrin, you will run," Ashriel continued in that same low, hypnotic tone.

"Yes," Rae said, her voice without inflection.

Lungs laboring for air, a flash of memory hit Jillian again, and she gasped. Clenching her eyes shut against another wave of pain in her head, lost moments from the past couple weeks fought for space in her mind, rushing in like a tidal wave.

The sensation of being crushed to the wall, a horrible power holding her captive.

"I love the fear in you."

Merciless, predatory gazes that watched her with a kind of hunger she didn't understand.

"Humans are such poor, magic-deficient creatures."

The shock of cold electricity against her skin when her captors touched her.

And at the center of it all, Ashriel's cryptic words. *"Breakable little humans shouldn't ask questions with answers that would make their heads explode."*

Her head spun dizzyingly, dread filling her. Trembling, she opened her eyes, only to find Ashriel staring directly at her from across the room.

"What are you?" Jillian whispered, remembering the gashes he'd left on the walls of her bedroom. The feel of slashed wood beneath her fingers, resembling claw marks. Clinging to the doorframe for support, she tried to make sense of what was happening to her, but the pieces her mind put together made no sense.

"Rae," he said without looking at the other woman. He held Jillian's gaze as if willing her to stay put. "It's time to leave. Get as far away as possible," he said, and Jillian felt some subtle shift to the air in the room. A brief pressure, and a strange tingle over her skin that was quickly gone. It was nothing like the forceful power in her memories, but she understood Ashriel was in full control of Rae in that moment. "Forget your cooking supplies and go."

When he dropped his hands from Rae's shoulders, she took a deep breath, blinking rapidly like she was waking up. "Right," she said, seeming a little disoriented. "You guys will visit me at the café sometime, right?"

A chill worked its way through Jillian. It was unsettling how unaware Rae seemed. Like she was just continuing a conversation she'd been having.

"Absolutely," Ashriel said, finally breaking his gaze away from Jillian.

"Yeah," Jillian said, keeping her eyes on Ashriel as she released the death grip she'd had on the door frame. Unsure if she could trust him, her legs were trembling as she came to stand protectively next to Rae, the fear of being so close to him nearly overwhelming. She wasn't about to abandon Rae, though, so she watched him cautiously as she set the water she was still clutching on the end table and grabbed Rae's hand. "Let's g—"

Pain lanced through Jillian's skull, and she sucked a breath in between her teeth. Cradling her head with her free hand, she breathed through the now-familiar pain. A memory of Petrin's mocking voice slithered through her head. *"Haven't you learned yet?"*

"You can't," Ashriel said, a bitter note to his voice, and she recognized the significance behind his words. Her mind and body wouldn't cooperate if she tried. There was a pause, and Jillian lifted her head to see his usual scowl. "I'll take her to the door." His tone left no room for argument. "Stay here and wait for me to come back."

She was still afraid of him, but she somehow knew he wasn't the one keeping her in that house. He wasn't the one who had hurt her. From the beginning, he'd done nothing but tell her to get out. It wasn't much to go on, but she knew she had to rely on him for the moment. She couldn't help Rae herself.

Reluctantly, she let go of Rae's hand and let Ashriel lead her away. The moment he closed the door behind them and she was alone, the strength left her legs. Crumpling to her knees, she leaned forward to press her hands against the floor. She was shaking, and it was hard to breathe, and for the first time in her life, she thought she might be having a panic attack.

She gave herself the luxury of freaking out for a minute, and then she got unsteadily to her feet. She took several deep breaths, trying to ease the pressure of fear sitting in her chest like a rock, while she tried to make sense of what she'd seen.

As crazy as it felt, there was no doubt in her mind anymore that her employers weren't human. She could barely wrap her head around the things they could do.

And what about Ashriel? He was as dangerous as the other two, but she got a totally different feeling from him. From the beginning, she had suspected he had some kind of issue with Odath and Petrin, but what did that mean for her and Rae?

Hearing the sound of the doorknob turning, Jillian spun around to find Ashriel in the doorway. His expression was hard, those mysterious purple eyes unreadable, and she couldn't shake the knot of fear she still felt in her gut.

"Was Rae able to leave?" she said. At his nod, she felt both relieved and scared. "Then why can't I?"

"I've been working on her longer than you," he said, closing the door as he came into the study. "And her mental barriers aren't as strong as yours."

"You've been *working* on me?" She narrowed

her eyes, not liking the sound of that. "My mental barriers—"

"You have to go," he said, obviously in no mood to explain.

"How?" she said, retreating a few steps when he would have come closer. He stopped, the length of the room between them, and she hoped he couldn't see how relieved she was. "I can't even think about it without my head feeling like it's splitting open."

"I'm working on it," he said, an edge of frustration in his voice. "But part of it will be letting me into your mind."

"What?" Her stomach sank. That was the last thing she ever wanted to experience again.

"If you willingly let me in, it won't hurt you," he said, seeming to understand her fear. "It was Odath and Petrin's forcefulness that damaged your mind."

Could she trust him? She wasn't sure, but she found herself wanting to. The worst thing he'd done to her was be rude and demand she leave, but the crazy things he'd said and done before were beginning to take on a new meaning to her.

Swallowing past the dryness in her throat, she tried to be rational about the situation. If she had to let him into her mind in order to get out, she'd find a way to do it. "I don't know how."

"I'll show you," he said, and she couldn't help moving back again when he took a step toward her. He stopped, putting his hands up for a moment as if to show her he meant no harm. "You don't have much time to get used to the idea," he said, backing away.

"There's no other way?" she asked, pushing down the anxiety in her chest. He was trying to give her a chance to wrap her head around what was happening, but this was all too much.

"No," he said, and she could sense the urgency in him as he glanced at the door. "You're stuck here as long as you're under their spell." Turning away from her, he walked toward the window, and she noticed he was careful to keep as much space between them as possible. He yanked the curtains open, letting more light spill into the room. He was quiet a long moment, giving her what time he could. "I can't stand how closed in this place is," he finally said, sounding like he was speaking more to himself than to her.

It could all be an act, but he didn't sound like he was trying to manipulate her. They both knew he could force himself into her mind any time he wanted, but it didn't seem like he wanted to.

Letting her breath out slowly, she braced herself for whatever strange reaction he would throw her way. "If I had my way, I would burn those curtains," she said, testing the waters.

There was a short silence, as if he were trying to decide what to do himself. Glancing back at her, he gave her a slight grin. "It could be arranged if you help me. Sadly, the spell I'm under won't let me do anything that could destroy the house."

"Now that I know your secret, do I still have to clean up afterward?"

Even though he turned his face toward the window again, she could hear his low chuckle. He still frightened her, but the sound of that deep rumble did funny things to her. Totally inappropriate, out of place things, considering the circumstances. Why did her strange fascination with him have to rear it's ugly head right at that moment?

As unbelievable as the situation was, they were talking easily for the first time, and it felt like she was meeting him all over again. Some of her fear was starting to subside, and she was second-guessing the opinions she'd had of him before.

"All this time, acting like a lunatic, you've been trying to help me, haven't you?" she said, really seeing him for the first time. "And Rae too."

He sighed deeply as he turned to face her, leaning back against the windowsill with crossed arms. "You're stronger than most humans, but the natural barriers in your mind are still no match for Odath and Petrin," he said, not really denying or acknowledging what she'd said. "Getting into the minds of the other humans that have been brought here was easier because their barriers were weaker. I don't want to risk harming you further. Let me help you."

"What about you?" she pushed, setting the issue of him being in her head aside for the moment because she didn't want to think about it. "Why don't you leave too?"

"You don't have time to worry about me," he said, sounding oddly resigned. "What do you think will happen once they realize Rae is gone, and you're the only human here at the moment? If it makes you feel better, I could take your memories of what happened here if I had more time to build my strength. But we're out of time."

He straightened away from the window, studying her. A familiar sensation moved through her, gentle and warm, and she somehow knew he was using magic on her, but she didn't feel threatened. "Your mental barriers are so fragile right now. I don't know what forcing you to go would do to you. What would it take for me to convince you to do this of your own free will?"

"Tell me the truth," she said firmly, her fear *of* him taking an unexpected turn into fear *for* him. She knew he was right. She had to get out. But she wasn't sure she could make herself do it until she knew he could get out too. "If you're not helping them, then you're as trapped as I am, aren't you?"

He scrubbed his face with his hands, looking weary as he muttered something in a different language. "I have never begged anyone for anything in my entire life," he said quietly, his gaze burning into hers when he lowered his hands. "And, believe me, that's saying something." The low laugh that followed this comment was bitter. Humorless.

"But I will drop to my knees right here and now and beg you to leave," he vowed with perfect sincerity. "I will promise you anything that is within my power to give. I will pay whatever price you ask. Just let me help you leave."

She stared at him, completely at a loss. How was she supposed to respond to that? She studied his troubled expression, considering her situation carefully.

"Letting you into my mind will help you undo whatever Odath and Petrin did to me?" she asked.

"Yes."

"And you can leave with me?"

There was a very brief silence, but she caught it. "Yes."

"You're lying."

"Tairi, gesja hano!" he growled, automatically taking

a step toward her before catching himself. Probably trying not to scare her, he kept his distance, but he glanced impatiently at the door again like he expected Odath and Petrin to show up any second. "There's no time for this! Just let me help you."

She didn't like it, but what choice did she have? Once she was out, she would check on Rae, and find a way to help Ashriel. She had no idea how, up against beings she didn't understand, but she *would* do something for Ashriel.

Swallowing her apprehension, she cautiously approached him. "How do I do this?"

The moment the words were out of her mouth, he was already moving, his long strides eating up those last few feet between them in seconds. She automatically stiffened when his hands reached for her. He hesitated briefly, seeing that telltale sign, before gently settling his hands on her shoulders.

Although her T-shirt separated his skin from hers, she could feel the effect he had on her immediately. A comforting warmth spread from where he touched her, and unlike with Odath and Petrin, it felt right. There was no shock of electricity, but she could feel the magic in him somehow, tingling over her skin.

"Keep your eyes on me," he said, his tone dropping into that hypnotic cadence she'd heard him use with Rae. He lowered his beautiful face a little closer, eyes capturing hers, and she felt heat flooding her cheeks. "I won't hurt you. Trust in me, and listen to my voice."

"Okay," she said, finding it extremely easy to stare at him. The magic moving between them intensified. Her energy and his, mixing together naturally. She struggled to stay calm, the sensation new and strange, and it was hard not to feel anxious. The inside of her left wrist tingled with warmth, and she unconsciously clasped it with her other hand.

His brows furrowed as he caught that movement, hands tensing on her shoulders, but he didn't say anything. When his eyes met hers again, there was something different about the way he looked at her. Searching, almost.

"Follow my breaths. Concentrate on me," he said. His hands ghosted down her arms, hesitating over her wrists, before silently coaxing her to let him take her hands. "Focus on opening your mind to me."

She instinctively knew what she felt then was his mind brushing against hers. Almost like a physical touch, she could tell he was being gentle with her. Following his lead, she closed her eyes as he did. Letting her guard down was easy with him, and just that quickly her mind was enveloped by his, the lingering pain in her head vanishing in an instant.

She should have felt as helpless as she had with Odath and Petrin. It would have been completely normal to be scared. But she felt none of that. All she had was an unexplainable sense that this was right.

"I didn't want to know your name," he said, his tone gentling as something shifted in her mind. Like rips stitching themselves back together, she felt healed. Freed. Complete again. "I can't fully protect you as I am now, and if I fail you, I know you will haunt me the most."

Connected as she was to him, she knew it was his voice she heard in her head. *"Your name will stay with me for different reasons now,"* his thoughts whispered through her mind.

Her eyes fluttered open at that, and she found him a little closer than expected, eyes still closed in concentration. The space between them was almost nothing. They were so close she could lean into him if she chose.

She was surprised by just how badly she wanted to.

"You're getting greedy, Ashriel," Petrin said from behind them, startling them apart. Ashriel quickly stepped in front of Jillian, and she was nearly paralyzed by the predatory gleam in the other woman's eyes as she watched them. "You know the rules of our little game," she said, as though there were any real hope for their victims. "You've already chosen who you'd save today."

"Leave her out of this," Ashriel said, a low, primal growl in his voice.

With her mind still faintly connected to his, Jillian knew this wasn't a game at all. That Odath and Petrin let anyone live was purely on a whim. She couldn't make out the full meaning of the impressions she was getting from Ashriel, but she understood Odath and Petrin let him get rid of a human here and there because it didn't matter in the grand scheme of things. There were other responsibilities that they had to split their attention on. They could always draw more humans to them, so him breaking one free meant little to them, except for the inconvenience of having to start over with their spells on a new person. He did the best he could to save as many as possible, but it was a doomed endeavor.

"You don't need her to complete your mission," he said, and the next thoughts Jillian could make out from him were much clearer. *"When they come for me, you have to run."*

She didn't like that at all, and she hoped what she was thinking got through to him. The last thing she wanted was to leave him to fend for himself.

"I think we've been over this," Petrin said as Odath joined her, leaning lazily against the doorjamb. "Where's the fun in only taking what we need?"

Jillian looked around, desperately searching for anything she could use as a weapon, but there weren't many options. Peering around Ashriel, she found Odath's calculating gaze waiting for hers.

Petrin and Ashriel moved at the same time, her hand going to her pendant as he launched himself at her. Jillian grabbed the nearest thing she could get her hands on, some small, metal sculpture, and hurled it at Odath as he moved toward her.

There was a flash of light, blinding her, and Ashriel's shout. She felt an impact to her chest and was falling before she could even grasp what had happened. Her body felt like it was on fire, nerves screaming at her as she hit the floor hard enough to lose her breath.

Odath's satisfied grin as he stood above her was the last thing she saw before her body wasn't hers again.

Chapter Eight

Jillian stood in front of the stairs, running the vacuum over the large entryway rug. She went over and over the same spot.

Had it been a day? Two?

Someone, a lady with light-blond hair and gold eyes, whispered to her.

She couldn't remember how she answered.

"Jilli—!"

There was a commotion somewhere. A man's familiar voice. Something breaking. But she didn't turn her head.

The vacuum went over the same spot, again and again.

CHAPTER NINE

A DIFFERENT DAY. THERE WAS LIGHT in front of her.

A window.

She moved her cloth across the glass in a slow circle.

Another lady came by, this one with darker, honey-blond hair and concerned, dark-brown eyes.

"I'm fine," Jillian said automatically.

Time passed.

More shouting, and something crashing to the ground.

A man's voice shouting for her. His strong hands shaking her by the shoulders. "Listen to my voice—!"

A flash of light in the periphery of her vision.

A cold laugh somewhere behind her.

She kept cleaning the window, her hand moving in a slow circle.

CHAPTER TEN

Another day had passed. Jillian stood motionless, staring at the broom laying on the floor beside her.

She couldn't sweep anymore.

Someone had ripped the broom from her hands and was holding her tightly in their arms, so she couldn't pick it up again.

A familiar voice begged her, "For the love of God, wake up!"

His touch stirred something in her. Some elusive memory.

"I'm fine," she said, and his arms tightened.

Someone appeared behind the man holding her, but the words the other woman said didn't make any sense.

Jillian knew she should be sweeping the floor.

But she couldn't reach the broom.

Chapter Eleven

"FOR CLAIMING NOT TO CARE about Jillian any more than you do the other humans we bring in, you seem unusually focused on her," Petrin said with a knowing smirk. "Why is that, Ashriel?"

"Anything I can do to fuck with you," Ashriel said, frozen in place by Petrin's power over him. Wherever she had the gegaji hidden, that damned blood contract that forced him to follow her will, he silently swore the first thing he would do after he found and destroyed it would be to kill her with his bare hands.

No longer held by him, Jillian mindlessly wandered over to the broom and picked it up. She began sweeping right where she was, in the middle of the library, with a blank look on her face.

"It's a little late to try and pretend you weren't just clinging to her a second ago," Petrin said, approaching Jillian without a care in the world. She knew Ashriel was helpless to stop her. "It's almost as if she's—"

"She isn't," Ashriel said, not even wanting to hear the words out loud.

"Then she truly is useless, and I can drain her right now," Petrin said, wrapping her fingers around Jillian's throat and lifting her off the ground. Jillian somehow kept hold of the broom even as she choked and gasped for air.

"Petrin!" Ashriel roared, fighting the invisible force holding him with everything he had. "Stop! Please!"

Petrin laughed, setting Jillian back on her feet. She started sweeping again, and Petrin looked at Ashriel with genuine shock. "That's the first time I've ever heard you say *please*." Her gaze narrowed, a mad gleam in her eyes. "I think I like it."

Ashriel gritted his teeth, holding back out of fear of what Petrin might do to Jillian if she stopped seeing the situation as amusing. He couldn't stand the thought of Petrin or Odath putting their disgusting hands on her again, or damaging her mind any further. "What do you want?"

Petrin tilted her head. "What do you have left to give me?" she asked, even though they both knew he had nothing. He was already under their control. What more did he have to offer? "Unless..."

There was something in her tone that made his blood run cold. Apparently, he *did* have something left for them to take, other than Jillian. Not that he knew what the hell that even was.

"Say it," he said, knowing he would regret asking. The terms of the gegaji were very specific. They both knew it would be incredibly hard to force him to do anything outside the contract already set for him.

"We need you to find Darenai," she said, and he stared at her.

Then he laughed, for the first time in a long time. Really laughed. "You let him get away? Is this a habit with you guys? Oh, you are so fu—"

"His soul is wandering, unanchored from his body," Petrin cut him off, her self-satisfied smile losing some of its strength. "You wouldn't want him to die, would you? After all you've sacrificed?"

He hoped she could sense from him all the colorful ways he was fantasizing about killing her. "I know he would rather be dead, than let you continue to use him."

"Fine," Petrin said, turning toward Jillian again. Her hand shot out to grab Jillian's throat, her hold rougher this time, and she squeezed. Jillian dropped the broom, but didn't have any will left to fight as the air was choked out of her.

"Stop!" Ashriel shouted, pulling so hard against the magic holding him that he felt the pain down to his joints. He didn't care if it broke every bone in his body. "Whatever you want!"

Petrin dropped Jillian in a heap on the floor, said a quick spell, and the light came back into Jillian's eyes. As she coughed and gasped for air, holding her throat, Petrin spoke to her coldly.

"I won't take your memories this time," she said, and Jillian glared up at her defiantly. "My attention needs to be elsewhere. But let me be clear." She glanced between Jillian and Ashriel to make it clear the warning was for both of them. "You try to leave, or get in my way again, and I will kill you both. Enalel may not approve, but she can find another way to accomplish her goals if necessary."

Jillian got unsteadily to her feet, and Ashriel had to admire her bravery. Her hands were shaking, but she didn't look away from Petrin.

Petrin smirked, getting some sick kick out of Jillian's nerve. She turned her back on them and walked toward the doorway, but glanced back at Ashriel one last time before she left. "Be ready to start hunting today," she said, and he knew she meant for Darenai this time.

He didn't say a word as she left the room, but he was already wracking his brain for a way out of it. The moment the power holding him was gone, he wanted to go to Jillian's side, but he made himself keep his distance. He knew how terrified she must be, even of him.

When she turned to look at him, her body trembling, he felt as helpless as when Petrin had held him immobilized. "Tell me what happened," she demanded, a waver in her voice despite her best efforts to hide her fear from him.

"They took control of your mind," he said.

"How long?" she said, her chest heaving like she'd just run for miles.

"Days," he said, barely able to stand the pain he sensed in her. Shock registered on her face, and she went pale. His dampened senses picked up on her accelerating heart rate, and he knew she was about to lose it, but he couldn't lie to her. "And they brought Rae back."

"What?"

"She doesn't seem to remember anything," he said, not wanting Jillian to find out in any of the horrible ways Odath and Petrin might come up with. "I don't know if she even remembers her friend died."

Jillian just stared at him like a wounded child, and he had to stifle a groan. He had spent the entire time she'd been mind controlled in his own private hell, afraid he would wake up from his forced sleep and find that they had killed her. Haunted by her, as he'd known he would be.

When she took a hesitating step toward him, he didn't have the strength to keep her at a distance. All he wanted to do was grab her and hold onto her, and reassure himself that she was really there in front of him, and out of immediate danger.

He opened his arms to her, and she came to him so naturally he should have been shocked. He would have been, considering the situation she was in as a human, but he understood that part of her knew she could trust him, as he inherently wanted to trust her. It was evidence of the bond with her he'd feared all along. He could barely believe it himself, but he could feel the truth of it deep inside. He still sensed her fear as he wrapped his arms around her, but he could feel her need just as strongly. Their connection made it instinctual for her to seek comfort in him, and he held onto her gratefully.

But it wasn't enough. Not nearly. Just the knowledge that she'd been at the mercy of his enemies for days had his blood boiling and his nerves on edge. He scanned her with his senses as best he could, magic moving between them everywhere they touched, but he couldn't calm his mind.

"I'm sorry I couldn't protect you," he said, hating himself for his helplessness. If he could just find the gegaji Petrin and Odath were using, he could break the spells he was under and fight them on equal footing. He knew it had to be in the house somewhere. A gegaji had to be relatively close to the person bound by it, or it wouldn't work. But no matter how many items he destroyed, none of them were his gegaji. Hell, it could even be an object he couldn't see, considering that he couldn't see the spell marks. "I couldn't save Rae's friend, or Rae, and I can't save you."

He sensed her trying to get a hold of herself, and let her pull away from him. She was a little calmer as she slipped out of his grasp, taking a small step back to look up at him. "You tried to get us to leave—"

"For all the good it did," he said harshly, not ready to let himself off the hook. He'd done everything in his power to help them, but it wasn't enough. "This is why I don't like dealing with humans. I never saw much good in your people before this, and now that I'm starting to, I have to watch you die because you're so damned breakable."

"What happened to us isn't your fault. There was nothing more you could have done," she insisted, trying to comfort him. It seemed like she could see right through him, and he felt exposed. She was far more forgiving than he deserved. "I'm safe for the moment, thanks to you. Not all of it made sense, but I get that you just agreed to something important in order to save me."

There was a question in her words that he was reluctant to answer, but he knew she wouldn't drop it. "She wants me to hunt someone close to me, and return him to her captivity," he said, and immediately saw the horror in her eyes. He searched for the words to comfort her. "You insist that what happened to you and Rae wasn't my fault, but you blame yourself for what Petrin is forcing me to do?"

"This is different," she said, unconvinced.

"No, it's not," he said. "Another person's evil isn't your fault."

Her brows furrowed in a frown, but she finally nodded, accepting his words. “And it isn’t yours either,” she said pointedly.

Uncomfortable, he began to look away from her, only to notice the faint bruises already beginning to darken the skin on her neck. Ugly marks left from Petrin’s cruelty.

He couldn’t help the low growl that rumbled from his throat, anger boiling inside him. He slid one of his arms around her waist, and she let him pull her closer. “You’re injured,” he said, brows snapping down into a scowl. She didn’t seem opposed to his touch, but she must have known he was on edge. Her breathing had picked up again, her fear spiking for a moment as he gently brought his other hand to her neck, but she settled down surprisingly quickly.

“What am I feeling?” she asked, and it took him a second to figure out how she meant that. Probably a product of their growing bond, she seemed to be getting more sensitive to the flow of magic between them.

“A sad attempt at healing,” he said, feeling her pulse thundering against his palm. Alive, and so precious to him. The warmth of her body seeped into him, their energy mixing, and he knew he was in trouble. He was still too unsettled by what she’d just been through, and he wasn’t sure he had it in him to keep his composure much longer.

“Right,” she said, still sounding unsure.

Her bruises faded away as he completed the healing, but he just couldn’t bring himself to release her yet. “This is all my fault,” he said, guilt eating away at him. “If something happens to you again—”

“How is this your fault?” she said, shaking her head

when he met her eyes again. "They were never going to let me go. You know that." Raising her chin, she put on a brave face for him, but he'd been in her mind briefly. He knew how afraid she really was, and he found himself admiring her all the more for her courage. "Now that I know a little of what's going on, I'll be careful to stay away from them as much as I can. Nothing is going to happen to me." He could sense the uncertainty she was trying to hide.

"It's a nice lie," he said, his already questionable self-control beginning to slip. Sighing, his eyes fastened on her lips, and he silently cursed the bond's magnifying effect on his need for her. He knew he should let go of her, and never touch her again. That's what he was supposed to do. And he had every intention of doing it. But somehow, he was leaning down, letting his thumb stroke up the column of her neck to tip her head to the side, angling the temptation of her mouth away from him before he gave in.

It was insanity, but he didn't care. Torture, but it was worth it.

His lips found the sensitive spot just under her ear, and he felt her tremble, hands clutching at his shoulders. When she didn't protest, he kept going, gently trailing kisses along her neck until he felt her pulse beating frantically against his lips.

"I hope you can actually keep that promise," he whispered darkly, forcing himself to stop while he still could. She stared at him with wide eyes as he lifted his head. Her cheeks were stained with a pretty blush. "For both our sakes."

"I thought you don't like humans," she said, but she still didn't pull away from him. "What was that?"

"Proof that I really am insane," he said, fighting the urge to search for more bruises.

He'd never realized how overprotective he could be. He was one wrong move away from wrapping his fragile human in blankets and hiding her away somewhere where Odath and Petrin couldn't break her.

That notion brought him up short immediately. *My human?*

Darenai would love that, if he ever heard of it.

Just as he managed to convince himself stashing her somewhere was illogical, and he needed to think about the situation rationally, she ruined it.

"I want to help you," she said, crushing any hope he had that she operated with any kind of common sense, or any general awareness of how squishy she was compared to the battle-hardened, blood-addicted maniacs she was talking about going up against. "We could call the police."

"With what?" he said, raising an eyebrow. "I don't know if you've noticed, but my kind and electronics don't mix."

"That's you?" she said, scowling as if he'd broken the electricity in the house on purpose.

"Not like we can help it."

"Then I'll find another way," she insisted.

"No," he said firmly. Maybe being as blunt as possible would work? "You will die."

"The police—"

"Would all die."

"But I could—"

"You could die."

"Stop it!" she said, exasperated. She planted her

hands on his chest and pushed herself out of his hold to glare up at him. "I have a plan!"

"Against monsters who use magic you could never understand?" He narrowed his eyes at her, crossing his arms over his chest. "Maybe if I say it slower, it will sink in. You. Would. Die."

"If they're so dangerous—"

He couldn't fucking believe it. "If?"

"All the more reason for me to do something—"

"I'm sorry, did you say, '*If* they're so dangerous?'"

"What am I supposed to do then?" she demanded, planting her hands on her hips like she was gearing up for an argument, as if this topic was really open for any kind of discussion. "I know they're killing people, and what? I hide in the pantry or something?"

"Great plan," he said, unwilling to budge on this. Never had he been so overwhelmed by the desire to protect someone. All he could think of was the self-satisfied smirk on Odath's temptingly punchable face, and Petrin's only slightly more controlled hunger. "Didn't you just get done telling me you'd be more careful and stay out of their way? Not that it will do much good, but attempting to make yourself somewhat less of a target by being out of their faces when possible would make my life easier."

"While they bring in more people to kill?" she said, and he had no answer for that. "What about Rae?"

His stomach sank. "I can get her out—"

"They brought her back like nothing even happened! So does she hide in the pantry with me?"

"No, but—"

"Is the pantry a fortress where these 'monsters who

use magic I could never understand' somehow won't find us?"

"There's a way—"

"Are they allergic to pantries?"

"Don't be ridic—"

"Let's cram the whole world in the pantry, Ashriel! Because even though they seem to think killing people is entertaining, I bet they'll just stop once they have whatever they want, right? And then we can all go about our lives without worrying about them, and never mind the people they already killed?"

"Fine!" Ashriel snapped, at the end of his patience. "Are you going to face them in hand-to-hand combat? Bend the laws of nature and develop magical abilities overnight? Because I'm no match for them right now. What exactly are *you* going to do?"

Jillian took a deep breath, raising her chin defiantly. "The marks or whatever," she said, pointing to a couple spots around the room. "You can't see any of them, can you?"

Heaven help him, she was a glorious, frustrating pain in his ass. "No, I can't see them," he said, glancing around to analyze the library and its contents. Books and bookshelves. A large couch and two matching chairs, and a coffee table in between. Nothing seemed out of the ordinary.

"And you've been breaking everything because whatever's controlling you might be invisible to you as well," she said, and he was glad she finally understood at least part of what was going on.

"It could be any object in this house, invisible to me or not," he said, raising an eyebrow at her. "And?"

"The marks affect you too?"

"Yes," he said, not sure he liked where this was going. "The ones in your room were directed at you or any other human staying there. But somewhere in this damned house is the contract binding me to their will."

"What's the contract?"

"Shimana call it a gegaji. An enchanted object, bound with the power of my own blood. It's normally used for criminals during their incarceration, to drain their magic and keep them in line while they serve their time," he said, stifling the urge to sigh. This conversation was pointless, but at the very least he felt like he owed her the truth of the situation. Maybe then she'd back off and just go hide somewhere. "Normally you couldn't do it with a gegaji, because there are restrictions on them, but my tampered with gegaji, with a little mind control added in, means I'll be forced to murder a ruler's son from a city neighboring my own."

He saw her go a little pale at that, but she pushed through her horror with that frustrating stubbornness of hers. "So if I help you destroy the marks, and find this contract, you might be able to fight them?"

"Yes, but you'll be hiding in the pantry, so you can't help," he said flatly, almost wishing that were actually a viable option at that point.

"It's the only way I can see," she insisted, rolling her eyes at him. "You need to break the power they have over you or, you're right, none of us will make it out of this."

"It's too dangerous."

"How long can you split your attention between trying to get the townspeople Odath and Petrin hire to stay away from here and freeing yourself? I get the feeling we're all running out of time," she said, pressing her point. "Remember when you asked me to let you into my mind? Same logic applies here. We don't have time to argue about this. It's your turn to trust me. Let me help you."

When he hesitated, she turned away from him and looked around the room. After a moment of searching, she impatiently grabbed a small metal statue off the coffee table and stalked toward one of the walls. Flipping the statue over, she clutched the figure in both hands and raised it over her head, one of the base's sharp corners angled toward the wall. "I'll do it alone if I have to—"

"No!" Even with his preternatural speed, he almost didn't make it in time. He caught her wrists before she could bring the statue down on the wall. "The magic in the marks could hurt you when you try to destroy them."

"It's a little late to worry about getting hurt," she said, struggling to wrestle the statue out of his grasp.

Sighing, he easily pulled it away from her and held it over his head, out of her reach. "The way you unthinkingly hurl yourself at death is starting to get disturbing." He held up his free hand when she rounded on him, ready to start arguing again. "Promise me you won't do anything without me," he said, narrowing his eyes at her.

"Fine," she said, crossing her arms in annoyance.

"Then we do this together," he said, feeling like it was a massive mistake the second the words were out of his mouth. Never in a million years would he have imagined a day would come when he would be relying on a human for anything.

Regret was already setting in, but what else could

he do? He couldn't keep his distance and keep an eye on her at the same time, all while looking for his gegaji. Since he was probably the only one who couldn't see the marks because of his damned gegaji, he could technically ask another human to help, but it was bad enough that Jillian was involved. The death of the one and only human he'd involved when he'd first been brought to the human realm still haunted him. Petrin and Odath had made an example of the defenseless human that he'd never forget. If he had his way, he wouldn't include Jillian in this madness either, but she wasn't leaving him much of a choice.

And how long had it been since anyone other than Darenai had insisted on fighting by his side? He reminded himself that she was a human. That she was stubborn. That she loved to argue with him, when no one in several hundred years had dared it. But they all sounded like admirable traits, just because it was her. He'd been trying to crush his growing need for her, but it wasn't working.

"Let's start here," she said, and something about the determination in her gaze, and stubborn set to her jaw, made him think of what Darenai had said to him on their last mission.

"Someday humans might surprise you," Darenai had said. *"There's good in them too."*

There was a warmth on the inside of his left wrist that he couldn't ignore anymore, and he stifled the urge to start cursing. Instead, he held the statue out to her. "Anything look funny on this?"

She took it out of his hands, turning it over to examine it from different angles. "No."

He took it from her and tossed it over his shoulder. It landed somewhere behind him with a satisfying crash, and he felt a smile pulling at his lips at her instinctual surprise. Raising a hand between them, he let her see his nails lengthening into deadly black claws, wanting to drive home exactly what she was getting herself into. "Next?"

"What are you?" Jillian asked again, unable to keep the thought to herself. "And don't try to tell me I wouldn't understand. I think we're beyond that right now."

"I'm a shima," he said, as if that should mean anything to her. "Now point me in a direction. Odath and Petrin might be busy doing something for Enalel right now, but we probably don't have a lot of time, and we have to be strategic about when and how often we do this. If we get caught, you're dead."

A sickening lurch of fear settled in her gut, and she had to remind herself to breathe. She walked to one of the shelves and pointed at a mark carved into the wood. "Here."

Ashriel followed her and placed his hand exactly where she was pointing. She saw him wince, but he didn't move otherwise. "As my realm is the opposite of yours, shimana are the opposites of humans," he said, surprising her. She noticed he was careful to only nick the edges of the mark in a few places with his claws, blending the damage in with the curves of the design. "Here you have technology. Electricity. No magic." There was a change to the air around him, a heavy, tingling kind of sensation, and she knew he was using magic to affect the mark somehow. "Where I'm from, we rely on magic. Some can change their shape.

Some control the elements. Some can even walk in your dreams and grant wishes. There are many kinds of magic, used by the different aspects of shimana."

"Aspects?" she said, trying to wrap her head around what he was saying. It sounded too unreal. She wouldn't believe a word of it, if she hadn't spent days being mind controlled and hadn't just watched his hand basically morph into a weapon.

"What you would think of as races," he said, sounding bored. She moved to the next mark when he turned to her and gave her an expectant look. He touched it briefly before shaking his head and gesturing for her to show him another. "You have some shima blood yourself."

That got her attention, and she stopped dead in her tracks to stare at him. "What?"

He laughed softly, the sound weaving its way inside her like another one of his spells. The brush of his lips on her skin was fresh in her mind, her neck tingling with warmth where he had kissed her, and she found herself blushing again. She wanted to ask him if the way he made her feel was a shima thing too, but she was afraid of his answer.

"It must have been far back in your family line, but there's just enough shima blood in you to make you a little harder to control," he said, looking at her with a mysterious expression. "It's enough for you to sense certain things too, like the hallways and rooms in the house moving, or the bad energy from the marks."

Taking a deep breath, she asked the question nagging at her. "Is that why I feel strange when I touch you?"

He hesitated, looking at her in an analyzing kind

of way with his mesmerizing purple eyes, and she instantly felt embarrassed. Maybe it really was just her, and he didn't feel a thing. She was ready for him to mock her, or blow her off and call her a weirdo or something, but he surprised her again.

"Partly," he said, and then quickly moved on before she could ask anything else. "I have to leave some of the marks alone," he said, disgust clear in his tone as he gestured for her to continue pointing them out. "I should have been more careful in your room and covered what I was doing there, but I was too angry to think about it. If we destroy too many, or we're too obvious, they'll catch on. They'll start to notice a change in the magic anyway, but hopefully, they won't be able to pinpoint where it's coming from immediately."

What he was saying made sense, but she didn't like leaving any of them. They continued that way for a while, working in silence until Ashriel said they had to stop. They'd destroyed about half the marks in the room by that point.

She looked around at their progress, feeling a little better already. Ashriel had done such a good job of hiding his tampering, all the marks seemed undamaged. The air felt just a tiny bit lighter as she went over to sit on the edge of the desk. "Should we go to another room?"

He shook his head. "We shouldn't press our luck," he said, eyeing the closed library door in a way that made her think he sensed someone nearby. "And we shouldn't seem like we're getting too close."

She laughed at that, but the sound was a little strained. "We've never really gotten along, so that shouldn't be too hard," she said, trying to gauge his reaction. What had it meant to him when he'd held her, kissed her neck? She was sure that wasn't part of the healing he'd done. Did he only want to protect her out of pity for a weak human? Or out of a sense of obligation because he felt responsible somehow? "Besides, you don't like humans."

"Not even a little," he agreed, leisurely strolling over to stand in front of her. His expression was unreadable again, and she wondered what he was thinking as he studied her. Her heart felt like it would beat right out of her chest, so filled with a mix of fear and excitement she wasn't sure if she wanted to run from this otherworldly man or throw herself into his arms again. She could sense the tension in him too, wound tight, even though he seemed so calm on the surface.

"You especially don't like me," she said, knowing what she was doing was insane. She tilted her head, hoping she looked more composed than she felt, and he immediately picked up on the silent invitation she was trying to convey.

"Can't stand you," he said, closing the small distance between them. It was too natural, the way he leaned in, hands landing on her knees and sweeping up along her thighs to coax her legs apart so he could stand between them. He crowded her space, and she was more than fine with it, leaning back on her hands a little to look up at him. Even though she could sense him trying to hold himself in check, her breath caught at the burning intensity in his gaze. There was no mistaking the longing in his eyes as one of his hands moved up, curving over her hip before following the line of her spine to her midback for support.

He stopped just short of kissing her, resting his

forehead against hers and closing his eyes, and it took everything she had not to pull him down with her onto the desk and let him have his way with her. The hand still resting on her thigh tensed as if he knew what she was thinking. He took a deep breath, and she knew she wasn't the only one struggling for control. She could feel the urgency in him, matching her own, and she closed her eyes too, trying center herself.

"Well," she said. "Now that we've established our mutual hatred..."

He laughed softly, and for a long moment, neither of them moved. He held on to her like he couldn't stand the thought of ever letting go again. Although the tension had left his body, his hands gentle as he held her close, she could feel how hard he was working to restrain himself. He seemed to need the comfort of her touch just as desperately as she needed his, but they both knew Odath and Petrin were still around. Who knew when they would show up out of nowhere again?

It was clear just how badly he wanted her, and with her new knowledge of him and their situation, for the first time, she felt an unspoken understanding pass between them.

If only...

It took him a moment to gather himself, but he finally lifted his head. "Come with me," he said, taking hold of her wrists and pulling her to her feet as he moved away. Keeping one of her hands clasped securely in his, he practically dragged her from the room. She almost had to jog to keep up as he led her down several hallways and up the stairs to the second floor.

Understanding what she was feeling for the first time, she recognized the magical shift in the air when the rooms and halls started changing somewhere ahead of them, and she heard him curse under his breath as he abruptly turned to lead her in another direction. When they finally reached her bedroom, he threw the door open and preceded her inside.

"They had you sleeping in a different room while you were under their control," he said, glaring around the room like he expected Odath or Petrin to jump out of the shadows at any second. "Are there any new marks here?"

She looked around carefully, paying attention to what she sensed too. "No, it's fine."

He turned and narrowed his eyes at her. "That is the worst possible phrase you could use right now."

"Really, I mean it," she said quickly, realizing her mistake. She squeezed his hand and that seemed to calm him down. "There aren't any new marks."

"Good. Listen to me carefully," he said, tugging her hand to pull her closer. "They're suspicious of my connection to you already," he said, speaking softly, and there was some weight to his words that she didn't understand. "Even more than your shima blood, it would tempt them if they knew for sure." His jaw clenched, and she could tell he was holding something back. Not wanting to push their new truce, she filed it away for later. "Don't do anything to draw their attention to you. I can't protect you as I am now."

Swallowing against the pit of fear in her gut, she nodded. "Believe me, I don't want them anywhere near me."

"Rest now," he said, and she recognized the sensation of his mind brushing against hers. It wasn't intrusive, and she got the sense he was just checking again to make sure she was all right. "I'll come get you tomorrow morning."

"What should I do?" she said, not really sure how she was supposed to act, moving forward. "Just keep being the housekeeper?"

"For now," he said, absently brushing his thumb over her knuckles. "Whether it's Rae, or any other human they may lure in, you can't act like anything's off in front of them."

Her brows snapped together in a frown. "But you—"

"Had nothing more to lose at the time," he said, probably sensing an argument coming. "I'm useful to them for the moment. They don't see me as a threat, and they get a sick thrill out of watching me struggle against them." He stared at her hard, trying to drive his point home. "You can't do that, Jillian. It's true that they initially wanted to use the power of your shima blood, but even as an extra means of keeping me under control, you don't have the same value to them as I do. So you can't interfere, remember?"

A vision of Petrin's cold gaze freezing her in place flashed through her mind and had the hair on the back of her neck standing up. They'd both been warned.

"Fine," she said, still frowning. "But I don't like it."

"Welcome to my world," he said, bitterness plain in his tone. He let go of her hand and headed for the door. "Lock this behind me, for whatever good it will do."

She watched him go, and she did as he asked as soon as he closed the door behind himself. She rubbed her arms against a sudden chill. Her eyes fell on her suitcases, still partially packed. Bits of memory started coming back to her when she looked at them.

She wasn't going to just sit back and let Ashriel do

everything, as much as he might want her to. "Sorry, Ashriel," she said, determined. Walking to one of the slashed-up marks on her wall, she ran her fingers over the splintered wood and broken plaster.

She would do whatever it took to help him and get them all out of this situation.

CHAPTER TWELVE

PETRIN STARED AT THE MESSENGER standing in front of her, more than a little unnerved. She was too silent, her dark-gold eyes sharp and watchful beneath the hood of her black cloak. Petrin's eyes flicked down to the slave collar she wore. The thick leather strap, embedded with different kinds of spell crystals, looked well-worn, the skin visible just under the edges scarred from the woman fighting her controller.

Of course, the bastard hadn't bothered to show up himself, and he wouldn't even send his messenger directly to Enalel. Too risky, she supposed, considering his position. There could be no potential ties between them if Enalel failed. Petrin didn't know who he was, only that he was a very powerful ancient, and a respected member of the Junak. Known only as 'the slavemaster' to Enalel and everyone else involved, very few had met him in person, and he was never referred to by his actual name. He couldn't afford to risk showing his hand just yet, and so he'd sent an underling. That he'd sent her all the way to the human realm to deliver his message in person did not bode well.

"Enalel has overstepped," the woman said. "Taking the warrior from Kretore was not part of the plan."

Petrin shrugged, unconcerned. "She was forced to improvise when he came searching for Darenai," she said, bored with the conversation already. She was much more interested in the puppet in front of her. "Tell me, how long have you been wearing that?"

"I feel I should remind you it's partly Enalel's failed attempt to use a slave collar on that warrior that has led me here," the woman said, and Petrin wondered if she had orders never to reveal the slavemaster's secret. He was the only one to ever perfect the use of the collars, so it would make sense that he kept it to himself to increase their value. "It would be unwise to waste time trying yourself."

Petrin narrowed her eyes, fascinated. The woman was controlled, but certainly not tamed. There was a fire in her eyes. It was clear she wanted to kill Petrin, and probably the slavemaster too, but she was helpless to do so. The collar she wore was too powerful.

"You're like a doll, fully aware that you're locked in your own body," she said, laughing at the hopelessness of the other woman's situation. She walked a circle around the woman, scanning her with her senses. Stopping beside her, she rested a hand on the woman's shoulder. "A bloodthirsty, rage-filled doll."

The woman slowly turned her head, the hood hiding half of her face, but what Petrin could see was expressionless. "Release me," the woman said, her tone flat. There was no anger or threat in her words.

"When I'm satisfied that I know how it works," Petrin said, ignoring the woman. "If I could get a slave collar to work on Ashriel, things would go much smoother."

She came around to stand in front of the woman and pushed her hood back, exposing long dark-red hair, streaked with deep gold.

No sooner had she reached for the collar than she was flung across the room. She tried to counter the overwhelming air magic, but she slammed into the wall so fast and hard, she bounced off of it and crumpled to the floor. Magic poured from the woman, a tightly controlled stream of air that easily held Petrin pinned to the floor like an insect. The woman hadn't moved an inch and continued to stare at her as she gasped to catch her breath. Before she could recover, she was lifted and smashed back against the wall hard enough that the plaster cracked. It took every ounce of magic Petrin had to erect a shield strong enough to keep the woman from killing her on the spot.

"My master has given me permission to defend myself in order to complete my task. Touch me again, and I will rip your arm off and beat you to death with it," the woman said, a hint of who she would be without the collar breaking through for just a second. And there was such a chilling cold in her tone that Petrin truly felt afraid. The promise of death in her eyes was no joke or empty threat. She was far more powerful than even Enalel, and Petrin wondered who Enalel had gotten her involved with, if this woman's master was more powerful than her.

Petrin tried to say something, but she couldn't get any words out as she struggled to draw air into her lungs.

"It was difficult to get our hands on an ancient," the woman said without inflection, continuing the conversation as if nothing had happened. No matter how

Petrin struggled, it didn't strain the woman at all. "Retrieve Darenai's soul so we can finish the ritual. Finding another ancient would be inconvenient and might draw attention."

"Ashriel will help," Petrin said, struggling for breath.

"Have you found Sijo Otharo?" the woman said, approaching Petrin. She didn't draw any kind of a weapon to threaten Petrin. It was unnecessary. Instead, she increased the pressure of the air pinning Petrin to the wall. She heard the wood framework of the house groan under the strain, and she felt several ribs crack.

"Ugh!" Petrin groaned in pain, clenching her jaw and sucking a breath in between her teeth to keep from screaming. "Not yet."

"You are running out of time," the woman said, dropping Petrin face first in a heap on the floor. Petrin was wiping blood from her mouth, dizzy from lack of oxygen, as the woman towered over her. "If you continue to fail, you will see me again."

Jillian made her way down the stairs to the first floor the next morning, Ashriel walking slightly ahead of her, so nervous she thought she'd be sick. She'd been up most of the night studying the complicated symbols on her walls so she'd recognize them. She didn't know what each one did specifically, but she knew if she saw them, she could rule them out as the ones controlling Ashriel, since he'd said they were aimed at humans. She wondered how much she could rely on her shima blood to help her find what she was looking for.

She was so lost in rumination, she nearly walked into his outstretched arm. She froze at his signal, following his line of sight to an empty hallway off the entryway. Seconds later, a frightening woman in a black cloak emerged from the darkness of the hall and strode into the foyer. She moved briskly, beautiful dark-red hair flowing below her shoulders, but paused as she reached the front door. She turned toward them, dusky-gold eyes pinning Jillian in place. No magic necessary.

She was hauntingly beautiful, even when her elegant brows drew together in a frown. She looked like she wanted to say something, her lips parting as if to speak, but no sound came out. She coughed, seeming to choke a little, and a drop of blood trickled from beneath the collar she wore. After a tense moment, she turned her back on them and continued out the door.

"Who was that?" Jillian said as they continued to the bottom of the stairs. She was still new to sensing different kinds of magic, but even she could feel the difference in that woman. She was extremely powerful, whoever she was.

"Bad news," Ashriel said grimly. "Enalel, the woman Odath and Petrin serve, serves a master herself. Someone I've never met, many times more powerful than Enalel could ever hope to be. That's one of his slaves. If he sent her, we might already be fucked."

"How astute, Ashriel," Petrin said, coming from the same direction the woman had. Jillian was shocked to see the smear of blood at the corner of her mouth, and the busted lip that was already sealing itself closed. She didn't have to ask to know it was the scary woman's handiwork, and she decided she might like the stranger after all. "But it's time to direct all that cleverness of yours to something useful. Time to hunt."

Ashriel stiffened at Petrin's words, and Jillian's stomach sank. Was it the ruler's son from his gegaji? Or the other man he'd agreed to hunt in order to save her? She wanted to beg Petrin not to make Ashriel do this, but Ashriel's mind brushed at hers, and she could feel his silent warning.

If she tried to interfere...

Clenching her hands into fists, she glared at Petrin. She'd never hated anyone the way she hated that woman. Petrin seemed to love that, and a smile twisted her lips. Jillian was careful not to react, and let Petrin think she was going to be an obedient human and do nothing.

"Ready to go?" a cheerful voice said behind her, an unexpected hand landing on her shoulder. Her first instinct was to defend herself, but Ashriel swiftly grabbed her wrist to stop her, and she froze.

She didn't know whether to feel relieved or terrified that it was Rae as her friend walked past her toward the door, not noticing the tension in Jillian. Trying to compose herself, she glanced worriedly at Petrin, and the other woman simply raised an eyebrow, offering no context to Rae's question.

How was she supposed to keep up appearances if she didn't know what was going on? On edge, she tried to make her voice sound normal. "Sure, where to?"

Rae grasped the doorknob, giving her a funny look, and Jillian noticed the homemade pie she was holding in the other hand. "To the barbecue!" she said, laughing. "We talked about this yesterday, remember?"

They sure the heck didn't talk about it, and everyone knew that except Rae. Was this how she'd been when she'd been mind controlled? "Yeah," she said, trying to hide her concern behind a smile. "Let's go."

The second the words left her mouth, Jillian expected instant pain, but instead she felt a brief pressure in her head that swept down over her body. Starting to be able to tell the difference between how different people's magic felt since she'd been on the receiving end of so much of it, she knew Petrin was doing something to her.

Rae frowned a little at the stiffness in Jillian's voice. "Are you all right?"

"Yeah!" Jillian said, quickly improvising. "I just didn't sleep well. I think my brain's not awake yet." She laughed, hoping it sounded natural. "Please tell me we can stop for coffee, or I don't think I can make it."

Rae laughed at that. "Sure thing!"

"You're okay with us going?" Jillian said, sliding an uneasy glance Petrin's way.

Petrin shrugged, unconcerned, and Jillian realized what she'd felt moments before had probably been Petrin allowing her to leave again. "I'll see you both later tonight for dinner," Petrin said, sounding innocent as she waved them off. But Jillian knew better. There was an underlying threat to her words that only Ashriel and herself understood. She seemed to want to keep up the pretense of freedom for Rae.

Rae nodded, giving Petrin a bright smile. "Absolutely!" she said, and Jillian followed her to the door, trying to keep sight of Petrin out of the corner of her eye without being too obvious. Rae gave an over-the-shoulder wave as she opened the door and sailed out. "See ya later!"

Jillian risked one more glance at Ashriel, meeting his unreadable gaze, and for a moment just before she closed the door behind herself, she sensed his pain.

Keeping up conversation as they drove to get coffee on the way to the barbecue nearly killed Jillian. Rae was full of stories about how her family had gotten together with Hasenda and Noren all the time when she was growing up, but it was hard for Jillian to keep up with the conversation. She was no actress, and trying to be cheerful when all she could think of was the anguish Ashriel must be going through as he was forced to hunt an innocent man was nearly impossible.

Rae pulled up to the coffee shop and parked in one of the spaces beside the little brick building. “You sure you’re up to this today?” she asked, looking at Jillian skeptically.

“I swear, I’m fine,” Jillian said, and ignored her inner knee-jerk cringe at the word *fine*. The least she could do was keep Rae away from the house for a while and give Ashriel one less thing to worry about. “The coffee will fix me.”

After they got their coffee, she focused on doing her part the rest of the way to the barbecue. She couldn’t let Rae worry and risk Rae wanting to go back to the house too soon. She wasn’t sure, but she hoped some time away from the house would weaken the effect of the marks on Rae as well.

The drive to the barbecue was short luckily, winding through quiet, tree-lined streets. Remembering the older couple who’d tried to help her when she’d passed out in town, she tried to relax. The neighborhood Hasenda and Noren lived in was beautiful, with older houses spaced apart with big yards. At least a dozen different cars were parked outside Noren and Hasenda's when they pulled up. It was nowhere near as big as Odath and Petrin's. It had the same Victorian-style architecture, but it felt a million times warmer.

They parked along the street, Jillian grabbed the pie Rae had stashed on the floor of the backseat for safety, and they headed up the sidewalk toward the house, chatting along the way.

"Noren has the best barbecue sauce recipe in the universe, I swear!" Rae said, and then she laughed. "I keep threatening to steal it from him, but I can't figure out what ingredients he uses."

"It's been so long since I've been to a barbecue," Jillian said, finally getting a little excited. She could already smell it, making her mouth water, and could see a little trail of smoke coming from somewhere behind the house. At least she could look forward to some good food and company to take her mind off things for a while. "Whatever his secret is, the way you talk about it, it sounds amazing."

It was as Jillian opened the gate at the end of the walkway leading up to the house and stepped through that she felt a sensation sweep over her, like she was passing through the water's surface in a warm lake. She froze in her tracks, heart pounding in her chest. It was an unfamiliar sensation, but she recognized it as some kind of magic at least. The fact that Rae seemed completely unfazed as she passed Jillian and then stopped a few steps ahead, turning to raise an eyebrow in question, wasn't comforting at all, considering the situation.

Senses on high alert, she tried to plaster an easy

smile on. "Sorry, I almost tripped and thought I was about to drop the pie."

"Hasenda would kill me," Rae said, eyes widening jokingly. "She always demands that particular dessert."

Jillian barely heard Rae joking with her as they walked the rest of the way to the door. She no longer felt that gentle pressure. Whatever the spell had been, it seemed to stay at the end of the walkway. It didn't feel anything like the magic Odath and Petrin had used on her before, or the gentler magic Ashriel had used, and it made her wonder if there might be another shima working with them that she didn't know about.

She wracked her brain to find the meaning behind Odath and Petrin putting spells so far away from the house. It seemed too far away from the house to draw more humans to them. So what was the purpose?

Rae walked into the house, comfortable enough not to knock, and Jillian followed her. Glancing around warily as she closed the door behind them, she was on the lookout for anything that felt off. She'd learned the hard way not to ignore her instincts.

"Rae!" Hasenda said, poking her head out of the kitchen to see who it was. Setting aside whatever she was doing, she rushed down the hall to greet them. She hugged Rae, then turned to Jillian. "Are you a hugger or a shaker?" She opened her arms for a hug anyway, and Jillian couldn't help being drawn in by the older woman's bubbly personality.

"Definitely a hugger," she said, feeling a little more at ease. Jillian went in for a hug, and as soon as Hasenda's arms wrapped around her, she realized she'd made a terrible mistake. Energy moved between them immediately, and something brushed gently at her mind. She realized with a start that it somehow *felt* like Hasenda's consciousness reaching for hers.

Oh no, oh no, oh no. She tried to keep calm, but adrenaline was rushing through her. A memory came back to her from when she'd blacked out on the sidewalk, of Hasenda's hands on her, and what she hadn't recognized at the time as the sensation of magic being used on her. *Keep it together.*

It took everything she had not to shove Hasenda away from her. The older woman had helped her before, and Rae loved her, but after everything Jillian had seen and been through, it was impossible for her to immediately trust that Hasenda wasn't just pretending the way Odath and Petrin had attempted to in the beginning. Jillian's pulse was pounding in her ears as she pulled away, and she noticed the sharp look in Hasenda's eyes, even though she kept the smile on her face.

She knew Hasenda was suspicious, and Jillian prayed she could fool her into thinking it was just the shima blood Ashriel had told her about. Clearly, there were humans out there with shima ancestors besides her, who had no idea. If she could play it off like she was still one of those, she could make it through this.

Jillian returned her smile, glancing at Rae. "Rae told me about Noren's barbecue sauce. Something about it being the most amazing thing in the universe?"

She felt the pressure on her mind get a little stronger, Hasenda watching her closely for any reaction, and she didn't resist. She filled her mind with thoughts of barbecue ribs, cheeseburgers, brats, and any other barbecue food she could come up with, but she never felt the sharp, cutting sensation of her mind being fully invaded.

"Oh, he knows it is," Hasenda said, with an affectionate laugh. The pressure on her mind disappeared, and Jillian was careful not to show the relief she felt. Hasenda hadn't forced her way in, never going beyond the surface, but Jillian knew she was being tested. For what, she didn't know. "It's his favorite recipe. He loves that there's one thing he knows how to make that Rae doesn't yet."

She knew it was too late to turn back without raising suspicion, so the tried to clear her mind and prepare herself for whatever happened next. Feeling like she was walking into the lion's den, she followed Hasenda and Rae through the cozy house, and out into the backyard where Noren was cooking at the grill. The yard was full of groups of people chatting and sipping drinks, or snacking on various foods from the folding tables that had been set out, rustic-looking tablecloths on them fluttering in the warm breeze.

It should have been a nice reprieve from the dark, closed-in house she'd been trapped in for almost a month, but she wasn't sure she could trust it. Were they all shimana? She thought it was safe to assume that if Hasenda was, then Noren would be too, at the very least.

She went with Rae and Hasenda to greet Noren at the grill, and his eyes met hers in a friendly way. Hasenda laid her hand on his shoulder, and Jillian could have sworn that some silent conversation passed between them. He didn't try to touch her mind, but she knew from the analyzing way he looked at her that she had been right about him.

"I'm glad you could both make it," he said, giving them a full grin that had the smile lines crinkling at the corners of his brown eyes.

"Yeah, I was worried you wouldn't be able to, with how hard you've been working on the café," Hasenda said, looping an arm around Noren's free arm as they chatted.

At the mention of the café, Rae's eyes got a little glassy, and Jillian could tell with a quick glance that the other two immediately noticed too. "I'm fine," she said, and something seemed off about her smile for a split second before she recovered. "The café's on hold for a while. The kitchen needs more updating than I'd originally realized."

Jillian hadn't seen the place herself yet, but she knew from experience that Rae was probably lying without even being aware of it. When Hasenda released Noren's arm and moved closer to Rae, putting a hand on her shoulder, Jillian almost slapped the woman's hand away. It was only barely that she managed to stop herself, and she felt Noren's gaze on her again, so she tried to act oblivious when she looked at him.

Doing her best impression of a serene smile, she made small talk. "I can't wait to see the café when it's ready." She mentally ran through a list of café foods, just in case, and worked on keeping her breathing even. From what little she knew, shimana could sense a lot that humans couldn't, and she didn't want to risk giving herself away.

"It's been in the works for a while," he said, and when he looked at Rae, Jillian could see the genuine pride in his gaze. Was he only faking? He should be in movies if he was. “She’s really good at what she does. I know it’ll be a success.”

When Jillian glanced over at the other two women, Rae looked a little better. Her eyes were clearer, and whatever fog had come over her seemed to have passed. Was that Hasenda’s doing?

She didn’t sense anything malicious about Hasenda and Noren. The very faint energy she could feel from them when she got close felt nothing like Odath’s and Petrin’s. She knew she couldn’t let her guard down, however. Ashriel hadn’t mentioned them, so she didn’t think he knew they were in town, and of the three shi-mana she’d met before them, only one didn’t want to drain her, kill her, or both. Not good odds.

Jillian wanted to get back to the house to warn Ashriel in case they were somehow involved with Odath and Petrin. She wasn’t sure either she or Rae were any more out of harm’s way than usual.

CHAPTER THIRTEEN

JILLIAN HAD NO IDEA WHAT she was going to do about what had happened to Rae when they got back to Odath and Petrin's that night. What *could* she do? Assuming Ashriel had returned to the house after hunting with Petrin, could he help Rae again?

Rae had seemed fine after that one incident, but Jillian was still worried, so she hung out and chatted with Rae in the kitchen, watching from her usual seat at the island while Rae was prepping for dinner and chopping vegetables. Before she searched for Ashriel, she wanted to try and make sure her friend would be all right on her own.

They were both stuffed, so the food Rae was cooking was more for the others in the household. Making food for Ashriel was fine, but knowing part of what Rae prepared would go to the monsters responsible for Rae's condition made Jillian's blood boil. Watching her friend be used like this, totally unaware, made her want to take up Ashriel's pastime of breaking things.

"Didn't I tell you it would be amazing?" Rae said, gushing about the food at the barbecue while she started some water boiling in a pot, and some olive oil, garlic, and spices heating in a pan.

Jillian had to agree. Whatever else Noren was, he was just as good a cook as Rae. "It was," she said easily, unable to deny it. "Mmm, especially the ribs. Noren is a genius."

"Just you watch," Rae said, pointing the business end of a spatula at her. "I *will* get that recipe from him." She turned back to the stove, stirring the contents of the pan a little before reaching for the towering plate of diced vegetables.

Jillian felt the spells in the house activate, hallways and rooms changing shape and shifting position, and had to stifle a sigh. So much for finding her bedroom quickly after dinner. "You never know," Jillian said, continuing as if nothing out of the ordinary was happening just outside the kitchen.

"I think he wants me to experiment and figure it out myself," Rae said, pretending to be annoyed, but it was clear she loved the challenge.

"I volunteer to try every practice version you come up with," Jillian said, completely serious. She briefly wondered if it were possible to get tired of barbecue and then just as quickly dismissed the idea as pure insanity. Not possible.

She opened her mouth to joke about needing to join Rae on her jogs to work off all the food, but she was distracted when the house shifted again. The second time felt different than the last. The shifts usually never happened so close together. It was possible the pattern had changed, but she wondered if the spells had been purposely reactivated that time.

The kitchen suddenly felt too quiet with only the

sound of sizzling food to fill the room, and she frowned at Rae's back. "Rae?" When there was no answer, Jillian got up from her seat and walked toward Rae. "Hey," she said, putting a hand on Rae's shoulder.

Rae didn't turn or react in any way. She just kept cooking. Her movements were so single-minded, Jillian knew right away that the spells were affecting Rae again. Leaning forward a little to peek around Rae's shoulder, she noticed the vacant expression on her face, and her gut clenched with fear. The house shifted a third time, and Jillian wondered why she wasn't affected too.

Was it because she wasn't being controlled at the moment herself? Her shima ancestry? Or was it her strange connection to Ashriel?

Remembering from firsthand experience that the spells Rae was under made it pointless to try and pry the cooking utensils from Rae's hands, and that the spells would make Rae complete her task without setting anything on fire, Jillian cautiously approached the open kitchen door. She didn't know what to expect, assuming she'd always been under mind control when this had happened in the past. Some of the spell marks she'd seen might have even been for the sole purpose of putting nearby humans into a trance while the rooms moved.

When she peeked out into the hallway, for the first time she caught the house shifting right in front of her. The dizzying effect of the hallway lengthening off to the right messed with her depth perception and made her instantly nauseous. Jumping as a door right across the hall from her slammed itself shut and morphed into the wall, she clutched the kitchen doorframe for support.

Farther down to the right, a door seemed to phase into existence right out of the wallpaper. Looking the other way down the hall, she flinched and automatically jumped back into the kitchen as the far wall down the hallway to the left came rushing right at her face. The kitchen door slammed closed. The floor beneath her feet rumbled ominously.

Backing away from the door, she turned and rushed protectively to Rae's side. She didn't know what she could do, but she tried to place herself between Rae and danger as best she could while Rae was in her helpless trance state. Rae was still cooking, however, so far away mentally that she had no idea what was happening around her. Dishes rattled in their cupboards, and Jillian found herself swaying slightly next to Rae as the room moved within the house.

When the shaking stopped and the groaning of the house grew quiet around her, Jillian took a few hesitant steps toward the kitchen door. Unsure if it was really over, she didn't know if it was safe to leave the room or not.

"Jillian?" Rae said behind her, and Jillian's blood went cold. When she turned to face Rae, it was as if the past couple minutes had never happened. The pasta was boiling, and Rae had added fresh tomatoes to the sautéing vegetables to make a sauce. "What's up? You look like you just saw a spider or something," she teased.

"I'm—" She refused to say it, out of pure spite. "Everything's okay," she said instead, even though changing the wording didn't make it any less of a lie.

Rae gave her a funny look. "If you're sure," she said, returning her attention to the food.

"I need to grab something from my room," Jillian said, studying Rae while she worked. Rae really did seem completely normal.

"'Kay," Rae said with a little wave over her shoulder, laughing a little. "I'm so full I could die. Don't know if you're even hungry after the barbecue, but it'll be ready in a few if you want any. See if you can find Ashriel too. I can never find him when I'm looking for him, for some reason."

"Will do," Jillian said absently, turning toward the door. She *really* didn't want to open it, but since hiding in the pantry wasn't a serious option...

When she opened the door, everything was eerily calm and far too ordinary. She looked to the left. There was a dead end with a console table that held a small lamp on top. To the right, the hall stretched on before disappearing at a corner and continuing another direction. Several doors lined the way that hadn't been there before, and she took a wary step out into the hall to investigate. She knew the hall she was in probably wouldn't move again for a while, but to be safe, she closed the kitchen door, hoping Rae would stay put for the time being.

As she walked down the hall, she noticed tiny changes here and there, but nothing big. She'd almost begun to relax again when a different section of the house started to shift. Stopping where she was, she waited, trying to determine if she needed to jump into a room to escape it.

There was a thud on the floor above her, and the sound of a scuffle. Something crashed to the ground, and she thought she heard a woman's voice. Frowning at the ceiling, she felt the house shifting above her, and she started moving in the direction of the first-floor stairway, led by some inner instinct.

She found her way to the stairs, and stopped, looking up into the shadows at the top. The cold, electric spark of magic tinged the air around her, flowing heavier from the second floor. The same instincts that had brought her there fought with each other. She wanted to run, but she wanted to press on just as strongly. She felt like it was important that she did, but she didn't know why.

A shrill, blood-curdling scream tore through the air from the second floor, and she was moving before she could debate any further, racing up the stairs faster than she knew she could. Trusting her instincts, she flew down one hallway after another, hurtling toward the last place she wanted to be. She could feel the house shifting ahead of her, and the notion of throwing herself back into that chaos terrified her, but she didn't let it slow her down. She couldn't.

Up ahead she could feel fear. Desperation. Someone was lost in the dark halls of the second floor while they moved.

And she wasn't alone.

Too late, she sensed the other presence ahead, and came face to face with Odath as she rounded a corner. She nearly slammed into him, but managed to stumble to a halt at the last second. His beautiful, twisted face broke into a smile, as if he'd been waiting for her. There was no mistaking the hunger in his light-brown eyes as he watched her. With a wall at her back, only a few short feet separated them. It was far too close for comfort, but there was nothing she could do about it.

Odath held a young blond girl, probably college age, close to his body, one arm around her back, the other hand cradling the back of her head. In any other situation this would have looked like he was embracing his lover, but there was nothing romantic about it. A bloody, ragged bite marked the space where her neck and shoulder met, and she was so still Jillian couldn't tell if she was alive or dead.

"Please, don't do this," Jillian said. She'd gotten this far, but she hadn't considered what she'd do when she got there. She may have some shima blood and a connection to Ashriel, but she was powerless up against Odath.

Odath chuckled. "Only if you take her place," he said, and the girl shifted weakly in his hold, hazel eyes fluttering open for a moment. He whispered something to her in another language, and her gaze grew glassy, eyes rolling back in her head as her body went limp.

"Stop!" Jillian begged, holding out a hand in front of her as if to ward him off. "Please. You don't need to kill her to drain her, right?"

Odath tilted his head at her, resting the side of his head against the girl's forehead in a sick caricature of what could have been an affectionate gesture. "Ashriel's shared a lot with you, hasn't he?"

Realizing her mistake, she said her next words carefully. Ashriel had warned her that the extent of their connection could make her more tempting to Odath and Petrin. So did she use it to save the girl, or did she hide it? Would it make Ashriel's situation worse if she confirmed it?

"That's right," she said, staring him down with disgust. She might be able help the girl without exposing Ashriel if she was careful. "I have that tiny bit of shima blood in my veins, don't I?"

Odath raised his head, and his knowing smirk nearly made her vomit. "Go on," he goaded her. "Say it."

"You can drain me again," she said, swallowing her fear and the instant revulsion she felt at the thought of Odath touching her. It was patchy, but she remembered the sting on her skin like electricity and a chilling cold sweeping through her when he'd used magic to drain her, but he'd never bitten her. She got the feeling she wouldn't be so lucky this time. "Just let her go."

Odath carelessly dropped the girl, never breaking eye contact with Jillian as she fell like a ragdoll in a heap at his feet. "Ah, the sweet illusion of choice." And then he was on her, grasping her shoulders to shove her back against the wall. A shocking electric cold shot through her where they touched, and she gritted her teeth against it. His face came so close to hers she could smell the blood on his breath. "I love the sensation of that moment of hope, followed by the crushing disappointment you feel right after. Give me more," he said, squeezing her shoulders painfully, but she refused to make a sound.

She swallowed her words and stayed still, even though she wanted to fight with everything she had. Odath sneered at her, and she felt some small satisfaction in his displeasure. "I won't put you in a trance for this," he said, his grin coming back. Fear and disgust wound so tightly together in her gut, it would serve him right if she threw up on him. "You'll give me what I need, whether you want to or not."

He dipped his head toward her neck, dark-red hair brushing her skin, and she clenched her eyes shut, trying to brace herself. She concentrated on Ashriel in that moment, calling to him in her head. *"Ashriel..."*

A savage growl filled her ears, and a bone-breaking impact hit Odath from the side, forcing him to release her. Without hesitation, she scrambled to the girl's side, away from Odath and his attacker. She expected to see a wild beast, but to her shock, the sight that met her eyes as she hunched protectively over the girl was Ashriel, his nails morphed into deadly black claws, and the backs of his hands covered in dark-gray, metallic, armorlike scales.

The two shimana tore at each other viciously, punching, clawing, and kicking. Blood splattered the wall, but she couldn't tell whose it was. Odath got a good punch in that made Ashriel stumble, putting some space between them, and Jillian felt the change to the air again.

"No!" She managed to throw herself between them just as Odath cast his spell. There was a blinding flash of light and an immediate impact that took her breath away and sent her flying back into Ashriel. The last things she was aware of were his arms wrapping around her protectively and his ragged voice shouting her name.

Chapter Fourteen

Jillian lurched up out of her bed, barely stifling the scream lodged in her throat as she fought with the covers tangled around her. Her heart beat frantically, and she was shocked she was still alive. It took her several seconds to realize she wasn't in the hallway anymore.

Looking around to assure herself she was alone in the bedroom, she took several deep breaths to try and calm herself. A glance at the clock told her it was early morning, and she winced at the pain in her body that she hadn't felt at first in her panic. She couldn't remember how she had gotten to her bedroom. There was nothing beyond her memory of being hit by Odath's spell.

How many times had something similar happened when she had been mind controlled? It was disconcerting to think about, but at least she was still alive.

She gasped when she tried to get up, every muscle in her body feeling like it had been torn. She hurt everywhere. Even breathing was painful. Her head spun, she was exhausted, and she couldn't seem to make her eyes focus. Looking down at herself, she realized she was still wearing the same clothes she had been the day before, plastered to her body from sweat.

Ashriel. He must have been the one who brought her to her room. Odath and Petrin certainly wouldn't have chosen this particular room, with its slashed-up spell marks. What had he been forced to do in order to spare her from the others again? By now she knew she would have ended up like Mindy if Ashriel hadn't kept intervening.

Ignoring the relentless aching in her body, she took a quick shower and started getting ready. She needed to know if Ashriel and the girl Odath had bitten were okay. Pausing at her door, she tried to center herself, feeling like she was going into battle. Pushing her fear aside, she left the room and headed to the first floor.

The house was uncomfortably quiet, and she remembered with a jolt of worry that she'd left Rae alone in the kitchen the night before. She muddled her way to the kitchen, and was relieved when she found Rae there with her back to the door, humming a cheerful tune to herself as she fixed breakfast. Quietly turning away before she was noticed, she set off to look for Ashriel. There was no sign of Odath or Petrin, but she wasn't sure if that was a good thing or not.

Did that mean they were out hunting someone? Ashriel's friend, or the man he was supposed to kill for them? She couldn't relax until she found Ashriel.

Remembering his words, she focused her senses on what she wanted to find. Making her way down a different hallway, she paused in front of the slightly ajar library door and pushed it open to peek into the dimly lit room. The curtains were cracked open a little, but it didn't leave nearly enough light for her to really see anything.

"Hello?" she called. It was the muffled groan that gave his presence away, and she thanked her freaky, shima blood for leading her there. "Ashriel?" She strained to see in dark room. Flicking the light switch, she grumbled under her breath when nothing happened. Of course, no lights would come on. That would make life too easy.

Frustrated and in pain, she didn't care about the rules at that moment. Closing the door behind her, she made her way carefully to the window and flung the curtains open to let the light pour into the room. She heard his low growl of annoyance from somewhere behind her, and turned to find him slumped back on the couch.

"First question," Ashriel snapped tiredly. "Why the hell did you have to do that?" Wincing, he leaned forward to lower his head into the cradle of his hands, attempting to keep the light out of his eyes.

"Are you okay?" she asked, immune to his rudeness.

"Dandy," he said, words muffled by his hands. "Don't I look dandy to you?"

She raised her eyebrows. "Not really. You're not acting like yourself."

Keeping one hand over his eyes, he let out a deep sigh as he dropped the other hand to blindly grasp at the items on end table beside the couch. Managing to grab a small figure from its surface, he returned to his slumped position with a pained grimace and tossed the figure carelessly over his head. There was a small breaking noise somewhere behind him.

"Better?"

She couldn't help smiling at his ridiculousness. "Almost. But now you have to scowl at me and say something rude."

He frowned convincingly, eyes still shielded behind his hand, but didn't say anything.

"Seriously, what did they do to you?" she said, noticing how pale and weak he looked. She saw the circles under his dark-violet eyes as he dropped his hand and raised his head to glare at her. Hoping to give him some relief from the light shining on him, she moved closer until her shadow fell across him.

"Nothing a little time regenerating wouldn't fix, if they'd let me get the full benefit of it for once," he said.

"Regenerating?" she repeated, wondering if this was somehow different than the healing he'd done on her before when under mind control.

"Second question," Ashriel continued as if she hadn't spoken. "How much of a fucking death wish do you have? I can take a hit from Odath. You can't." He pointed to himself. "Nearly immortal, magical being that can regenerate." He pointed to her. "Squishy, breakable, foolish human who can't regenerate." The last bit was an angry growl. "What were you thinking?"

She'd be offended if she didn't know being unpleasant was his extremely skewed way of showing concern. She shrugged in the face of his frustration. "You would've done the same for me," she said, knowing it was true, and his eyes widened a fraction.

"You are un-fucking-believable, you know that?" he said with a weary laugh, but he sounded suspiciously impressed, despite his words.

"What did you have to sacrifice to save me this time?" she demanded, asking the question that had been plaguing her since she'd woken up. "And what happened to the girl?"

He stared at her silently for a long moment, his mind brushing at hers, and she accepted the connection without even having to think about it. "Come here," he said quietly.

"Why?"

"Less questions, more getting your stubborn ass over here."

She took a small step toward him, not sure what to make of the look in his eyes.

"Closer."

She moved another tiny step forward, unsure if it was really safe to be within arm's reach at the moment. She wanted the comfort of his touch, but knew it could be disastrous if she gave in.

"Dammit," he muttered, rising to his feet faster than he looked capable of in his current state. She gasped as his arms locked around her, pulling her down with him onto the couch. She ended up sitting across his lap, hands braced against his chest, her face only inches from his.

"What are you doing?" she said, nervously shooting a glance at the door. "Petrin and—"

"They were called away before you woke up," he said.

"Let me up," she said, trying to sound like she didn't want to be there, but she knew her blush gave her away. A strange warmth was spreading through her body, and her left wrist tingled strongly. She pushed against his chest, but his arms didn't budge. "I need some answers, and I'm not going to let you distract me."

"Shhh..." he mumbled, leaning his head back against the couch and closing his eyes. He sighed as if even talking was too much effort. "I'm healing you, because your pain is harder to bear than my own."

That left her momentarily speechless. His energy flowed through her easily, and she felt oddly comforted. She sensed that he took his time with the healing, focusing on all the little details of the injuries in her body, and her discomfort started to ease.

Reluctantly, she let herself relax for a moment, trying to decipher the different things she was sensing and feeling. With his head tipped back, she could see that faint scar on his neck again, and without thinking she lifted a hand to trace it with her fingers.

"Enalel's failed attempt at using a slave collar on me," he mumbled, seeming to sense her unspoken question. He didn't bother to raise his head. "It takes a lot to scar a shima, but that'll do it."

Frowning at the thin line of scar tissue, she remembered the intimidating shima woman who had visited Petrin, and the collar she wore. What had she intended to say before the collar had stopped her? And what kind of power would it have taken to stop her from speaking? And did slave collars not weaken their victims like Ashriel's gegaji did?

"Wait," she said, a thought occurring to her. "Won't this weaken you more, using your magic like this?" She tried to push herself off his lap, but he barely seemed to notice. In fact, he almost looked like he was falling asleep, which frustrated her even more. "Stop. I'm all right."

Ashriel laughed softly, barely opening his eyes to look at her. "You know if you'd said, 'I'm fine,' I would have had to expend more energy breaking something." His hands tensed on her slightly, his hold getting a little tighter for a moment. "Odath could have pulverized you easily, naori," he said, using an unfamiliar term in his language. "Never do that again."

She stilled at his quiet words. "What does that mean? Naori?" she asked, brows furrowing. She sighed after a long moment, rolling her eyes when he didn't answer. He wasn't ready to go there yet, so he had no intention of explaining.

He tried to ignore what having her in his arms did to him. He had been oblivious to almost everything else all morning, but his damned body chose that moment to wake up. After he healed her, he would try to convince her to go back to her bedroom and rest—for her health as well as for his sanity.

He had no idea how he was going to persuade her, however. He had sensed her determination when she had entered the room. She was on a mission, which meant aside from a natural disaster or a freak house fire, nothing could distract her from her goal.

She pushed against him again, trying to get up, but he continued to ignore her. "Fine!" she snapped. "If you're not going to let me up, I'll just ask you right here."

He peered at her from beneath lowered lashes. "Ask me what?"

"What happened to that girl last night?" she demanded. "Is she okay? Where is she? Did you take her to the hospital? What did they do to you? Are you all right? And then what happened to me after Odath's magic hit me? And how did I get to my room? And why do I feel like I was hit by a bus? And—"

"Shhh," he grumbled, frowning. Sighing deeply, he closed his eyes again. "The girl was unconscious, but she's fine now. I got her to the hospital." He didn't want to bother with elaborate details. "Don't know why Odath attacked her, beyond the obvious draining and blood. Don't care why. Maybe another of his games. She's at home now, sleeping it off. You apparently want to die young and joyously threw yourself into the path of your own death in order to shield me, and mysteriously, *shockingly*, ended up unconscious yourself." The sarcasm was evident. "I carried you to your room. You slept it off. Now, here we are."

She raised her eyebrows at him, and he could practically feel her praying for patience. "I see."

"Yep," he said, and left it at that. Talking was too much trouble.

His lack of a response seemed to make her forget she was annoyed at him. "You're not okay, are you?"

Sensing her genuine concern, Ashriel opened his eyes again. She watched him silently, her brows furrowed in worry. He must have finally gone completely mad. He'd long since stopped caring that she was a human, and his restraint wasn't what it should be at the moment.

And he really couldn't make himself care. It took too much energy.

Her body felt so warm and soft against his, and he'd been dying to hold her for so long. He had never been all that good at denying himself anything. But he had tried this time. He really had.

"Blood is a powerful source of magical energy,"

he said reluctantly, trying to choose his words so he didn't worry her further. "My gegaji doesn't require that I allow them to take mine, so normally attempting to take it by force would result in a battle to the death. Enalel doesn't want me dead for the moment, so they hold back. I offered them blood more tempting than yours, and they backed off for the moment."

"They use your blood for magic?" She sounded as disgusted as he felt.

"And to drink."

She looked very much like she wanted to gag. "Like, as in—" she hesitated, and he sensed her fear again "—vampires or something?"

"Petrin is a sathra aspect," he said, glad the conversation seemed to have distracted her enough to keep her sitting still in his arms. "A vampire, in your language. Odath is not. He just likes the rush it gives him."

"I'm sorry—"

"Don't," he said, not wanting her to feel guilty. "It was my choice."

She went quiet, but he could sense her concern for him. After a moment, she shifted to raise a hand to his forehead. "You're freezing!" she said, shocked.

"And you're so warm," he groaned. Unable to help himself, he raised a hand to clasp hers, bringing her hand away from his forehead.

Closing his eyes in pleasure, he rubbed his cheek against her palm, reveling in her touch and the warmth that radiated from her. "Just once," he murmured against her skin. "Just once, let me have this much of you."

It was a damned lie, and he knew it. Once would never be enough, but he'd have to make do.

She froze, and he waited for her to pull away. He wouldn't stop her. If she had any sense at all, she'd smack him and leap out of his arms any second. He planted a kiss in the middle of her palm, fully expecting her to be the sensible one out of the two of them.

She didn't move at all for a long moment, and then she shocked the hell out of him by snuggling closer, leaning into him until her head rested on his shoulder. Relief soared through him because this meant she wasn't going to move yet. He began trailing soft kisses from her hand down to her wrist.

"Mmm," she sighed. "Better?"

He shifted his hold on her, his hand leaving hers to cradle the nape of her neck.

"Almost," he said softly, and then he did the stupidest fucking thing he could've possibly done.

He gently lowered his lips to hers, and time seemed to stop.

"Finally." The thought whispered through his mind, and he could have sworn in his exhausted, half-delusional state that he heard her voice mingled with his own in his head.

The kiss was fleeting at first. Teasing. Learning the shape and feel of her lips with his own. Only short, caressing kisses, but euphoria was singing through his veins already. His whole body was suddenly awake and on fire, burning for more of her touch.

Melting into his embrace, she parted her lips, tracing his with the tip of her tongue, urging him closer. One arm slid around his neck for balance, leaving the other hand free to tangle in his hair, and he was almost certain he'd die right there.

With a shuddering groan, he deepened the kiss, his tongue sliding against hers. Devouring her and demanding more, he drew on her tongue, wrenching another moan out of her. She seemed as greedy as he was as he shifted them to lay on the couch, her body blanketing his.

Just a kiss, that's all. No more. He kept telling himself this over and over, even as his hands smoothed down her back, inching toward her hips. Even in his lust-fogged state, he knew he had to stop before things got out of hand.

Shifting her weight to the side a little and leaning away from him, she broke the kiss, and he instantly felt the loss. Sliding one of her hands down to the top buttons of his shirt, she started tugging them free, and he was suddenly content to wait for her to finish before he kissed her again.

Good intentions wavering dangerously, he took advantage of her position. His hands found their way to her bottom, squeezing gently. Leaning forward just long enough to slide one of his palms down along her leg, he hooked his fingers behind her knee and pulled her thigh across him.

Immediately understanding what he wanted, she sat up to straddle him. Her gaze scorched him when his chest was finally exposed to her wandering fingers. Such a small thing, but so rewarding as her palm smoothed over his cool skin. Her fingertips traced along his chest before moving down his abdomen, and he couldn't help a groan of appreciation.

His eyes drifted closed in pleasure as she leaned

forward to kiss him again, her warmth searing him. And it wasn't nearly enough. He wanted more. Much more. Of her skin exposed to his greedy eyes. Of her hands teasing him. Of her mouth making good on the promises her hums of pleasure made as she touched him. Of her body heat seeping into him, and her energy mixing with his own.

He could feel it even now. A faint connecting of their energy. Each of them drawing just a very little from the other.

He knew he was reaching the point of no return, but he couldn't seem to rein himself in. Especially not when she sat up, hands leaving him to wrench her shirt over her head, exposing more of her perfect, creamy skin to his hungry gaze.

He swept his hands up from her hips, smoothing his palms up along her sides, watching the way her nipples hardened in response beneath the flimsy black satin of her bra. Sitting up to wrap his arms around her, he took her mouth again. Holding her close, he reveled in all that warmth and softness pressed against him. He felt her shiver as she wound her arms around him, holding him close.

For almost a month he had given himself reason after reason to keep his distance. And he knew she had been doing the same. Such a short amount of time that managed to feel like forever. Wanting. So close. So aware of each other. Denying themselves. Constantly circling each other like some kind of dance that had them edging closer but then always retreating again.

It was all of that denial, and the dozens of reasons why this shouldn't happen, that brought an edge of desperation to their embrace. Their bodies entwined so tightly that they could each feel the thundering of the other's heart. Feel the way the other trembled with need.

He swallowed her delighted gasp as he easily lifted her, smoothly switching their positions. Lying beneath him, she clung to him until his mouth left hers to kiss a burning path to her chest. He felt her tremble as he pushed her bra out of the way, arching up, inviting more, and he cupped the weight of one of her breasts, kneading gently before bringing the nipple to his lips.

"Ashriel," she moaned, tangling her fingers in his hair, holding him to her as he circled her nipple with his tongue before gently sucking her into his mouth. Greedy for more, he shifted his weight, his other hand snaking down between them to undo her jeans.

Impatient, he tugged the material out of his way, pushing her jeans down what little he could in their current position. She lowered a hand to help him shove at them, lifting her hips, and he gently bit her nipple as she managed to wiggle her way out of them. He sensed her pleasure spike, excitement burning through her as sharp and primal as his own, and she couldn't contain a low gasp. Another rasp of his tongue, and he was switching his attention to her other nipple, his hand slipping inside her panties.

"Oh, mmm," she moaned, trailing off as his fingers parted her, finding the sensitive bud of her desire. He was on fire, needing to make her as crazy for him as he was for her, and completely drunk on the knowledge that she wanted him.

He teased her relentlessly, applying just enough pressure to bring her to the brink, until she was begging him. "Please," she panted, writhing against him. "Oh, please more."

He left her breast, drawing a faint protest from her that made him smile. Nuzzling kisses along the column of her throat, he murmured endearments in his own language, his fingers sliding teasingly lower.

He was nearly mindless with his own need as he found her opening, gently pressing inside. His palm pressed against her most sensitive spot as his fingers moved, and he felt her release crash through her in shuddering waves. Taking her mouth again, he swallowed her cries as she clung to him, felt her muscles clenching hard around his fingers. He felt a possessive kind of satisfaction, knowing he had brought her to that point.

After he felt her shudders subside, he smoothed his hand upward again to rest on her trembling stomach. He gentled their kiss, leaning away to study her expression as she relaxed back into the couch.

A lazy smile curved her lips. Her eyes fluttered open to look up at him, and she was so viscerally beautiful to him it was like a punch to the gut. His body raged at him to take her, right then and there, and claim her as his own. But for the first time ever he thought about holding himself back. Could he afford to lose control for a while?

In his moment of indecision, one of her hands slid its way lower, cupping him through his jeans. "Stop overthinking," she said, running the flat of her palm up along his length.

He sucked in a deep breath, a shiver wracking his frame as her fingers moved to undo his jeans. She fumbled with the button, laughing softly at the groan she pulled from him, and he caught her wrist, desperately trying to regain his senses. The tiny voice of sanity that had been mysteriously absent up until that point had reared its ugly, sadistic head. “Wait,” he almost begged, his restraint hanging on by a pathetic little thread of pretty damned much nothing. Common sense was beginning to intrude as he gazed down at her. His fragile little human.

Mine...

He fully embraced that possessive claim as it burned itself into his soul. Letting go of her wrist, he lifted his hand to touch the softness of her cheek.

She looked up at him questioningly, waiting, a smile kicking up the corners of her mouth. “You want to stop now?” she asked teasingly, her gaze hot.

“I think I'd rather die,” he admitted, almost physically pained. At that moment, he wanted her more than he wanted his next breath.

What had he been thinking? His scent and energy were all over her after their make out session, and then some, screaming like a neon sign to any shima who cared to look at her that she belonged to him, and guilt swamped him. He knew better. This was another reason he'd been trying to hold back.

If Enalel found out...

He couldn't do this. He had to stop right that second, even if it killed him. Before it was too late. Cursing, urgency still pounding through his body, he knew it already was.

He gently pulled away from her, shifting again so that they were laying beside each other, her head resting in the groove of his shoulder. If he hadn't been in agony, he might have been impressed with himself as he gently tugged at her clothes to cover her again. He wasn't going to endanger her further just to satisfy his own needs.

He curved his arms around her protectively, pulling her tighter against his chest. Forcing himself to take several very deep, very long breaths, he began counting backward from about a trillion. In as many languages as he could remember at that moment. At the same time. Anything, *anything* to distract himself from the terrible need that still tore at him.

"We have to stop now," he said softly, impressed by how even he could make his voice sound. He knew she could feel his chest moving beneath her with his ragged breaths, his heart still pounding beneath the palm she left splayed over his chest, but he stood his ground.

"Ashriel," she began to protest, lifting her face to frown at him, but he silenced her with another deep kiss. He trembled as she nibbled on his lips, trying to entice him into changing his mind. When he finally pulled away again, he didn't hide his burning need from her, but he had to remind her of their situation.

"They could be back anytime," he said, regret thickening his voice as he watched her eyes widen, reality crashing back down. He sensed the fear rise up in her, cooling her desire, and he hated it even though he knew it was necessary. "Just rest with me and heal. I can feel how tired you are." He closed his eyes, trying to act like he could actually sleep. Every little shifting movement she made against him only made him burn more. "Don't worry. I will be able to sense them when they come back," he reassured her.

He felt her hesitate, then settle against him, grumbling something about stubborn men even as she tried to stifle a yawn. He focused on trying to calm himself, thinking of anything and everything he could besides the warm curves pressed against him. After several endlessly agonizing minutes, he felt her drift off in his arms.

Sighing deeply, he cradled her close and finished the healing he had started earlier. Afraid to rest for fear of Odath or Petrin returning and finding them together like that, he kept watch over her while she slept.

The capital city, Neluk, in the shima realm
In the meeting chamber of the Junak

Petrin stood beside Odath in the middle of the large meeting chamber of the Junak, posing as the Telesil and Ushara, first and second protectors for the city of Orilia. Well prepared for this moment, they had even done cleansing rituals and kept their energies masked to hide the dark magic that clung to them. Luckily, it hadn't been necessary for the illusion to extend to her forming the usual telepathic bond between a Telesil and an Ushara. They had mutually agreed that neither of them wanted to be inside the other's head.

As first and second protectors of Orilia and its ruler, Jiru Otharo, they were a few steps behind him, according to traditional etiquette. He reported to the ruler of Neluk and leader of the Junak, Jiru Ferven Talura, without even one mistake. It had taken a lot of planning to get to this point undetected, but it looked as if everything would go smoothly.

"Orilia was infiltrated by the rogue shimana?" Jiru Talura said, pale-blue eyes studying the three of them closely. There were murmurs around the room, other Jiruna and their protectors from different cities whispering among themselves. "Humiv, you said they called themselves?"

He was an imposing man, with short black hair and a tall, muscular build. Although he wore a decorative white cloak, embroidered in black with the patterns of Neluk and the Junak, he wore his silver armor and sword beneath, a sobering reminder that the realm was gradually erupting into war, city by city. As a powerful ancient in his own right, he would be one of the hardest to fool.

"Yes," Jiru Otharo said, and Petrin was extremely impressed by how natural he sounded. No more tremors or glassy eyes. As much as she hoped to never meet the man Enalel served, she had to admit, he had really done the impossible with the slave collars. Keeping her smirk to herself, she remained silent and listened. "My Ushara and Telesil gave their lives trying to protect the city, and my son, Banen, was taken. If it hadn't been for them, Orilia would have fallen to Humiv." Jiru Talura's gaze briefly swept over Petrin and Odath when Jiru Otharo gestured to them. "My new protectors have found the trail of one of the attackers."

"I will offer what resources I can to help you capture them," Jiru Talura said, glancing to one of his own protectors and giving her a silent signal. His Ushara left quickly, following whatever order she had been given through their bond.

"Thank you," Jiru Otharo said, and Petrin was careful to keep her expression blank, knowing what his next words would be. "That's one of the reasons I requested this meeting. We've uncovered who this man is, and who he serves."

The whispering in the room got loud again, until Jiru Talura raised a hand for silence. "Name them."

"He serves Kretore—"

Jiru Otharo's words were quickly drowned out by shouting from different parts of the room, many of the Junak members abandoning etiquette. While some Jiruna loudly voiced their support of Kretore, others turned suspicious eyes on Kretore's Jiruna and their protectors. The Jiruna in question protested the loudest, demanding proof that one of theirs was responsible.

"Do not make such accusations lightly," Jiru Talura said warningly, narrowing his eyes. If Jiru Otharo hadn't been under deep mind control, he might have flinched, but not even a bead of sweat gave him away. "You've collected proof?" At Jiru Otharo's nod, he continued, "Can you name him?"

"He's one of their warriors," Jiru Otharo said. "Ashriel Teleshani."

CHAPTER FIFTEEN

JILLIAN GOT UP EARLY THE next morning, raced through her morning routine, and got ready in record time. Ashriel had told her Odath and Petrin would be gone again for a couple hours on Enalel's orders, doing whatever horrible thing it was they liked to do, and she wasn't about to waste this chance to look for his gegaji.

Considering she'd spent the better part of the day before recovering with Ashriel, they'd been lucky that Odath and Petrin hadn't returned until late that night. He'd sensed them when they'd gotten back, and he had sent her off to her room with obvious reluctance.

There was a knock at her bedroom door just as she was pulling her hair back into a ponytail. Seeing the way her cheeks instantly flushed in the mirror, she took a deep breath to steady herself.

Time and place, she sternly reminded herself. Not that it helped all that much when all she'd been able to dream about the night before had been his hands on her and his lips scorching a path across her skin.

But what exactly were they? What had it meant to Ashriel? Was it any different for a shima than it was for a human?

Pushing the question of their relationship to the back of her mind for later, assuming they could free themselves and would have an opportunity to explore it, she turned and headed for the door. Whatever weird thing was happening between them, she instantly knew it was him on the other side as she approached it. She could actually *feel* his presence on some level she didn't understand yet. So when she opened the door, it was no surprise at all when she was immediately enveloped in his strong arms. He captured her mouth in a fiery kiss, walking her backward into her room a few steps. She clung to him, a now-familiar warmth and energy moving through her, and hoped he'd always greet her this way.

It was over too quickly for her liking, but she understood when he pulled away to look down at her. "Morning."

"You're killing me," she said, laughing breathlessly.

"We're probably going to die," he said, keeping her in his arms. "Just making sure I regret nothing when I go."

"Stop being so morbid," she said, knowing he was only half joking.

Releasing her, he sighed, brushing a stray strand of hair behind her ear. "We need to be quick," he said, but she stopped him before he could turn for the door.

"Wait," she said. She went around him to close the bedroom door. "Something happened while I was out with Rae yesterday." That immediately got his attention. "Are there other shimana in town, helping Petrin and Odath?"

"It's not impossible, but I haven't seen anyone," he said, frowning. "Why?"

He listened carefully as she told him what she'd sensed around Noren and Hasenda. "I can't be sure, but they didn't seem like bad people. I can tell they honestly care about Rae, and I'm pretty confident they were the only shimana at the barbecue. The other guests all just felt like normal townspeople."

"Rae obviously doesn't know they're shimana," he said, and she was relieved and a little surprised that he wasn't suspicious of Rae. Despite what he said about humans, he seemed to consider her a friend. "Otherwise, she might know enough about our culture to have at least some idea she's being controlled here."

"Shouldn't we—"

"No," he said flatly.

"You don't even know what I was going to say."

"Shouldn't we tell Rae what's going on?" he said, raising an eyebrow.

"Yeah."

"Answer's still no," he said, frowning at her. "She has even less value than you to Odath and Petrin. She's nothing more than an expendable energy source to them. If she finds out what's going on, they might just kill her to avoid the hassle. Whatever's happening with Enalel and her master right now, they don't seem to have the attention to spare."

Jillian felt a chill at that. The last thing she wanted was to put Rae in harm's way.

"Fine," she said, remembering her own experiences with Odath and Petrin. "Do you think we can go to Hasenda and Noren for help?" she asked, hopeful. This opened up more options for them—*if* she could get out of the house with the excuse to do some shopping again. "We can't go to human police, but your people can do something, right?"

"Assuming Hasenda and Noren really aren't involved in what's happening, maybe," he said, but he held a hand up before she could get too excited. "That's a big *if*, Jillian. My people are getting ready for war right now. There's no telling who these shimana really are. So until I meet them myself, I'm not going to feel very optimistic."

"Okay, so they're the last resort if we don't find your gegaji soon," she said, not willing to completely give up on the idea. He hadn't seen the way Noren and Hasenda had been around Rae. She wanted to give them the benefit of the doubt, and so far, her instincts had been good.

"Fine. Last resort," he said, agreeing surprisingly easily. He crossed his arms, giving her a hard look, like he fully expected her to disagree with what he was about to say. And he was right. "If something happens to me, go to them. Even if that means leaving me behind."

Raising her chin, she returned his frown as she grabbed his hand. "It's not going to come to that." Tugging to get him to follow her, she turned and headed for the door again. "Let's start with the third floor."

He squeezed her hand briefly. "There's probably a reason they don't want you up there."

"Exactly," she said, more determined than ever. He seemed to have this thing about sacrificing himself for her, and not that she didn't appreciate that he cared, but she'd rather him not die trying to save her. Every time he faced off with Odath and Petrin to help her, it made his situation worse.

They made their way to the third-floor staircase, still hand in hand. For whatever time they had, she'd decided she wouldn't hide her feelings from him. Whatever that meant between a human and a shima, she didn't particularly care. They'd worry about that once they got out of there.

When she got to the top of the staircase and had her first good look at the third-floor hallway, she stopped. Looking first one way and then the other, she blinked a few times, trying to figure out what she was seeing and feeling. It was overwhelming to look at, let alone process with her weak senses.

"Jillian?" Ashriel said beside her, and she sensed him tensing. He must have felt the change in her because he let go of her hand and moved forward to look around himself, as if he could defend her from something he couldn't even see.

"I, uh..." She cleared her throat, unsure what to make of it. "I'm going to assume you don't see any of this?"

"Nothing but walls," he said impatiently. "What is it? What do you see?"

Jillian moved toward the wall opposite the stairs, reaching out a hand, but she stopped short of touching it. Just having her hand close gave her the chills. "Large, interconnecting spirals with all kinds of symbols inside them. Some I recognize. Some I don't," she said, looking at him quickly. Maybe this was it. Maybe they'd actually found something related to his gegaji. "And different sizes and shapes of gray and black crystals."

His brows snapped together in a scowl, and he pulled her away from the wall. "Crystals?"

"Yeah," she said, pointing toward the wall and following one of the spiraling lines with her finger. "Like some big, creepy mosaic. I don't like how it feels."

He went to where she pointed, hands morphing into claws, and did the same thing he always did. He carefully sliced into the wall, making the tiniest cut possible. After a moment, she heard him cursing under his breath. He followed the lines of the spellwork with his own eyes.

"Much more powerful versions of the spells downstairs, but directed at shimana," he said after a moment.

"Nothing to do with the gegaji?" she said, disappointed.

"Not directly," he said, shaking his head. His hands returned to normal as he turned to face her. "But they do add to the magic affecting me, so they might come in handy later. If things start looking bad, I might be able to free up more of my sealed powers by slashing these up. It wouldn't be much, but anything would help."

"You're not going to destroy any now?"

"No," he said. "These are more powerful. Petrin and Odath would notice too quickly. These marks will have to be the last resort before the Hasenda and Noren last resort." He scowled at her as if he were reading her mind, which wasn't outside the realm of possibility. "And before you try, don't. These would absolutely hurt you if you tampered with them yourself."

"I promise not to touch them," she said, then lowered her voice to mutter in a pretend whisper. "Unless things go sideways."

"Jillian—"

"No," she said, stopping him before he could tell her she was being an idiot again. "I get it. I'm out of my league. But if we get to the point where that's my only option, and we're going to die anyway, I *will* do it."

He sighed, looking very much as though he still wanted to pretend he could forbid her from doing it. "Now who's being morbid?" he said instead, giving her a tight smile as he took her hand again. "Let's search the other floors. We probably don't have much time left, and I don't want to be caught up here with you."

They went back down to the second floor, which they hadn't searched as thoroughly yet, hoping to find something new. The occasional shifting of hallways and rooms made it harder to keep track of where they'd looked, but she was grateful at least not to be in the middle of it when things started moving.

"Do the spell marks we've seen make the house move too, or is that something else?" she asked. She opened a door to a room they'd already checked, only to find that it had switched to a different room. Annoyed, she stepped into the unfamiliar bedroom, seeing only the usual patterns on the walls, matching the ones in her own room. "And why would anyone purposely make a house impossible to navigate?"

"Could be a defense mechanism in case any uninvited shimana find this place. Could be a way to confuse the humans they lure in," he said, throwing out a couple possibilities. Working carefully to destroy a couple of the marks she pointed out, he shrugged. "And probably to keep me from figuring out a way to do what I'm doing now. The only reason I've even gotten this far is because you're pointing the marks out to me."

She studied his back as he worked, wondering if she could ask more. Now that she was in the loop on everything, and they'd gotten a lot closer, he was more talkative. He'd stopped with most of his rude, cryptic comments and wasn't actively trying to irritate her anymore. They were kind of a thing, so she could ask, right?

Seeming to sense her eyes on him, he turned, lips kicking up at the corners like he was amused. "Why do I get the feeling you're not staring at me for any of the kinky reasons I'm hoping for?"

She felt her cheeks warming. Well, *now* she was, despite knowing he was only teasing.

"The people they want you to hunt..." She didn't know how to be delicate about asking, knowing he was close to one of them.

"I don't know what Enalel's plan is," he said, gesturing for her to precede him out the door into the hallway. "But the men I'm hunting have become involved in the war in my realm, whether they meant to or not."

"Your friend?"

"Darenai," he said, and although she could only see his face in profile as they walked toward the next room, she could tell he was a little sad. "I don't know how he got involved with Enalel. Only that, after a whole century of looking, he had suddenly found some clues about the murder of his brother."

The way he talked about a century passing felt too surreal, but she pushed her shock away and focused on the rest of what he'd said. "That's...convenient."

"I thought so too," he said, a hint of anger slipping into his tone. The next door they opened somehow led to the study that was supposed to be on the first floor, but she was beyond disbelief at that point, so she just stifled a sigh and started pointing while he talked and scored different marks with his claws. "When I didn't hear from him after a few weeks, I followed his trail, and was eventually led to Enalel myself. She captured me and held me for a month before you arrived, extracting information from my mind and trying to make a slave collar work on me. Fortunately, the closest she could get to controlling me fully is the gegaji. During that time, if I wasn't hunting for them, I was trying to free as many humans as I could from their clutches. And here we are. I was brought here specifically to keep me hidden until I can successfully hunt and kill the Sijo, and make Kretore look suspicious."

"That's horrible," she said, knowing firsthand the pain of having someone force their way into her mind. She couldn't imagine what it would be like to have some kind of device, like the slave collar, keeping her in that state she'd been in before. "How did Darenai escape from Enalel?"

There was a heavy silence, and for a moment, she worried she might have pried too much. "He didn't. She has his body, apparently, probably still in the shima realm," he finally said, that somber tone back in his voice. His back was to her as he worked, and she approached him silently, listening. "Whatever dark magic they used on him has separated his soul from his body. His spirit is wandering."

Wrapping her arms around him from behind, she rested her forehead on his back and closed her eyes. It was really hazy, but she recalled bits of his conversation with Petrin. "I'm sorry."

His hands settled over hers, and she felt him take a

deep breath. "Without it, he will wither away and die. With it, Enalel will use him in whatever scheme she's come up with, and he will die. Either way..."

The situation sounded so hopeless, she felt like any reassurance she tried to give would be hollow. So she just held on to him. She knew nothing about magic, but she understood the kind of evil it would take to do what he was describing.

"And the Sijo," he said, using another unfamiliar shima word. "I guess you would call him a prince? I thought she only wanted to steal the throne from him at first. But I think that's just her reward from her master for adding to the chaos in the shima realm. Raising the tension between the different cities and their rulers, making them doubt and suspect each other, I think that's what this is really about with the Sijo." She could sense the anger and frustration in him. "I serve a different city under a different ruler. If I were the one who killed him, and Enalel managed to make it look a certain way..."

"Your ruler would look guilty," she said, raising her head and loosening her grip on him as he turned to face her.

He glanced at her before looking over her shoulder, toward the doorway, as if he'd heard something she hadn't, and she automatically stiffened. "We're okay," he said after a moment, but he gently set her away from him. "They've returned, but they aren't searching for you right now. We need to go downstairs, like usual. It should be time for breakfast by now."

She resisted the urge to take his hand as they left the room and headed for the stairs to the first floor. She couldn't show her affection in front of Odath and

Petrin. They would only use it as a weapon. So instead, she kept a good amount of distance between them as they walked.

Petrin was waiting for them at the bottom of the stairs. "Still sticking close to your favorite human, I see," she said, giving them an unpleasant, self-satisfied smile. "I wonder what you'd offer me this time to spare her? You haven't got much left to give." She glanced at Jillian with a knowing look in her eyes, as though she could see right through them. Jillian had never considered herself a violent woman, but the more time she spent in that house, under Odath and Petrin's thumb, that was quickly starting to change. "Lucky for you, it's time to hunt instead this time."

Jillian felt her blood run cold at that, but she was careful to keep her expression blank. She knew she had to stay calm, or Petrin would sense it, but it was hard to push away the fear she felt for Ashriel.

"Let's get this over with," Ashriel said, heading for the door without a backward glance at Jillian.

Knowing better than to show a reaction to anything happening, Jillian gave Petrin a bland look as he wrenched the door open and started toward the driveway without her. She had to keep up the pretense of obedience so Odath and Petrin would keep ignoring her. She couldn't help Ashriel and Rae otherwise. "I'll start cleaning after breakfast."

Petrin smirked, looking awfully pleased with herself as she turned to follow Ashriel. Pausing on her way out the door, she leveled a piercingly cold glare at Jillian. "Don't do anything stupid while we're out."

It wasn't until the door was closed behind Petrin that Jillian let herself relax the death grip she had on her emotions. She wasn't prone to cursing much either, but in that moment, she was thinking some seriously unkind things about Petrin that didn't extend far beyond four-letter descriptives.

Would she do anything stupid? No. She wasn't a fool. She was determined to be so careful, they'd never see it coming, magic or not. She was banking on what Ashriel had told her. Even she could see that they were a little too comfortable with their positions, assuming they would always have the upper hand.

She couldn't wait to make them regret that.

Knowing Odath was most likely lurking somewhere in the house, probably waiting in some darkened corner like a creeper, she was mindful to act as if it were business as usual. Turning on her heel, she headed straight for the kitchen.

She needed to eat, but she also wanted to check in on Rae. Now that she knew her friend was mind controlled, she wasn't sure what to expect. She remembered, from her own experience, it would only get worse as the days passed.

When she reached the kitchen, Rae was humming to herself and cooking as usual. They chatted over breakfast, and Jillian was relieved that Rae seemed to be in a good place for the time being. She was careful not to say anything that would make Rae compulsively tell her she was fine.

"Where's Ashriel?" Rae asked, taking both their plates to the sink when they were done. "Normally, he doesn't miss a meal."

"He's helping Petrin with something in town, I think," she said, trying to stick as close to the truth as possible.

Rae laughed, obviously not expecting that answer. "Really? I assumed he hated everyone, especially her and Odath."

Jillian had to work to keep the smile on her face. "Oh, I'm pretty sure he still does. How long are you here today?" Rae spent a lot of time there, but she lived in a house she'd inherited somewhere across town.

Rae froze for a second at the sink, going completely still and silent, and then continued on as if everything was normal. "I'll be staying here tonight, I think. Petrin offered me a room so I wouldn't have to commute."

Even though she wanted to push the issue, she knew it would only hurt Rae if she did. Instead, she got to her feet, determination renewed. "Okay, I'd better get started. Thanks for breakfast!"

"Anytime!" Rae said cheerfully, giving Jillian one of her over-the-shoulder waves.

The rest of the day, she went from room to room, cleaning. Sometimes she took wrong turns on purpose, even though she knew the house had already shifted ahead of her, keeping up the appearance of ignorance.

It was getting rarer every day to find a room she hadn't searched already with Ashriel, but when she did find a room, she took careful note of every spell mark she could find. So far, there still wasn't anything new.

She'd even gone back to the mural on the wall across from the entryway, knowing it had to represent some place in the shima realm, but she didn't sense any kind of magic coming off it, and there were no spell marks on or around it. It was just there for some reason. She'd ask Ashriel about it later, but it wasn't a priority at the moment.

She made quick work of the actual cleaning part

of her process on the first floor because she couldn't care less about doing a thorough job for Odath and Petrin. Screw them. She hoped they would choke on a particularly unpleasant and large dust bunny, among other, much pointier things.

Then she headed to the second floor and did the same thing, combing over each room and taking note of any room she hadn't already searched with Ashriel. Still no new symbols, but at least she'd found more spells for him to destroy.

It was getting late when she heard movement on the floor above her, and she realized Ashriel must have gotten back from his hunt. Anxious to check in on him and make sure he was all right, she made her way to his room. She was extra careful, stopping at the bottom of the third-floor stairs and concentrating on what she felt in the house around her. She didn't want Odath or Petrin to see her going up there.

When everything felt normal, she hurried up the stairs as quietly as she could and crept down the hall. She probably didn't have too much time before one of them would show up out of nowhere. That seemed to be just another of their things on the ever-growing list of creepy and horrible things about them.

Reaching his room, she knocked lightly, hoping his superhuman hearing would pick up on it, or he'd sense her, or the planets would align and send him a magical telegraph to open his door before she was noticed. When there was no answer, she looked both ways down the hall before quietly turning the knob. She just prayed the door didn't squeak as she opened it.

Peeking into the room, she saw Ashriel standing

in front of the window across the room, his back to her. He didn't seem to have noticed her open the door, and that worried her. It seemed as though he was lost in thought, and through their weird connection, she could sense the chaos in his mind.

He was so preoccupied he didn't even notice when she stepped into the room, closing the door behind herself with a nearly inaudible click. "Ashriel..." Faltering when he startled at the sound of her voice, she saw the way his eyes widened in shock as he partially turned to face her, and then he froze.

The same kind of unnatural stillness came over him that she'd seen in Rae, but it only got worse. She heard the air leave his lungs in a low sigh, his eyes going glassy as she watched.

"Ashriel?" Worried, she rushed to his side. What magic was this? Another part of the gegaji, or something else she didn't know about?

She grabbed his hand, gasping at how cold it was, and quickly looked down. Stifling the scream that rose to her throat, she saw that it had turned gray, and was hardening like stone beneath her touch.

CHAPTER SIXTEEN

ASHRIEL FELT THE HORROR IN Jillian as she jerked her hand away, stumbling in her haste to put space between them. It was a natural reaction from a human, seeing something she couldn't understand, but it still stung. He felt the panic in her and heard the rush of air in and out of her lungs, the pounding of her heart echoing his own.

Unable to do anything for her, he roared in frustration inside his prison. Throwing his energy against the power of the gegaji controlling him, he tried to free himself even for a moment to reassure her, but it was too late.

The process had already begun, his skin fading to gray all the way past his wrists and up his forearms to disappear under the rolled sleeves of his shirt, until his clothes began to change as well. With her directly in front of him in his frozen state, he had a closeup view as she helplessly watched the spell's progress creeping down his legs, up along his neck, over his face and hair, and finally into his eyes. The magic of his aspect allowed him to keep his senses, but the gegaji kept him trapped in his body, unable to reach out and reassure her.

But it was she who moved, shocking him. "What is this?" she said, slowly approaching him and reaching for his hand again. For once, he appreciated her penchant for touching magical things she didn't understand. He felt her mind brush at his, and welcomed the connection, trying to relay to her that he was all right. "I can feel you in there, but what do I do about it?"

"Nothing," he thought, willing his words to reach her across their partial bond, new as it was. After a handful of weeks, he already felt as if he knew her well enough to be sure she was about to do something reckless to try and help him. *"You do nothing until I wake up in the morning."*

His hopes were in vain.

"There's something I missed," she said, glancing around his bedroom. "There has to be."

"Just wait," he thought, an edge of desperation in his frustration. *"Now is not the time to hurl yourself at death again!"*

"Is this because of that mural?" she wondered out loud, searching his face as if she could find the answer there. "I know you wouldn't like it, but..." She turned away, ready to head toward the door.

"Dammit, Jillian, just wait until morning!" his mind shouted, and she whipped around to look at him.

"What was that?" she said, eyes wide. He wasn't sure if he wanted to kiss her or shake her or both when her surprise turned into a mystified smile. "That was actually kind of cool." She moved closer to him again, lifting a hand to touch his cheek. "See you in the morning, then."

After hearing Ashriel's voice in her mind, Jillian had tried to keep a level head, but it still ended up being the longest night of her life. She just tossed and turned in her bed, unable to sleep and constantly fighting the need to go check on him and make sure he was still doing all right. Knowing it was too risky, she'd finally managed to catch a few hours of sleep.

Not sure what time he'd meant when he'd said *morning,* she got up early again and snuck up to his room. Rubbing her eyes in exhaustion as she closed and locked the door behind her, she walked over and slumped down on the edge of Ashriel's bed to wait. Looking out the window, she saw the sky was already starting to lighten as the sun came up.

It wasn't long before she heard a soft gasp, and her gaze immediately went to him, searching for any change. Any sign at all that he was waking up. As she watched, his skin began to fade to a more normal color. She slid off the edge of the bed and rose to her feet, approaching him warily as his clothes, hair, and skin visibly softened until they were normal again.

"Ashriel?" she said hesitantly as he blinked, taking several deep breaths. When he silently opened his arms to her, she threw herself at him, and he caught her easily, holding her close.

"Thank you for waiting for once," he said, laughing against her hair. "I was sure you would've challenged Petrin to a duel or set the house on fire or something to free me."

"Shut up," she said, pulling away to glare up at him. "Explain. And then tell me why you *didn't* explain that was going to happen before I could freak out about it."

"It's how my aspect normally regenerates when we're badly injured or when we need to defend ourselves," he said, as if that should make any sense. "What you saw last night isn't normally how it goes. The gegaji has twisted it. I usually do it by choice when I'm injured, but Enalel forces me into this state every night. She feeds off the power I should be replenishing, keeping me weak and my powers locked away. My gegaji connects me to her, so even across the distance of the barrier between the realms she can take the energy that's supposed to go to me."

"Your aspect..." She hesitated, floundering. A lifetime's worth of confidence that magic wasn't real and creatures like vampires didn't exist had crumbled to dust weeks ago, but she still felt weird saying the words out loud. Taking a steadying breath, she just threw her question out there. "Are you like Petrin? A..." She searched her memory for the shima word he'd used for vampire.

He shook his head. "Sathra?" he said, his expression unreadable as he loosened his hold to look down at her. "No, I'm not a sathra."

When he didn't seem like he was going to offer any more information, she forced herself to ask the next question. "What are you?" she said, somehow feeling like an even bigger idiot with this question, even though she'd asked him before.

"I'm a jahuni aspect," he said, as though that should mean something.

"You're not a sathra," she said flatly, giving him a

blank look. It didn't sit well with her that he was holding back again. "You're a jahuni."

He nodded, waiting for a reaction.

"Okay," she said, raising an eyebrow at him. "Is there a reason you don't want to come out and say it?"

"Making you terrified of me isn't what I'm going for anymore," he said, not helping matters at all.

"Your aspect is scarier than Petrin's?"

"Depends on my mood."

"So, yes then?"

He grinned. "Maybe." Tilting his head, he studied her, as if trying to anticipate her reaction. "In your language, the closest word I can find would be *dragon*."

She stared at him a long moment. "Of course," she finally said, deciding he was right about the terrifying part and proud of how nonhysterical she sounded. "Why couldn't I tell just by looking at you?"

He chuckled, his mouth curving into a genuine smile. "Not what you would expect?" Taking a step back from her, he extended his arms away from himself, inviting her to really look at him.

Mutely, she shook her head, her eyes traveling over him like she had never seen him before. He looked pretty much the same as before. Still mouthwateringly gorgeous. But she noticed more now. She let herself really pay attention to what she was feeling, not dismissing it this time. She could feel that same attraction. The pull that drew her to him. And energy. An intense, swirling energy that clung to him.

"But you look so human," she said.

"This is my natural form," he said, seeming to understand her confusion. "But I can transform, either partially, as you've seen with my hands, or fully." When she continued to stare at him, trying to imagine what he was describing, he smiled. "I could—" he hesitated again, and she could tell he was weighing his words "—show you, if you like. I don't sense Odath or Petrin nearby, so we have time."

Forcefully pushing aside her nervousness, she raised her chin, determined not to be a coward. "How?"

Lowering his arms, he gave her a measuring look. "You would have to open your mind to me again."

She stood her ground as he took a step toward her again. "That sounds too easy."

"I know you can feel it," he murmured, tilting his head. "The connection between us."

"You know I do," she said, and his expression warmed. He looked pleased by her words. "I have for a while."

"Good," he said, his voice taking on a low, seductive quality. Gently tempting her. "You can use that to touch my mind anytime you like."

"As in... telepathy?" she said, a little excited. "Like last night?"

He nodded. "Over time, if we want to, we will eventually be able to hear each other's thoughts whenever our minds are connected." He was close enough to touch, but he kept that little bit of space between them. He extended his hand to her, palm up, and waited. "But for now, all we can do is touch."

Her eyes darted down to his hand, feeling the energy surge around him, reaching out to her. Letting her instincts lead her, she met his gaze again and slipped her hand into his.

He lifted her hand gently, raising it to his lips to trail a brief kiss across her knuckles. "I'm going to reach out to you with my mind," he said, lowering her hand again to clasp it between both of his. "Just like last time. There's nothing to be afraid of."

She tilted her chin up at him. "I'm not afraid," she said, more used to the sensation than she had been before.

His lips curved up in a knowing smile, and she felt his energy move across the distance between them, surrounding her in a comforting warmth. "Relax," he coaxed her, enticing with his voice and the gentle pressure of his hands around hers. "Your body automatically wants to reach out to me." His eyes drifted closed. "Trust me. Let yourself reach for me."

Taking a deep breath, she followed his lead, letting her own eyes close. She concentrated on his warmth, his breath, and then the steady rhythm of his heartbeat when she began to feel it, the pace matching her own.

Another deep breath, and she let go of her resistance. She felt a faint sensation, not exactly thoughts, brushing at her mind. She envisioned herself opening to him, letting him in. Energy swirled around them. Between them. Their minds met, and she began to see vague flickers of light behind her eyelids. Then the outside world was gone. She was only aware of him and the connection they shared.

What she saw was hazy at first. Cliffs. A clear, blue sky. A form was beginning to take shape in her mind. Huge. Powerful. Terrifying.

She was vaguely aware of Ashriel's hand squeezing hers gently. She felt the question in his mind, and sensed that he was considering breaking away. Keeping her eyes closed for fear of losing the connection, she shook her head, hoping he would understand. She wanted to see more.

The vision became clearer, a great beast looming in her mind. Sleekly muscled, it was strangely majestic for a creature of its size as it perched on the edge of the cliff. Dark-gray, metallic scales shimmered as it moved, stretching great, batlike, leathery wings out away from its body, ready to take flight. Powerful arms and legs ended in wicked-looking claws, with talons the color of onyx. Spikes ran in a neat row from the crown of its head, down the long, lithe neck, between strong shoulder blades, following the spine all the way to the heavily spiked tip of the tail, the spikes all in that same onyx.

The neck curved around gracefully, until she was face to face with the dragon, its gaze boring into her. Two long black horns curved away from his head on either side. She had the impression of a low, rumbling growl. Thin tendrils of smoke escaped its maw before the pearl-white teeth snapped shut.

She felt a shiver of fear until the head tilted in a familiar way. The dark-violet eyes were much gentler than she would have expected, black pupils narrowed to vertical, serpentlike slits. It lowered its great body, curling its tail and wings around until she felt enveloped. Protected.

And then the vision faded.

Reality came flooding back gradually as Ashriel eased his hold on her mind until they were two separate beings again. The connection was still there, but faintly. In the background.

Keeping her eyes closed, she wanted to draw the moment out. She felt him inhale, breathing her in, and realized she was tucked close against him. She wasn't really sure when that had happened. He clasped her hand tightly to his chest, his forehead resting against hers as he held her, their breaths mingling.

"That's..." She trailed off, at a loss, unused to this strange intensity.

"Spiritual," he gently supplied. "The connection between us is a bond of lovers."

She missed his warmth immediately when he reluctantly released her, wrapping her arms around herself as she let her eyes open again. "Do all shimana have this connection with each other?"

His lips curved in a smile that had her digging her fingers into her arms to stop herself from reaching for him again. "Some." There was longing in that one word. In his searching expression as he watched her.

An answering heat was beginning to curl through her. She cleared her throat, trying to distract herself. "And that's how a jahuni heals themselves?" She waved her hand toward the window, not sure what else to say.

"It's usually the most efficient way, but I have what amounts to a magical parasite," he said, bitterness plain in his voice. "It's necessary for the gegaji to force me into that state every night. Otherwise I wouldn't survive being drained over and over again like this. I never fully regenerate, though, especially now that my magic is mostly sealed away. I can do small amounts of magic with what Enalel has left me, but my powers are nothing compared to what they should be."

"Then there's no time to waste," she said, taking his hand and pulling him with her toward the door. She could tell he was just a little weaker every day. What would happen if they decided he wasn't strong enough to do what they needed anymore? "Where should we start today?"

The morning passed the same as it had for over a week, with her surreptitiously examining anything in the house that looked even the smallest bit unusual as she cleaned. She was very aware that she couldn't afford to draw attention to herself, but she couldn't just stand idly by either. When they'd first started working together to find his gegaji, she'd been covert about it, just glancing around, not really moving anything unless she was cleaning it. But as the days wore on, she'd become bolder, even hurling a few things herself when she thought she'd found something. She was starting to get why he preferred that way of searching.

She'd also started checking in on Rae since the incident after the barbecue. There wasn't much she could do, but at least it gave her some small peace of mind to see Rae was still acting normally the majority of the time. She hadn't seen Rae that day, however, so she was starting to get worried. She doubted Petrin would let her have a day off, considering they'd started noticeably controlling and draining her.

Ashriel distanced himself from her a few times, going to work in different parts of the house, just in case Odath and Petrin were lurking somewhere. It was clear he wanted to stay near her for her safety, but he didn't want to seem too attached to her. Honestly, she was a little relieved when he'd leave. She knew, if something did happen between her and the other shimana, he'd do whatever it took to protect her, even if that meant hurting himself in the process.

Sighing as she trudged across the entryway with

her cleaning supplies, she paused in front of the shima mural again. That was next on her list to ask Ashriel about, but it was so out in the open she hadn't been able to find a good opportunity. Odath and Petrin passed by the area frequently, so she'd concentrated on the areas she could go with Ashriel relatively safely. Honestly, she'd dismissed it at first, since it felt nothing like the spell marks all around the house. It didn't give her the same bad vibes the spell marks did, but who knew? Anything could be important.

Sensing someone coming, she busied herself with wiping down the mirror on the wall above the small entryway table. In the mirror's reflection, she saw Petrin strutting toward the door, looking really pleased with herself. She was wearing dull silver armor and a dark-brown cloak. She had a long dagger strapped to a weapon belt at her waist, and Jillian's eyes widened at the sight.

Could things get any stranger or any worse?

Yes on both fronts, apparently.

Following Petrin with an angry, pained expression, wearing his usual not-suitable-for-a-deathmatch clothes, Ashriel caught Jillian's gaze in the mirror for a split second, his mind brushing at hers. *"She found one of them."* His words whispered through her mind, and her stomach sank.

They were out of time. The only question was, who had they found? The Sijo? Or Darenai?

CHAPTER SEVENTEEN

The capital city of Neluk, shima realm
In the meeting chamber of the Junak

LANSA FERUMA, JIRU OF URUJEK, slouched back in his seat, putting on a disinterested air as he listened to the testimony of two shimana who had been living in the human realm for decades. His son, Gajano, sat to his right in his position as both Telesil and Sijo of Urujek, his usual scowl firmly in place.

Covertly scanning the cavernous, semicircular room with his pale-violet eyes, he took stock of who was in attendance from his vantage point toward the center. The room was made up of rows of tables, several levels high, aisles of stairs connecting them. Brightly lit with crystal wall sconces, with natural light shining down from a large, circular window at the apex of the vaulted ceiling, it was easy to pick out the ones he'd been keeping an eye on.

Noren and Hasenda Gaisudji stood before Jiru Talura's throne at the front of the room, in the center of the flat of the semicircle, sharing their concerns. Their voices, magnified by the spells on the light-gray stone tiles under their feet, carried around the room, and Lansa listened intently.

"Humans have been showing up at the hospital with strange symptoms," Hasenda said calmly, not showing even a hint of nerves in front of Jiru Talura. As a healer in the shima realm, it had only been natural for her to follow the same course in the human realm, and she'd picked up on what no human doctor could. "At first, it was small things. A human with memory lapses. Another with splitting headaches and nightmares. Now, some of them, their minds are so fractured it's impossible to miss. They're being mind controlled by someone, and drained, but I can't figure out why or who is responsible."

"I was a bidkoil for centuries before moving to that town," her prasuri, Noren, added. His experience reading the weak spots in the barrier caught Lansa's attention immediately, even more of a red flag than his mate's statements had been. "For almost two months, the aragna in and around the town have been behaving strangely."

Lansa shifted in his seat, catching a certain Jiru's reaction to that. Jiru Otharo's accusation against Kretore didn't sit well with him. Having recently formed an alliance with both Kretore and the city of Amvitum, unbeknownst to the Junak, he knew without a doubt there was more to Jiru Otharo's claim than there seemed, and that Jiru Otharo had lied in front of the entire Junak. A risk not many would take under Jiru Talura's scrutiny.

He also knew Kretore had been searching for the accused warrior, Ashriel, for nearly two months at this point. As far as Lansa had observed, it hadn't been an attempt to cover their tracks. They had truly looked, and had eventually listed him as a possible victim of Humiv's kidnappings. Members of Ashriel's family had stepped forward as well, vouching for the warrior and continuing the search for him.

"Gajano," he said across their telepathic link. *"Pay attention to Jiru Otharo and his Ushara."* He sensed Gajano's focus shift from scanning the rest of the room to zero in on his new targets.

Rising to his feet, Lansa's pulled-back, nearly waist-length, dark-golden-blond hair slid back over his shoulder, the decorative bloodred beads in the mix of wavy hair and braids clinking together as he moved. In keeping with the Junak's etiquette, he stood silently and waited to be acknowledged by Jiru Talura. At the Junak leader's nod for him to speak, Hasenda and Noren turned to look at him as he spoke.

"Something similar happened to an arag in Urujek, just before we were attacked by Humiv," he said, his voice magnified by the room's spellwork, as theirs had been. "I'd be interested in seeing readings from these aragna."

He heard Gajano's chuckle in his mind. *"That got a reaction."*

Tamping down on the triumph he felt at finally finding a lead, Lansa kept his expression blank as Jiru Otharo rose to his feet as well. At Jiru Talura's nod, he spoke, "We have more pressing matters to deal with than a few strange readings in the human realm and some humans with explainable human illnesses. A few headaches and memory lapses don't necessarily mean mind control. Meanwhile, Humiv still has my son." He glared at Lansa convincingly, but Lansa noticed the way his hand trembled at his side just slightly. "How many times can we divide our focus before the Junak is spread too thin to do anything? What if that's what Humiv wants? To keep us chasing leads to nowhere while they take more of our people and attack more of our cities?"

"I apologize," Lansa said, giving a slight bow to Jiru Otharo. "It wasn't my intention to dismiss what has happened in Orilia. You're right. We should stay focused on the most immediate threat." Holding Jiru Otharo's gaze, he felt the weight of the room's attention on him and their exchange, which was exactly what he'd been hoping for. "Let me know if I can assist you in your search for your son."

Jiru Otharo nodded, and they both took their seats again. Hasenda and Noren continued making their case to the leader of the Junak, and Lansa was careful to appear like his attention was on them.

Gajano had kept his dark-blue eyes trained on Jiru Otharo and his Ushara throughout the exchange. Taking a deep breath, he pushed a hand through his black hair, meeting Lansa's gaze briefly. *"Jiru Otharo's Ushara reacted before he did. For a second, he looked so worked up I thought he was about to stand up and say something to you himself."*

Lansa laughed softly as he leaned back in his chair. *"Interesting. It's impossible to tell from all the way across the room, but I didn't see any noticeable scars on Jiru Otharo's neck from a slave collar."*

"I'll find a way to take a closer look."

"Don't be reckless," Lansa said, unable to shake the memory of Gajano nearly dying by Humiv's hands when Urujek was attacked.

Gajano raised an eyebrow beside him, shooting him an amused glance. *"You can say that with a straight face? Between the two of us, that's never been me."*

"It is concerning that the aragna are giving off strange energy readings in the human realm," Jiru Talura's voice rang out across the room. "But there's no real proof that humans are being mind controlled, or that the two situations would necessarily be connected if they were."

"Their symptoms—" Hasenda began, only to be silenced by a narrow-eyed glare from Jiru Talura. Neither her or her prasuri had said so, but they seemed to have a personal reason for stepping forward.

"Whatever game Humiv is playing, waging war on the entire shima realm, why would they bother with humans?" he said coolly. "What benefit could they possibly get out of it?"

Noren took Hasenda's hand in a comforting, protective gesture. "We don't know that it's Humiv, but—"

"Then it's not an immediate threat," Jiru Talura said, his hard tone conveying that he'd brook no argument. "We will look into it when we have resources to spare."

Lansa could tell Noren was biting his tongue to keep from saying exactly what he thought of Jiru Talura's dismissal, but he wordlessly bowed beside his prasuri without further argument when they were excused from the Junak chamber.

Everyone in the room stood and bowed low as Jiru Talura rose to pronounce the meeting over. "We will reconvene next week," he said before bowing slightly and exiting the chamber through a door at the far end of the room, between the central rows of tables.

"Set up a meeting with the Jiruna of Kretore and Amvitum," Lansa said across his bond to Gajano. They would have to move very carefully if Orilia was involved with Humiv, voluntarily or not. He'd suspected since the initial attack on his own city that the Junak had already been infiltrated. The question was, who were they, and what were they planning with all of this?

Gajano got to his feet unhurriedly, rolling tense shoulders under his black armor. *"You've attracted someone else's attention,"* he said, subtly moving so that he was free of the confining space behind the desk, always ready for battle.

Lansa sensed the other man walking down the stairs from one of the rows above and behind him, but didn't look toward him until he heard him speak.

"Excuse me, Jiru Feruma?" the man said, and Lansa turned around to see Saisha Aniyu, the Jiru of Majit, standing there. "It's been a while," he said with a broad smile, extending his right hand. Usually they would just offer a slight bow to each other, but Jiru Aniyu had always been much less concerned about convention, and more about making a warm impression on others. "Do you have a moment?"

It was second nature at that point for Lansa to muffle his energy down to nothing before he clasped the other man's forearm in a friendly greeting, naturally putting up an impenetrable barrier in his mind. For the time being, he chose to trust no one outside the small circle he'd formed behind the Junak's back. Not that he'd ever been particularly forthcoming about the level of his own powers, even in more peaceful times.

"Good to see you, Jiru Aniyu," Lansa said easily, offering a smile of his own. Just as cautious as Lansa, he could feel Gajano's imperceptible shift behind him, relaxing when Jiru Aniyu released Lansa's arm. "How can I help you?"

Unlike Lansa, Jiru Aniyu seemed to feel at home in the formal clothing all Jiruna wore in front of the Junak. The black hide pants and boots, with a white, wide-sleeved shirt and matching cloak bearing black-embroidered designs representing his city suited him. His deep-brown hair, falling below his shoulders, was pulled back, and his ever-present smile always reached his dark-blue eyes, adding to his natural harmless charm.

"I think Jiru Talura may have been too hasty in ignoring what was said about the aragna," he said, moving a little closer and lowering his voice.

"Do nothing," Lansa warned telepathically, sensing Gajano's unease. As innocuous and pleasant as Jiru Aniyu seemed, he was a powerful ancient, far older than even Lansa, and under that cheerful demeanor he was known for being surprisingly ruthless to his enemies.

"I don't trust him," Gajano said stiffly, remaining outwardly calm.

"Agreed," Lansa said aloud, answering both of them as he crossed his arms over his chest. "He didn't seem overly concerned about the readings in Urujek either, calling them a fluke."

"What are the readings like now? If there's even a hint—"

"Stable," Lansa said, shaking his head. "Like the fluctuations never happened."

"That should be more reassuring than it is," Jiru Aniyu said, smile dimming a bit. "Those weak spots in the arute are too dangerous to overlook something like that, even if it was only temporary."

The barrier between the realms, the arute, had been closely monitored since the beginning of time. If any of the aragna ever deteriorated, allowing the two realms to touch, neither realm would survive the fall-out. For Jiru Talura to be so unconcerned over this possible second instance of changes in aragna was out of character, even in a time of war.

"I'd be more convinced of Jiru Aniyu's sincerity if he'd cared when this happened in Urujek," Gajano muttered across their link.

"I thought so too," Lansa said, answering them both again. "But there's nothing that can be done about it. The decision has been made to focus our energy on Humiv."

"I'd like to help you," Jiru Aniyu said. Lansa sensed a change in the air. Unfamiliar magic crept toward him, and the other Jiru's magic swept over him and everything else in the room moments later, scanning for listeners. He only barely managed to stop himself from reacting. Dropping his hands to his sides, he gave Gajano a subtle signal for silence—both voiced and telepathic—as Jiru Aniyu continued as if nothing had happened.

"I believe Humiv and the temporary changes in aragna are connected, and it would be foolish to underestimate either one."

"What do you have in mind?" Lansa said, tilting his head and narrowing his eyes. "Going against a direct order from Jiru Talura, especially with these tensions between the cities, could make things worse."

"He didn't forbid us from investigating on our own.

He only said our focus should be on Humiv," Jiru Aniyu said, giving him a measuring look. "Let's see what we can find on our own with the aragna and share what we discover. We can't dedicate a lot of resources without going against Jiru Talura, but with both of us working together we won't have to. We can split the burden."

Lansa extended his hand to Jiru Aniyu again, smiling in a friendly way. "Give me a day to think about it."

Jiru Aniyu nodded, clasping Lansa's forearm without hesitation. "Thank you for considering it," he said, giving Lansa another of his blinding smiles before turning away. "I'll be in touch," he said over his shoulder as he headed for the door.

"Let's go," Lansa said the moment Jiru Aniyu left the room.

"What do you—"

Lansa gave him a sharp look, quickly grasping Gajano's shoulder and shaking his head. "We need to get back to Urujek," he said out loud, hoping Gajano would hear the weight in his words.

Understanding Lansa's meaning, if not the reason, Gajano quickly turned and led the way to the teleportation chamber in the open courtyard of Jiru Talura's castle. It was the only place within the castle grounds that anyone could teleport, and it was restricted to be used by Jiruna and their protectors only. On guard, Lansa was careful to take note of whether or not he felt eyes on him as they made their way. Placing a hand on Gajano's shoulder the instant they entered the courtyard, he took his teleportation crystal from a pocket in his cloak, whispered the incantation that would bring them back to Urujek, and they were gone. Whisked away in an instant and a flash of light.

Finding himself in his own throne room in Urujek, he greeted the small figure lounging on the arm of his throne chair. "Navin," he said, giving her a nod while waiting to see her reaction to them.

Navin, his Ushara, jumped up off the arm of his chair as soon as they appeared, hopping down the couple steps from the dais to jog over to them. Light reflected off her silvery-white armor and shimmered in the gold streaks of her short, white-blond, spikey hair. She stopped dead in her tracks several feet away, though, eyes going wide, and Lansa knew he'd been right to silence Gajano.

Silently, Lansa lifted a hand to Gajano's eyes, signaling him to keep them closed. Gajano raised an eyebrow, but obeyed, and then Lansa followed suit. He sensed Navin approach them, a scorching, uncomfortable heat washing over him, and felt Gajano tense beside him in surprise. Seeming to grasp the gist of what was going on, however, he didn't move otherwise. Light slowly began to penetrate his eyelids, until he had to clench them closed and duck his head to keep from being blinded.

After a long moment, the light and heat faded, and he heard Navin's voice. "Lansa?" she said, one of two people in the world who were allowed to address him informally.

Raising his head, he met her concerned pale-blue eyes and held them. "Is there something on my cloak?" he said, purposely vague.

"Not anymore," she said, brows snapping together. "What was that? I didn't like the way that felt."

Gajano looked between the two of them, not having

picked up on what happened. "Will either of you explain?"

Navin waved her hand though the air, looking at some spot above Gajano's head. "Your energy was all messed up. Cloudy, nasty stuff with ears," she muttered.

Gajano stared at her. "I had ears."

"Yes," she clarified, as if it should be obvious. "Someone was listening."

"I do believe we've made a new enemy," Lansa said, crossing his arms over his chest as he considered his next move. "Jiru Aniyu must have felt it too when our minds were attacked by an ancient, powerful kind of dark magic."

"I didn't feel it," Gajano said, obviously unsettled.

"I wouldn't have either if it weren't so sticky and gross," Navin said, distaste clear in her usually perky expression. "The energy was all over both of you. Luckily, I saw you right after the spell was cast, and it didn't have time to really settle in." She paused, looking between the two of them. "And it was sloppy, like someone only put half effort into it."

"I'm glad they were incompetent," Gajano said.

"Were they?" Lansa said, signaling for them to follow him into his office behind the throne room. "Why bother with that kind of high level, complicated magic if you're going to do it poorly? The risk of being caught is too great if it's done improperly."

He directed his energy at a certain stone in the wall behind his throne. The stones in front of him pushed back into the wall, folding in on themselves until they formed an opening big enough to be a passageway. Gajano and Navin followed him through, and the passageway sealed itself closed behind them as he headed for his large desk at the far end of the room on the other side. Taking a blank piece of paper and a crystal pen from a drawer, he started taking notes, planning where he would go next with his investigation.

"Everyone knows you're ancient, but not quite how ancient," Navin said, leaning over to look at his notes. "Do you think whoever did it was testing you?"

"It's possible," Lansa said.

"Or they wanted to give you a push toward trusting Jiru Aniyu," Gajano added. "What better way than to clearly attack you while the Jiru is right in front of you, and you know it isn't him?"

"Also a possibility," Lansa said, straightening away from his notes to look at his protectors. "Go to the Jiruna of Kretore and Amvitum and set up a meeting. We have several new leads to follow."

Jillian was in a frenzy, tearing haphazardly through the house like a madwoman. There was no sign of Rae still, no response anywhere in the house that she could hear when she called out, and Ashriel and Petrin had been gone almost an hour already. She no longer cared if she got caught. Even when rooms shifted, she didn't care. She threw herself at room after room until she'd exhausted every option on the first floor. All that mattered was finding the contract that bound Ashriel.

If she didn't...

She refused to think beyond that.

Taking the stairs to the second floor two at a time, she raced through the hallways, shattering as many things as possible. Wherever Odath was, he hadn't appeared out of the shadows to stop her yet, and she wasn't going to stop until he did, or Ashriel came back, or she found his contract. End of story.

Once she'd destroyed that floor, there was only one option left. Out of breath, dark-brown hair a disheveled mess, she swiped the sweat from her eyes and ran for the third-floor stairs. *Last resort before the last resort,* she thought grimly.

Coming to the top of the stairs, she came face to face with the eerily glowing crystal mural. Knowing better than to touch it directly, she grabbed the nearest object, a small lamp sitting on yet another decorative narrow hallway table, and hurled it at the wall as hard as she could.

An electric crackle rent the air, stinging over her skin. Whatever magic was in the stones rebounded the energy of her throw back at her hard enough to shove her back into the wall behind her with a painful impact.

Determined, she flew back down the stairs, headed for the first floor again. Like hell she'd let that be the end of it. She was going to find a way to get one of those crystals out of the wall without killing herself, if it was the last thing she did. And it might be. But she'd cross that bridge later.

Reaching the first floor, she made her way purposefully across the entryway toward the supply closet. She'd seen metal tools in there before. There had to be something she could use.

She glanced at the entryway mural on her way by out of habit, before continuing on her way.

About ten feet down the hallway, she stopped. Then she turned around and retraced her steps. Moving to stand in front of the mural, her eyes were drawn to the directional compass at the bottom right of the map. It was a little four-pointed star, with a teeny, tiny figure carved into the center.

What was the figure?

What was that teeny, tiny thing that had been staring her in the face for a month?

What was making her want to scream with anger until the universe exploded?

A dragon.

It was a freaking dragon.

Resuming her trip to the supply closet, she made it there in record time, guided by rage, adrenaline, and her freaky shima blood. She threw things around until she found what she was looking for, having zero concern for anything that broke in the process. She found a crowbar and lifted it to the dim supply closet light triumphantly like it was the sword Excalibur. She felt a short-lived rush of victory.

Oh, she was going to destroy everything. *Everything.*

Dashing back to the mural in the entryway, she raised the crowbar above her head and brought it down as hard as she could. The result was so much worse than the creepy crystal mural. That had been nothing.

A jolt wrenched through every muscle in her arms the second the crowbar made contact with the mural, so painful she wondered if her arms had just been ripped from her body. And then she was airborne, a *boom* like thunder filling her ears as she sailed through the air. Hitting the floor so hard she bounced, she ended up crumpled on the ground in front of the door, the breath knocked out of her and her mouth full of the taste of blood.

Looking down at her body fearfully, she was momentarily relieved to see she still had arms. That quickly transformed into fear when she realized she couldn't move at all, just like the spell Odath and Petrin had used on her before.

How had she broken free before? She remembered scratching Odath's face and kneeing him, so it was possible, right?

Ashriel's words filled her head. *"Follow my breaths. Concentrate on me,"* he'd said the first time he'd fully shared her mind. Concentrating on her breathing, she tried to compose herself. Her freaky blood was more reliable when she was calm.

Move, she thought, focusing what she now recognized has her own tiny amount of magical energy. *Get up!*

Suddenly, like someone had lifted a thousand-pound lead blanket off her body, she was free. Struggling to her feet, she made her way back to the mural.

"Understood," she muttered, glaring at it. "No hitting, then."

Reaching toward the wood, she hovered her hand over the mural. She'd touched it many times before and had never been hurt. So maybe it only reacted to force? Hesitantly, she lightly brushed the carved map with one fingertip and immediately leapt back like it was going to bite her.

When nothing happened, she tried again, trailing several fingers over the wood. When nothing exploded, and she didn't die, she counted that as a victory and moved on. Placing her fingers over the tiny dragon, she felt an electric tingle of warning move up her arm.

"Okay," she breathed, heart pounding. "I'm playing

nice, see?" she said to the mural—because why not? She was officially in crazy, upside-down, magic land, and nothing made sense anyway. So why not talk to the mural?

"When something feels like it's different, stop and focus your mind completely on the room you want to find. Your instincts will lead you," Ashriel's words whispered to her. It had been a totally different context at the time, but maybe the same concept applied?

Taking a deep breath, she tried to channel her energy into the tiny dragon. It felt sloppy, even to her inexperienced senses, but again, nothing was exploding, and she wasn't dying, so all was well for the time being.

After several agonizing seconds where she wondered if she was going to die, she finally, *finally* felt a soft, nearly imperceptible click.

Chapter Eighteen

"Now we'll end this," Petrin said, feeding the building storm with her bloodlust. Dark, thick clouds rolled in out of nowhere, blotting out the sun to protect her from the light.

She'd brought Ashriel to a different house several miles away from where he was being kept, not far enough from town to be safe. There was a good chance humans would see and hear the battle, but she didn't seem to care. Just as concerning, Odath was nowhere in sight, and was probably acting on Enalel's behalf elsewhere.

Beside her, Ashriel fell to his knees, clutching his head. He could feel Petrin's energy reaching out to him, adding her will to Enalel's. The gegaji was demanding to be fulfilled.

"Kill him."

He felt his body begin to move against his will and fought with every ounce of strength he had left. He struggled until he felt like his body would be torn apart from the strain.

He felt himself stand up, his gaze turning to the house in the clearing ahead. As he stumbled forward, he saw the back door of the house open. Sijo Otharo stepped out, already knowing Ashriel was there.

Wind whipped through the Sijo's light-blond hair. His pale-green eyes fixed on Ashriel. To Ashriel's dismay, he was dressed in casual shima clothes again—brown hide pants and a white linen shirt instead of the fire-resistant armor he sorely needed at the moment. A simple dagger in a sheath was at his waist.

Heart sinking, Ashriel prayed the Sijo was as good a fighter as he remembered from their first encounter. Normally, it would require several shimana to take down a fully transformed jahuni, but Ashriel had been kept weak for too long. Even with Petrin's energy feeding the compulsions he was under, it might not be enough if his opponent was as strong as he seemed. The Sijo had a chance, at least.

One look at the Sijo's grim expression as he enclosed the area in a sphere of illusion to hide the battle from the eyes of any nearby humans told Ashriel he was thinking the same thing. If the forces struggling for supremacy in his body didn't tear him apart, the Sijo would be forced to kill him in order to save himself and stop Enalel.

Ashriel struggled to hold on to his control. He could feel the pull of the magic in every cell of his body. The gegaji demanding to be fulfilled. Enalel's demand for the Sijo's blood burned into his brain. Petrin fed the compulsions.

All he had was his own determination to fight those powers to the death if he had to.

Gasping, his body shaking violently with the effort to stop himself, he stumbled to a halt several yards away from the Sijo. He felt the agony of the change being forced on him, and fell to his knees again. The pain crippled him, made it hard to breathe. Sweat drenched his body.

The whole time, the Sijo's calm gaze never left him. He felt the weight of it and understood the other shima would have helped if he could have. They both knew he was fighting a losing battle. Ashriel would attack, no matter how hard he tried to stop himself. The only thing the Sijo could do was wait to kill him.

Glancing up, despite the pain, he saw the way the Sijo took a defensive stance in front of him. The fire inside Ashriel reached a fever pitch, pain tearing through him as his bones began to shift, and he let out a roaring scream. He fell forward onto his hands. The fingers that dug into the ground elongated into deadly black claws. He labored for breath.

He raised his head, gaze locking on to the Sijo. "Run," he growled menacingly, the beast inside him so close to the surface that his voice echoed eerily.

It was all he could manage before the change took him. He felt the wings explode from his back, shredding through his shirt easily, stretching wide. His tattered clothes morphed with him, and he felt his body become stronger, larger, full of power he couldn't control. Thick, dark-gray, metallic scales covered his skin. Bones changed. Realigned. Fire burned in his throat.

Light enveloped Ashriel, and the last of his control was gone. As the light faded, he felt like he was watching a movie. None of it felt real. He was nothing more than a spectator looking through a jahuni's eyes as smoke curled from his nostrils and he craned his neck to look down at the Sijo. Tucking his wings close to his body, he growled threateningly, lowering himself into a crouch and shifting his weight restlessly.

"Come on. Draw your weapon!" Ashriel shouted into the void, even though he knew the Sijo couldn't hear him. *"Defend yourself!"*

Letting out a thunderous roar, Ashriel charged, driving the Sijo back toward the trees. Drawing in huge lungfuls of air, he breathed a deadly stream of fire at the Sijo. Spinning around quickly when the Sijo teleported behind him to avoid the fire, he followed the momentum through with a vicious swing of his spiked tail.

The Sijo flung an energy spell at Ashriel's eyes, and he jerked his head to the side to avoid it, shifting his weight to tear at the Sijo with a massive front claw. He felt the impact when he hit the Sijo, flinging him several yards across the clearing.

"Get up, damn you!" Ashriel raged from inside his prison. *"Don't take pity on me! End this before it's too late!"*

Seeing an opening while the Sijo was dazed from the blow, clutching his wounded left side, he brought down his other claw hard enough to crack the earth where he hit, but the Sijo teleported out of the way just in time. Throwing another energy spell at Ashriel's eyes as Ashriel turned his head to locate the him again, the Sijo finally hit his mark.

Roaring in fury, Ashriel stumbled and shook his head violently from side to side. *"This is it, Sijo,"* Ashriel thought, thinking of Jillian regretfully and praying she would take Rae and go to Hasenda and Noren immediately. *"This is the only chance you're going to have."*

Through streaming eyes, Ashriel caught the glimmer of a blade lengthening into a deadly lance as the Sijo raced toward him, taking the opening he'd made. Ashriel breathed a sigh of relief. He didn't want to die. Not at all. But he also didn't want to murder an innocent man. And on the off chance he won this battle, what other horrible things would Enalel make him do? He prayed that Tairi would take care of Jillian and Rae if he couldn't himself.

Feeling the Sijo leap onto his back, Ashriel spread his wings wide, raising onto his back legs and tearing at his own shoulders to try and reach the Sijo. Bringing his head around, he snapped his teeth at the Sijo, managing to graze his arm and make him stumble, and he jerked to the side and made another grab for the Sijo with his claws.

Grasping one of the black spikes on Ashriel's back, the Sijo swung himself up again and began making his way up Ashriel's spine. Ashriel shook his head, breathing fire into the sky. With a sickening lurch in his stomach, Ashriel felt himself gathering energy he shouldn't have been able to tap into in his weakened state, preparing to blast the whole area with the raw energy of a jahuni pulse.

Ashriel tried to control it, but he felt the energy rise up inside him anyway. He felt Petrin's perverse pleasure as she fed him her energy. Bile rose in his throat at the thought of what he was about to do, willingly or not. The surrounding area would be demolished for miles. All that would be left would be a desolate, charred crater, painted with the blood of humans.

Sensitive to the dark magic Ashriel was being filled with by Petrin, he felt the Sijo stumble again. In his momentary distraction, Ashriel nearly bit the Sijo in half with the next snap of his jaws, but the Sijo teleported at the last second. Reappearing farther up Ashriel's spine, the Sijo threw energy at his eyes again and managed to stun him. His movements slowed for just a moment. He hestitated just enough to give the Sijo his opening.

With the Sijo charging toward Ashriel's head, he knew this was the end. Even as he recovered and began to thrash around again, he knew the Sijo wouldn't miss when he struck. It almost felt like he was watching in slow motion as the Sijo leapt into the air directly above Ashriel's head, lance flashing with the Sijo's energy.

Twisting at the last second in midair, the Sijo hurled his weapon into the trees.

"Wait, what?" Ashriel couldn't fucking believe it. Yet another suicidal idiot who enjoyed throwing himself at death? *"What are you doing? Strike while you can!"*

He heard Petrin's screech of pain somewhere in the distance. Suddenly he was dizzy and disoriented, and he realized he could feel his limbs again. The Sijo had stopped attacking him, teleporting somewhere else instantly, and Ashriel heard the sounds of weapons clashing from the trees where Petrin's scream had come from. He quickly realized the Sijo had given him one last chance to free himself while he and Petrin were battling each other somewhere out of Ashriel's line of sight. The only thing holding Ashriel on his current course was the gegaji, and the pull was weak.

"Fight!" he ordered himself, heart pounding in his chest. Now that he had an opportunity to do something, he wasn't about to give in. His full concentration shifted to resisting the gegaji still dragging at his will.

Thrashing, eyes still streaming, he struggled to regain control.

A cold draft moved past Jillian as the mural moved back an inch, then slid open to the right side, disappearing into a nook built into the wall. Just as she was about to move closer, she heard a distant sound, like the roar of some gigantic beast.

Whipping around, she looked back at the front door. Whatever part of her was connected to Ashriel was telling her it had been him she'd heard, somewhere far away from the house in another part of town probably. She could sense that he was in trouble, and the urgency she'd been feeling since he'd left just kept building.

God help her. On top of everything else, she had no idea where Odath was. He hadn't been with Petrin, so she prayed he was somewhere else, on one of his missions for Enalel.

Turning back to the opening that had been hidden behind the mural, she tried to push away the fear she felt. A darkened passageway stretched out before her, leading downward into what she assumed was a basement. The passageway was almost pitch black, except for a dim light she could see farther down. Taking a few cautious steps forward, she craned her neck, trying to make out if there was anything potentially deadly in the shadows leading downward.

There was a faint stirring of air and a hollow grating noise behind her that made her spin around in alarm. Fear beginning to creep in, she realized the wall had closed behind her.

She ran her hands along the surface but couldn't find any latch or button on that side of the door. It made her uneasy that she didn't know how to get back out, but she forced herself to turn away from the door all the same.

She knew what she was looking for had to be down there. Running a hand along the cool wall and keeping the other out in front of her, she made her way carefully down the passage.

As it angled farther downward, the smooth plaster of the wall stopped abruptly about a quarter of the way down. Then the walls were packed dirt and rock, like the sides of an underground tunnel would be. The ground beneath her feet was uneven, leading steadily downward. The air smelled damp, like dirt and decay.

Her way became easier to see as she neared the end of the passage. There was a door there, almost exactly like the one she had come through to get into the passage, only it swung inward rather than sliding into the wall. It had been left partially open, the faint light from the room beyond spilling out. Jillian reached out an unsteady hand and pushed the door the rest of the way open.

The sight that greeted her made her stomach lurch. The metallic scent of blood mingled with the scent of decomposition. The room was large and rectangular in shape. Large bowls sat in each corner, filled with fire that seemed to need no fuel. And situated in two rows of six, on either side of a walkway leading to a stone altar against the far wall, were coffins made out of stone. Strange symbols marked everything in the room, different than any of the others she'd seen so far, and she prayed one of them would help Ashriel.

Some of the coffins were open and empty. Some were closed. But all of them had smudges of dried blood on them. The altar and the dirt floor around it were almost black with it. She had the sickening feeling this was where Mindy had been taken, along with the other victims of supposed animal attacks.

As she studied her surroundings, she noticed a figure inside one of the open coffins. Fear nearly choking her, she cautiously moved toward it. There, laying silently in the coffin, was Rae.

"Rae!" She knelt down and shook Rae by the shoulders. Her head lolled to the side, but she didn't respond. She was pale, except for the dark blood running steadily from gashes in her right forearm. They looked like deep teeth marks, like someone had gnawed through her skin. Only her shallow, uneven breathing reassured Jillian that she was still alive.

Yanking the dust rag she hadn't used out of her pocket, she quickly tied it around Rae's forearm and pressed on it. Heart racing, she tried to figure out what she should do now.

"Were you looking for something?"

Jillian jerked her head around to see Petrin leaning against the open doorway. She was covered in blood and something had cut right through her armor like butter in several places. Her jaw had a ragged tear, and was hanging at an abnormal angle. She looked weak, using the doorway for support, but Jillian knew better. She had seen how Ashriel moved when he was weakened.

Setting Rae's arm back at her side, Jillian rose carefully to her feet to face Petrin.

"What were you searching for, I wonder, that led

you down here?" Petrin taunted, pushing away from the doorway. A sick clicking sound could be heard as her jaw slid itself back into place.

Swallowing her fear, Jillian scowled defiantly at Petrin. "What have you done to Rae?" she demanded. Some angry, feral part of herself she hadn't known existed was bristling inside her like an enraged lion.

Petrin narrowed her eyes, laughing low in her throat. "I see it clearly now, your connection to Ashriel. The beastly side of a jahuni is in you," she said cryptically. "That fierce protective instinct will land you in the same position as Ashriel, if you aren't careful."

Ignoring Petrin's taunting, she chose to file those comments away for later, and mentally prepared herself for a *really* uneven fight. "Please just let us go, Petrin."

"You humans can be so amusing sometimes," she said with a chuckle, a twisted smile curving her lips. "You think you can help her?"

Jillian looked around her for anything she could defend herself with, not bothering to waste time with an answer.

"You think you can help Ashriel?" Petrin asked mockingly. "You really think you can save either of them?"

There was nothing Jillian could grab except the bowls of fire, but they were too far away.

Petrin's pendant glittered in the dim light as she took a step forward, catching Jillian's eye. There, wrapped around the bloodred hilt of the dagger, was a golden dragon. She'd noticed it before when they'd first met, but hadn't paid it any mind since then, dismissing it as just an unusual piece of jewelry.

Petrin smiled knowingly, bringing a hand up to grasp it. “You want this?” she goaded. “Come and take it from me.”

CHAPTER NINETEEN

ASHRIEL STRUGGLED AGAINST THE GEGAJI'S hold on him. Without Petrin adding her power to the gegaji, he knew he could break free.

He felt the brush of a mind reaching out to his, and automatically stiffened, ready to fight. Vision still blurry, he tucked his wings close, dropping into a defensive crouch, all four claws digging into the earth as he braced himself.

"Let me help," he heard the Sijo call out to him, approaching from the tree line.

Blinking his sore eyes, he angled his head around so he could focus on the Sijo as he lifted his free hand toward Ashriel. Although he normally didn't like to let strangers touch his mind, he wouldn't turn down the Sijo's assistance. This was the second time the Sijo had intervened on his behalf, so he decided to take a chance.

Forcing himself to calm, his great chest heaving from exertion, he opened his mind to the Sijo. It was uncomfortable at first, having the Sijo's foreign energy in his mind, but before long, he felt the pull of the gegaji fade away.

As soon as he was able, he transformed back to his shima form. Light surrounded him, and his ragged clothing morphed back onto his body as he changed. His initial transformation had been so sloppy his jeans were torn in several places, and his back felt cool from the two large, frayed holes where his wings had ripped through, but none of that mattered as he knelt on the ground, weak from fighting Enalel and Petrin's compulsions, the gegaji, and the Sijo on top of it all.

"The enemy escaped me, but I doubt she got very far in her condition," the Sijo said, and Ashriel sorely wished he'd been able to witness Petrin getting the ass kicking she deserved. Dropping his hand, the Sijo strode toward him, returning his lance to its dagger form before sliding it back into its sheath. His right sleeve was torn and stained with blood from the deep gash in his arm, and he was favoring the ribs on his left side, but he seemed otherwise unharmed. "Are you all right?" he said, eyeing Ashriel closely for any sign that Petrin and Enalel's magic would overtake him again.

"You must go," Ashriel managed between gasping breaths. "Enalel won't stop coming after you."

"I know," the Sijo said, and Ashriel noticed the way he glanced at the house he'd come out of. Raising a hand over Ashriel, the Sijo started healing him. His body began to regenerate, his system flooded with energy the Sijo shared with him. "There's one more thing I must do, and then I'll be gone."

"Thank you, Sijo Otharo," Ashriel said formally, shifting his position so that he was kneeling before the Sijo properly. He bowed his head respectfully. "I am Ashriel Teleshani, a warrior of Kretore."

"There's no need for such formality," the Sijo said lightly, extending an arm to help Ashriel to his feet. "Call me Banen."

Ashriel nodded, grateful for Banen's help as he rose to his feet.

"I can still feel Enalel's hold on you. I haven't repaid my debt to you yet," Banen said quietly, regret coloring his voice, surprising Ashriel. "I would be dead now if you hadn't saved me from Enalel."

"You owe me nothing, Banen," Ashriel said, smiling grimly. He was uneasy, not knowing where Petrin had gone, and whether Jillian was safe. He needed to set something in motion with Banen and get back to Jillian quickly. "I believe I just tried to rip your head off. That kind of cancels out the initial good deed, don't you think?"

Banen shook his head with a wry chuckle. "When you say it like that..."

"Can you make it to the Junak?" Ashriel said, even though he was doubtful. He remembered what he'd felt outside the Hidga Mountains. There were probably still ambushes waiting for Banen there.

"I can't even get close," Banen said, wincing and placing a hand over his ribs when he shifted his weight. He held up a hand to assure Ashriel he was fine before he continued, "Enalel has those void creatures waiting at every entrance into the valley, and my teleportation stone was taken. It was only the kindness of another, who gave me an empty teleport stone, that allowed me to get to the human realm."

Neluk, the capital city and seat of the Junak, was protected by the magic in the Hidga Mountains. No one could teleport in or out of Neluk, except at a handful of designated teleportation sites. The trek to get to Neluk through the mountains was long and dangerous, but necessary if a shima wanted to be allowed to get their hands on a teleportation stone that would allow them to teleport directly to Neluk. Without his teleportation stone, Banen would have to risk the mountain paths with who knew how many void creatures on his heels.

"I was afraid of that," Ashriel said.

"Between the two of us—"

"I'm still a danger to you," Ashriel said, shaking his head. "It wasn't only mind control affecting me. I'm under the influence of a gegaji as well." He felt the pull of it still, even though it was weakened after Banen's intervention.

Banen glanced at the thin scar on Ashriel's neck. "She used a slave collar on you as well," he said, brows furrowing in disgust.

"She tried at first," Ashriel said, remembering the searing pain of it. "She wasn't strong enough on her own. Whoever her master is, they are the one who has mastered the slave collars."

"I will come with you to find this gegaji," Banen said, his voice edged with menace. It seemed like he was more than ready to pursue Petrin. Drawing his dagger, he turned away from Ashriel and started heading for the tree line again.

"You can't," Ashriel said, jogging to catch up with him. "The place is a deathtrap. There are spell marks engraved in every room of the house."

Banen cursed, pushing a hand through his hair in frustration as he stopped. "What is Enalel doing here?" he said, turning to Ashriel as he angrily resheathed his dagger. "She didn't just bring you here to track me down. The arute is dangerously unstable in this town. Several aragna are reacting to *something*, and I have neither the knowledge or the skill to balance them myself."

"She's commanded Odath and Petrin to gather energy where they've been holding me, including my own, and luring in humans for sacrifice," he said, trying to make sense of this new information with what he already knew. "At least a dozen so far."

"The new slave collars, void creatures, the unstable arute, and now energy gathering and human sacrifices in a concentrated area?" Banen said, considering. "I'm familiar with some of the darker magic, but I have no idea how any of this is related or what it's building toward."

"For now, go to the Jiruna of Kretore," Ashriel said, anxious to get back to Jillian. There was nothing more Banen could do for him, and the longer he stayed, the greater the risk that Enalel would show up with her void creatures. "Tell them what has happened to me and what's going on here. If you can't get to the Junak yourself, Kretore can protect you and get you to there. I have to return to Petrin and Odath."

"I don't like leaving you under Enalel's control," Banen said, brows snapping together in a frown. "If you stay, won't they kill you for your failure?"

Ashriel shook his head. "They have me hunting someone else as well. I'm still useful," he said, not wanting to get into the details. "But I could not leave regardless, even if I had my gegaji in my hand right now." He held Banen's gaze and told the truth. The one thing any shima would understand. "They have my prasuri."

Banen's eyes widened. For the first time, Banen seemed unsure. "I'm sorry," he said, and Ashriel could tell he understood perfectly.

"I will do what I can to prevent any more deaths until I can find my gegaji and get my prasuri out of there. I'm hoping all of us can make it out of this, but you need to assume I might not, and you're the only one who's seen what Enalel is doing here and what she's done in Orilia," Ashriel said, taking on the unfamiliar role of the voice of reason. Normally, he'd be all for having Banen's help carving a bloody path through Enalel's underlings until they got to her, but there was too much at stake, and they both had people depending on them. "You need to go."

Ashriel could tell Banen hated that he was right, but Banen finally nodded with a heavy sigh. "You are too weak to return as you are," he said, extending his hand again. "Let me lend you some more of my energy."

"Thank you," Ashriel said, kneeling in front of Banen again in a show of respect. He lowered his head as he felt the energy pour into him, replenishing a little of his weakened powers along with his body.

"I will come back to help you as soon as I can," Banen said after a moment, lowering his hand.

Ashriel nodded, rising to his feet. "May the Light of Tairi shine upon you," he said, asking for God's protection from their enemies.

Banen extended his hand to clasp Ashriel's forearm, a sign of their alliance and Banen's trust. "And upon you as well." It was as he was letting go of Banen's arm that he felt the first prickle of unease. Banen picked up on it immediately. "Ashriel?"

The unease turned to fear as Ashriel sensed the

barely there echo of Jillian's panic across the distance that separated them. Their connection was so new and weak he couldn't get a clear read on what was happening.

"Something's wrong," Ashriel said, already focusing all of his senses on Jillian as he turned away from Banen. "Leave now." And then he was racing through the forest toward Jillian, his mind full of her fear.

Jillian glanced at the pendant Petrin held lightly between her fingers.

"That's right. His gegaji is right here," Petrin taunted. A sly smile curved her lips, exposing fangs, and just like with the mural, Jillian felt a million different kinds of stupid. She'd been so desperate to keep away from Odath and Petrin that it hadn't occurred to her one of them might be *wearing* the freaking gegaji. "Right under his nose the whole time. Hidden by the spells he's under."

Jillian's mind raced. How could she get close enough to take it from Petrin?

"Don't you want to save your own prasuri?" Petrin goaded, twirling the chain of the necklace around a slender finger. "Your mate?" she elaborated at Jillian's blank look, her voice taking on that falsely pleasant tone that made Jillian want to grind her teeth.

"My mate?" she said distractedly, Petrin's meaning taking a second to sink in.

Petrin shrugged with her good shoulder, the gaping wound in the other one beginning to close. "Not like it matters," she said, reading Jillian's confusion. "I'm going to take your blood. Fix my little problem." She indicated her wounds with a wave of her hand. "And then I'm going to kill him. Maybe I'll leave you just enough blood to be able to watch as I do it."

"I'm right here, if you really think you can accomplish all that," Ashriel growled from the open doorway, and Jillian felt as if she could have passed out at the relief she felt. But it was short-lived. As grateful as she was to see him alive, she could tell he'd been through an ugly battle.

He looked much more like the feral animal she pictured when she thought of a jahuni than a man at that moment. Clothes ripped in several places, he was streaked with dirt from head to toe. His black hair was loose, wildly framing his face as if he had run through the woods to get there, and there was a murderous gleam in his dark-violet eyes.

Petrin turned her back on Jillian, dismissing her to meet the real threat. "I may be weakened, but it'll take more than the energy the Sijo gave you to stop me."

Petrin drew her dagger and charged Ashriel, the blade slicing toward his throat. Jillian watched helplessly as Ashriel was forced to face his enemy without a weapon or anything else to protect himself from her blade. He was on the defensive, ducking and leaping away as Petrin slashed at him. A few times, she was repelled by some magic Ashriel cast, but she just kept attacking.

Desperate to help somehow, she watched them anxiously. The next time Petrin drew back, prepared to strike again, Jillian leapt onto her back, wrapping an arm around her neck and squeezing with all her strength.

"Jillian! No!" Ashriel shouted, lunging at Petrin despite the dagger she still held. Jillian caught a glance of his angry, horrified expression over Petrin's shoulder, but there was no going back at that point.

Petrin growled, grasping Jillian's arm in a punishing grip. She barely paused as she twisted Jillian's arm cruelly and flung her into a wall like a rag doll.

Tasting blood for the second time that day, Jillian briefly shut her eyes against the pain and clenched her hands, struggling to get back up. Her arm ached, and she knew it was broken, or at the very least pulled out of the socket. Maybe both. But she tried to ignore it. She had to keep going.

Out of the corner of her eye, she could see Ashriel fighting Petrin like a possessed man. Striking out with his hands. Dodging. Blocking as best he could. Hurling balls of fire and streams of energy at her. In his blind rage, he didn't even let up when Petrin's dagger sliced into his limbs several times. Breathing hard, blood streaming from his wounds, he tried to get between Petrin and Jillian, but Petrin was faster and stronger, even with as many injuries as she had herself.

Managing to get to her knees, Jillian crawled toward one of the stone caskets, determined. There was only one way to help Ashriel. She couldn't give up. *Just a little farther,* she urged, gritting her teeth against the pain and exhaustion.

"Give up, and maybe I'll go easy on her," Petrin said, an ugly sneer twisting her beautiful features. "Maybe I won't hand her over to Odath after I feed on her."

Ashriel roared in fury and charged her again.

Petrin lowered her stance, prepared to make another attack.

It was the sound of delicate glass shattering that made them both freeze.

Jillian coughed, leaning sideways against the stone coffin on the floor beside her. Breathing carefully as she clutched her possibly broken arm, she managed a smile as the others stared at her. Just for Petrin. Because screw her.

It was a gleeful, triumphant moment as Petrin's hand flew to her throat where her pendant *used* to be. If it wouldn't have hurt to do it, Jillian would have laughed at the dumbfounded look on the other woman's face. Instead, she raised the pendant between them, the tiny hilt shattered and emptied of the blood that had been inside it.

Petrin took one threatening step toward Jillian, the bloodlust clear in her eyes, before she was stopped again.

"You have no idea how many creative ways I've dreamed of killing you," Ashriel said from behind Petrin, his voice deepening ominously. "This is going to be fun." His voice was filled with deadly promise as Petrin spun to face him again, lowering herself into a defensive stance.

Jillian watched in amazement as flames spread from his hands, coating his skin and flowing over it harmlessly like water. His body glowed as energy poured into him. His hands clenched and unclenched, and through their connection, she could feel the rush of power flowing through him, almost intoxicating as magic flooded his starved body.

His wounds sealed up. Scales rippled over his body protectively, giving a dark, silvery hue to his skin as wings grew from his back. He rolled his shoulders back in a stretch, and his body lengthened, muscles straining as he towered over Petrin. Black horns grew out on either side of his head, curving back and up. His nails became black talons as he extended a hand in front of himself, crooking a clawlike finger at her.

Ashriel cocked his head to the side, giving Petrin a cold smile as the light around him faded. "Well?" he growled, his fangs flashing. "What are you waiting for?"

"Eri rahunit, lathir karekit jenwe!" Petrin hissed savagely, cursing him in their language as she held her dagger out in front of her. She touched the crystal at the end of the dagger's hilt. "This isn't over," she promised, her eyes glancing to Jillian.

Ashriel tried to get to her, but it was too late.

She activated the crystal before he could even get close. There was a flash of light, and then she was gone.

CHAPTER TWENTY

"WHERE ARE WE GOING?" JILLIAN asked dazedly from the cradle of Ashriel's arms. Her entire body throbbed with a relentless, bruised kind of pain. She held her injured arm close to her body, not wanting to jostle it or make it worse.

In his regular shima form again, he glanced down at her. "To Rae's," he said quietly, walking easily through the thick trees even in the darkness. "I have no idea where Odath is, and I want to be as far from that place as possible when he returns."

The mention of Odath made her stiffen. "Won't he find us?"

"Yes," Ashriel said, and she found herself wishing he would lie to her. "How soon depends on how badly Enalel wants us. That Enalel sent Petrin with me alone to attack the Sijo tells me Odath's on another mission for Enalel, so Petrin is a more immediate threat. She drank Rae's blood, and a sathra's pull on their donors can be used to control them or track their location just as surely as any spell, especially with humans."

"She took your blood too," Jillian said, feeling a little sick. "So she can still control you?"

"I'm too strong for her to control now, but she could easily track me," he said, before making an obvious attempt at steering the conversation away from the topic of Petrin drinking his blood. "We'll stay at Rae's long enough for Rae to heal, and then we'll have to find somewhere else to hide for a while."

"Oh," she answered, not having the strength or desire to press for more information just then. All she wanted to do was bury her face against his chest and shut everything else out. She'd have plenty of time to worry about Petrin and Odath while Rae recovered, so for the time being, she tried to take comfort in the small victory of being out of the house they'd been trapped in.

There was a gentle warmth emanating through her, beginning to ease her pain, and a soft tingle in her left wrist. She instinctively knew it was Ashriel somehow. He was healing her again, but it felt much stronger than it had the last time he'd done it. She already felt a great deal better, and her arm wasn't killing her anymore.

Glancing down over her shoulder, toward the ground in front of them, she saw Rae floating ahead. She was several feet above the ground, keeping pace with Ashriel as he walked. She looked peaceful, like she was sleeping, but it still gave Jillian the creeps.

"She's okay," he said, seeming to sense her fear. "She's in an enchanted sleep right now."

She nodded, even though she didn't completely understand that either. She was just glad Rae wasn't dead.

She relaxed again, closing her eyes and just listening to his heart beat against her ear and the sound of leaves and twigs crunching beneath his feet. Bugs made noises all around, and an owl hooted from high above. She could hear cars in the distance, so she knew they weren't far from the main road. They might have even been traveling alongside it.

"Why are we going through the woods?" she asked absently, trying to distract herself from thinking too much about the floating woman in front of them or the cursed house they'd just left behind.

"If we get too close to the main road, there's a chance someone will see Rae floating," Ashriel said, a hint of amusement coloring his voice.

"I guess that could be a problem, huh?" she said, trying to sound like the whole floating thing didn't really bother her.

"Just a bit," he said.

"How do you know where Rae's is?"

"As she is now, her mind is quiet," he said. "Complacent. I can pick little bits of information out of her memories without harming her mind."

After several minutes of easy silence, an old Victorian house came into view. It was deep in the woods, away from the main town. There was a large garden and a long, tree-lined driveway that led to the road.

The door opened on its own as Ashriel climbed the steps up to the front porch, and it closed behind them just the same after they went inside. Without a pause, he went straight to the second floor, locating Rae's bedroom easily. Sitting Jillian on the edge of the bed, he levitated Rae carefully onto it beside her.

Jillian winced, turning gingerly so she could see what was going on as Ashriel went over to Rae's side of the bed. Jillian got a sinking feeling in her stomach when he placed his fingertips on Rae's temples. She quickly grasped one of his wrists. "What are you doing?"

"I'm going to alter her memories," he said, like that should be totally obvious.

"Why?" Jillian demanded, scowling at him.

"She will remember what happened to her in that house," he said, frowning right back at her. "It's dangerous for humans to know about my people."

"Dangerous how?" Raising an eyebrow at him, she released his arm. "As far as I can tell, you can take care of yourselves just fine."

"You have no idea what your own species is capable of," he said darkly. "Trust me. Over the centuries that I have been alive, I have seen how humans treat my people with my own eyes."

"And how have they treated you, exactly?" she asked, unable to contain the edge of anger in her voice.

"They experiment on us." His voice became cold. "They take us apart piece by piece to try and figure out how we work. Or they just torture and kill us."

"They who?" She still wasn't backing down.

He gave her a long look. "You think you're the first person in the history of this planet to find out about us?" he asked sarcastically. "You think someone didn't manage to figure it out before you? There are people who know, and they hunt us. Maybe the police wouldn't believe Rae if she tried to tell someone, but these people would."

"Rae wouldn't do that. She wouldn't tell anybody," she insisted.

"How do you know?" He dropped his hands from

Rae's temples to scrub them over his face in frustration. "Look, she may not want to remember anyway."

"Do you think I would hurt you?" she demanded. "I am a human, after all."

"Dammit, Jillian, I'm not accusing you."

"But you're accusing Rae?" She crossed her arms over her chest, raising an eyebrow at him. "She was a victim of the same kind of treatment you're talking about, and so were a bunch of other people from what I saw in that basement. It wasn't humans who did that."

"I get what you're saying, but it's not the same," he said.

"Yeah, it is, but that doesn't mean I see you the way I do Odath and Petrin. I know better, and so do you." She knew she was getting through to him when he started grumbling to himself in his own language, head tipped back and eyes closed like he was praying for patience. "I'm not saying let's announce the existence of shimana to the world. I'm just asking you not to mess with Rae's memories," she said, hoping he'd see reason. "There are bad people on both sides, but you know Rae isn't one of them."

Sighing loudly, Ashriel shifted to put a knee on the bed and leaned across Rae to softly grasp Jillian's chin. Before she could react, he kissed her, giving her bottom lip a playful bite. "Please stop being a pain in my ass," he said, but he didn't put his fingers back on Rae's temples when he pulled away.

"That's not a good way to dissuade me," she said, grinning at him with her heart on her sleeve.

There was a short pause while some kind of mischief danced in Ashriel's eyes. "I'm weak to temptation. Stop it." He quickly returned his attention to Rae. "I'm going to wake her up," he said, placing his fingers on her temples. "Who knows what kind of state she'll be in or what she'll remember right away? Be ready."

Jillian nodded, worried. "Okay." She remembered how disorienting it was waking up after being mind controlled. The panic she'd felt when Ashriel had turned to stone and the fear she'd experienced when she'd discovered the existence of shimana and how powerful they were was still fresh in her mind.

He softly chanted a few words, and she felt the air shift around him. Magic moved between him and Rae, and after a few breaths Rae's eyes snapped open. Gasping, she tried to scramble away from both of them. Jillian couldn't read what Rae was thinking, but she was sure her friend's mind was still firmly locked in the basement with Odath and Petrin.

"No!" Rae screamed, kicking at them and backing herself up to the headboard. Her brown eyes were wild, her dark-blond hair a tangled mess around her shoulders and face as she gasped for air as if she'd run for miles. "Don't touch me!"

"It's all right!" Jillian said, holding her hands out toward Rae. "You're safe."

Ashriel stayed quiet, standing up from the edge of the bed and taking a step back. He kept his distance, clearly concerned for Rae despite what he'd said before. Jillian knew he'd moved for Rae's sake. She probably knew now that Ashriel wasn't human either, and she might be just as afraid of him as she was of Odath and Petrin.

"Where am I?" Rae croaked, her voice hoarse like she'd been crying.

"You're home, Rae," Jillian soothed. "Odath and Petrin are nowhere near us."

Rae closed her eyes, trying to pull herself together, but she couldn't seem to slow her breathing.

"Let me ease her panic," Ashriel's voice whispered into Jillian's mind, drawing her attention to him. He was frowning, but she knew him well enough to know he was worried.

"Okay," Jillian thought, hoping he heard her.

"Rae," Ashriel said, his voice lowering to that hypnotic tone he'd used before. "Rae, look at me."

His voice was commanding, compelling Rae to obey. When Rae met his steady gaze, Jillian felt the air change around him again.

"Remember that you are safe with us," he said, and the magic felt different than when he'd told her to leave Odath and Petrin's home. He took several deep, even breaths, coaxing Rae to follow his lead.

Rae looked at him a long moment, her breathing evening out, but the fear was still in her eyes. "You're one of them."

"You know Ashriel's not like them, Rae," Jillian quickly reassured her, scooting closer and gently taking Rae's hands. "He saved us both."

"What was that?" Rae said, looking between the two of them. Her grip on Jillian's hands tightened, and she could feel Rae trembling. "What happened to me?"

It took a while to work their way through it, but Jillian started to share what had happened at the house. At some point, Ashriel went and got a glass of water for Rae while she listened in contemplative silence. It was like the wind had been taken out of her sails, and she was lifeless.

The worst part was when she got to Mindy. Rae buried her face in her hands and just cried.

"I'm so sorry," Ashriel said, and Jillian could hear the pain in his voice clearly. He still seemed to blame himself to some degree for not being able to get everyone out of that house.

"You tried to save her," Rae said, sniffling and wiping at her eyes. For the first time since she'd woken up, she looked at Ashriel directly. "Odath and Petrin are the ones who did this. Not you."

Jillian could tell he was still struggling with it, but he smiled at Rae weakly, nodding his acknowledgement of her words. Silence descended after that while Rae digested what she'd learned.

"It's important that you don't tell anyone what you know about us," Ashriel said after a while.

"No one would believe me anyway," Rae said, swiping at her eyes again with a hollow smile. "Who would I tell?"

"There are other humans who know about my people, and they would love nothing more than to get their hands on me," Ashriel said, his usual sarcasm strangely absent. "Or even you, now that you've been touched by magic."

Rae took a deep breath, nodding. "Got it," she said with a shaky laugh. "Don't tell anyone that I've met a vampire and a dragon and whatever Odath is."

"Tifire," Ashriel said.

Jillian raised an eyebrow. "A what?"

"Faerie."

Rae blew out a breath and leaned back against the headboard tiredly. "Right. Bloodthirsty faeries."

"Give it time," Jillian said, patting Rae's shoulder.

It was news to her that Odath was a faerie, but at that point she was beyond being shocked by anything. Up was down. Pigs were flying. And a faerie had tried to suck her blood. Why not, right? "It won't sound any less crazy tomorrow, but it's going to be all right."

"Wait," Rae said, getting tense all over again as she quickly looked between Ashriel and Jillian. "Aren't Odath and Petrin just going to follow us? They know where I live."

"We're loose ends, so it's only a matter of time until they do," Ashriel said, never one to sugarcoat his words. Rae looked like she was about to catapult herself out of bed when he quickly continued, "We can't move until you're strong enough. As I've explained to Jillian many times, with great futility," he said, shooting Jillian a quick glare while she tried to keep a look of innocence on her face. "Humans are weak, easily breakable creatures. So unless you have a hidden arsenal in your house somewhere and a weaponized wheelchair to keep you from collapsing from the trauma your mind and body have been through, I can't protect you both while fighting and carrying you."

Jillian tried to cover her laugh with a cough, but Ashriel still scowled at her. "That's his way of saying he cares and doesn't want you to die."

Rae smiled weakly, and Jillian could tell she was trying to keep calm when she took a deep breath, settling back against the headboard again. "Okay."

"You need to rest now," Ashriel said firmly. "For a couple days at least. In the meantime, I'll put up a protective barrier around the house."

Rae gave him a skeptical look. "This barrier can keep Petrin and Odath away?"

"It will buy us time if they get here before you've had time to heal," he said. "But we really can't stay here long."

Seeming to understand that was about as good as it was going to get, Rae nodded. "All right."

Ashriel did his magical scanner thing on Rae one last time, and then they left her alone to rest. She'd told them where the guest rooms were, but they wanted to check out the rest of the house before turning in. Ashriel set a barrier around the property, explaining that it would prevent anyone with bad intentions toward them from getting close. If they managed to break through, he would know immediately.

As reassuring as that was, Jillian knew better than to get too comfortable. They were still being hunted by monsters, and although Ashriel had his powers back, it was still two against one, assuming their master, Enalel, continued to stay out of it.

The last thing Ashriel asked Jillian to do was unplug any electronics she thought Rae may want to keep, including lamps. When she would have asked why, he raised an eyebrow and placed his hand on a digital clock sitting on a table. It started to flicker, making an unnatural crackling noise.

"I can suppress my energy so this doesn't happen. But if my concentration slips, things will start exploding," he said. She could sense that he wasn't using any magic at all. It was just his proximity to the clock that was affecting it.

"Right," she said, thinking about the house they'd just escaped and how unreliable the electricity had been on the rare occasions it had worked at all. She'd tried replacing both her charger and her phone when they'd broken, but nothing had worked.

He dropped his hand. The clock stopped sounding like it was cooking from the inside, but the display had gone dark. "I'd do it myself, but..." He gestured to the broken clock.

"Probably for the best," she said, deciding it was better not to question his uncharacteristic care for other people's things.

Digging her cell phone out of her pocket, she saw that the screen had cracked, undoubtedly at some point during the fight with Petrin. When it turned on, she saw there was barely any battery left. She made a quick call to her parents since she'd been out of touch for so long, careful to make sure she kept her tone cheerful and hoping they wouldn't ask too many questions. When she was done, she shut the phone off, tossed it on the coffee table in the living room, and went about unplugging everything.

Once Ashriel was confident they were safe for the moment and nothing would blow up if he let his guard down, they went back up to the second floor and headed for their rooms.

Pausing in front of her room, Ashriel turned to her. "You need rest too," he said, brushing a strand of hair behind her ear.

Debating on whether or not to push it after the day they'd all had, she bit her lip, studying his face. His gaze zeroed in on her mouth, a smoldering heat coming into his violet eyes, and the decision was made for her. Before things went any further, she needed clarification on one thing.

Taking his hand and entwining their fingers, she dragged him into her room and closed the door behind them.

The second she closed the door, Ashriel mentally ran through the fantastically exhaustive list of reasons he *hoped* she'd brought him into her room. But seeing the determined set to her shoulders and the gleam in her eye when she faced him, he quickly switched to the much shorter, much less enjoyable list of topics that came to mind next.

"Petrin said something to me," she began, and Ashriel felt the immediate urge to murder the person in question. No conversation beginning that way would end well. The only thing Petrin had to offer was poison. "Something I think I kind of suspected, but I need you to explain it to me yourself, so I'm sure I understand."

Well, this certainly didn't sound good. "Go on," he said, uneasy.

She took a deep breath, and he could tell she was bracing herself. "Do shimana take mates?"

Okay, he could work with that. It's a question he would have expected sooner or later. She was an intelligent woman. It would be obvious, even to a human who had lived their whole life without magic, that their connection meant something.

"Prasuri," he said, trying to read her reaction. "That's the shima word for *mate*."

"She said I'm your prasuri," she said, tilting her head at him. "Is that true? Is that why we're so connected, or is it my shima blood?"

"I believe you are my prasuri," he said, and just

being able to say it out loud finally felt amazing. "Magical bonds are present in bloodlines, or they can be forged through rituals." He'd spent so long keeping his distance, now that he could get close to her, he couldn't resist. He approached her slowly, giving her time to back away as he closed the short space separating them. But she stood her ground, as always, looking at him with an impressive lack of fear for a human.

"Our bond has grown on its own, naturally. Telepathy, sharing magical energy, and you showing the very beginning of jahuni characteristics." He stopped within arm's reach of her, his gaze dropping to her left wrist. "There's a possibility that we bear matching marks on our wrists. These are all part of the developing bond we share."

"So it's another spell," she said, sounding a little disappointed. Meeting her eyes again, he found her frowning slightly, and he immediately understood what she meant.

He shook his head, smiling slightly. "You know me better than that by now," he said with a chuckle. "I don't respond well to being controlled. The magic makes us aware of each other, and draws us together, but the choice to complete the bond is ultimately ours. Even magic cannot force love where there is none."

He tried to ignore the pang in his chest. It was clear she felt the same attraction as him, but love was another thing entirely. Could she come to love him? "You can reject the bond and go back to living normally, as a human, if that's what you really want."

She took a deep breath, as she always did before

she stepped out of her comfort zone. "I don't see any marks."

"It only appears at the touch of your prasuri, or after you're fully bonded with them," he said, clenching his hands at his sides to keep from reaching for her. "When we offer ourselves to our partner, there are traditional words we say." He kept a firm leash on himself. She needed to know what she was getting herself into before they went any further. "That's when we check for the mark. Just grabbing another's wrist without permission is considered invasive and rude."

She laughed softly, raising an eyebrow. "You're worried about being polite?"

"Only with you," he said, smirking. "There's no denying I want you, but bonding yourself to me is something you really need to think about. You would become immortal and take on my jahuni aspect."

"Wait, wait, wait," she said, holding up a hand. "Does that mean—"

"Eventually, after a hundred or so years of practice, you could transform into a full jahuni form, like I can?" He grinned, loving the stunned look on her face. "Absolutely."

She dropped her hand, and after a moment of contemplation, she squared her shoulders. "Say the words."

Taken aback, he tried to wipe the incredulous look off his face, but couldn't quite manage it. "Do you realize you're asking me to propose to you, more or less?" He grinned. "Take me to dinner first."

She blushed, laughing nervously. "I just wanted to see if we have the mark," she said, and he found her embarrassment endearing. He could sense the indecision in her, but it wasn't in her nature to turn away from the conversation now that they'd started down this path. "I may not understand it all yet, but I trust you when you say I can think about it."

"I have waited over three hundred years to say the words," he said, and almost laughed at the way her eyes widened at that. "I'll keep waiting until you've put thought into what they mean. If you truly are my prasuri, just saying the ritual words to propose would connect us more deeply. This is the kind of life-altering decision you shouldn't just jump into out of curiosity. Later on, going through with the bonding ritual to fully become my prasuri would change you. You would no longer be human."

"It's weird to hear you saying something so reasonable," she said, trying to ease the tension between them with a joke. "I was kind of expecting you to say eff it and just go for it."

He laughed. "I'm an ass, but even I have to draw the line somewhere," he said, and then extended his left wrist to her in invitation. "You know I'm a big fan of breaking rules, though, among other things, so find out for yourself if I bear a mark, if that helps you decide. But don't ask for the words again until you've fully considered what you're committing to."

She gave him a searching look. "I'm sorry," she said after a moment, as if she could see right through him. She must have guessed what he wasn't saying. A shima offering their wrist to their partner was a very personal and meaningful thing. "I didn't realize what I was asking—"

Before she could second-guess herself further, he grabbed her hand and gently wrapped it around his wrist. "It doesn't matter," he said, holding her surprised gaze. He could feel energy moving between them where they touched, and it felt natural, right. "I'm already sure."

He waited with bated breath as she stared down at her hand, clasped over the inside of his left wrist. Part of him was afraid to move, or even to speak. He was scared that if he even blinked, she might change her mind and just walk away. Rationally, he knew that her being curious wasn't the same as her agreeing to be his prasuri. But it would at least be a place to start.

Seeming to come to some kind of decision, she loosened her grip, trailing her fingertips over his skin. Magic moved between them, and his wrist grew warm as the skin darkened like a birthmark, forming a faint circular pattern, curves and lines intertwining inside it like an intricate knot.

Unable to help himself, he pulled her close and captured her lips, swallowing the sound of surprise she made. The satisfaction he felt at seeing the mark finally appear—after *centuries*—

was beyond anything he'd imagined. She wrapped her arms around him, and he didn't release her until they were both breathless.

She laughed softly when he pulled away slightly, resting his forehead against hers and closing his eyes. "Enough for today," he said, trying to regain control. "I intend to give you time to think, but I'm not the best at self-restraint."

"For the record, I'm totally fine if you restrain yourself less," she said, and he wondered if she was some kind of closet sadist.

Crowding her space, he kissed her again, resting

his hands on her hips as he walked her backward. She wound her arms around him as her back came up against the bedroom door, exploring his body with her hands as greedily as he did hers.

He was on the verge of shredding clothes with his bare hands when he broke away again. Her gazing up at him with flushed cheeks and kiss swollen lips was not helping matters. “Be careful what you ask of me, naori,” he said teasingly, brushing her cheek with the backs of his knuckles. “I will give you anything you want.”

She laughed, eyes narrowing seductively. “You'll do whatever I say?”

“If it means I get to touch you and do unspeakable things to you, abso-fucking-lutely,” he said, completely without shame. “I think you've proven by now I'm not above begging when it comes to you.”

“Then—”

“You're killing me. You know that, don't you?” he said, quickly circumventing whatever she was about to say because he knew exactly where this was headed, and he was at the end of his limited capacity to deny himself. “At least take tonight and let me believe you've thought about this. Again, I proudly acknowledge that I'm an ass, but I don't want to feel like I'm taking advantage of you not understanding the gravity of shima bonding rituals.”

“If you say so,” she said with the kind of obvious reluctance that made him feel immeasurably stupid for insisting on taking the damned high ground. She knew exactly what she was doing, sliding her hands up his chest and gently pushing to put a little space between them. "But don't think I'm going to forget that you offered me anything I want."

"This is it. This is how I die," he said as she left the circle of his arms with an alluring smile, and every cell of his body responded with an all-consuming, fiery desire.

"So, what's our next move?" she said, and he watched her saunter away from him. His brain was so fogged with lust it took him a moment to interpret what she'd said in any way not involving her naked. She turned to look at him, tilting her head. "Are you paying attention?"

"Yep."

"To the conversation?"

"Nope."

She laughed, clearly enjoying herself. "While I'm thinking deeply of my life choices, what should we do about Odath and Petrin? I doubt they'll just leave us alone." Although she was still smiling, the mention of their enemies sobered her a little.

He blew out a breath, forcing himself to focus. "First, we need to find out if Noren and Hasenda can be trusted," he said, considering their options. "I need to know if it's only Odath and Petrin after us or if there are others in town we need to worry about."

"I want to go with you," she said immediately, and he gritted his teeth.

"What have I said about gleefully hurling yourself at death at every damned opportunity?" he said, narrowing his eyes. "Stop it. We don't know yet if they can be trusted, and you barely survived a fight with one shima. I'm not leading you into a potential battle with two others."

She opened her mouth to say something, considered, then shut it. After a moment, she nodded, crossing her arms over her chest. "Fine."

He narrowed his eyes, knowing better. She never agreed to keep her nose out of a situation so easily. Especially, for some reason, any situation that could lead to her immediate death. "You should rest now too."

"Sounds good," she said far too easily for his liking.

Approaching her, he planted a kiss on her lips and glared at her from close range. "Seriously, don't do anything to get yourself killed overnight."

"Will do," she said, again way too agreeably. "Er, won't do, I mean."

He sighed. "Tying you to the bed is becoming more tempting by the second," he said, and was about to stalk from the room when she caught his hand.

When he looked back at her, she gave his hand a gentle pull. "Stay—"

The last of his composure snapped and she barely got the first word out before he turned and ducked to wrap his arms around her hips, lifting her off her feet and drawing a surprised sound from her somewhere between a squeal and a giggle. Her arms went around his neck while he quickly moved to the bed, her laughter filling his ears as she clung to him.

"I was trying to give you space," he said, gently tossing her on the bed.

She landed with a little bounce, eyes sparkling with amusement, and immediately opened her arms to him. "Don't need it."

Not sure if he wanted to curse or laugh, he climbed onto the bed beside her and dragged her close. "Good," he said as she snuggled her back to his front, magic and energy moving comfortably between them. For the first time since he'd been captured by Enalel, he let himself relax.

It went unspoken between them, but he could sense that she needed the comfort of his presence as much as he needed hers. They'd almost lost each other. If Banen hadn't helped him break free, or if Petrin had been alone with Jillian just a few minutes longer...

"Don't think about it right now," she said, interrupting the dark train of his thoughts. Taking the hand he had splayed against her stomach and pulling it up so she could plant a kiss against his palm, she easily brought his attention back to the moment. "There's plenty of time to worry tomorrow."

"I don't worry," he said, kissing the curve where her neck met her shoulder and lightly giving it a playful bite. "I break things until the problem is solved."

She laughed, clasping the hand she'd kissed and hugging it to her chest. Despite what he said, he realized this really was the first time he could hold her without being on high alert. There was no one to snatch her away. No danger lurking nearby.

Content to live in the moment, he held on to her until they both drifted off.

CHAPTER TWENTY-ONE

Shima realm
The throne room in the city of Orilia

PETRIN KNELT BEFORE ENALEL, HER head bowed, knowing this was not going to go well for her. After her fight with the Sijo, she hadn't been prepared to fight Ashriel at his full strength. She'd failed Enalel on two counts, which was an extremely dangerous position to be in. She could practically *feel* Odath silently gloating beside her because he'd had nothing to do with either event, and swore to herself she'd kill the disgusting little bootlicker the second she had an excuse.

"Not only did you fail to kill Banen," Enalel said disdainfully, her voice carrying a deathly quiet edge to it. She could feel the weight of Enalel's cold gray eyes resting on her, but didn't dare raise her head. "You lost the Kretore warrior as well. Now both of them are on the loose and could be anywhere."

"I have Ashriel's dagger with his teleport stone in it," Petrin said, beat-up armor creaking as she flipped the edge of her cloak open to show the dagger strapped to her weapon belt at her waist. "He can't cross the barrier without it, and I've taken his blood, so I can still track him."

There was no way to form another gegaji with Ashriel without him present, so it was the best Petrin could do. She was afraid it wouldn't be enough for Enalel, however, or Enalel's master.

"You'd better pray that you can," Enalel said, a distinct growl in her voice. Petrin knew it was the displeasure of their master, whoever he was, that was putting Enalel so on edge. Remembering his fiery-haired messenger, she couldn't blame Enalel. He was not a man one would ever want to disappoint. Luckily, he'd laid enough false trails to keep the Junak busy for a century. "Raising the tension between the cities is necessary moving forward, and to do that we need this to go as planned, without raising the suspicion of the Junak or the attention of Kronen."

Kronen, the most ancient and powerful shima, and Jiru of Iseyba, was the only one who could really ruin their plans completely. Humiv could always plot other ways to get the different Jiruna at each other's throats, but having Kronen involve himself too soon could be catastrophic to their plans.

"I'll stop Ashriel before he can find a way back to the shima realm," Petrin said.

"Maybe this time I should go after him," Odath interjected, and Petrin gritted her teeth at his overly pleasant, ass-kissing tone.

"I have other plans for you," Enalel said, dismissing his request, and Petrin smirked to herself. "You will pursue Banen. He may be back in the shima realm, but he's still always a step ahead. Track him down and bring him to me. Dead or alive, it doesn't matter anymore. Kill anyone who gets in your way. He can't make it to the Junak."

"Consider it done," he said, and Petrin rolled her eyes.

Enalel's next words rang through the quiet throne room, sending a chill of apprehension through Petrin. "If either of you fail me again, you will pay very dearly."

It took two full days for Rae to wake up on her own. Jillian had begun to worry that she might not be healing correctly or that Odath and Petrin had hurt her so badly that she couldn't recover. Only Ashriel's assurances kept her from rushing Rae to the hospital.

"Human doctors can't do anything for her," he said for what was probably the dozenth time, but Jillian couldn't help but worry. "Besides, that'll be one of the main places they keep an eye on. Humans don't regenerate like shimana do, so it would only make sense that you and Rae would end up there at some point to get treated." She opened her mouth to argue. He raised a hand to stop her. "Healing magic is not my strength, but you know I like Rae at least enough to ensure she doesn't die. If she were in danger, I would do what I had to do."

She looked away from him to hide her smile. "Okay." He liked to act tough, but she knew he really did consider Rae a friend.

Rae, finally up on her feet again, was busily weeding her garden to distract herself. They'd tried to get her to rest more, but she'd insisted she needed some fresh air. Although Ashriel didn't say as much, Jillian knew he was keeping an eye on Rae to make sure she didn't overdo it.

"She's strong for a human," he said, watching Rae as she worked. "She'll be all right."

Sitting beside him on the steps of the porch, she studied his profile. "Can I ask you something?"

Leaning back on his hands, he gave her a sideways look, head tilted. "I think we've covered that you can ask me anything," he said, a teasing smile turning up the corners of his mouth.

Feeling herself blush, she narrowed her eyes at him. "I won't be distracted."

"Pity," he said.

Biting her lip, she tried to shake off years of *knowing* magic didn't exist. "So dragons are real." Even with the memory of him covered in metallic scales, with horns and wings, fresh in her memory, she felt silly saying this out loud.

He nodded, raising an eyebrow. "Yes?"

"And vampires and faeries?"

Knowing she was floundering, his grin got bigger, and she had the urge to punch him in the arm. "Yes?"

"So are other things real too?"

"You're going to have to be a little more specific," he said innocently. "What kinds of things?"

Sighing, she playfully slapped his arm lightly with the back of her hand. "I'm new to this, but you're not going to make this easy on me, are you?"

"Absolutely not," he said cheerfully. When she narrowed her eyes at him, he merely smiled patiently and waited.

"What about witches?"

"Real."

"Do they—"

"No cauldrons, no brooms," he said, laughing.

"What about garlic and vampires?"

He sighed dramatically. "*One* guy has an allergy, and it's recorded for all time."

"Crosses?"

"Shimana are actually very spiritual in general, regardless of aspect," he said, totally serious. "We believe we're all following the same God, but in different ways and by different names. Our spiritual path closely resembles Christianity, and although we don't wear jewelry until we find our prasuri, we do have crosses embroidered in the designs of many of our garments or carved into beads some of us wear in our hair."

"No jewelry?" she said, surprised.

"Only one piece that we wear once we're bonded with our prasuri," he said, watching her in a way that had heat creeping into her cheeks again. Sitting forward again, he reached over to trail his fingertips across the inside of her left forearm and down toward her hand. The mark appeared on her inner wrist, and he smiled with a gentleness she wasn't used to seeing in him. "Enchanted to become whatever we wish to wear." He started drawing lazy circles across her skin, raising goosebumps on her arm. "Not that I mind, but why so curious about the aspects today?"

"I want to learn everything I can," she said, glancing down at his hand, unable to contain a slight shiver. "I can't make a decision until I know what I'm getting into, right?"

Stopping the movement of his hand with her own, she intertwined their fingers and lowered their joined hands to her knees. Smoothing the palm of her free hand over the back of his, she traced her fingers along the backs of his until his hand was clasped between both of hers.

His hands had protected her. Fought for her. Driven her crazy with their surprising gentleness. In her heart, something had been growing for a long time, and she might already have an answer for him.

Feeling his gaze on her, she looked up at him. He watched her silently. His expression was unreadable.

Ashriel cleared his throat, glancing down at their joined hands. "I was just thinking of all the other things I could teach you," he said teasingly, lifting his gaze to hers with a heated look. "The many things I would like to show you."

Oh, she was very sure there were many, many things he could teach her. Anytime. Any place. On any surface.

Seeming to sense the direction her thoughts were taking, he tugged gently on her hands, drawing her closer until her thigh pressed against his. Eagerly leaning toward him, she anticipated the feel of his lips on hers.

There was a needy edge to his kiss as their lips met. No teasing this time. Just the full force of his desire washing over her, answering her own and building on it until she was ready to crawl onto his lap.

She heard his low groan, and then, mid-make out session, an image flashed through Jillian's mind, vivid and intoxicating, and she knew these were Ashriel's desires. Her thighs parting as she straddled him. Her palm pushing him down onto the porch.

Totally on board with what he wanted, she sucked on his bottom lip and nibbled persuasively before her tongue passed his lips again, intent on torturing him. She reveled in his helpless shudder, ready for more.

Rae cleared her throat loudly, reminding her that they weren't alone, and this wasn't their porch. Blushing so hard she was afraid she'd catch fire, Jillian pulled away from Ashriel, dazed, to see Rae standing there, openly amused.

"When exactly did this become a thing?" she asked, raising an eyebrow at them as she shifted the basket of vegetables she was carrying to one hip.

"How are the..." Ashriel eyed the basket of vegetables dubiously. "Whatever all that is?"

"The whatevers are ready to be prepped for dinner," she said, laughing at his blatant attempt to change the subject. "And don't think I won't get details out of Jillian, because I will."

Jillian fanned her face, trying to get her mind out of the gutter. "What's for dinner?"

"Mmm hmm," Rae hummed, grinning knowingly. "I see you trying to dodge too, but it's no use. Anyway—" she drew out the word as she eyed them both "—when are we going to Hasenda and Noren's?"

Jillian met Ashriel's scowl head on, knowing he wasn't going to like this new turn to the conversation. "They've been like family to her since she was born," she said, feeling like she should probably explain herself. "She needed to know what was going on."

"Rather than trying to get yourselves killed for the hundredth time, you should both go somewhere safe now that Rae's well enough," Ashriel said, looking back at Rae with a withering glare as he attempted to talk some sense into them. "Odath and Petrin can easily find us right now."

Apparently, it was a hopeless endeavor.

"Noren and Hasenda are family," Rae said, as if that should settle everything. "I'm going nowhere until I talk to them."

"I don't want to be caught by Odath and Petrin either," Jillian chimed in, not helping matters at all. "But Rae needs to do this."

"Neither of you are going," he repeated, narrowing his eyes at Jillian. As usual, she wasn't the least bit fazed.

"You going to mind control us like the others did?" Rae said, no real malice in her voice.

A tic started in his jaw. "You know better."

"Exactly," she said, shooting a wink at Jillian and patting him on the shoulder as she moved around them to climb the steps to the back door. "So when are we going?" She threw the last words over her shoulder, obviously not intimidated by the glare he shot at her back.

Gajano took a deep breath as he left the empty house in the human realm, Navin at his side. She looked as disgusted and nauseated as he felt.

The place was full of dark magic and spell marks for binding, draining, and mind control. Whoever had placed the marks had cursed the place so that it continuously shifted, hiding the caster's secrets.

One secret they'd found easily, however. The sacrificial chamber beneath the house.

"I need a bath," she groaned beside him, looking down at her spotless silvery-white armor as though it were covered in something so disturbing it was beyond words. "And possibly the cleansing fires of Iseyba to melt down my armor and make me a new set. I'll never get the stink of that place off me, otherwise."

"Agreed," he said, uncomfortably aware of the cloying dark magic that stained his energy and clung to his own black armor as well. It was an insidious kind of power, and it left a nasty mark on everything it touched. The darker the spells, the worse it was, and as a sathra, the aspect with the highest natural concentration of dark energy, he would need to thoroughly cleanse himself to rid himself of the taint. "I could smell blood everywhere we went, both human and shima."

"Whatever was going on here ended days ago," she said, eyeing the house as though she thought it would grab her and pull her back inside. Her gaze followed some invisible line he couldn't see around the house, and she frowned. "No one has reinforced the spells recently, and the air feels stale."

Wrapped in cloth and tucked away inside an inner pocket in his black cloak, he carried the evidence of a broken gegaji in the form of a shattered pendant. Just having it so close to his body gave him the chills. "You have all the readings you need?"

She nodded, showing him a handful of glowing crystal vials before she tucked them inside her white cloak. "We need to keep moving," she said, again analyzing energy patterns he couldn't see himself, her gaze wandering off into the woods.

With a flick of her wrist, white light filled the house. It shone through the windows and the still-open front door, nearly blinding, and he had to shield his eyes. He felt the impact in the air, a small light explosion, and the loud crumbling of the structure as it collapsed into a pile of rubble and burst into bluish-white flames. The white fire of purification would cleanse the cursed remains of the house, and the corrupted land it had sat on.

He knew it was necessary, and they couldn't allow any humans to wander in or for Humiv to return to such a place and use it again, but he got the sneaking suspicion she had enjoyed that. As a tifire aspect, she was especially vulnerable to the sickening effect of dark magic.

"Feel better?" he asked, chuckling as he lowered his hand.

She didn't even bother to deny it. A wide grin spread across her innocent face. "Much," she said, then turned on her heel and beckoned for him to follow her down whatever trail she'd found leading into the woods and away from the darkness of the house.

CHAPTER TWENTY-TWO

Ashriel stood on the back porch later that evening, reinforcing the protective barrier he'd placed around Rae's house. The tension of waiting for Enalel's next move was getting to him. He wanted to be out searching for evidence of whatever she was doing, and finding a way back to the shima realm, but he was stuck babysitting his damned humans.

Now I have two humans throwing themselves directly in the path of their own death, he thought tiredly. It was no wonder they got along so well. Neither seemed to have any sense of self-preservation where his kind was concerned.

Noren and Hasenda sounded like they could be potential allies, but he wasn't ready to risk either Rae's or Jillian's lives on that gamble. Not that either of them was listening. That would just make his life too damned easy.

It wasn't uncommon for shimana to come to the human realm, especially those who had given up their immortality to age as humans. They tended to live in fairly unpopulated areas, since it wasn't always easy to suppress their energy, but as long as they hid their powers and blended in, it was fine. It sounded as though Noren and Hasenda had integrated themselves well, living lives that didn't attract either human or shima attention, but that didn't mean they could automatically be trusted.

He was so lost in speculation that he nearly missed the soft sound of someone approaching behind him. He didn't have to turn to know who it was, though. He could feel Jillian's presence now, even more than he could before. The connection between them had grown stronger, and it was to the point where it was second nature to reach out to her in his mind.

Her perfume reached him first, a delicate blend of some kind of flowers and the soap she used. He closed his eyes to savor it. That was all it took. Just her nearness was enough to make him ache to touch her.

This was what he had waited his whole life to feel. What he had nearly given up on ever finding. Now that he had it, what could he do to keep it? How could he protect her?

He knew he should be taking things slow with her. It was a litany he told himself about a billion times a day, but he had never been very good at being patient when he wanted something.

The gentle touch of her hand on his shoulder had his pulse speeding up. It was a perfectly innocent action, but to someone who was only vaguely aware that such a word as restraint existed, it was like a match to gasoline.

"Brooding again?" she teased, her hand trailing down along his arm as she came around to stand beside him. "Is there anything I can do to help take your mind off whatever it is?"

Ashriel clenched his teeth and had to wait a long moment before he could answer. He gave her a measuring look, telling himself she couldn't possibly be aware that she was torturing him, but the mischievous smile that played around her lips said otherwise.

His gaze traveled hungrily over her body. She wore her hair loose tonight, falling in gentle waves over her shoulders. A white spaghetti-strap shirt and tight blue jeans hugged every curve, making his mouth go dry.

"You prefer me destroying things?" he asked to distract himself, flashing her a wicked smile. "I'm sure I could find some fields to burn somewhere."

"I thought only half of what's in our legends is true?" she teased.

"Well," he murmured, tilting his head. "I have to admit I have a weakness for sacrifices." Gently pulling her over to him, he backed her up against the railing of the porch, resting his hands on either side of her to cage her in. "Are you going to be my sacrifice?" he whispered, leaning nearer until their bodies were so close he could feel the warmth that emanated from her.

Her hands moved up along his arms, to rest on his shoulders. "Hmm," she said, considering. "It doesn't sound so bad when you say it like that."

It was a very clear invitation that he didn't need to hear twice. With something close to a growl, he captured her lips in a deep kiss, his hands rough and possessive on her hips, dragging her against him to press her against his hardness.

She gasped in surprise, but his kiss swallowed the sound. She slid her arms up and around him, one hand tangling in his hair.

He drew away from her slightly. "You know," he

said, his voice a low rumble against her mouth. He trailed kisses along her jaw toward her ear. "To do this whole sacrifice thing properly would require restraints of some sort." He nibbled gently on her ear then, his arms encircling her.

She laughed softly, and he felt her shiver in his embrace as he began to kiss his way down along her neck. "When you say it like that..."

With a soft sigh, he inhaled the scent in her hair. "I want to show you something," he said softly, turning her in his arms until her back was pressed up against his chest, her head resting back against his shoulder. He curled his arms around her waist, lowering his head to nip playfully at her shoulder.

"Mmm hmm," she sighed, tilting her head to the side to give him better access as she covered his hands with her own to intertwine their fingers, and he knew he was in serious trouble.

Nuzzling her neck gently, he savored the way she melted into him. "This is important," he murmured, nibbling gently at the spot where her neck met her shoulder. "Do I have your attention?"

"Completely," she said, and he could hear the smile in her voice.

"Close your eyes," he whispered against her ear. "And share your mind with me."

"Okay," she said, opening her mind to him without hesitation, and he led her awareness to the things he wanted her to feel. The low, humming energy all around them. In the trees, plants, and dirt. Even the house itself.

"The energy of the earth," he said. "Of nature and life."

"It's in everything," she said, sounding awed.

Leading her mind still, he showed her the distinct energy around each of them. Thick, like water almost, pulsing and swirling around them as they met, intertwined, and broke apart again.

"Our energy," he whispered. "The energy of a person or animal is always thicker. Stronger. Easier to pick out."

"Beautiful," she said, seemingly content to just experience what he was showing her.

"Breathe, and imagine spreading your awareness to everything in your surroundings," he said, helping her learn how to fan out her senses, like fingers searching for something. He showed her the human presence in the house. Rae came into focus, and the awareness became a brief vision.

Rae, humming to herself as she put away the leftovers from dinner. Plates and glasses stacked in the sink, ready to be washed. The pale, sunny, yellow paint on the walls. The sound of the radio in the background.

Next, he led her senses out farther. There was the familiar hum of nature's energy. The pulse of theirs. He became aware of small animals in the woods around them. Then, like the shimmering threads of a spider's web, he showed her the little lines of energy all around them. It was like a globe surrounding the house and the land several yards out in any direction. The lines glowed dimly in the blackness, crossing and intertwining until there wasn't any empty space in the web.

"Concentrate now," he whispered, continuing to lead her so she could learn to do this herself. "Reach out with your mind."

He helped her reach out to the web, a tingle of

magical energy moving through them as they worked. More glowing lines began to fan out in her mind, a little dimmer than the rest. They followed the lines Ashriel had set down, weaving between them. Strengthening them until the web was a solid wall of pale light.

"You've added your power to mine, strengthening the spell and protecting this place alongside me," he said, impressed by how quickly she caught on. "No one meaning us harm will be able to pass through this protective barrier without breaking it."

"That's amazing," she breathed, and he brought their awareness back to themselves, allowing her mind to relax. "But it makes me nervous that you're showing me a way to protect myself right now."

"Whether I'm here or not, the barrier I placed around the house will still work. But it makes me feel better if you know how to do this yourself and understand a little of how it works," he said, and then sighed against her hair. "I can't wait any longer to look into Hasenda and Noren."

"Rae and I are ready to go with you," she said, shifting a little to glare challengingly at him over her shoulder. She seemed to sense his denial before he actually spoke, and he was half proud, half exasperated.

"I can't put you in danger again," he said, unable to help the roughness in his voice. He still remembered how helpless he'd felt when she'd been under Odath and Petrin's mind control, or when she'd been hurt by them, and a gut-wrenching fear settled in his chest.

"You won't be able to concentrate on defending yourself if I'm there," she said after a long moment, sensing where his mind was going.

There was a long silence. "I've never been afraid

before," he said finally, remembering the searing pain he'd sensed in her when her arm had been dislocated during his battle with Petrin. "Not like that."

"Stop it. I'm here now, with you, and I'm all right." Jillian settled her body back against his again. She stroked her thumbs over his comfortingly. "But how do you think I feel?" she asked softly. "Knowing what they did to you before?"

Ashriel suddenly saw himself through her eyes. The pain on his face as he was compelled to hunt Banen. His body covered in bloody wounds as Petrin attacked him, and him without a weapon.

"If this were Odath and Petrin we were talking about, I wouldn't ask," she persisted. "But at least with Noren and Hasenda, two people who have been close friends of Rae's family since before she was born, let us be there. I don't see it turning into a battle."

"You're far too trusting," Ashriel said darkly.

"I promise we'll stay far back, like good little humans fully aware of how squishable we are," she said, trying to ease his fear.

He got that he was being overprotective. Hasenda and Noren would have done something horrible long before now if they were involved with Enalel. But that wasn't much of a comfort when up against Jillian's safety.

"I'll consider it," he relented, attempting to be reasonable even though letting her anywhere near possible danger went against all of his instincts.

He was still very aware of her body, warm against his. Her curves fitting so perfectly against him. Their energies combined as she happily relaxed against him again, swirling together and intertwining like lovers.

Slipping one of his hands beneath the hem of her shirt to smooth over bare skin of her abdomen, he lowered his head to kiss her neck again, his need eating away at him. He wanted her so badly that he was nearly shaking with the force of it. He knew he should release her, and insist she go inside, but he wasn't sure he had the strength left to do it.

"You should go in now," Ashriel whispered against her skin, making no move to release her.

Jillian lifted a hand over her head, tangling it in his hair as he swirled his tongue over a sensitive spot just below her ear. "Probably," she agreed shakily, but she wasn't about to stop him.

Sliding his other hand out of her grasp, he trailed his fingers lazily over the waistband of her jeans. His fingertips snagged on the button and she couldn't help the way she shivered in anticipation.

"Tell me to back off," he said, his voice hoarse. "Because I don't do the whole willpower thing." There was a note of possessiveness in his voice. A very clear warning. "Unless you push me away, I can't make myself let go of you."

"So don't," she said without hesitation, and she felt him grow still.

"You need to—"

"I thought about it, like you told me to," she said.

"It's only been a couple days."

"It's been a month since we met," she corrected him. "I've wanted you since the beginning, even when you were breaking things."

"You have terrible taste," he said, laughing even as he tightened his hold briefly.

"I know. But you said you would give me anything I want, right?" she said softly, turning in his embrace to face him. "So I want you." Sliding her arms up and around him, her mouth found his.

Groaning, his hands started moving. Down her back and over her hips. Cupping her bottom and tugging her against him. She snuggled her body close to him, silently offering everything.

"If you don't leave me now," he warned, his voice rough with need, and she could feel the barely leashed tension in him.

She briefly remembered protection, or the lack thereof, but just as quickly dismissed it. She had her answer. She would be his mate, and she accepted everything that entailed. She could tell he heard the train of her thoughts because his hold on her tightened a little bit.

"I don't want to," she whispered, urging him on. "I want this, Ashriel. I want you." She kissed him deeply then, offering up all the feelings that whirled chaotically inside her. "Please—"

The word had barely passed her lips before he swept her up in his arms, carrying her inside the house and up the stairs so fast that everything around them was a blur.

She could sense that he was done denying himself, and she'd never been so thrilled to push someone to their breaking point before. The gnawing desire she had felt for him from the very beginning had built to the point of making her crazy, and she could feel the same urgency in him.

When they reached her room, he kicked the door closed behind them and she heard the lock click even though his hands never left her. He was already kissing her again as he stopped beside the bed, letting her body slide down along his as he set her on her feet again.

Her hands shook as she began unbuttoning his shirt. Impatient, he ripped it the rest of the way, buttons flying everywhere, and threw it on the floor.

Giddy with excitement, she laughed breathlessly. “You tore it.”

“I don’t care,” he growled, and she could feel the urgency in him as he reached for her. “It was in the way.” He pulled her roughly against him, startling another heady giggle out of her as he rained kisses along the length of her neck. He found that place just below her ear that made her shudder, sucking gently at the skin there.

She lowered her arms from around his neck, pushing away just enough to flatten her hands against his chest, savoring the warmth of his skin against hers. He gasped at her touch, capturing her mouth in another ravenous kiss as her hands continued to move lower, his tongue swirling against hers in an erotic dance that left them both dizzy.

Smoothing her palms down over his abdomen, she felt the muscles clench in reaction when her nails grazed the sensitive flesh below his belly button. She promised herself that she would take her time, intent on letting her hands roam all over his warm skin and tense muscles.

She gentled their kiss, breaking off to nibble teasingly at his lips before her mouth drifted to his neck, and his hands left her to undo his jeans. She loved the low growl in his throat as her wandering hands covered his to help him shove his pants down off his hips. Lightly kissing a path down his chest, her fingers slipping from his as she tugged his jeans all the way down, she teased her way down his body as she lowered herself to her knees. Light nibbles with her teeth. Soothing swirls of her tongue when he shivered in reaction. Hands smoothing back up his calves. Nails gently dragging up the outsides of his thighs.

She curled her fingers around his rigid length, delighting in the choked sound of pleasure her touch inspired. His breath gusted out of him as she stroked him. She felt him bury his trembling fingers in her hair as she swirled her tongue around the head of his penis. In a smooth gliding motion, she took him into her mouth.

He moaned, mindlessly whispering something in his language as his head tipped back, his eyes sliding shut in ecstasy. She loved the way he trembled as she pleasured him, one of his hands fisting in her hair. It wasn't long before she sensed him teetering close to the edge, ready to explode.

Pulling away from her, he grabbed her shoulders, urgently tugging her to her feet. His mouth found hers again, kissing her deeply. "Naked," he managed, almost panting against her sensitive lips, pushing his hands beneath the material of her shirt to roam the length of her back, pressing her body close to his again. "Now. Or the clothes die a horrible death." With an impatient flick of his wrists he fisted his hands in the back of her shirt, ready to start tearing if she didn't move fast enough.

Jillian giggled and pushed away from him, her eyes greedily drinking in the sight of his naked body. It didn't matter that he wasn't human, or that he had powers she couldn't even imagine. The only thing that was important was the connection they shared. Her heart pounded in her chest as he stalked her across the room, missing his touch already, and she found herself wishing he hadn't felt the need to save her clothes. She backed away from him, and he froze, momentarily paralyzed as he watched her reach for the hem of her shirt and draw it over her head. His gaze narrowed as she dropped the shirt on the floor and took another sauntering step away from him.

A reckless kind of excitement soared through her as she knowingly pushed his restraint. The hunger in his eyes was like a physical touch as she trailed her hands sensuously down her body. Over her breasts, still covered by a lacy, white bra. Over her abdomen, raising goose bumps on her soft skin. Down to the button of her jeans. He drank in every move she made, following the movement of her fingers sliding beneath the material of her jeans and pushing them down over her hips, exposing matching panties.

His eyes had darkened with his need for her, and he watched her like a starving man, egging her on. At the edge of her own control, she extended her hand to him, coaxing him to her, and it was like she had unleashed a storm.

He moved faster than she could see again, closing the distance between them in a second. And then she was in his arms again, and he was tumbling them both onto the bed. He came down on top of her, careful not to crush her with his weight, his deft fingers finishing the job her teasing ones had abandoned. He lifted himself away from her just long enough to remove her panties, and then he settled his hips between her thighs. A hand roamed covetously over her ribs, maneuvering beneath her to unclasp her bra with surprising care.

"So cautious suddenly?" she teased. It was her turn to moan as he nuzzled one of the flimsy cups of her bra out of the way to suck on an aching nipple.

"Mmm," he agreed with an appreciative growl as her fingers threaded through his hair, holding him to her. "I like this." His voice was a dark whisper against her skin, his breath warming her nipple before he lapped at the very tip. "I want to see you in it again."

She lifted her arms complacently while he removed that last thin barrier between them. He tossed the bra away, his eyes devouring every inch of her like he couldn't get enough. Curling her legs over his hips, she lifted a hand to trail her fingertips over his lips, inviting his mouth back to hers.

Clasping her hand, he kissed the delicate pads of her fingers before twining them together with his own and lowering them to the bed. The depth of feeling behind his violet eyes mesmerized her, and he took her by surprise when he kissed her with a tenderness he'd never shown before.

"You are so beautiful," he whispered, his voice ragged against her mouth. "Hanotse navoj," he murmured as she glided her hands along his back. "Hanotse prasuri." He kissed a path to her ear, pausing to take the lobe between his teeth.

She arched beneath him, moaning low in her throat at the tingles that swept over her body. Feeling him pressing at her entrance, she almost forgot how to breathe.

"Iyo kawey eri," he whispered into her ear, thrusting into her welcoming body.

Gasping, she dug her nails into his back as he began to move, and she rolled her hips to meet him. She couldn't understand his whispered endearments, but she knew what *prasuri* meant.

"H-hanotse prasuri," she softly repeated, shuddering in ecstasy.

Despite his best intentions, he seemed to lose all control when he heard her tentative words. Their bodies moved together more urgently. He thrust harder. Deeper.

With a low growl, Ashriel captured her mouth, swallowing both of their moans. Pleasure rolled over her in waves. Building with every stroke. Every trembling breath. Every gliding touch.

Ashriel's hand tightened in hers as she got closer to her peak. Quivering beneath him, she couldn't hold back any longer. She rode out the tremors as he lengthened his strokes, touching her core as they came undone together. Release surged through them both, and they held tight to each other.

She felt their bond deepen, her mind open to him, their very souls coming together in that moment of rapture. His mouth gentled on hers as the tremors slowed, and she cradled him with her body as little aftershocks swirled through them.

It was several long moments before either of them could summon the strength to move. He buried his face against her neck, kissing her softly, and she made a satisfied noise, somewhere between a hum and a sigh.

Collapsing next to her on the bed, he pulled her close, curling himself around her back as he tugged the tangled sheets over them, and she snuggled against him with a contented sigh. Nothing else mattered as he wrapped an arm around her, kissing the nape of her neck. She could feel his smile in her mind, and for the first time since the whole ordeal with Odath and Petrin had started, she felt safe.

"So you're going to say it now, right?" she said, gazing happily at the mark on her left wrist where it laid on the pillow beside her head.

She felt the warm gust of his laugh against her neck, and he shifted so he could pull her onto her back again to face him. Propping himself up on his elbow, he gazed down at her, a smile kicking up the corner of his mouth in a lopsided grin.

"I freely offer myself to you," he said, smoothing runaway strands of hair out of her face with his free hand. "Both my light and my darkness." As he spoke, a now-familiar warmth began to spread through her body, their energies naturally reaching out to each other and mixing together to become one. It was like a part of herself was holding its breath, waiting for the rest of what he would say.

"All the rest of my days and my nights," he said, trailing his fingertips over her lips. "Now say, 'I accept and offer all that I am to you in return.'"

"I accept," she said, so happy she didn't know what to do with herself. She couldn't help her sappy smile as she reached for him and pulled him down to her for a kiss. "And offer all that I am to you in return."

"I accept," he said against her lips, and the instant he said it, she could feel their bond grow. Exchanging these words, it felt like they had exchanged a small part of themselves as well, on a spiritual, soul-deep level.

His hands moved over her body with an agonizing gentleness as he deepened their kiss, and she welcomed him eagerly as he settled himself above her again.

CHAPTER TWENTY-THREE

"MMM..." JILLIAN WOKE WITH A lazy stretch, taking stock of her sore muscles and actually feeling happy about them. She knew Ashriel was already awake even before she rolled over to find his side of the bed empty. She could easily sense him in the house now without really having to concentrate.

She smiled to herself and cracked her eyes open, squinting a little at the light streaming through the windows. Something sparkling on the pillow next to her drew her attention.

Lifting her head, she saw a slender stream of light that seemed to be suspended there. Curious, she sat up, knowing Ashriel had left this for her. Little points of light reflected off each other, forming the shape of a flower. It glittered, all different colors, hovering in front of her.

She brushed one of the petals with her fingertips, and it shattered, the little lights raining over her hand. She immediately felt warmth spread through her. Happiness. Affection. These were his emotions. The mark on her wrist tingled pleasantly.

Ridiculously happy, she showered and got dressed,

throwing on jeans and a tank top. Even the prospect of checking into Noren and Hasenda later that morning couldn't dampen her mood too much. Her instincts told her they were good people, but Ashriel needed to be sure, for all their sakes.

Pulling her hair back, she studied herself in the mirror, wondering if she should be wearing camo instead or something. Not that it would help, considering the people in question would be able to sense her presence anyway.

Feeling optimistic, despite the challenges ahead, she wandered downstairs to the kitchen, following the smell of breakfast. Unlike Odath and Petrin's house, Rae's was so warm and inviting it felt like home already. It was refreshing after being locked up in the gloominess of the other place.

Early morning light streamed through all the windows, giving a cheery feel to the house. There were a lot of antiques and pieces of furniture that had belonged to Rae's grandparents, mixed with a few more modern touches Rae had added, resulting in a charming hodgepodge of styles.

When she entered the kitchen, Ashriel was at the stove for once, checking the scrambled eggs in the skillet on the burner in front of him. Moving up behind him, she wrapped her arms around his waist.

"'Morning," he murmured, lowering the heat and setting the spatula he was holding aside. Turning he wrapped his arms around her, kissing the top of her head.

"Good morning," she said brightly, nuzzling her cheek against his chest and breathing him in. "You're cooking?"

"While Rae's on the phone with her family, far away from me and what she calls my *weird shima electricity thing*," he said, sounding amused. In comparison to how he'd been at Odath and Petrin's, seeing him doing something so normal and mundane was hard to get used to.

"I loved the flower," she said, and sensed his smile. Smoothing her hands down his back, she thought vividly of all the ways she'd like to show him just how good she felt this morning. She knew at least some of the images in her mind made it across when she felt him tense, growling low in her ear, his arms tightening around her.

"Go. Sit," he said with a chuckle, gently disentangling her and turning her toward the table. "Otherwise, you're going to end up right back where you started."

Sauntering over to the table, she shot him a heated glance, mentally replaying a few specific moments of their night together in her mind for him. "Promise?" she said, enjoying her effect on him.

His violet eyes seemed to catch on fire as he watched her, and her breath came a little faster as heat crashed through her. She could feel his desire, intoxicating her. Leaning back against the counter, hands clenched on the edge like he was stopping himself from going to her, he gave her a slow, predatory smile. Holding her gaze, he reached for her with his mind.

Her breath caught when she felt a ghostly hand shackle her wrist. He remained where he was, hands anchored to the counter still, his expression smoldering. "You really should eat some breakfast," he said, his voice dark with promise as that invisible hand began to softly inch its way up the inside of her forearm. "You're going to need your strength."

The sensation faded just as it reached the inside of her elbow, leaving her breathing a little faster than she had been before.

"Good morning!" Rae said brightly, marching into the kitchen, her sudden presence surprising Jillian out of her lust-fogged trance. "Breakfast will be ready in a few."

It took a moment before Jillian could respond in a normal voice. "Good morning," she said distractedly, her eyes devouring Ashriel as he turned to get the plates out for Rae. "Thanks." She tried to calm her racing heart as Rae handed her a glass of orange juice. She raised it to her lips, watching Ashriel over the rim as she took a drink.

Ashriel piled a plate with food, much more than she could eat, and set it in front of her with a wicked look that made her choke.

Rae gave her a concerned look. "You okay?" she asked as Jillian continued to sputter and cough, her face turning red as she grabbed for a napkin.

Jillian nodded with an embarrassed smile, waiting until Rae turned her back again to glare at Ashriel over her napkin.

"Are you feeling all right?" Ashriel asked, all innocence as he sat across the table from her.

Jillian narrowed her eyes at him. Had she imagined the slight emphasis he put on the word *feeling*?

"You felt fine last night," he continued in a conversational tone, thoroughly enjoying himself as Jillian's eyes widened. "I can't wait to taste—" He took a deliberately long swallow of his orange juice in the middle of his sentence "—this breakfast, Rae." His eyes burned into Jillian, and it was clear he was enjoying his little game.

"It's nothing fancy," Rae said over her shoulder with a good-natured laugh, completely unaware as she put a plate together for herself. "I need more ingredients."

Jillian clamped her lips together to stop a moan as that phantom hand returned to trail along the inside of her knee. She gasped softly as it inched dangerously higher, and Ashriel covered the sound with a well-timed cough.

Narrowing her eyes at him, she envisioned Rae's shocked face and herself climbing over the table to attack him, clothes and dishes flying everywhere, and it was his turn to choke.

He silently held up his hands in a gesture of truce as Rae finally came to sit with them.

Jillian watched him carefully through breakfast, but he behaved himself for the most part, aside from a few teasing glances at her plate.

As they finished their breakfasts, a tense silence settled between the three of them. They all knew what was coming next, and none of them were looking forward to it for various reasons.

Rae grabbed their empty plates and took them to the sink, probably looking for something to distract herself, and Ashriel sighed.

"Before we go, I need both of you to promise me something," he said, sounding weary and resigned.

Rae turned away from the sink, drying her hands on a towel, and glanced at Jillian. It was new and strange to her, but she knew the anxiety she was sensing was Rae's.

"We're going with you," Jillian said, ready for an argument as she shifted her attention to Ashriel. *"Rae can't just sit here, wringing her hands, while you confront some of her oldest friends,"* she said across their link.

Jillian heard his mental sigh loud and clear. *"Don't worry. I've given up on convincing either of you to act logically here."* He glanced between the two of them, saying the rest out loud. "Do *nothing* to attract attention to yourselves," he said, as if this wasn't obvious. "If I tell you to run, you do it. No heroics. No doing anything stupid that ends with either of you dead." He glared hard at Jillian. "You are no match for a shima. Do not attempt to help me fight anyone."

"Got it," Rae said, and Jillian sensed her fear skyrocket. She couldn't tell for sure, but she thought Rae's fear was probably more for her friends than herself.

Biting her lip to keep from pointing out that she'd helped last time, Jillian nodded. "Of course," she said, and Ashriel's eyes immediately narrowed on her as if he knew what she'd been thinking.

"Tying you up really is more tempting every second," he said telepathically.

Knowing this was not the time to get caught up in an argument with him, she got up and led the way out of the kitchen. Quickly heading for the front door before he could change his mind, Jillian snagged Rae's car keys from the little entryway table and held them out to her. "Let's go."

Ashriel had made it clear that, while it was possible if all shima parties suppressed their natural magical energy so as not to accidentally fry their phones, talking that way wouldn't give him what he needed to trust the other two shimana. He needed to get a sense for them in person. Something about their energy. She may not have understood it completely, but she got that it was important to him.

Squaring her shoulders, the usually cheerful Rae took the keys with a serious look on her face. For better or worse, they were about to find out just who Rae's friends really were.

The drive to Noren and Hasenda's was short, but it felt like hours to Jillian with the way Ashriel was silently brooding in the back seat, arms crossed as he glared at the back of her head. *"Have I mentioned that this is a terrible fucking idea?"* he grumbled across their bond, and she could feel the tension in him too.

"We'll stay out of your way. I promise," Jillian tried to reassure him, but she had to admit even she was on edge, despite her earlier confidence that she could trust her instincts where Noren and Hasenda were concerned.

"You both realize that if they do turn out to be enemies, and Odath and Petrin show up, it'll be four against one?" Ashriel said.

"Four against three," she corrected him, but he apparently was not in the mood to see the humor. She got the distinct impression he was considering tying her down again, and not in a kinky way this time.

"I am not amused," he said, reading her thoughts, but she saw his lips twitch like he wanted to smile, despite himself. *"In fact, I'll* refuse *to tie you down if this defiance continues."*

Jillian had to turn her face toward the window to hide her smile, not wanting to have to make up an excuse to Rae as to why she was trying not to laugh.

As far as Ashriel could remember, he had never voluntarily done something so stupid in his entire life. Tactically speaking, bringing his still mostly human prasuri and his entirely human friend to a potential battle was the worst possible decision he could make. He'd been enslaved, tortured, and drained, and yet the prospect of disappointing his prasuri seemed so much worse that he was actually going along with this madness.

On top of that, he was currently *supposed* to be mad at her about this whole situation, but there he was, grinning like an idiot because he could see the reflection of her blushing in the glass of the passenger-side window, and he thought her damned smile was gorgeous.

What the hell is wrong with me? he wondered, mystified by Jillian's power over him.

Rae pulled up to a curb along a quiet street and shut off the engine. Looking back at him in the rear-view mirror, she was so tense he was surprised she could keep her voice steady. "The house is up ahead," she said, pointing about four houses down. He'd told Rae to park a good distance away so he could get a feel for the area, and this was about as good as it was going to get inside a human neighborhood.

"I'll scout ahead," he said, casting a quick protection spell over the two of them to make them harder to detect before getting out of the car. He made it three steps away from the car before he heard two car doors shut behind him. Stopping, he closed his eyes, tipping his head back to the heavens to pray for patience. Without looking back, he walked on ahead, sensing them both trailing behind him at a good distance.

They were silent, thank Tairi, as they followed him. Circling around behind the row of houses, he approached Noren and Hasenda's from the back. It wasn't long before he felt the pressure of a protective barrier, just like the one he'd placed around Rae's house, and held up a hand to signal the others to stop where they were.

"Take Rae and hide in the trees," he thought to Jillian, glancing back at them briefly.

When they were safely out of line of sight of the house, he cautiously moved forward. Crossing the protective barrier would have announced their presence, and it wasn't long before a shima he assumed to be Noren stepped out onto the back porch, followed by his prasuri, Hasenda.

There was no doubt they were shimana, but they could have passed for humans easily, dressed in casual human clothes. They had given up their immortality to age as humans did, appearing to be in their late fifties or early sixties, by human standards. Noren's black hair was liberally sprinkled with gray, and Hasenda's light-blond hair was streaked with white, but looks could be deceiving with shimana. Who knew how old they actually were? Ashriel knew better than to underestimate them. They were much more powerful than the humans they imitated.

"Why are you here?" Noren said, brown eyes narrowing with mistrust. "Are you from the Junak?"

Ashriel shook his head. "No—"

Noren took a defensive stance next to his prasuri, flames erupting in the palms of his hands. "Then are you responsible for what's been happening here?"

"Where's Rae?" Hasenda demanded, taking a threatening step forward, her hazel eyes fierce.

"I mean you no harm," Ashriel said, holding his empty hands out from his sides in a sign of peace. Right away he could tell Jillian had been right. He sensed no deception in either of them.

"If you aren't from the Junak, you need to leave," Noren warned, the flames in his hands burning higher as he stepped off the porch.

"Stop!" Rae shouted from behind Ashriel, and he sighed, dropping his hands to his sides. Glancing over his shoulder, he saw that Rae and Jillian had both jumped out of cover, despite their promises.

"He was the one who saved me," Rae insisted, sticking up for Ashriel.

"It's a damned good thing they appear to be who Rae says they are," Ashriel grumbled to Jillian and saw her eyes flick to him with a mildly apologetic smile.

"She thought you were going to fight," Jillian said.

A second later, Hasenda was flying past him to grab Rae up in a big hug. At first, Rae appeared unsure, but then she seemed to come to some kind of internal decision and hugged the other woman back.

"You hadn't been back to your house in days, your family hadn't heard from you, and when we found the place you'd been working it was covered in dark magic," Hasenda said, pulling away enough to hold Rae by the shoulders so she could look her up and down, checking for any obvious injuries.

"We've been going back and forth to the Junak, trying to get them to do something," Noren said, walking over to join him, the fire in his hands extinguished.

"I'm sorry for jumping to conclusions, but we can't be too careful with Humiv on the loose."

Ashriel raised an eyebrow. "Humiv?"

"Let's go inside to talk," Hasenda said, ushering Rae toward the house.

It was probably a good idea not to be so out in the open, especially with what he wanted to discuss, so he nodded and followed them inside. Beside him, Jillian's hand brushed against his in a comforting gesture and he threaded his fingers through hers. Only then did he realize how tense he'd become during that exchange.

Ashriel was leery of going inside at first, a little twitchy after being locked inside his captors' house for so long, but Noren and Hasenda's home felt similar to Rae's. It was inviting and warm, and full of furniture he recognized as shima in design. Various trinkets made of materials that could only be found in the shima realm. Paintings of familiar shima landscapes. Woodwork detailed with different intertwining, swirling patterns and carvings of vines, leaves, flowers, and trees.

All the electronics were shima items that had been redesigned to look more human. Appliances, clocks, and lamps with crystal lights and useless cords plugged into equally useless electrical sockets. A necessary deception in order to blend in. Even when a shima wasn't using magic, the natural energy in their body interfered with anything run by electricity. There were ways to guard against that, but it would be too exhausting to keep it up all the time.

Following Noren and Hasenda through the house, they made their way to the living room. Two large, light-gray sofas dominated the middle of the room, situated on either side of a coffee table with shima vine carvings along the legs and edges. There was no television, for obvious reasons, but there were several shelves filled with books along the walls.

Gathering in the living room, they all sat down and exchanged the information they had. Noren and Hasenda went over what had happened with Humiv in the time Ashriel had been held captive, and Rae explained what had happened to her while the other two shimana listened carefully. She explained about the mind control, while Ashriel and Jillian filled in the blanks about the spell marks and the gegaji controlling Ashriel.

"Ashriel and Jillian had to fight to get me out of that place," she said, clenching her hands in her lap.

"I'm so sorry," Hasenda said, taking Rae's hand. "We knew something was going on. So many humans were getting sick, and no matter how many times we cleansed them it just kept happening. We thought the source of whatever was affecting everyone was in town somewhere, so we've been searching there to try and find a way to fix it. When we saw you at the barbecue, and realized you were being influenced too, we went straight to the Junak for help. We didn't realize—"

"It's not your fault," Rae said, squeezing her hand. "But why didn't you tell me?" Looking between the shimana, she waved her hand to encompass the three of them. "About all of this? Does the rest of the family know?"

Noren shook his head. "There are laws forbidding us from sharing what we are, for our safety as well as yours."

"So can we just go back to the Junak?" Jillian

asked, and Ashriel could tell she was attempting to turn the conversation back to their enemies for Rae's sake.

He sensed Rae's relief, and she gave Jillian a small, grateful smile. This was a personal conversation Rae needed to have with Noren and Hasenda.

Hasenda sighed. "I doubt it would do any good," she said to Jillian, before glancing over at Ashriel. "You said you were being forced to hunt Sijo Otharo?"

"I was," he said, already guessing where this was going. "Don't tell me. They used me to implicate Kretore?"

"Yes, and Kretore spoke for you," Hasenda said.

"As Enalel expected they would," Ashriel said, wishing he were still in a place where he could break something.

"The Junak is divided now," Hasenda said. "Everyone is suspicious of each other. Nobody knows who could be involved with Humiv."

Cursing under his breath, he glanced at Noren. "What about the readings you mentioned?"

"The leader of the Junak dismissed them," Noren said, getting up from his seat. "I'll show you what I've recorded." He went out into the hallway and disappeared into another room.

"If we can't go to the Junak, what *can* we do?" Jillian said, and he could feel her worry through their link. "The town is still in danger, not to mention whatever this Humiv is doing on your side."

"This is all Humiv's doing, in both realms," Ashriel said. "But what they hope to gain here in the human realm, I don't know."

"I think I have an idea," Noren said, returning with

a large, rolled up map in his hands. Ashriel recognized it as a tool bidkoilna used to document their findings on different weak spots in the barrier between the realms. Noren spread it out on the coffee table, and Ashriel immediately recognized the layout of the town. He'd been forced to hunt in the area enough times that the landmarks were familiar.

"Some of these aragna are new," Noren said, pointing to several of the weak spots he'd marked on the map. "And they are all giving off strange readings."

"The Jiru of Urujek mentioned this had happened in his city before it was attacked," Hasenda said.

"Jiru Otharo shut him down quickly, though," Noren added, a frown furrowing his brows. "And the leader of the Junak was swayed by Jiru Otharo's argument."

"Then let's see what the Jiru of Urujek has to say," Jillian said.

"The entire shima realm will be hunting for me," Ashriel said bitterly. Technically, he could use one of Noren and Hasenda's teleport stones to cross the barrier between the realms, but he knew better. "Whether they believe I attacked Orilia or not, they will be forced to arrest me if they see me."

"We'll go," Hasenda said.

"Thank you," Ashriel said, relieved that he was finally getting somewhere.

"Told you they weren't bad people," Jillian's voice flitted through his mind, sounding very pleased with herself.

He shot her an amused glance. *"Yeah, yeah,"* he said. *"You were right. Should I show my appreciation now or in private?"* he said, ghosting his energy along the side of her neck to touch her telepathically. He was immediately rewarded with the blush staining her cheeks.

"I'll stay here and look into the aragna," Ashriel said out loud, returning his attention to the others in the room. He was the one teasing her, and yet it was hard to stay focused when she looked at him with such open affection. He wanted to grab her up and take her someplace where they could be alone right that second. "If you'll let me borrow your tools? I may not be able to fix any anomalies I find, but I can at least gather evidence and track any changes or deterioration."

"And you," Hasenda said, giving Rae a stern look. "Will be going to stay with your family, out of harm's way. Odath and Petrin know where you live, but they don't know where your family is."

"I don't want to draw them to my family," Rae protested immediately.

"They'll be more worried about me," Ashriel said. "They won't care if you tell the whole world about what happened to you. It wouldn't affect their plans. The three of us are the ones who could potentially get back to the shima realm and ruin everything if we talk to the right people."

"So they're coming after you now too?" Rae said to Hasenda and Noren, and Ashriel could sense her anxiety going up again.

"We'll be with the Jiru of Urujek long before they can do anything about it," Noren said, and the confidence in his tone helped ease Rae's worry a little.

"All right. I'll call my parents and let them know we'll be visiting for a while," Rae said, glancing at Jillian.

Ashriel's faint glimmer of hope that Jillian would follow Rae's example and hide somewhere was immediately crushed, and he almost laughed at how predictable it was.

"I'm staying with Ashriel," Jillian said. Everyone in the room had something to say about that, but Ashriel kept his mouth shut while the others tried to persuade her. He knew better.

"They could use you against him," Noren said reasonably.

"What if they mind control you again?" Hasenda pointed out.

"What if you get hurt?" Rae said, clearly afraid.

"He's my prasuri," Jillian said, and that quieted everyone more effectively than if she'd shouted. "My place is with him."

Ashriel stared at her. He hadn't expected that declaration. He knew he was smiling like a dopey, lovestruck fool, but he didn't care.

"His what now?" Rae said with a raised eyebrow, not understanding why the others had accepted that so fast.

"His mate," Hasenda said.

"Oh," Rae said, looking between Ashriel and Jillian. "Oooh." A wide grin curved her lips. She may not have understood the full implications of that, but she got the general idea. "So that's what's going on."

Jillian blushed, smiling in an adorable, embarrassed kind of way that only reinforced Ashriel's desire to monopolize her for the rest of the evening, but she stood her ground against the others. "I promise I'll stay out of the way. But I can't leave him."

"You'd better text me all the time," Rae said, growing serious again. "I'm *not* going to lose another friend because of those monsters. If I don't hear from you, I'm calling the police, or the FBI, or the president. I don't know. I'm calling somebody with bazookas and tanks."

Ashriel refrained from his usual cynicism, skipping his whole they-would-all-die speech he'd given to Jillian. Who knew? He hadn't been up against tanks and bazookas personally. It could work if there were enough of them.

"All right," he said instead, leaning forward to examine the map. "Let's plan how we're doing this."

CHAPTER TWENTY-FOUR

Shima realm
The city of Urujek

LANSA SIGHED HEAVILY AS HE glanced between the map he was holding and the papers spread out on his desk in the hidden study behind the throne. He'd just spent several hours marking the map where all the known Humiv attacks had taken place and detailing what had happened at each encounter in his notes. There was no discernable pattern in location or in who was attacked or when. The details he'd noted were more troubling, however. More shimana were being abducted with each attack.

He glanced up as the enchanted doorway appeared on the far wall, the stones moving to create space as Gajano and Navin passed through. They both stopped in front of his desk and knelt before him, lowering their heads respectfully.

"Please, rise," Lansa said, waving away the formality. He had never required it of either of them. "What news do you bring me?" He dropped the map onto his desk and leaned back in his chair.

Now that the traditional show of respect was out of the way, Navin bounced to her feet, unceremoniously dropping her pack from her shoulder with a loud thunk. Marching across the room, she hopped up to sit on the edge of Lansa's desk. Gajano sighed heavily and got to his feet with more restraint, although he did approach Lansa in a much more relaxed manner than any others aside from Navin would dare.

Navin leaned across the desk toward Lansa, slapping a hand down against the wood for emphasis. "That woman is one plague away from the apocalypse!"

Lansa raised an eyebrow. "Woman?"

"Jiru Otharo's sister, Enalel," Gajano said.

"It's even worse than you thought," Navin continued as if they hadn't spoken. "All secrets and empty eyes and she's talking to someone higher up, I'm telling you!" Her brows drew together over light-blue eyes that blazed at him. "All those warriors in Orilia are just stumbling around, falling all over each other, with their eyes all..." She shuddered, wincing at the memory of what she'd seen. "Ugh...and Humiv has the Junak running in circles so well that they haven't noticed a damned thing!"

Impassioned, she threw her hands up in exasperation. "And don't get me started on that town in the human realm. We found this place that was *covered* in so much blood, even *I* could smell it. And now I need a bath," she said with feeling. "A dozen baths. And new armor." She sniffed indignantly, fluffing her short, spikey white-blond hair with her fingers. She offered him a dazzling smile then, completely at odds with what she was saying. "I say you let me go back to

Orilia and rain some unholy death upon her. Somebody needs to."

Lansa calmly raised an eyebrow at Gajano, as always waiting for him to translate Navin-speak into some kind of sense. She was eccentric as it was, but when she got worked up, she tended to go off on tangents.

"Both Orilia and that town in the human realm are in danger," Gajano calmly explained, used to translating.

"That's what I'm saying," she said as she studied her neatly trimmed nails, frowning at the chipped, white polish. "You should just let me kill her already." Dropping her hand, her head swiveled around to look at Gajano. "Tell him about the eyes!" She sounded greatly disgusted.

"There are signs that slave collars have been used in Orilia," Gajano clarified. "All the warriors I spotted were—"

"Standing around, staring off into space when they weren't following Enalel's orders," Navin chimed in.

Gajano looked mildly pained, and Lansa tried not to laugh. "Do you want to—"

"No," Navin said, smiling at him. "Go on."

"The Jiru, as well," Gajano said. "I couldn't get anywhere near him, but from what I could see he didn't make a move without her command either."

"He was so normal when he was in front of the Junak, though," Lansa said, considering.

"She's probably worked hard to get him to act like that when necessary," Gajano said. "She probably hasn't had the time to make sure each individual warrior is controlled as smoothly."

"It's true!" Navin said, nodding. "I even ran up and pushed one of the warriors over."

"Tell me I misunderstood that." Lansa looked hopefully to Gajano only to be disappointed by the weary expression on his son's face.

"You know I couldn't stop her," he said defensively. "You know I tried, but it's just not possible."

Lansa scrubbed his face with his hands. "Okay. So you ran up to a possible enemy warrior, out in the open where anyone could see you, and just tipped him over?"

"I was stealthy about it!" Navin said, frowning as though she were greatly offended. "And not even a blink or a twitch or a 'why the shit did you just tip me over?'"

Lansa looked at Gajano for further explanation, but he appeared to be at a loss for one.

Navin's expression turned unexpectedly serious. "It was sad, Lansa," she said quietly, a rare note of solemnity in her voice that he knew better than to dismiss. "There was nothing left of those warriors. They wouldn't even defend themselves against me because she hadn't directly ordered them to. I doubt the one I knocked down would have even gotten up if I hadn't stood him back up myself. He felt so...stiff. Like every movement was a struggle." She shivered, a look of revulsion crossing her features. "If we need to take Orilia back from her by force, we will have to find a way to spare the warriors. I will not fight someone so helpless."

Lansa nodded, knowing when to take her seriously. "We won't do anything that would take innocent lives," he reassured her. "We will begin working on something to take them out without harming them."

"I want a shot at Enalel when the time comes," Navin said, her voice steely. As a tifire aspect, one of the closest to the Light, she was extremely sensitive to the kind of dark magic and cruelty she'd seen in Orilia. "I want to pay her back for what she did to those warriors, and to her own brother."

"What about the townspeople in Orilia?" Lansa said. "It's not a good sign that no one has reported anything unusual about the warriors there, or about Ashriel's alleged attack."

"Half have been convinced by Enalel's story, it seems," Gajano said.

"And the other half?"

"Aren't there anymore," Gajano said grimly.

"Mysteriously visiting family in other cities for a few months without notice, and with no way to contact them?" Lansa said, raising an eyebrow. If it wasn't a sure thing at this point that the Junak had been corrupted, he would have thought the governing body of Ejoma was officially incompetent beyond redemption.

"Pretty much," Navin said, back to picking at her nail polish.

"The town we scouted in the human realm was just as bad," Gajano added.

"The place Navin mentioned?" Lansa asked, glancing between the two of them.

Gajano nodded and went over everything they'd found, from the house to the weak spots in the barrier. The more Lansa heard, the more concerned he became.

"If it's anything like what happened here, they

could actually be trying to make the realms collide," Navin said.

"Why would anyone do that? It's suicide," Gajano said, obviously uneasy. It was a sentiment everyone had shared during the incident in Urujek half a year before, and there was still no logical answer.

"And what does that have to do with the creatures Humiv has created?" Lansa said, considering. He knew of only one person he could ask. "Send for Triaris." He rose from his chair and gathered up the map and notes to place them in a pile at one end of his desk. As his most talented spy, Lansa knew Triaris could complete this task without being captured. "I need him to get a message to the Jiruna of Amvitum."

Gajano and Navin both inclined their heads respectfully, offering a slight bow as Lansa took a fresh piece of paper and wrote out a quick note. Placing his hand over it when he was finished, he enchanted it so that it could only be read by the intended recipients.

When he was done, he folded and sealed the letter, and raised his head to look at Gajano and Navin. "We need to find Sijo Otharo and the warrior from Kretore," he said, gesturing for them to follow him out of the study.

Once they were out, the doorway resealed itself behind them. Stopping, Lansa turned to the two of them, giving them a hard look. "Do not do anything foolish that could place you in danger." His tone was a very clear command, and he knew they both heard it, although his gaze rested slightly longer on Navin than it did Gajano.

Knowing better than to be flippant on this subject,

Navin inclined her head again. "Of course, Lansa. We will be careful."

"Good," he said, turning to continue on his way to the door. "Those involved will answer for the crimes they have committed," he vowed. "When the time is right, we will destroy them all. But not at your expense."

His mind was already on the next moves he wanted to make as he headed for the hallway outside the throne room, when there was a knock on the large, closed double doors.

"Enter," Lansa called out, stopping where he was in the middle of the room. Navin and Gajano immediately flanked him, waiting a step behind him on either side.

A warrior came in and bowed low. "There are two visitors here, demanding to see you," he said, raising his head when Lansa acknowledged his bow with a nod. "Noren and Hasenda Gaisudji. They say they have vital information on Humiv they need to share with you."

Lansa smiled, sensing that those familiar names got Navin and Gajano's attention immediately too. "Bring them to me."

Ashriel wandered through the trees, exploring an area just outside of town that Noren had marked. Holding the map up, he checked the landmarks to make sure he was headed in the right direction still.

Jillian and Rae were safely back at Rae's house, thank Tairi. He could breathe a little easier, knowing if he ran into trouble, they would be far from it this time. He'd had a hell of a time convincing Jillian to wait at home, but when he'd reminded her he could concentrate better while not worrying about her possible impending death if Odath and Petrin found them, she'd grudgingly agreed. But not without a fierce scowl on her face and a demand that he return to Rae's in a couple hours, like he'd promised, or she'd go out looking for him whether he liked it or not.

It was beginning to get dark when he began to feel the change in energy in the area. Pausing, he let his senses fan out, analyzing everything around him. The flow of energy was just a little disjointed. Uneven. Pitted almost.

Nothing had been disturbed. None of the trees or plants had been marked by dark magic. No runes were carved into the earth. There was no obvious difference between this area and any other part of the woods, but he could tell it had been cleansed recently. It had been sloppily done, however, letting little telltale signs slip into his senses.

Scowling in distaste, he recognized the tainted feel of void energy. Thicker. Stagnant. Unnatural. It saturated the whole area. The cleansing hadn't been enough to hide that.

Moving forward purposefully, not wanting to miss anything, Ashriel trailed his hands over whatever he passed. Trees, bushes, leaves. Trying to pick up anything that might have been left behind. Hoping more clues had been missed in the cleansing.

He didn't have to search long.

With his senses analyzing everything so closely, the metallic tang of blood was like a slap in the face. Kneeling, he brushed his hands over the fallen leaves at his feet. Specks of blood dotted their surfaces. Gliding his hands farther out from his body, he felt his stomach lurch. Just beyond the reach of his fingertips, he could sense what felt like the edges of a large pool of blood that had seeped into the soil. A blemish on the earth that could not be cleansed. On top of that, very faintly, he could sense the foulness of Odath and Petrin's energy where they had repeatedly tried to cleanse the blood from the area.

They had sacrificed people there, and no amount of cleansing could erase the trauma caused to the area by what they had done.

Pushing his senses farther, he realized it wasn't just human blood. They had sacrificed their own people as well.

Saying a silent prayer of thanks that none of the blood was Darenai's, he used several large leaves to gather samples of the stained soil and blood-spattered leaves. Encasing the samples with his energy to keep them safe, he tucked them away in the pack Noren had given him and began trying to purify the area the best he could.

As a jahuni, being farther from the Light, he only had limited abilities for purifying and healing. For the most part he could only heal himself and other people to a certain extent. Healing the earth was far beyond his skills.

Rising to his feet, he checked the map to confirm what he was feeling. He sensed the arag right in front of him, near the dried pool of blood. Not having a lot of experience dealing with these weak spots in the barrier, he couldn't be sure, but something felt very wrong about it.

Taking a small crystal vial out of the pack, he said

a quick spell Noren had taught him and very carefully took a sample of the arag. After he was finished, he added his own mark to the map before putting everything away and moving on.

By the time he returned to Rae's for dinner, he'd checked three aragna and felt completely saturated in the darkness he had been trying to purify. He felt so unclean he wanted to burn everything he was wearing and scrub his skin raw. It felt like death was clinging to him.

He saw Jillian waiting for him on the porch as he approached the house and held up a hand to stop her from reaching for him. "I need to purify myself before you touch me," he grumbled. "I feel like I just got done rolling in excrement." He shrugged out of the pack and held it out toward her just enough for her to sense the nastiness inside.

Jillian's nose scrunched up in disgust. It was obvious the part of her that was becoming more like him was as repulsed by what he had found as he was. "What is that?" she asked as he opened the pack for her to peer inside. The neatly folded leaves and crystal vials looked innocent enough, but Ashriel needn't have worried. She instinctively wanted to keep her distance from them.

"Evidence," he said with distaste. He got permission from Rae to put the pack in a room by itself, where Jillian and himself wouldn't feel sickened by it, and Ashriel filled them in on what he'd found at the arag sites he'd visited.

Rae looked over the map he'd spread out in her living room to show them. "At least none of those weak spots are near here."

"I'll keep working on purifying these areas as I visit them, but I'll probably have to go back several times to make any real difference," he said. Glancing over at Rae, he narrowed his eyes, hoping she'd been busy doing what she'd promised. "Are you ready to go for tomorrow?"

Rae raised her hands in a sign of surrender. "I'm packed, I swear. I won't make a fuss," she said, but she glanced worriedly at Jillian. "But I don't like leaving you guys here."

"We'll be fine," Jillian reassured her, waving her cell phone at Rae. "I'll keep you posted on how we're doing."

"I need a shower," Ashriel said, deciding to grab dinner later. Purifying himself was his top priority at the moment. He waved to them over his shoulder and trudged off, anxious to take off his clothes that reeked of blood and dark magic.

Petrin stood outside the charred remains of the house she'd been living in here in the human realm. Whoever had been there had been powerful. She could still feel the sting of pure light magic in the air.

It had taken her longer than she would have liked to heal from the injuries she'd sustained in her battles with the Sijo and Ashriel, but she wouldn't let the Kretore warrior slip through her fingers again. If she displeased Enalel one more time, she would lose more than Enalel's favor.

She couldn't allow this new threat to make her hesitate.

Odath's hunt for the Sijo had led him back to the

human realm as well, but she wouldn't have to deal with him, luckily. He had his own orders from Enalel to attend to, so Petrin was left to hunt on her own, as she preferred.

Turning away from what was left of the house, she centered herself and fanned out her senses. She had a fair idea of where Ashriel might have fled to with two humans in tow, but she couldn't leave anything to chance.

After hours of scouting the surrounding areas, the sathra part of her nature that had attuned itself to Ashriel when she'd tasted his blood finally picked up on something. It was very faint, but it was enough to tell her that her guess about his whereabouts had been correct. He was still in town with his humans, and he was searching for clues.

Sighing, she dug in the pocket of her cloak for her communication crystal. Unfortunately, she'd need a little help after all for the plan coming together in her head to go smoothly. There were other loose ends that needed taking care of besides Ashriel.

"Odath," she said, when he answered across the distance through his own crystal. "I have a favor to ask that I actually don't think you'll mind granting."

Chapter Twenty-Five

A depressing kind of air settled over Jillian and Rae as they discussed their plans for the next day while they ate. Jillian could tell Rae was as worried as she was, but she was putting on a brave face.

Ashriel had one more place he needed to check first thing in the morning, and after that, she was going with him to escort Rae to her parents' house. She didn't want to scare Rae, but she couldn't shake the feeling of urgency that had settled over her. She almost wished they could go that night.

Odath and Petrin would not give up easily. Ashriel was a threat they would be looking to take care of. With his powers restored, could he take them both on?

Pushing those thoughts away, Jillian tried to lighten the mood, joking with Rae like everything was normal. She felt herself blushing again when the conversation turned to her and Ashriel.

"Honestly, I'm really happy for you guys. I'm kinda surprised, though," Rae said, a mischievous gleam in her eyes. "You've come a long way from him flipping out because he didn't want to know your name. I still feel like I need details on how this happened."

They chatted for a good while, and by the end of it Rae looked a lot more at ease. After dinner, they said good night and headed off to their rooms. She wasn't sure either of them would sleep very well, but they had to try.

When Jillian walked into her bedroom, she found Ashriel there, resting on the bed. She was startled at first, seeing him in that same petrified state that had terrified her before. The next thing that crossed her mind was to wonder how he wasn't crushing the bed with his weight, but figured that must be just another strange jahuni thing she didn't understand.

She remembered he'd said this was natural for his kind, especially when they needed to heal. Able to sense the steady pulse of his energy, she was reassured that he was fine. He felt cleaner than he had before too, having purified himself of the dark magic that had soaked into him.

Her eyes never left him as she closed the door behind herself. Unlike the first time she'd seen him like this, she had some sort of idea what she was looking at, and she was curious. Abandoning any hope of sleeping, she approached the bed.

Not wanting to disturb him, and unsure if she even could, she kicked off her shoes and climbed carefully onto the bed, tucking her legs beneath her so she could lean over him a little. He looked completely relaxed. His eyes were closed and his ankles were crossed, hands resting on his stomach.

She was pleased to see he had taken off his clothes, and they were nowhere to be seen. They were probably in the same room as the pack. The covers were pulled low over his hips, and she couldn't help the sappy smile that curved her lips as she looked at him.

It hadn't taken him long at all to work his way into her heart. She thought she was starting to understand what he'd meant about the prasuri bond being a deeper kind of love.

Stretching out beside him, she propped herself on her elbow, resting her cheek on her palm. Unafraid, she touched the fingertips of her free hand to his arm. He was warm to the touch. Much warmer than she remembered the last time he'd been petrified. The flow of his energy was much stronger too, and even though he appeared to be a statue, there was nothing lifeless about him. The idea rose into her mind that it was because he was healthier now.

Trailing her fingers up the length of his arm, she was surprised by the smoothness of the stone. By the life she could feel in it. He was beautiful, from his wickedly teasing mouth to the rough hands he used to drive her crazy.

The warmth she felt in her heart was quickly spreading until she was on fire. Impatient for him to wake up so she could feel his hands on her body.

Her eyes lifted to study his face, and she trailed her fingertips along his cheek. His lips. Then she let them glide down his muscled chest, until she covered one of his hands with hers. Leaning close, she pressed her lips to his skin, just beside his ear.

"Wake up, hanotse prasuri," she whispered.

As if he had been waiting just for that, she felt his skin giving beneath her hand. Softening. Warming even more. She was close enough, her lips still moving along his neck, that she felt his first deep breath, and took it with him. Breathing in his scent.

She only had a moment to enjoy the change in the skin beneath her hand before she found herself pinned beneath him. His mouth claimed hers hungrily, his hands as impatient as hers had been as he cupped her breast through the material of her shirt.

Her other hand too busy pushing beneath the blankets still tangled around his waist, she tugged at the hem of her shirt one-handed. Wriggling a little, she managed to shimmy the material up enough for him to pull it up the rest of the way.

His chuckle was husky as he pulled away from her slightly, his eyes devouring her. "So impatient," he murmured teasingly, tugging the cup of her bra out of the way to circle her nipple with his fingertips.

Tangling her hand in his hair, she arched beneath him. "Ashriel, please..."

"Mmm," Lowering his head, he cupped her breast again, flicking his tongue over her nipple. "Is this what you want?" He sucked her nipple into his mouth, gently at first, then with stronger pulls. Flicking his tongue and swirling until she was panting.

Sensation shot through Jillian like lightning. Her body burned with need, the ache between her thighs almost unbearable. Greedy for more, she moved her hands to undo her jeans.

When he pulled back and grabbed her wrists to stop her, she would have protested, but he brought her hands up to pin them to the bed on either side of her. The nails on one of his hands lengthened into black claws, and he very carefully trailed the sharp point at the end of his index finger down the soft part of her inner forearm, toward her elbow. Knowing where this was headed, she felt a thrill of excitement, fully embracing this side of him.

Openly enjoying tormenting her, he trailed his razor-sharp nails along the material of her jeans, the deadly points catching and tearing through as if it was nothing. Her breath picked up at the faint ripping sound, and then he grazed the newly exposed skin of her hip bone and upper thigh with the backs of his knuckles before moving on. Working with maddening slowness, he gave the same treatment to the remains of the jeans over her other hip and then to her shirt and bra, shredding the material until she was free, and he could toss it all away.

"Ashriel," she moaned, her skin oversensitized to his soft touch as he slid his palm up along her thigh until he could grip her hip.

"More?" he said, gazing down at her with barely leashed desire. "Tell me where." His lips covered hers again before she could respond, his tongue dancing against hers teasingly.

"Show me." The words whispered into her mind as his nails caught on the edge of her panties and tore through them with one careful slice so he could remove them too.

When she reached for his hand, his nails had already returned to normal, and she shamelessly led him to where she most wanted to be touched. Gasping into his mouth when he complied, she laced the fingers of her pinned hand through his and held on tight.

Her breath hitched as his fingers played against her. And then all she could do was cling to him as he quickly drove her over the edge. She heard his groan as she shook beneath him, clenching around his fingers. He leaned away from her only long enough to kick away the blankets that were still in the way, and then he was settling between her thighs, lowering himself into her waiting arms.

Hands smoothing over the taut muscles of his shoulders, she wrapped her legs around his hips and urged him closer until she could feel him pressing against her. Moaning low in her throat, she delighted in the muscles that flexed beneath her hands as he slowly entered her, drawing out that first stroke.

Sliding her palms down his back, she arched beneath him as their bodies moved together. Muscles bunched and relaxed beneath her fingers, his spine bowing sensuously with every gliding thrust. She held him tighter, moving to meet him.

Their energy rolled together. Their senses and feelings overlapped until they were one in mind and body. Sharing each other's pleasure. Building on it.

Curling his arms around her, he rolled them easily so that she was on top of him.

Leaning up and bracing her palms on his chest, she rocked against him, driving them both closer and closer to the edge. Tipping her head back, she moaned, feeling the beginning of her climax.

Gripping her hips, he pulled her down harder against him, and she gasped. Feeling her release seemed to trigger his own, and they found their peak together, moving greedily against each other until the last tremor had eased.

Panting, she collapsed against his chest. His arms curved around her, his hands smoothing over her skin lovingly, and she raised her head. Kissing him languorously, she hummed in pleasure when one of his hands came up to tangle in her hair.

"Want me to move?" she mumbled, lowering her head to rest her cheek on his chest again.

His arms tightened around her. "Mmm...stay just where you are."

Her lips curved into a satisfied smile at the lingering heat in his tone. Wallowing in the afterglow of their lovemaking, she sighed contentedly.

They were quiet for a while, each just enjoying the closeness of the other. But, with their minds open to each other, he must have felt it when her thoughts began to turn toward the evidence he had collected.

"Do not think of that now," he soothed. "I will keep them stored where they won't disturb you."

"Why do I feel like that?" she said.

His hands stroked down her back comfortingly. "It's natural, since you share some of my power now. Dark magic puts my kind on edge. We're careful about how we use it, if ever," he said quietly. "It's something we all have to face at some point, though, regardless of if we use dark magic or not. Whether we use the power, or the power uses us."

She shivered. "And when the power uses you?"

"It becomes an addiction. A sickness that we call *hajithra*," he said, managing to tug the blankets over them. "Dark sickness." His hands smoothed down her thighs in a caress. "When we're controlled by the hajithra, we lose sight of right and wrong. The power becomes everything. We are capable of anything."

"Like Odath and Petrin," she said, remembering how they'd been.

"Yes," he said, absently drawing little circles on her

thighs with his fingertips. "You become convinced that it makes you stronger. Which it does, in some ways, but you hand your freedom over in exchange. Recovery from hajithra almost never happens."

"How did you get past it?"

"It was Darenai, telling me not to be a dumb ass," he said, and she could hear the smile in his voice. "I didn't make it easy for him, though." He laughed at the memory, the sound rumbling against her ear, and she couldn't help but smile herself.

He didn't say it out loud, but as connected as they were, she knew when his mind took a darker turn. "Don't think like that," she said. Crossing her hands over his chest, she rested her chin on them to gaze up at him. "When this is all over, you're going to introduce me to him. Then you'll both be there to help me learn, and to help me face the temptation when it comes."

He was quiet a moment, and she waited, knowing he was mulling something over. "You're not afraid of it?" he finally asked. "Of no longer being human?"

She understood the rest of that question, even though he left it unspoken. Was she afraid of what he was? Of tying herself to him, *literally* forever?

Leaning up, she kissed him, nibbling at his lips playfully. *"You share my mind,"* she teased, whispering into his mind as she deepened her kiss.

"I try to give you your privacy, navoj, as much as possible." His hands began moving on her again. Caressing. Teasing.

"Are you listening now?" she said, feeling him stirring to life beneath her again as her own hands began to roam.

She knew he was reading her thoughts, and felt him

still, his breath catching for a moment at the words that flitted through her mind. And then he was rolling her beneath him again, bracing himself above her. His hand was gentle as he caressed her face, leaning away from her just enough to study her expression.

"Say it out loud," he softly demanded, and she could feel the need burning through him. "I need to hear it. I don't want any more confusion between us."

"I want to be your prasuri," she repeated, smiling up at him. "I love you."

He captured her mouth in a passionate kiss that had her breath picking up again. "Rivishne," he whispered, his hands exploring her. "Again. Say it again."

"I love you," she said on a sigh, arching into his caresses, her eyes fluttering closed. "More than I have ever let myself love any other." Her gaze met his again. "More than I knew I could love."

"I love you too," he murmured, raining kisses against her skin. "Forever."

For the next few hours, nothing else mattered. There was nothing else to think about—not the threat of Enalel, not even the darkness that stained the woods around the town.

There was only this bright spot that they had found together in all the uncertainty. This perfect moment God had given them. There was only each other, and the love they could finally share freely.

The next morning, Jillian was in high spirits, optimism undampened by their precarious circumstances. There was still a sense of urgency in the back of her mind, but at least they were moving forward now.

Meeting with Hasenda and Noren had given them a direction, and the possibility that the ruler of Urujek might help them. There was hope for the town and the people in it if they succeeded in getting word to that Jiru.

She threw on shorts and a tank top and pulled her hair back, not bothering with shoes. Catching a glimpse of a shredded pile of material that had been tossed across the room, she blushed and made a mental note to toss them when Rae wasn't looking.

Skipping down the stairs, she met the others for breakfast in the kitchen, appreciating the way Ashriel's gaze swept over her when he saw her.

"Got everything you need?" Ashriel asked Rae after they finished eating.

The three of them gathered at the front door as Ashriel double-checked his pack to make sure he had the tools he needed. The evidence he'd collected the day before was upstairs in an unused room, but the pack was still stained by the dark magic from those items, and it made Jillian want to wrinkle her nose.

"Ready to go when you are," Rae said with a nod. Jillian could sense her nervous energy, but she seemed to understand it was too dangerous to stay.

"I'll only be a couple hours, and then we're going straight to Rae's family," he said, turning his attention to Jillian. He narrowed his eyes, frowning slightly. "Please don't do anything dangerous while I'm gone."

"You say that like I do it all the time," she said innocently.

"Because you have no survival instinct," he said, lips twitching in the beginning of smile, despite himself. He leaned in and kissed her quickly before she could respond. "Seriously, if anything feels even the slightest bit off, reach out to me with your mind. I'll hear you."

She nodded, and he turned and was out the front door before she could give in to the urge to throw herself at him again.

"I'm still not used to it," Rae said, chuckling behind her. "This whole new softer side of Ashriel. It's actually kind of scary the way you have him wrapped around your finger."

Jillian grinned. "He's still a jerk," she said jokingly and then shrugged. "He's just *my* jerk now."

Laughing, Rae shook her head. "I'll be right back," she said, heading for the stairs. "I actually just came up with one more thing I want to bring with me."

"All right, I'll be in the kitchen," Jillian said. "I'm making some tea. Want some?"

"Sure," Rae said, jogging up the stairs. "Be down in a few!"

Humming to herself, Jillian wandered into the kitchen. She filled the kettle and set it on the stove, then went to the cupboards for the tea bags.

Leaning back against the counter, she lifted her left wrist and trailed her fingers over the inside of it. The prasuri mark slowly appeared, darkening the skin, and she smiled to herself. It was a pretty pattern. She couldn't wait to see what the jewelry would look like that shimana wore when they found their prasuri. Ashriel had told her it was unique to each couple.

Hearing the kettle whistle, she removed it from the heat and started steeping the tea. Several minutes passed while she happily imagined what the shima realm would be like, based on what Ashriel had described. Preparing a cup for Rae and herself, she added a little sweetener to both mugs and brought them to the table.

Sipping her tea while she waited for Rae, Jillian wondered what was taking so long. Just because she could, and Ashriel had said to be wary while he was gone, she fanned her senses out to scan through the house. She didn't expect to find anything unusual, but she figured she might as well practice the very small amount of magic she knew.

Frowning when she didn't sense any other presence in the house, she set her tea down and concentrated. Scanning more carefully the second time, she specifically searched for Rae. Still feeling nothing, she got up and made her way to the stairs.

"Rae?" she called up. When there was no answer, a tingle of unease moved through her.

She made her way up the stairs and toward Rae's room. The house was unusually gloomy without sunlight streaming in through the open windows. She could hear thunder rumbling ominously in the distance, adding to the heavy atmosphere that suddenly had her on edge.

"Rae?" she called again. She knocked on Rae's door, and it was slightly ajar, so it swung open a little. Pressing her palm to the wood, she opened it the rest of the way and went into the empty room.

Something felt wrong. There was a familiar, but very unwelcome, charge of magic in the air, just like she'd felt at Petrin and Odath's. Rae's duffel bag was on the bed, halfway zipped up, but there was no sign of Rae.

Jillian's gaze was drawn to the open window across

the room, curtains fluttering in the breeze. She only got a couple steps closer before that magical energy she'd felt intensified. Pushing past the instinctive revulsion she felt, she moved to the window, trying to keep from moving directly in front of it where she could be easily seen, and peeked around the window frame down into the back yard.

Ashriel's warning about Petrin's hold on Rae was fresh in her mind. Would a sathra's power over a victim need eye contact, like the mind control she'd experienced before had? Could it take effect across a distance? The protective barrier around Rae's property hadn't reacted, so no one could have gotten close to Rae physically.

"Jillian?" Ashriel's voice whispered through her mind, and she latched onto the comforting sound. It was fainter than usual, as if he spoke to her across a great distance. *"What's wrong?"*

"I can't find Rae," she said, trying to keep the fear out of her voice and failing miserably. *"And I think they've found us."*

"I'm on my way," he said immediately. *"Do not so much as* consider *taking a step out of that house. I'm warning you!"* he nearly growled, seeming to read her intentions.

The fact that he was on his way back helped, but she was still scared.

Hurriedly turning around, she rushed through the upstairs, checking the rooms in case she'd missed something when she'd scanned. Rushing down the steps, her eyes were searching the living room before she even reached the bottom. Seeing the front door was still bolted, she ran down the hall toward the kitchen.

Where is she? She frantically wondered. Looking out the window at the back of the kitchen, she peered into the garden.

Pausing as she felt something new, she straightened away from the window and concentrated. Ashriel had warned her that being so close to the contaminated energy around the weak spots all morning would put him on edge, and that she'd probably sense it through their bond. But what she felt from him now was more than simple disgust or uneasiness. Much more. Something was happening on his end too, but she was powerless to help him.

Just as she was about to reach out to him, that's when she felt it. The mental equivalent of a tornado siren blaring in her brain. All of her senses were screaming at her.

Going to the back door, she opened it and took a cautious step out onto the porch. She felt Ashriel's horror at the exact moment she spotted Rae.

Rae had wandered far beyond the back gate, and was getting closer and closer the edge of the barrier. Her steps were uneven and staggering, and Jillian instinctively knew she was being controlled.

She knew what the screaming was now too. Having added her own power to the barrier, it was warning her.

There, just a few feet in front of Rae, sheltered from the sun by trees and heavy cloud cover, Petrin waited on the other side of the barrier. In her dull silver armor, she smiled at Jillian across the distance.

CHAPTER TWENTY-SIX

ASHRIEL APPROACHED THE MAIN PLACE on Noren's map that he was interested in with a great deal of apprehension. Noren had warned him that there was a particularly nasty altar there, covered in the blood of humans and shimana alike, and that he would need to cleanse himself thoroughly after interacting with it.

He was glad it was unlikely any human would venture this far into the woods. Humans may not have been nearly as sensitive to dark energy as shimana, if at all, but they could still be affected by it in various ways. He'd chosen to travel to this location on foot, miles away from any road or hiking trail, unused to driving and a little worried he might blow up Rae's car, however unlikely. He could run far faster than any mortal anyway, and it was the closest he could safely get to flying in the human realm, so it hadn't been a problem.

Folding the map and shoving it into the back pocket of his jeans, he scanned the area, knowing he was close. After a while, he began to notice the scent of stale blood, becoming stronger and fouler as he followed it, until he finally came to a small clearing in the middle of the woods.

Whatever he had expected, it was not what he found.

He had thought to see bloodstained earth. Tainted energy. The trauma left at the site of such brutal murders. It made sense that it was stronger here than at any other site. He was disturbed and repulsed by the stone altar at the center of the clearing, etched with all kinds of dark spell marks.

But what froze him in his tracks and had his senses on high alert, were the blackened and scorched gashes in the trees all around him. Gouged into the earth at his feet. The altar was in shattered pieces, the spell marks ruined and powerless now.

The shattered altar was good. The scorch marks were not. There was no mention of signs of a battle in Noren's notes on this location.

Placing his hand to the nearest scorched tree, he could feel tainted energy of one of Humiv's void creatures seeping from it in sickening waves. The battle had been recent. Maybe only hours ago.

He could sense the remnants of Banen's energy. He must have been the one who destroyed the altar and the runes. There was no sign of where Banen went, but at least it didn't appear he had been killed in the fight.

Moving toward the altar, he examined it closely. Repelled by the darkness he felt rolling off of it, he kept what reasonable distance he could. Banen had managed to begin the purifying process, but it looked like he had been interrupted.

Why would he have come to this place when Ashriel

had warned him that Enalel had servants here? Why risk it? Something must have changed his mind.

What had he been looking for?

As in tune with nature as the yalirna were, Banen would have felt the disturbances in the energy all around him acutely, to the point where the dark magic would have made him ill. It was possible, considering the power he had displayed in their battle, that he could have felt the unusual spikes and pits in the energy levels affecting the barrier as well.

Staring at the altar, he knew he was missing something. Something Banen had picked up on since their battle.

What changed?

"Kaitsa aro Tairi," he murmured, lifting his hands to the sky. Calling on the Light of God, he closed his eyes and chanted the spell that would let him see beyond the distractions of the tainted energy, and beyond the limits of his normal scanning abilities for a short time. "Yasuwo hano um niyuk."

His senses intensified dizzyingly, and he stood very still, getting used to the unfamiliar heightening. Moving by instinct, his eyes still closed, he let his body move on its own.

He could sense every living thing for miles. Could feel the darkness of the evil that defiled the trees around him. The contamination of the partially purified altar just ahead of him. But he was protected from it all by his spell, allowing him to remain free of distraction.

Although his skin crawled, he felt himself lower his hands and place them firmly on the stone of the altar. The spell protected him from the crippling nausea he knew would have overtaken him. There had been too much suffering there, too much evil, for him not to have been affected.

Energy swept up his arms, and through his enhanced awareness, he could see what had drawn Banen there. What Banen had tried unsuccessfully to stop. This was the weakest spot in the barrier he had come across so far. The scars Odath and Petrin had left in this place were deep, but his instincts told him there was more to it than just their desire for the power in blood.

Human energy. Shima energy. Both were there. But not just any shima energy.

He sensed the power of ancients.

Feeling Darenai's energy there, he cursed. This was where his friend had been separated from his body. He'd been expecting to run across it eventually, and had tried to prepare himself, but it didn't sting any less.

Lifting an unsteady hand up away from the altar to get a sense of the open space above it, he felt a burning pain singe his fingers and yanked them swiftly back, his eyes snapping open in horror. Backing away from the altar as quickly as he could, he tried to analyze what he was feeling.

Shimmering in the air above the altar, a barely visible cloud even to his shima eyes, was very carefully controlled dark magic. They were suspended spells he didn't recognize, executed with meticulous precision. Enalel had already punched a tiny hole in the barrier, and the energies were beginning to mix together.

Completely unequipped to deal with a hole in the barrier that could potentially end all life in both realms,

Ashriel dropped the pack and rummaged around inside. Noren had given him a vial of water from Iseyba and had taught him a spell that was supposed to help in stabilizing the barrier, but would it be enough to do anything about an actual hole?

Feeling a ripple of unease in his mind, he paused. It was very faint, but he could sense that Jillian was upset. Glancing at the space above the altar, he grabbed the vial of Iseyba water and approached it carefully.

"Jillian?" he called out to her across their bond, hoping she could answer him across the distance. Telepathy was still new to her, but she seemed to be taking to it quickly. *"What's wrong?"*

"I can't find Rae," she said, and he could sense the fear she was trying to hide. *"And I think they've found us."*

"I'm on my way," he said, using his energy to float the water out of the vial and curl around the pool of dark magic above the altar. Knowing she was likely to find a way to get herself killed if he wasn't careful, he paused, emphasizing his next words. *"Do not so much as* consider *taking a step out of that house, I'm warning you!"*

He chanted the spell Noren had taught him, working as cautiously and precisely as possible, and all the while his instincts were shouting at him to get back to Jillian. He couldn't afford to be sloppy with this, however, so he couldn't rush it.

The water glowed, infused with white light, and it gradually began to swirl around the dark magic, forming a sphere. As it moved faster, a funnel formed, disappearing into nowhere, and he sensed the water being pulled into the hole in the barrier. When all the water and light had been consumed, the shimmering dark magic vapor was no longer visible. Scanning it with his senses again, he could feel that he had managed to patch the hole. But just barely. It was weak, and it wouldn't hold for long, but at least it would buy him time to find someone who might be able to fix it.

In the midst of throwing everything back inside the pack and slinging it over his shoulders, he felt a jolt of pure terror from Jillian. Petrin was there, right in front of her. The air left his lungs in a rush, fear overwhelming him. Being so far from her when something was happening was like a nightmare he couldn't wake up from. He turned to run in the direction of Rae's, all of his heightened senses focused completely on Jillian and Rae, miles away.

He was so distracted that he didn't see what direction the attack came from.

Something hit him square in the back with enough force to slam him to the ground. Whatever it was clung to him, shocking him repeatedly. If it weren't for the pack, it would have burned right through the top layers of his skin.

Drawing on his energy, he sent a pulse out from his body, blowing the creature off him.

Please, Tairi, he silently begged. *Not now!*

Leaping to his feet, he brought up his shield, eyes and senses scanning, the flesh of his back throbbing in pain. A few feet away he saw a scorch mark where the creature must have landed.

"Very good, Ashriel," a familiar voice called behind him.

Turning swiftly, he dropped into a defensive crouch.

Odath stood several yards away, leaning nonchalantly against a tree. It was obvious Banen had managed to wound him in their battle. Dried blood smeared his forehead at the hairline, and stained his shirt in several places. A broad smile twisted his features as he straightened and took a few steps closer. Raising his hands, palms down, he summoned more creatures.

Ashriel recognized them as lisudari. Beings of unclean energy. Black sparks erupted all around Odath, the lisudari exploding into existence at his command. With no will of their own, at least a dozen of them awaited his command.

They had no features that could make them comparable to a living creature. They didn't breathe, or need to eat or drink, and had no heartbeat. They were a weapon, deadly and precise in their simplicity. Balls of sparkling, pulsing energy, they could form tentacles from their main mass to latch on to their victims.

At least they weren't like the void creature he'd faced in Orilia's throne room.

"Don't worry about Jillian," Odath taunted, knowing Ashriel's fear and trying to use it against him. "Petrin will take good care of her for you, I promise."

Ashriel took a threatening step forward. "I'd call her back if I were you," he said with a sneer. Calling on the power of his aspect, light enveloped him as he morphed into his second form. His skin took on the dark-gray, metallic sheen of his scales. His nails lengthening into deadly black claws, and black horns grew out on either side of his head, curving back and up. Without his adaptive armor to morph with him in this form, his wings ripped through his shirt as they extended from his back. "It will take both of you to kill me."

"Doubtful," Odath said confidently. He felt more lisudarina appearing behind him, surrounding him completely. He was badly outnumbered. Just the kind of odds, Odath preferred.

"Coward," Ashriel muttered, disgust thickening his voice. "What's the point in going after Jillian?"

Odath shrugged. "I'm not foolish enough to question my orders." He smirked. "Enalel has taken an interest in her. Seems to think your little prasuri is a liability. Knows too much." Odath flexed his hands and the lisudarina shuddered, ready to move at his signal.

"Still can't face me on your own, can you?" Ashriel taunted, his tone dripping with mockery. Fire rippled along his arms.

"Guess we'll never know," Odath said, flinging his arms wide. The lisudarina hurled themselves at Ashriel.

Ashriel's pulse spell took out about half of them, but the next wave that followed slammed against his shield, making him stagger. They clung to it, sapping his energy.

"Let's find out if you can hold your shield longer than I can hold the lisudarina," Odath said, narrowing his eyes.

Ashriel knew Odath had the upper hand. Without any weapons, he would tire quickly using only magic. And he couldn't fight the lisudarina with hand-to-hand combat without being burned.

It was as his mind was racing, considering his limited options, trying to figure out a way around Odath, that the area was suddenly flooded with light. Momentarily blinded, he felt the lisudarina dissolve from his shield, hissing loudly as they died. Hearing Odath shout in pain, he reinforced his shield and waited with bated breath to face the newcomers.

When the light cleared, he saw two shimana he didn't recognize standing between him and Odath, their backs to him. One a small, pixie-like, blond woman with short, gold-streaked, spikey hair and the silvery-white armor of an Ushara. The other, a tall man with black hair and the black armor of a Telesil.

Raising her arms, the woman called on the energy of the forest. Groaning loudly, the trees all around the clearing began to sway and move to her will. Their branches swinging around toward Odath with deadly accuracy, they shot down toward him like spears, tearing into the ground all around him, most of them tearing into part of his body before he could move out of the way.

Blood splattered the ground, running from multiple wounds all over Odath's body as he tried to maintain his shield against the woman's relentless attacks.

The man pulled two long, wicked-looking swords from the belt at his waist and turned to toss one to Ashriel. Catching it easily, fire roared down Ashriel's arm and along the magical blade as though it were an extension of himself.

The man's dark-blue eyes met Ashriel's steadily. "Go to your humans now," he said. "We will follow once we have killed this one."

Ashriel nodded grimly. He had no choice but to trust that they were on his side. He had to get to Jillian immediately, and the absolute confidence in the other man's voice allowed Ashriel to turn his back on Odath, heart pounding as he raced toward Rae's.

In a panic, Jillian felt Ashriel's pain and knew he had been injured. Gasping, she had to remind herself to breathe. She could feel him coming closer. He was rushing back to her.

But Rae needed her now.

Leaping off the porch, she raced after Rae and managed to reach her before she got too close to Petrin. Yanking hard on Rae's arm, she managed to drag her a little farther away from the invisible barrier that stood between them and death.

Pulling Rae around to face her, she grasped her friend by the shoulders. "Rae!" she yelled, shaking her a little. "Snap out of it!"

Rae didn't even blink. Her glassy eyes stared blankly, looking right through Jillian as if she wasn't even there.

"Did Ashriel forget I took Rae's blood?" Petrin murmured with that sickening false sweetness that made Jillian want to hurl. Jillian glanced over Rae's shoulder, her stomach sinking as she took in Petrin's self-satisfied smirk. Petrin raised a hand to trail her fingertips over the barrier, little sparks fanning out from the contact. Holding Jillian's gaze, she raised her other hand and made a grasping motion. "Rae, bring her to me."

Jillian only had a fraction of a second to register what that meant before Rae slammed into her, making her stumble as the other woman's arms snaked around her in an iron grip. As she tried to struggle free of Rae's hold, she saw Petrin make a pulling motion with her clenched hand, and suddenly they were both flying, hurtling those last few yards toward Petrin.

Instinctively, Jillian thrust her arms around Rae, palms out, and focused on pulling them back again. They slowed a little, almost stopped, and Jillian pulled harder, gritting her teeth. They lurched to a stop, and taking a deep breath, she managed to force them back several feet.

Petrin's grin faded a little, and she clenched her hand harder, making a jerking motion.

Rae's hold tightened to the point of pain, and Jillian felt the violence of Petrin's energy surrounding them, viciously ripping into Jillian's much weaker energy. Feeling the pain of it in her body as well as her mind, Jillian gasped as her much weaker energy faltered, and they were flying again.

"Concentrate!" Ashriel commanded, his presence filling her mind, his power flooding her system so quickly that it stole her breath. *"Just hold on, navoj. Just a little longer. I'm almost there."*

Jillian didn't even try to contain the energy surging through her as his mind enveloped hers. It was way too much all at once. Much more than she had ever drawn from him. She prayed that Ashriel had control of it, because she certainly didn't as it flowed unchecked through her body and down her arms. They came to a sudden, bone-jarring stop again just at the inner edge of the barrier, and Jillian was shocked and thankful when her arms didn't snap from the force of it.

With barely two feet separating them, palms flat against the barrier, Jillian stared into Petrin's disbelieving eyes, the part of herself that was already becoming a jahuni resonating in Jillian's mind. Feeling her power mixing with Ashriel's again, she was ready for the shock of it this time. She mimicked Petrin's earlier smirk and tilted her head in a very Ashriel-like way, completely unimpressed as Petrin made another jerking motion with her hand.

"You know," Jillian murmured. "I do believe I'm going to enjoy this part." The pulse she sent out from her body was so strong that it sent all three of them flying.

Wrapping her arms around Rae, she had a satisfying view of Petrin being flung through the air before she hit the ground herself. She felt Petrin lose her grip on them immediately.

Shoulder aching from the fall, the relief she felt was short-lived as Rae began to struggle to get to Petrin again, the sathra compulsion still strong in her mind. Desperate, Jillian wrestled the other woman onto her back and sat on her stomach to try and keep her still. Rae struggled, but with Ashriel's power bolstering Jillian's, Rae couldn't push her away. Placing her hands on Rae's temples as she remembered Ashriel doing, she looked directly into her eyes and willed her to focus.

"Wake up!" she commanded, focusing her power on the unnatural energy she could feel surrounding Rae and pushing at it with her own.

Petrin laughed behind her. "It's no use," she said, her voice dripping false pleasantness. "I am much stronger than you."

Risking a glance over her shoulder, she saw that Petrin was on her feet again, stopping just outside the barrier, her dagger clutched in her hand. With a bestial snarl, she plunged it downward. The dagger stopped suddenly as it tore into the barrier. Sparks flew, and bright tendrils of energy sprang from that point, curving along the surface of the barrier. Muscles standing out in her arms, Petrin used both hands to work the dagger down, cutting farther and farther into it.

Keeping one hand against Rae's shoulder to hold her down, Jillian flung the other out toward Petrin. Gritting her teeth, she poured all of her energy, every last drop of it, into maintaining the barrier.

Slapping a palm against the top of the jagged tear she had created, Petrin hissed in pain as the barrier burned her skin, but she didn't pull her hand away. Black energy, slithering like worms, swirled at the edges of the tear, eating their way through. Breathing labored as she visibly fought the urge to yank her hand back, smoke curling from between her burning fingers, Petrin sneered at her. "Enalel will have you," she swore. "One way or the other."

Jillian felt the change in the energy around them at the same moment Petrin did.

Petrin flung out her burned hand to deflect the wall of fire that came at her from the side, the black energy in the tear fizzling out as she shifted her focus. Stumbling from the force of the energy pushing against her, she lost hold of the dagger stuck in the barrier and it dropped harmlessly to the ground without her power pouring into it.

Relief sang through Jillian as she got up and began dragging Rae back toward the house. She could feel Ashriel's energy coursing through her even before she saw him, lending her more strength even as Rae continued to struggle.

As he had been in the basement at Petrin and Odath's house, he was beautiful and terrifying in his second form. His shirt was scorched and ragged, his jeans torn in several places, and it was obvious that he'd been through battle already. Fire rolled down his arms in violent waves as he tossed his singed pack aside, extending down the length of a sword he held in one. Unlike anything she had ever seen, the sword was long and curved, with jagged points jutting out at odd angles and curving forward along the length of the blade. Deep-red runes glowed along its length, reminding her of blood.

Although his eyes didn't leave Petrin for a second, Jillian could feel his mind centered solely on her in that moment. An invisible hand stroked her cheek lovingly.

"Try to get Rae into the house if you can," he said. His tone made it clear that there was no questioning him on this. She would not put herself at risk trying to help him this time.

Switching his attention to Petrin, Ashriel sized her up, trying to gauge her next move.

"Nice try," he taunted her, reading her intentions when she finally made her move. Shifting his weight to the side as she scrambled for the dagger, he extended his free hand and shot several more blasts of fire at her, forcing her to bring up both hands to hold her shield. She was pushed back several steps, far away from the dagger. "You won't run away this time."

Never taking his eyes off her, he crouched to pick up the dagger and tucked it into his belt. Tilting his head to the side, he smirked at her, eyes narrowed. "Now stand and fight me, or run away and give me a clear shot at your back. Make your choice." More than ready for this fight, he took a fighting stance, crouching slightly and shifting his body to bring the shoulder of his sword arm back to extend that arm behind him, sword tip angled toward the ground. He raised his other hand slightly in front of him for defense, tucking his wings close to his body, and waited for Petrin's next move.

Shaking out her burned hand, the skin began to heal as she studied Ashriel. Drawing a short sword from a scabbard behind her back, she flung her arms out. The black sparks of lisudarina began appearing all around her.

"Good choice," Ashriel murmured darkly. Rushing forward he sent out a pulse of energy, obliterating the sparks before they could fully form. "But not nearly good enough!" Leaping, wings extending to lift him higher, he swung his sword in a deadly arc, using both hands on the hilt for more force.

Petrin brought up her own sword to deflect it with a deafening clash, and Ashriel shoved her back hard. Off balance, she was forced to quickly meet several slashes of his sword, falling into a defensive stance.

"What are you waiting for?" Ashriel said, his tone full of disdain as he tucked his wings close again. "Or am I too much for you when I can fight back?"

"Eri beshek!" she cursed him, deflecting several more blows. "I can take you, with or without your power!" Screaming in rage, Petrin saw an opening and lunged for it, swinging her blade at his midsection.

Turning away at the last moment and using his energy as a shield to shove her to the side, he let her momentum carry her past him and followed his own through with the blade, swinging at her exposed back.

"Ahh!" Petrin staggered as the blade tore through

the flesh of her back, blood spraying the air. Knowing any hesitation would get her killed, she stepped to the side, twisted, and swung her blade up.

But Ashriel was too quick, the tip of her sword only managing to make a shallow slash that was deflected by his scales before he brought his own blade down to block the rest of her swing. Striking out with her free hand as he shoved her sword away again, she blasted him with energy, tearing into his shoulder and making him stumble. His scales absorbed most of the damage, but she did manage to injure him.

Sweeping his blade up to his side again, he circled her, ignoring the blood that dripped from his wound. “Now, that's more like it,” he said, smirking at her. “An actual challenge. Located what's left of your spine, have you?”

Leaping away from him, Petrin swung her free hand down in a cutting motion. Thunder rumbled, and the sky darkened even further. Lightning rained down from the sky, slanting relentlessly down on Ashriel, pummeling his shield repeatedly. Knowing she was no match for him in hand-to-hand combat, she called more lisudarina to buy time, using his distraction as he was forced to fall back momentarily to defend himself. Slitting her hand with her blade, she dropped to one knee and slammed her palm to the earth.

“Gensa yokeshi,” she said, calling on the favorite minion of sathrana, a blood golem, as she dug her fingers into the soil. “Teles hano.”

The ground heaved in front of Petrin, spraying soil into the air. A form began to take shape as the ground shifted, lifting and cracking open like a fault line.

Ashriel maintained his shield through the assault

of lisudarina, dodging the lightning slamming to the ground all around him. He slashed at the lisudarina as he hurled himself across the distance at Petrin, trying to get to her before she could complete her summoning. The longer she had to pour her energy into the yokeshi, the stronger and more destructive the golem would be. Already, he could see the hulking shoulders and long, powerful arms as it began to pull itself free of the earth.

Destroying the last of the lisudarina, he didn't waste precious time going after the partially formed yokeshi. Yokeshina couldn't be taken down quickly, even in their weaker summoning states. Launching himself at Petrin, he struck downward, trying to take her head off.

Rolling swiftly to the side, she broke off her summoning and brought her sword back up to deflect his next few swings.

And then the gensa yokeshi was free of the earth.

His back to the yokeshi, it was on him in seconds as he fought Petrin. Before he could turn to face it, Ashriel felt an excruciating impact to his ribs and was hurled several feet through the air. Extending his wings, he managed to slow his fall and land in a crouched position again to face the yokeshi as it pursued him. With arms and legs thick like tree trunks it was nearly twice Ashriel's size, the soil that made up its body blackened with Petrin's blood. As imposing as this yokeshi was, Ashriel knew it could have been much worse as it struck out at him, forcing him to retreat farther.

Breathing labored, his ribs aching with every movement, he was forced to turn and meet Petrin's attack from behind. Metal rang against metal as he parried and sidestepped her, desperately trying to keep the yokeshi away from his back.

Leaping to the side as the yokeshi took another swing at him, Ashriel ducked beneath its arm, bringing his sword around at Petrin. She dodged behind the yokeshi at the last second, and Ashriel's sword tore into its chest instead.

Cursing, Ashriel had to release his sword as it stuck in its body to avoid the next swing of its arms.

Petrin was waiting for him as the yokeshi stumbled with its momentum, her sword arcing toward Ashriel's unprotected chest. Dodging, he rushed her, hands coming up to grasp her wrists, twist, and hurl her away again.

Turning as the yokeshi lumbered around to face him again, Ashriel lunged beneath its arms, grabbed the hilt of his sword, and ripped it free in time to parry as Petrin darted out from behind it again.

The yokeshi raised its arms as it loomed over him, ready to crush him into the ground.

Ashriel stepped close to Petrin again, shoving hard against her blade with his. And when she stumbled, one of the points along the length of his blade caught the edge of hers. With a twist of his wrist, she lost her grip on her weapon, and with the next slash of his sword, he felt his blade tear into her.

And then everything stopped.

He sensed the yokeshi grow still behind him, halting just as it began to bring its arms down. And as he yanked his sword free of Petrin's body, it crumbled back to the earth it came from.

Petrin gasped, head tipping back as she slumped to the ground.

This battle was over. Finally. But he knew the war with Enalel had only just begun. Odath was still out there, serving Enalel and her master and tracking Banen. Tairi only knew what damage they had done in the Junak with their scheming in the shima realm.

Ashriel knelt, his body and his heart weary, wiping the bloody sword clean on the grass. Wordlessly leaning over Petrin's body, he placed a hand on her arm. Taking a deep breath, he closed his eyes and purified her as best he could. It's what Darenai would have done, despite the evil inside her.

Feeling a hand on his shoulder, he looked up to find Jillian at his side. Despite his monstrous appearance, she didn't look at him with any fear as her hand lifted from his shoulder to cup his cheek.

Dropping the sword, he surged to his feet, wrapping his arms around her. Carrying her back several steps away from Petrin, he spread his wings to spare her from the sight. For several long moments, they comforted each other with their embrace, and he allowed himself to just silently breathe her in and collect himself. He held her tightly, never wanting to let her go again.

EPILOGUE

Shima realm
On the outskirts of Kretore

BANEN HAD SCOUTED SEVERAL AREAS along miles of labyrinthine tunnels and caverns leading to Kretore, but no matter where he approached from, he sensed the tainted energy of the void creatures. They were waiting in ambush, and he knew he wouldn't be able to get anywhere near the city.

But where else could he go? He was hunted and unsure of who he could trust. His own aunt was the one who had betrayed him, joining forces with Humiv. Who else had been corrupted? Of those he believed to be innocent, who else could he risk involving in his problems?

Gripping the hilt of his dagger, he turned away from Kretore with grim determination. He would have to find another way.

Human realm
Unknown location in the woods

Darenai wasn't sure how long he'd been wandering, or where he even was. One thing he could be sure of, however.

He was running out of time.

Tipping his head back, he wished he could feel the rays of sunlight beaming down through the gaps in the leaves of the trees high above. As he was, though, he couldn't feel anything.

Not the wind. Or the rain. Or the fallen leaves crunching beneath his feet. In fact, they didn't crunch at all.

Why would they? He didn't have much of a concept of time anymore, but he'd learned long ago that ghosts couldn't affect anything around them, not even the leaves on the cold ground below them.

Human realm
Outside Rae's house

"Rule number one," Navin said, eyeing the human in her charge closely. "No leaving the perimeter at any time, for any reason!"

She narrowed her eyes at Rae speculatively. "Rule number two," she continued in cheerful tones, "I have TV control from nine to midnight, and all day Wednesday!"

Gajano closed his eyes and rubbed at his temples silently as he listened to Navin's other demands, which for some reason now included pistachio ice cream and her own personal cabinet full of extra spicy beef jerky that Rae wasn't allowed to even look at.

"Can I leave her here?" Gajano quietly begged no one in particular. "Please?" He added the last for good measure. "Or do you need a pet?" His eyes slanted open to peer at Jillian hopefully. "She's house-trained, I think. And she fetches when you throw shiny things."

Ashriel blanched as though worried Gajano may actually be serious. “No,” he said adamantly.

Navin huffed and jabbed Gajano in the ribs. “Yeah, yeah,” she said and giggled at his expression. “You’d miss me so much you wouldn’t be able to last even an hour without me. You’d come crawling back to bask in my awesome.”

Gajano’s lips twitched in what could have been the beginning of a smile, despite the continued rubbing of his temples. “Bask in your awesome?”

Without bothering to explain, Navin hugged Jillian goodbye, waved at Ashriel, and stuck her tongue out at Gajano. Proclaiming her intentions to explore the human dwelling, she practically skipped away, humming.

“I promise you,” Gajano said in pained tones, glancing at Jillian again. “She is reliable. She’ll keep Rae safe while we’re away.”

She nodded, not doubting Navin for a second. Although Odath had managed to escape Navin and Gajano once, Jillian truly didn’t see that happening a second time.

Rae hugged them all goodbye, much to Gajano and Ashriel’s obvious discomfort. “You be careful,” she said, giving Jillian an extra squeeze with her hug.

“We’ll be back soon,” Jillian reassured her. “In the meantime, you have Navin, and Noren and Hasenda will be back before us too.”

Rae nodded, and turned to join Navin in the house. Jillian chuckled, hearing the two women talking animatedly about the culinary masterpiece that was the human recipe for queso. Navin seemed to have an obsession with human junk food.

"Ready?" Ashriel asked, slipping his hand into hers.

Jillian nodded, smiling up at him, her heart overflowing. Giving her hand a gentle squeeze, he flooded her mind with his love.

She didn't know what to expect on the other side of the barrier. The thought of leaving her world for Ashriel's was scary, but any fear she might have had because of her dad's injury was alleviated when his leg mysteriously healed, seemingly overnight.

Doctors were astounded. So was her dad. It was a medical miracle.

Ashriel refused to make eye contact, insisted he knew nothing, and complained humans were still far too breakable. He felt this meant they should check on her family frequently.

She was more than ready to tie herself to this man forever.

Jiru Feruma, the ruler of Urujek, had offered her and Ashriel his protection and had already sent some of his people to start working on the weak spots in the barrier, scattered on the outskirts of the town. Although Odath and Enalel still needed to be dealt with, she knew they couldn't hide for long with Jiru Feruma hunting them. She and Ashriel were finally safe, the town was in good hands, and she could finally breathe easier.

They were getting closer to finding Banen and Darenai. She could feel it. Once they found the Sijo and Ashriel's friend, they would finally have the upper hand on Enalel.

And they could complete the prasuri ritual. Little butterflies danced in her stomach at the possibility, and she found herself grinning happily.

Reading her mind and feeling her joy, Ashriel drew her into his arms. He kissed her briefly, sweetly, before burying his face in her hair to breathe her in.

"And then forever," he whispered into her mind.

"Forever," she echoed, feeling like she was glowing with happiness.

"Hold onto me tightly," Ashriel murmured as Gajano's hand settled on his shoulder.

"Always, hanotse kawey," she responded, full of love and trust. And even when she felt the world shift and change around her as she was swept into the shima realm with them, she had no doubts or fears. Only a soul-deep certainty. He would never leave her, and she would stand beside him always. *"Always."*

Kronen: Standalone Two – Waiting

~ For my favorite ghost hunter. In loving memory of SLS. ~

Hidga Mountains
South of Iseyba

Kronen could sense the hungry beasts in the shifting darkness. Their orblike forms, glowing at the periphery of his vision, were rarely there if he glanced in their direction.

They hungered for the energy that shima travelers naturally emitted, especially those who favored darker magic. They stalked their prey from the shadows. Waiting for the foolish or the unwary to step off the path.

He had walked these shadowy trails many times before, however, and understood their dangers well. He knew the faint hums he heard on occasion, like someone quietly singing, were meant to lure him deeper into the trees. He recognized the soft lights he saw out of the corner of his eye from time to time, blending in with the shimmering colors around him, as inviting distractions meant to make him lose focus. To follow them.

From the multihued glow of the crystal trees, iridescent trunks growing from the dark-gray stone of the mountains, to the steady pulse of magical energy in the air, everything about the Hidga Mountains was deceptively beautiful and calming. The dense canopy of deep-blue leaves high above, blocking out the sun's light, made the mountains feel like they were cut off from the rest of the world. This place could easily lull travelers into a sense of complacency, and lead the overly comfortable astray.

Sensing they were in no immediate danger, Kronen kept his dark-silver gaze trained on the path ahead. Neither him or his companion relied too heavily on the kind of darker magic that would tempt the creatures closer.

One of the bluish-white orbs drifted near the path, just out of his line of sight, before fading away again, and he sensed the tension spike in his Ushara, Varuk Iyadeyros. As Kronen's second protector, he had insisted on accompanying Kronen, and had been going on about what a bad idea it was for them to leave Iseyba for nearly an hour.

"Is a wendja following us?" Varuk asked beside him, sweeping their surroundings with his verdant eyes. Shifting colors kaleidoscoped over every surface, reflecting off Varuk's silvery-white armor and painting Kronen's long, white hair, cloak, and garshik robes in different hues. It was the perfect environment for wendjana, their glowing forms dancing gracefully through their surroundings, mostly undetected.

"Yes." Kronen shook his head when Varuk reached for his sword, signaling with a raised hand for him to stand down. As a garshik, the only aspect created without emotions, Kronen felt no fear himself, but understood he should probably say something reassuring to ease Varuk's mind. "The wendja is curious, but we are in no danger. We would make a poor meal."

Varuk heaved a sigh, pushing a hand through his shoulder-length, dark-blond hair in frustration. "This whole thing makes me uneasy," he said for the fifth time. "The last thing we need are wendjana."

"It's tracking us, but I doubt it will come any closer," Kronen said, confident in his understanding of that particular beast. "It probably senses I would kill it."

"Again, with the total certainty about all the killing," Varuk said, chuckling.

"It's true, and the fastest way to solve the problem."

"Your honesty scares me sometimes."

"Lying in this situation would only waste time." Kronen mimicked a smile. "Besides, you are partly here to stay my hand when appropriate."

"Truly, you terrify me, my friend," Varuk said with a laugh, shaking his head. "I still say this is a mistake." His disapproval was clear. A glance in his direction showed the grim furrowing of his brows as he walked beside Kronen on the wide path. "What if they find out you've left the protection of Iseyba and try to attack you next?"

"The wendjana—"

"You know what I mean," Varuk said, heaving another sigh. He did that a lot when he was frustrated.

"The rogue shimana?" Kronen asked.

"Yes," Varuk said, scanning the trees around them before turning a narrow-eyed gaze on Kronen again. "The ones setting fires to cities, setting loose some sort of unknown void monstrosities, and kidnapping people. Even high-ranking people, such as Jiruna."

There was a short silence, and Kronen felt the pressure of Varuk's glare but decided not to make eye contact. He had learned to do so in this kind of conversation was to unwittingly admit some form of guilt. Since Kronen knew he was acting appropriately, according to his mission, he chose to ignore him.

Varuk made some sort of noise then that was a mixture between a loud sigh and a groan of irritation. "Jiruna like *yourself*," he said in a tone like he was explaining something complicated to a misbehaving child.

"They haven't shown an interest in garshikna yet," Kronen pointed out.

"That we know of! What if they're plotting against you specifically? It wouldn't be the first time people have wanted to kill you or take your powers for their own," Varuk nearly shouted, clearly at the end of his patience. "With the way the arute has been fluctuating, you're slowly weakening as you take on the burden of maintaining the balance of magic."

Kronen couldn't find a logical argument to this, because it was true. Forced to stay in Iseyba, the source of magic in Ejoma, in order to keep a close eye on the ebb and flow of light and dark energy, he had begun to experience the first signs of strain in himself.

It was a very real possibility that Ejoma's new enemy, Humiv, was actively working to disrupt the stability of magic. Unable to deny Varuk's words, Kronen opted to try and appease him. "Being in a slightly weakened state means nothing to me."

"So far," Varuk said, not bothering to hide his frustration. "But it's taken up so much of your attention, you were obligated to put balancing the arute above going after Humiv yourself."

"I will remedy this," Kronen said, because there was no other option. It was his duty to protect the realm. The priority was always Iseyba, for the sake of both the human and shima realms, but he would not continue allowing his focus to be so divided. Dedicating almost all the garshikna in Iseyba to holding the balance in the brief absence he could afford, this excursion would ideally allow him to see with his own eyes the damage done to the realm outside Iseyba so he could plan how to stop it.

"How?" Varuk demanded. "The problems keep adding up. The very presence of the void creatures Humiv uses is making the imbalance worse by the day. We know next to nothing about the void creatures, except that they're living weapons and are more powerful every time we encounter them. Maybe the goal is to refine them and weaken you until they can stand up to even you."

It was Varuk's duty to protect Kronen, but he also recognized the genuine concern Varuk had for him. Friendship was a rarity between a garshik and any other aspect. His aspect's emotionless state didn't normally endear them to others. Although Kronen had never felt this sentiment for himself, he understood the significance of it.

"I would destroy them," Kronen answered, attempting to reassure Varuk. It was true, and he was sure Varuk knew that, but he continued anyway. "It doesn't matter how strong they believe they can make their creatures. I am the oldest living being, and the most powerful. Attacking me would be futile and the most foolish move they could possibly make."

He stopped in his tracks, remembering his manners as Varuk paused beside him with a raised brow. From studying other aspects, he had learned considering the opinions of others was the polite thing to do, despite the fact that he was right. He tilted his head thoughtfully, and Varuk waited with an openly amused expression.

"No," he said, clapping Varuk on the shoulder once in what he assumed would be interpreted as a friendly gesture. "Even if they managed to get past you, which is extremely unlikely, and attacked in my sleep, they would all die."

Varuk laughed, shaking his head. "It's unsettling when you say it with such confidence."

"I'm simply addressing your concerns," Kronen answered, then added a shrug as he'd seen Varuk do. "My intention is to ease your anxiety about me leaving."

"I'm suddenly much more worried about our enemies, to tell you the truth."

Kronen recognized this as humor and that killing him would be the incorrect response. Prone to taking things very literally, jokes usually escaped him, but he'd been around Varuk so long that he had learned the subtle differences between when someone was serious and when they weren't. It was also obvious Varuk would never betray him, so he returned his attention to the path ahead and started walking again.

"What was that pause just now?" Varuk asked, jogging to catch up with him.

Kronen wondered if this was one of those times where he should not say what he had truly been thinking. It might make Varuk uncomfortable. "It was nothing."

"I feel like I almost died again," Varuk said, unexpectedly entertained by the idea. "I did, didn't I?"

"Why do you seem further amused by the idea of me killing you?"

"Because it appears to be an inevitable risk, serving you." Varuk laughed, some of his tension beginning to fade as he talked. "Everybody outside Iseyba looks at me with awe for lasting this long."

"I don't kill my protectors," Kronen said, raising an eyebrow for effect. "But you have stayed much longer than any before you."

"Can't imagine why," Varuk said, still greatly entertained for reasons beyond Kronen's comprehension. "At first it made me uneasy, the different ways garshikna can interpret things without their emotions. You especially, my friend. One misstep and you may see me as a threat to be wiped out of existence."

Kronen couldn't argue, since it was true, so he merely nodded in agreement.

Varuk smirked at that, calmly tracking a wendja alongside the path for a moment before glancing at Kronen again. "Now it just makes me laugh. I understand you better, and why you take everything so seriously."

"It's—"

"Yes, it's your duty to remain serious and vigilant," Varuk said with a chuckle. "I feel like I deserve some kind of reward for having the world's most dangerous job. I should keep a tally of my near-death experiences, just in casual conversation with you."

An unfamiliar feeling of lightness came over Kronen then, almost dizzying in its intensity, and he found the corner of his mouth curling up slightly. A noise that could have been a laugh left his throat, followed by such an odd mix of sensations that he had to stop walking to keep himself from stumbling.

"That was more convincing than your last attempt," Varuk said, spinning on his heel to walk backward a few steps. He froze when he saw Kronen's expression.

Kronen wondered if there was some danger in the Hidga Mountains that he was unaware of, after all. Resting a hand against a crystal tree for support, he used his magic to scan himself for anomalies or injuries.

It was like somewhere inside himself there was a subtle change. Something vital shifting. Familiar and not. Uncomfortable but necessary. Like a missing piece of himself he'd never been aware of was trying to slide back into place.

Just when the chaotic feelings sweeping through him began to weaken, another sensation moved through him, as foreign and indecipherable as the rest. He turned his head to the west, squinting through the fluctuating lights of the woods, unsure what he was even looking for. Whether it was the high concentration of magic in the Hidga Mountains, or some unexplainable instinct, he suddenly felt like there was somewhere else he was supposed to be.

Where, he couldn't say.

He unthinkingly brought his free hand to his chest, taking a deep breath to ease the strange pressure he felt building there, and then whatever it was just... stopped.

"That was new," Varuk said, eyeing him warily. He glanced to the side, following Kronen's line of sight, before giving him a worried look. "What was that?"

"I don't know," Kronen said, still a little unsteady on his feet and unable to explain anything that had happened.

This response seemed to upset Varuk, based on the way his eyebrows shot up, so Kronen decided full honesty was unwise in this situation. He shrugged, straightening away from the tree. "I mimic others to make them more comfortable," he said, determined to quickly return to the task at hand.

Whatever those sensations had been, they were completely gone. He would consider them further later, but for the time being they were merely an unnecessary distraction.

"No, I know you do that all the time, but this was different." Varuk seemed unusually serious, but Kronen had no idea how to reassure him. "You always think about what mannerism to use before you use it, but that laugh was automatic." He narrowed his eyes, studying Kronen with suspicion like he expected him to burst into flames at any second. "And you looked like you were in pain for a moment."

"I don't know what it was," Kronen said. Even though it had happened only moments before, he found the sensations impossible to describe. Without them, it was as though they had never existed, or they had happened to someone else. "Maybe I have some illness."

Varuk crossed his arms, eyeing Kronen doubtfully. "You don't get ill," he said flatly. "Is this the first time this happened?"

It was obvious what Varuk was concerned about—the very real possibility that Kronen had just had the first definite signs of the biranij, the onset of emotion for a garshik. An extremely dangerous time for a garshik and anyone around them.

For Kronen, many believed it would be catastrophic.

"Yes, but now is not the time to worry about it," Kronen said, continuing down the path. "This does not change our task, and I will not allow it to get in the way."

"That sounds like you," Varuk said, catching up with him again. He could feel Varuk studying him closely, despite his easy tone. "Your nearly obsessive garshik focus on the mission is more comforting than it was before, but are you sure—"

"There is no foreseeable scenario where you could convince me to turn back," Kronen cut him off, adding a sigh because it seemed like it would fit the situation.

"Yes, but it's the unforeseeable scenarios I'm suddenly concerned about," he muttered, but continued to follow Kronen.

It took the better part of the day to reach the southern edge of the Hidga Mountains, and although Varuk made his usual small talk along the way, Kronen could sense a new tension in his Ushara. He kept stealing glances at Kronen, and it was clear he was looking for any changes in behavior.

As the crystal trees thinned, the terrain flattening out into a grassy plain, they reached their destination. One of the larger shima graveyards, the architecture was all open archways, decorative pillars, and stone walkways that led to gravestones housing cremated shima remains. Parts of the cemetery had been converted to sky gardens, honoring those that had passed into the next life.

At the center there was a large stone ring. Hollow in the middle, translucent smoke shimmered and moved inside the open space like water. Dark gray and about a foot thick all around, the ring was a perfect circle and twice as tall as a shima. Carved in graceful spirals and intertwining lines, and etched with ancient, powerful spellwork, it served as a window into the land of the dead.

It was there that shimana could sometimes communicate with their loved ones who had passed.

"So?" Varuk said, keeping his voice respectfully low. "Anything out of the ordinary?"

Kronen scanned the area with his senses, able to detect things in the arute as a garshik that no other aspects could. As the barrier between the human and shima realms, the arute was carefully monitored and maintained.

It was an unknown imbalance that had drawn him to the cemetery. Something he'd never felt before. It was similar to an arag in some ways, a weak spot in the arute. If it were only that, however, he would have sent someone else to investigate. The imbalance was unusual enough that it demanded immediate attention. Any change in the arute could be deadly, for both the human and shima realms.

"It's too quiet," Kronen said after he swept the area a few times. Varuk followed his lead when he suppressed his energy to make himself harder for others to sense. "There are no spirits here."

"None?" Varuk raised his eyebrows, glancing around uneasily. There should have been traces of them all around.

As they moved farther into the graveyard, Kronen could feel others there, hiding their own energy. This wouldn't be cause for concern under normal circumstances, but the mysterious nature of the disturbance in the arute made him cautious.

"There are three shimana at the ring," he said, using his bond with Varuk to communicate. *"Watch them."*

Varuk silently unsheathed his weapon, giving Kronen a quick nod. Keeping to the shadows at the edges of the cemetery, he went to find a good vantage point where he wouldn't be spotted or sensed by the others.

Confident he was undetectable to their senses, Kronen moved between gravestones and archways for cover as he closed the distance between them. Three men stood in front of the ring, the hoods of their black cloaks drawn up to hide their identities. Their attention was on the ring as he moved closer, but he didn't want to risk getting too close.

He waited behind the cover of an archway, near enough to catch bits and pieces of their conversation.

"—have to bring back more this time—"

"—it's too risky—"

"—experiments have failed—"

"—make them stronger—"

Varuk heard everything Kronen did through their bond, and he could feel his Ushara bristling at those words. *"Do you think they're causing the disturbance you felt?"* he asked, and Kronen sensed him settling into cover somewhere on the opposite side of the ring.

"Most likely."

One of the three stepped forward, drawing a silver dagger with a jeweled wooden hilt. Even from a distance, it was so heavily enchanted that he could feel dark magic pouring off it. The feeling was so repellant to him it made him nauseous, but he stood his ground and ignored it.

The one holding the dagger whispered a spell of some kind, slashing at the smoke swirling inside the ring. At once there was a terrible screaming in Kronen's mind, silent to anyone but a garshik. The arute tore dangerously, and he winced at the pain slicing through his head. It was so strong he could feel Varuk doing the same, even though he was only getting the sensation second hand through their bond.

The dagger glowed with dark energy, and Kronen could see souls of the dead being sucked into it. Their cries of pain echoed in his mind, and he decided he'd seen more than enough.

Teleporting himself to stand in the middle of the group, he grasped one by the neck, then outstretched a hand, and blasted another in the face with light magic at close enough range that he felt the man's gasp against his palm. The one with the dagger tried to escape, not even bothering to try and help the other two.

"Capture him," Kronen said, already sensing Varuk moving.

The second man was on the ground, unconscious. His face was blistered and burned from the light, but he would live. The man he held onto was choking in his grasp, clawing futilely at his hand. Kronen turned his attention to him first.

"What you have done is against several of our laws," he said, glancing at the damaged ring. The smoke was heaving inside it, flickering with sparks, and he wondered if even he could repair this kind of damage without assistance. A coldness came over Kronen as he looked at his enemy and dropped him in a heap on the ground. "I sense nothing but darkness inside you. Why would you ruin yourself by absorbing the souls of the dead?"

The man's hood fell back, and Kronen could see the signs of the unchecked later stages of hajithra, severe dark sickness, marking his skin with sores. The odd twitches and sheen of sweat on his brow and drenching his dark-blond hair showed him as being hopelessly addicted, and Kronen knew it wouldn't be long before the darkness burned its way through him. Killing him would be a mercy.

Bloodshot green eyes stared up at Kronen in fear. "I didn't!" he croaked, holding up a hand to beg for his life. "It wasn't for us! It—"

Kronen shielded himself just as there was a flash of light, and a jagged shard of crystalized air ripped through the man's chest, killing him before he could say anything more. Blood spattered the ground around Kronen while the crystal projectile shattered harmlessly against his shield.

Calmly stepping over the dead body in front of him to search for the new attacker, he used his magic to scan the area. Whoever they were, they were powerful enough to sneak up on him and hide their energy, which was a rarity.

It wouldn't be nearly enough to save them.

He could sense Varuk returning to him, having dealt with the man with the dagger, incapacitating and restraining him for later questioning. *"Watch yourself. There's one more,"* Kronen said through their bond, but his warning was too late.

As Varuk came out from behind a tree at the edge of the graveyard, tucking the dagger inside his cloak, Kronen caught a movement out of the corner of his eye. The last of the four enemies teleported behind a gravestone, holding a hand out toward Varuk, who hadn't seen him yet.

Time seemed to slow, and that unknown, fragmented part of Kronen reacted again, more powerfully than before. It happened so quickly he could have imagined it. Not pain. More like a sinking in his stomach that stole his breath. An unexplainable compulsion he couldn't ignore. He teleported before he could process any of it.

He put himself between Varuk and the cloaked man, meeting the deadly magic head on and easily deflecting it. Dirt and rock flew from the impact as the spell crashed into the ground several feet away. The cloaked man was already moving to attack again, but it didn't matter. The feeling that had made Kronen teleport in front of him began transforming into something sharper. Focused on his enemy. Boiling through his blood like fire.

This man would pay dearly for trying to kill Varuk.

The man hurled spells at him. Some, Kronen deflected; others, he absorbed. And he felt the corners of his mouth curl up in a cold smile. The man hesitated, suddenly unnerved, and Kronen latched onto the man's mind with his own. Mercilessly tearing through the man's mental barriers, he permanently ripped his enemy's powers from him. The man howled in agony, collapsing onto the ground and clutching at his head.

This should have been enough, but the fire in Kronen's veins had him convinced only blood would make the offense right.

"Stop!" Varuk shouted, racing to intercept him as he raised a hand to crush the man. Through their bond, he heard Varuk's words in his mind. *"If this is the biranij, you have to control your anger!"*

The sound of urgency in Varuk's voice stopped Kronen cold. Quickly, like someone had snapped their fingers, that fire in his blood was extinguished, leaving the familiar calm.

Anger? Was that what he'd felt? Disoriented, he remained still and took stock of what was happening in his body.

Varuk paused several feet away, sensing the chaos in Kronen's system. "Kronen," he said, before cautiously moving closer to rest a hand on his shoulder. Not wanting the enemy to overhear him, he spoke through their bond again. *"Are you all right?"*

The man's eyes widened in horror when he heard Kronen's name. "The Sight of God," he said under his breath. He crawled backward away from Kronen, weakened and unable to scramble back to his feet.

"I'm fine now," Kronen said, glancing at Varuk

before turning to the enemy again. Unwilling to let the man get away, he moved to close the distance between them.

"Wait! Please! I didn't know it was you!" The man raised his hands, flinching away from Kronen. He looked to Varuk for mercy. "Please, stop him!"

Kronen could still sense the tension in his Ushara, but Varuk returned his attention to the man anyway. They had a job to do. Kronen slowed his steps while Varuk approached the man with a smirk.

"You think I have any say in whether or not he kills you?" Varuk asked, a cold glimmer of amusement in his eyes. "It's true, part of my job is to be his conscience. I could *try* to convince him, but that only works if you're useful." He tilted his head, staring his adversary down. "*Are* you useful?"

Kronen watched his enemy sputter and beg for a few moments, before he decided he had waited long enough. Unmoved by anything the man had to say, Kronen raised a hand, ready to finish him off.

"No, I can help you!" the man shouted, scrambling back a few more feet before Kronen slammed him down into the dirt with a thought.

"Speak then," Kronen said. "You're wasting time."

"It's for the creatures," the man said, desperate to save himself. "We're bringing the souls to them."

Kronen stared down at the shaking man before him, considering. "Bind him," he said to Varuk. "We must bring him back with us for questioning with the other two."

While Varuk tied up and gathered the surviving three men and contacted Iseyba for assistance in bringing them back for interrogation, Kronen found his gaze drawn to the west again.

The fight was over, and everything was calm. The spirits were at ease, and would be safe until the ring could be repaired. But deep inside his chest, he felt an inexplicable pull. Like the touch of a hand so gentle it could have been imagined. It reminded him of something he'd experienced in the Hall of Memories, studying the emotions of others. But it was so much clearer than those echoes that it made him want to follow it.

It lasted only a moment. There in one breath and gone the next. But that moment made the whole world shift around him. It was clear this wasn't a fluke or some random illness.

It was impossible to tell how close it was, but he would finally have the biranij.

Varuk came to stand beside him, following Kronen's stare again. "Is something wrong?"

In the absence of those earlier feelings, he couldn't be sure if they were good or bad. They were just something that had happened.

"Maybe."

Varuk clasped his shoulder, gently drawing Kronen's attention back to him. "We need to return to Iseyba. If your time for the biranij is coming, you need to be in seclusion when it happens. It's too dangerous to have you around others until you know you can control yourself."

Neither of them mentioned the possibility everyone feared. That the shock to his system could drive him into the darkness, and Iseyba was the only place that could hope to contain him, aside from an act of God.

"Or you could follow the pull," Varuk said, clearly

uncomfortable with his own suggestion. "Get it over with and pray I can help you through it until you return to Iseyba."

For the first time in his long life, Kronen hesitated to respond. Varuk noticed immediately, but didn't comment on it.

Every garshik would have the biranij at some point in their life, and the warning signs, flashes of intense emotion and a compulsion to fling themselves headlong into the biranij, had become known as premonitions of an upcoming event in a garshik's life. Whether the event was good or bad, it was always life-changing.

"Would it be worse to postpone it, if that's even possible, in order to help fight this new enemy?" Kronen wondered out loud. "Or to pursue it, and fight two battles at once, possibly losing myself?" He shook his head. "We can't risk it right now. I will do what I can from Iseyba."

"Either way, the timing could be better," Varuk said grimly. "These imbalances in magic are already weakening you. We mustn't let word get out for as long as possible. Otherwise, who knows what the enemy will do while you're unable to leave Iseyba?"

"If the attacks on the cities get much worse, I may have no choice but to intervene anyway," Kronen answered, knowing he had to maintain peace and balance in the realm before concerning himself with the biranij.

"I pray it doesn't come to that," Varuk said.

With no words of reassurance to offer, Kronen stole one last look toward the west before turning back toward Iseyba.

Aruna: Standalone One – Fire

Shima realm
Inside a dimly lit interrogation chamber

Aruna was careful not to react to the sharp edge of the dagger pressing into the front of her neck. The sting as it pierced her skin was nothing. She'd endured much worse and knew she would again.

She kept her gaze straight ahead, unflinching, as her master's new interrogator towered over her. A good foot taller than her, at five-five, and completely solid with muscle, he should have been terrifying, staring her down with cold brown eyes. But to her, he was as easily dismissed as any of the enemies that had come before.

"Look at me," he said, truly believing himself to be enough to intimidate her.

Feeling a bead of blood welling up to drip from the fresh wound, she raised carefully blank eyes to stare at the man in front of her. She could smell the stench of blood and sweat on his black shirt and pants, and his shaggy brown hair was wet with both, but she didn't react to that either. She had to protect the illusion that she was still mind controlled. "Release me," she said, keeping her tone even.

"Don't think I didn't see what you did," he said, ignoring her.

Having only recently broken through the compulsion of her latest collar, she'd known it was a reckless risk to take, with no real gain for herself, but she'd been unable to stand by and let the interrogator continue to torture his victim. The stone walls and floor had been spattered with the captive's blood, his screams deafening in the mostly empty interrogation room. Under the glow of crystal lights in sconces on the walls, she'd seen he was beyond his breaking point, strapped to a table in the middle of the room and bleeding from numerous wounds of varying severity.

She'd seen many horrible things in the castle she was captive in, and over time she'd convinced herself she'd been desensitized to this sort of thing, but there were certain lines she still couldn't cross. Deeds she still wouldn't do or allow to be done to others in her presence, as long as her mind and her body were her own.

But it was a tricky balance. It was vital that it appeared she was completely under her slave collar's control. If she acted on her own, she risked exposure and punishment. Another turn under her master's experimentation as he worked to further perfect the effectiveness of his slave collars.

"I hit the man you're questioning," she said matter-of-factly.

"You knocked him out before I could get what I needed," he accused.

She had. The interrogator could go fuck himself as far as she was concerned. "You lack restraint," she said without inflection. "And patience. He can't divulge anything important if you kill him within the first couple hours of interrogation."

"Your job is to fetch," the interrogator said, roughly grabbing the front of her black cloak with his free hand and clenching it in his fist. "Not to try your hand at mine."

As intimidation tactics went, it was a classic. She was unimpressed.

"My job is whatever my master commands," she said blandly. Growing tired of wasting her time with this moron, she wondered if no one had warned him to keep his hands to himself where she was concerned. "I was ordered to assist you."

"I didn't ask for your help."

"My master has given me a task to complete," she continued as if he hadn't spoken. "If I allow you to kill this man, I can't do that."

"Is that really all?" he said, sneering at her. "I think your collar's control over you is slipping again."

"It would be foolish to continue this," she said when he glanced at her collar. She'd learned long ago that one of the more excruciating pains was caused by someone other than her master touching her collar. "I will defend myself if you don't release me immediately."

He laughed, slamming her back into the wall behind her. "Does a puppet like you really have permission for that?"

Tired of the pissing contest, she bit back a sigh. Lifting her hands, she clasped both of his as she called on the element of fire. Her palms ignited, and he shouted in pain, leaping away from her. When he lashed out with his dagger in anger, slashing toward her throat, she shot a blast of air at him powerful enough to hurl him back against the far wall. Pinning him there, she approached him slowly.

"Do not interfere in the task that has been set to me," she said, and after all her decades of practice, it was easy to keep her anger outwardly in check, showing nothing of her emotions. "Report what you have learned to our master. Nothing further can be gained from this captive today."

When he tried to speak, she pulled him a foot away from the wall and slammed him back a second time. "You also do not have our master's permission to touch me. Do so in the future at your own peril."

Dropping him unceremoniously in a heap on the ground, she turned on her heel and left the interrogation room, ignoring his curses behind her. Anything more, and she'd give herself away.

Everyone she passed very wisely gave her a wide berth as she walked the halls of the castle on her way to her room. No one who'd been there any length of time and knew the rules would dare lay a hand on their master's favorite plaything. Not without his permission, at least.

Pretending to be placid, she kept her expression blank no matter what whispers she heard or sights she caught out of the corner of her eye. She'd trained herself not to react unless she absolutely had to.

The more they believed they had her under control, the better off she was. She would use their oversight against them when the time came.

For over a century, she'd been beaten down. Tortured. Experimented on. Pain was nothing new to her. The scars marring the skin beneath her dull silver armor and under her slave collar were evidence enough of that.

How many slave collars had her master gone through before he'd managed to create one that could control her for any real length of time? The one she currently wore was about a hundred times more powerful than the first prototype he'd tried.

Apparently, she was more resilient than the average shima. Her powers already rivaled those of an ancient. It was this strength, the power in her bloodline, that had tempted her master to capture her when she was just a child. Ironically, it was this same power that always eventually thwarted her master's attempts to completely control her, and had helped her free herself of the mind control this time as well.

Making her way down the silent hallway, the hood of her black cloak still pulled up to lessen the chances of accidentally making eye contact with anyone, the only sounds that reached her ears at this late hour were hushed conversations behind closed doors and the distant footsteps of patrols.

Although she was regularly sent out on missions to spy on her master's enemies, or to eliminate them, she worked alone. Just as no one would lay a hand on her, no one would acknowledge she even existed, under pain of death.

She carried no weapon, for obvious reasons, even when she was sent out to complete a task. Her master was no fool. He suspected even now that she wasn't fully his yet. She would also never be allowed to move about freely, as his other puppets did, without wearing the slave collar. He'd learned from his arrogance a hundred years before, during his first attempts to control her. She was too strong to be without the collar's punishing influence.

In fact, as she entered her room and locked the door behind her, she was wondering how long it would take her master to reprimand her for her sloppy work that day. Hidden away in the meeting room of the Junak, she'd been tasked with casting a telepathic eavesdropping spell on some other Jiru her master wanted to keep tabs on. She'd hoped to warn this other Jiru in some small way.

Had her master been able to tell her misstep had been on purpose? Had she left enough time between this incident and her last "mistake" while under the influence of her current slave collar? She hoped she hadn't been too obvious. If she had to acclimate herself to a newer, stronger slave collar, she would lose weeks, possibly months of time building up her resistance to it. And in the meantime, she would be forced to do terrible things against her will.

At first, she'd come to believe she had all the time in the world. But she knew now that she'd been horribly wrong. He'd already begun using the slave collars on others, and if he succeeded in his plans, there would be many suffering lives under the control of slave collars.

Undoing the clasp of her cloak, she tossed it on her bed and crossed the room to stand in front of her mirror. Her bedroom was sparse—a bed, one dresser, a mirror, and a bathroom. No decorations or trinkets. Nothing to show her personality or preferences. When the slave collars worked properly, she had neither, so it had never bothered her. When they weren't working, she couldn't risk taking an interest in anything.

Taking a deep breath, she looked at herself in the mirror. She barely recognized the gilt eyes staring back at her. It wasn't often that she really looked at herself. Pushing her long, gold-streaked, dark-red hair over her shoulders, she examined the fresh cut on her throat. It was shallow, and would heal quickly, but her main concern was the collar barely an inch below it. The cut might draw attention to the fresh burns under the edges of the collar, caused when she'd broken free of its control, but she'd learned the hard way that if she were fully under the collar's control, she would have ignored the interrogator's cut unless her master told her otherwise.

She'd cleaned her newest burns carefully, leaving no trace of blood, but the magic of the collar wouldn't allow her to heal the damage it had inflicted as punishment, so she had to do her best to hide it. When she'd been a child, inexperienced with magic, lacerations from the collars had covered most of her neck, but she'd learned quickly how to work carefully and slowly.

Deciding it would be wiser to leave the cut, she turned and walked toward the window. She leaned her shoulder against the sill and crossed her arms, her gaze following the quickly darkening skyline.

Recently, she'd found a glimmer of hope. Her master had taken her on a mission with him to capture a jahuni aspect trainer several months before, and she'd finally been spotted by people who weren't under her master's thumb. They'd gotten a good look at her and the slave collar she wore, and she prayed that would be enough to give them a hint as to her master's plans.

Just hold on a little longer. She kept telling herself this every single day. Memories of the years she'd spent without hope were vivid and painful, and those thoughts came back to haunt her often. But she knew every day she was able to fight, every collar she was able to overcome, brought her closer to freedom.

She *would* be free someday.

Eymka: Standalone One – The Traveler

Shima realm
The city of Amvitum

"Eymka!" the owner of the tavern greeted him warmly from behind the bar at the far end of the room. "Welcome back! Come to show me your new goods?"

"Good evening!" Eymka said, grinning in the direction of the owner's voice. "Not tonight. All I want is good company, conversation, and drinks."

"I think we can accommodate you," the owner said cordially.

He made his way carefully through the tavern, using his knobby wooden staff to help find his way. It was tiring to constantly rely on magic to get around, so the other shimana who knew him had grown accustomed to seeing him use the staff as a human would a cane. With practice, even crowded places such as this tavern, with its booths along the walls and tables spaced out in the middle of the room, were fairly easy to traverse.

They were also used to his eccentric attire. He always wore his dark-brown cloak with the hood pulled up to cover his head and a strip of cloth tied around his eyes like a blindfold.

Showing his hair and eyes would raise too many questions. As it was, the little bit of white hair that could be seen under the edges of his cloak, despite him being young by shima standards at a thousand years old, had many assuming he was a garshik who had gone through the biranij and gained his emotions.

He didn't intend to correct them.

He'd been asked many times how he'd been injured, since it was rare for a shima to scar, let alone be so gravely injured that he was blinded and brought to the point of death, and he enjoyed making up a different tale for each person who asked. To a lady he sold a basket of fruit to, he'd said he'd lost his eyes in a life and death battle with a deadly usiri in the vast desert surrounding the city of Majit. To a child he'd given a toy warrior to, he'd said he'd earned his scars in a legendary battle against a crazed earth yokeshi in the labyrinths of Kretore. And to this particular tavern owner, he'd claimed it had been during a valiant mission to infiltrate a dark magic obsessed cult. He had no intention of ever giving anyone a straight answer, and it had become somewhat of a game to those familiar with him to guess what kind of story he'd tell next.

As he navigated his way to his usual table in the middle of the room, he sensed the presence of one of the waitresses behind him. As soon as he sat down, she placed his favorite drink in front of him, and he felt the change in energy as she placed her palms on the table and leaned toward him a little.

"It's been a while," she said, and although he couldn't see her face, he could hear the hint of invitation in her voice. "Can I get you anything else?"

"No, thank you," he said easily, giving her a friendly smile. As much as he enjoyed the company of the people he met, he was always careful to keep a certain distance from them—for their sake as well as his own. Not that he wasn't tempted by the idea of spending the night with her again, but his magic felt more unstable lately with the growing void creature presence. Changing his hair and eye color for her again would be difficult. "How've you been? What's new in Amvitum?"

"I'm doing well," she said cheerfully, unoffended by his light refusal. Their relationship was casual on both sides, never stepping over the bounds of affectionate friends. "And you? Visited anywhere new?"

He shook his head. "Not with war breaking out. I'm sticking to safer routes until things calm down."

"Probably for the best," she agreed. "Since your last visit, we've finished rebuilding and cleansing the last of the taint left from the void creatures." He could hear the smile in her voice as she sat down across from him. Taking a sip from his drink, he was content to listen to anything she had to tell him. "It only took a few weeks, but it felt like forever."

"I've felt the void energy left by the creatures during my travels too," he said, grimacing. "It's not a pleasant sensation, and it's becoming uncomfortably common to run across."

"I know a warrior from the castle who saw one of the creatures close up," she said excitedly. "Apparently, Jiru Kanas befriended one."

This brought him up short, and he tried to cover

his surprise with a laugh. "I never heard about this," he said conversationally, trying to keep her talking.

"It's true," she insisted. "Some of the warriors were talking about how it helped Jiru Kanas and his new prasuri escape Humiv when they were captured after the city was occupied, but then the creature was killed by Humiv and nothing came of it. Think of what we could have learned about them!"

"That's a shame," he said, frowning slightly. Had the Jiruna of Amvitum really gotten close to one somehow? In his experience, the creatures were without conscience or emotion. It shouldn't have been possible. "Our side could have gained a lot of valuable information from the creature." There was a brief silence, and he sensed she was holding something back. Tilting his head, he lowered his voice conspiratorially. "Who would I tell?" he coaxed.

She snorted, making a scoffing kind of sound. "You're a master storyteller—"

"I tell no one's stories but my own," he said, offering her a grin. Resting his forearms on the table, he cradled his drink between his hands and waited.

There was a short pause, and he sensed her lean forward again. "Well," she said, lowering her voice. "You know how Urujek was the first city to be attacked by Humiv?"

"I remember."

"It seems Jiru Feruma of Urujek has been in contact with the Jiruna here ever since then. They may have formed some kind of alliance behind the Junak's back to track down Humiv. It's not like they've been seen meeting or anything, but my warrior friend thinks something's definitely going on."

"I get why you were hesitant to say anything now," Eymka said, suddenly a little worried for the waitress. With her innocent and open personality, she wasn't being cautious enough with this information, and he knew it could get her into trouble. "You mustn't share this with anyone else who comes asking," he said, using a small amount of magic to find her hand so he could clasp it, momentarily ignoring the shima etiquette that said he shouldn't.

He muffled the magical energy he gave off down to nothing, so there would be no transfer between them, and "saw" her aura fill his vision, changing the blackness behind his eyelids into vivid, swirling colors. The natural energy that flowed from every shima formed her silhouette, and he could make out the lines and details of her face. He sensed her surprise at his suddenly grave manner, but pressed on. "I'm serious. I consider you and everyone else here a friend. If the Jiruna here have made a secret alliance, it must remain a secret. Your warrior friend should not speak of it again either."

She nodded, the colors in her aura shifting as she became nervous. "If you insist," she said, seeming to understand his implication. Maybe she hadn't thought of it as anything more than gossip, but what she'd just shared could bring Humiv or the Junak right to her doorstep if it was true.

He gave her hand a squeeze before releasing her, letting his vision fade, and changed the subject. "Tell me you made pie today," he said, pressing his hands together like he was praying. "Of all the places I've traveled, and all the pie I've eaten, yours has ruined me for anyone else's."

Giggling, she relaxed again. "I thought you weren't hungry?"

"I tried to resist, but you know I never can," he joked.

"I'll grab you a slice," she said, getting up from the table. "But you know that's not really a meal, right?"

"Agree to disagree," he said with a grin.

Talking to different patrons as they wandered through, both familiar and not, he spent the rest of his time at the tavern making light conversation. The waitress came back to sit with him when she wasn't too busy, and the owner stopped at his table to chat as well.

All the while, in the back of his mind he was wondering how seriously to take what he'd heard from the waitress. The cloth covering his eyes felt especially noticeable for once as he pondered his own personal reasons for being curious about Humiv's void creatures, and the meaning behind a possible alliance between the Jiruna of Amvitum and the Jiru of Urujek in the wake of the attacks on their cities.

He had hoped Humiv wouldn't be able to perfect their void creatures, but it appeared they were getting closer every day. The attacks were growing bolder and were happening more often.

Could he really do nothing? Just sit back and watch it all unfold? Could he afford the risk of taking action himself? The consequences of involving himself could be a great deal more than he wanted to pay, and they wouldn't just affect him.

There was a lot to consider.

After he finished his pie, he paid, made his goodbyes, and headed for the door. Everyone wished him well and safe travels, and he promised he'd be back with some rare items next time.

A soft wind rustled his cloak as he walked through Amvitum, passing the new and improved gates that had been reinforced after the attack. Out in the open, away from the crowds of people, he was able to relax a little more and think about which direction to go.

Sighing, he took his teleport stone out of the pocket of his cloak. He knew he couldn't make an informed decision yet. Not until he'd heard a little more. If there was an alliance, and if the attacks continued to worsen, he needed to know if he could trust these Jiruna.

If they weren't working with the Junak, they already had a point in their favor.

Uneasy about what he would find, he chanted a few quick words and was immediately whisked away to Urujek.

Coming Soon

Stay tuned for Banen and Darenai's stories!

What will become of the Sijo? Cut off from his allies and relentlessly hunted by Enalel, where can he turn? And what about Darenai? Left on the cusp between life and death, his soul severed from his body, what hope does he have?

Glossary

arag—weak point in the *arute*, a gateway where *arute* jumps can happen

aragna—plural form of *arag*

aro—of/from

arute—barrier that separates the realms

beshek—cuss word/insult: asshole/bastard/bitch

bidkoil—profession/title: reader, keeps track of the *arute* and any *aragna*

bidkoilna—plural form of *bidkoil*

Ejoma—*shima* realm

eri—you

gan—am

gegaji—ceremonial/traditional term: blood contract

gensa—blood

gesja—help

hajithra—illness: dark sickness

hano—me

hanotse—my

hathun—thank

Humiv—the name of the rogue *shima* group waging war on the *shima* realm

ith—in

iyo—I, referring to oneself

jahuni—aspect: dragon

jenwe—creature: lizard/reptile

jerutoj—cuss word/insult: hell

Jiru—profession/title: ruler

Jiruna—plural form of *Jiru*

Junak—council

kaitsa—light, capitalized when speaking of God or making a religious reference

karekit—sucking

kawey—love

lathir—dirt

lisudari—spell: dark energy creature

lisudarina—plural form of *lisudari*

naori—endearment: a poetic endearment meaning roughly "star of my night" or "star that guides me"

navoj—endearment: darling/sweetheart

niyuk—path/pathway/way

prasuri—life mate

rahunit—stinking

rivishne—again

sathra—aspect: vampire

shima—immortal

shimana—plural form of *shima*

Sijo—profession/title: future ruler

Sijona—plural form of *Sijo*

Tairi—God

teles—guard/protect

Telesil—profession/title: first protector of *Jiruna* and *Sijona*

Thavos—human realm

tifire—aspect: faerie

um—the

Ushara—profession/title: faerie-bonded of a *Telesil*, second protector of *Jiruna* and *Sijona*

usiri—creature: wild sand cat

wendja—creature: wisp

wendjana—plural form of *wendja*

yalir—aspect: elf

yalirna—plural form of *yalir*

yasuwo—reveal/show

yokeshi—spell: golem

ACKNOWLEDGEMENTS

THANK YOU AGAIN TO THE amazing team at The Pro Book Editor and Indie Author Publishing Services for all of your hard work and thorough attention to the details of Ejoma. I really appreciate everything you've done to make my stories more complete!

And thank you again to Glendon Haddix of Streetlight Graphics for my awesome book cover! And to Cornelia Yoder for my map!

And to you, dear reader, for going on another adventure with me through the realms of Ejoma and Thavos. Happy reading, and I hope to see you again in book three! I'd love to hear feedback from you guys, so please leave a review. I hope we'll connect on social media too!

ABOUT THE AUTHOR

Paige Addams lives with her very patient and amazing husband and their dog in Ohio. When she's not writing, she's growing her business as an LMT, practicing aikido (while trying not to kill herself in the process), and trying to learn contact juggling (like that scene from *Labyrinth*). Otherwise, she's generally procrastinating with video games and far more YouTube than is probably healthy. Stay tuned for more books in the Dual Realms series!

Made in the USA
Monee, IL
25 July 2021

73870350R00256